Furever Mated

The Crimson Hollow Series

Marissa Dobson

Published by Dobson Ink
Printed in the United States of America
ISBN-13: 978-1-946474-01-8

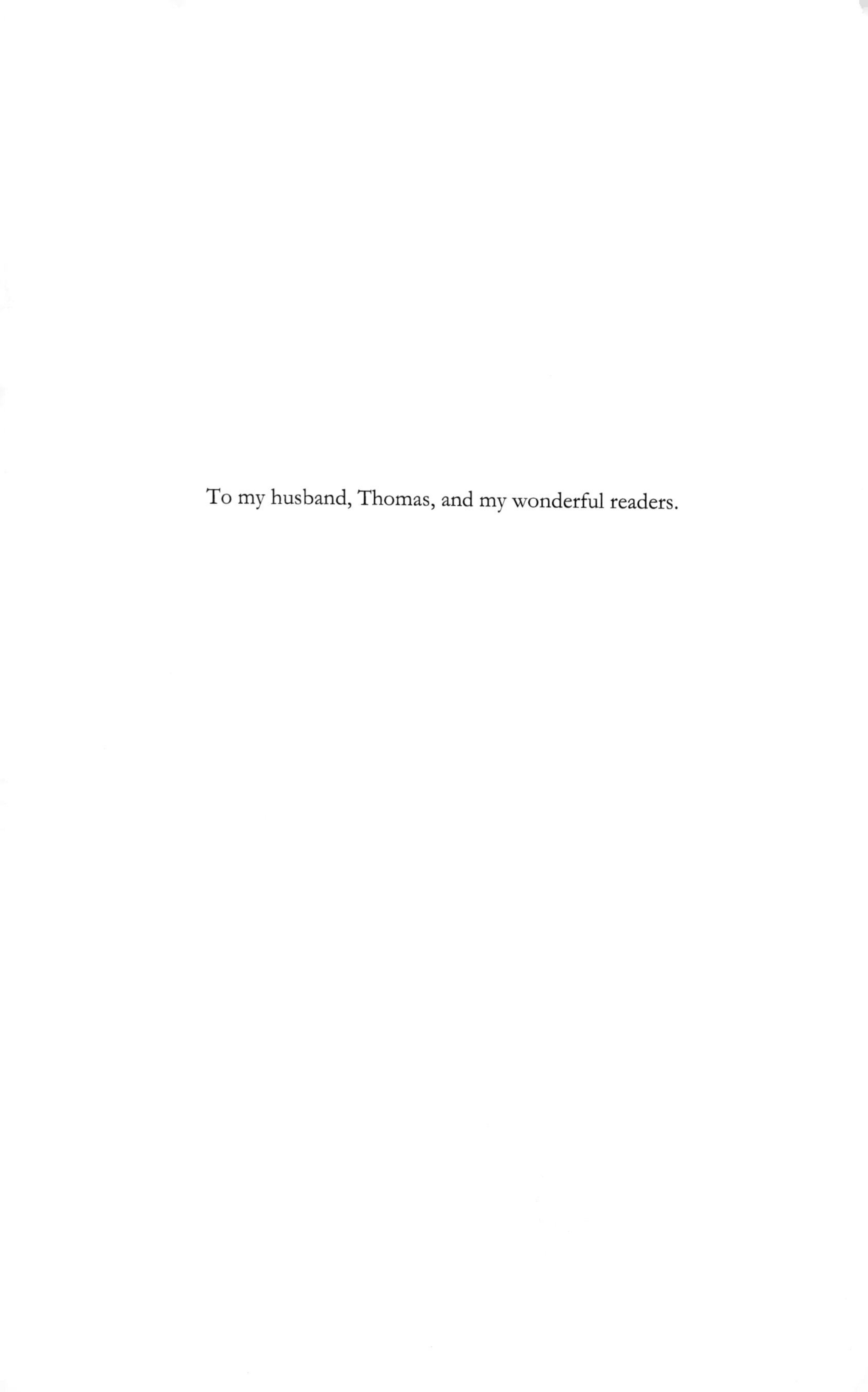

To my husband, Thomas, and my wonderful readers.

Contents

Romancing the Fox

No matter how far up the rungs of corporate success Sinopa Locklear climbs, her family will never be satisfied. To them, she's worthless because she refused to live out her destiny among the tribe and produce cubs. Her decision left an impassable bridge between her and those she loved.

When an offer to wipe the slate clean comes up, Garret Fox can't pass up the chance. All he has to do is spend a week with Sinopa, and pretend to be her fiancé. Seven days and they could go their separate ways. How hard could it be?

Both are running from something, afraid of getting too close and too intimate—until they are forced to behave as a couple for her family. Who'd have thought a fox would chase after a wolf of her own? Or is she his prey?

Chapter One

Sinopa Locklear poured her fifth glass of wine with hopes of drowning the panic rising within her, and leaned back against the sofa. Outside, the wind howled, a warning she tried not to hear. All she wanted to do was sit in her living room, alone, and drink until she passed out. She didn't want to think of what the week ahead of her was about to bring. For five years, she had stayed away from Crimson Hollow, using one excuse or another to get out of the family's yearly reunion. This year, her grandfather had made a special request for her to return home, therefore, tying her hands. No one disobeyed Granddad. He was the Chief of their tribe, and it was obvious he needed her for something.

She had been dreading the reunion for weeks, but in the morning, she would make the drive to their land. Crimson Hollow was isolated, more than an hour's drive from any real town in Montana. At one time she had loved it. The tribe had been self-sufficient, not relying on anyone but their own people. But she knew better now—that apparent freedom had been a lie, and now, she had a taste for city life and wasn't going back—even if her stubborn family welcomed her.

The doorbell rang, pulling her from her thoughts and making her want to put a pillow over her head. Likely, it would be Jenna on her doorstep, armed with another argument for why she should go to the reunion. "Go away, Jenna...I just want to be alone." She took a deep drink of wine, downing nearly half the glass.

Rather than Jenna going away, the doorbell shrieked again, ringing in her ear drums at double-time. "I told you earlier I didn't want company tonight." Even as she bitched, she got off the sofa and staggered toward the front door. As she swayed down the hall, she wanted to kill Jenna, not for interrupting her but for not just coming in like she normally did. Sinopa was too messed up for this; even with her shifter nature to process booze quickly, she was drunk.

Without looking out the glass window surrounding the door, she pulled it open. "Jenna, I told…" Her words died off as she realized it wasn't her best friend standing on her porch but a man—no, a wolf. His wide shoulders took up most of the doorframe, but it was his eyes that got her. The deep whiskey brown eyes stared back at her, stealing her breath and making her stumble back. Taking a deep breath, she caught the scent of his wolf. Her mind tried to process everything that was happening but the fog wouldn't lift. Still, she tried to keep the anxiety from her expression. Normally, she could hold her own against a wolf, but plastered, she stood no chance. If he was here for a fight, she was dead.

"Well, you're not what I was expecting."

Expecting? "Who…" She clung to the door, unsure if she did that to keep herself on her feet or because she wanted to slam it in his face. "Who are you?"

"The name's Garret Fox. I'm…I guess you could say, I'm your saving grace." He adjusted the duffle bag on his shoulder and nodded. "May I come in? It doesn't look like your legs are going to hold you up much longer."

"You're a wolf…" She couldn't stop herself from saying it.

"I am, and you're a fox. What a foxy woman you are." He let out a deep growl as his gaze traveled down her body. "I bet you look even better when you're not drunk and about to pass out."

She squared her shoulders and tried to give him her best glare. "I don't know who you are or why you're here, but I'd appreciate it if you left."

"A mutual friend asked me to help you." He reached out and caught her around the waist as she began to sway in place. "Let's get you sitting down and I'll explain."

"I didn't invite you in." She tried to get her legs to support her but they were like wet noodles. Even as she fought to stand on her own, she couldn't stop the urge tingling within her to lean against his rock hard body. She wanted to let her fingers run over his chest and feel the toned muscles hiding beneath the shirt.

Keep it together girl. He's a wolf. She wanted to blame her overreacting hormones on the wine, but she knew there was more to it than that. It had been too long since she'd had the company of a man. Shifters were sexual creatures and foxes were social too. She wanted to be around others who had a second nature. After spending much of her life around those who weren't foxes, it didn't matter what they changed into, only that they understood what she was.

Settled back onto the sofa, she grabbed her wine glass again, and glared at him. "I'm really not in the mood for company, let alone a stranger."

"How about you hold off on any more wine until I explain why I'm here?" He wrapped his hand around the rim of the glass, blocking her from taking another sip.

"Then you better get explaining because I have a bottle of wine to polish off before I pass out." Her stomach roiled in protest of more liquor and her head pounded a warning tempo at her temple that she needed to sleep. "I might just have to call the police on you. First you invite yourself into my home, and now you're taking away my one enjoyment tonight."

"I want to say this only once and not have to go through it again when you're sober." He took the glass from her hand and set it aside before he lowered his duffle bag to the floor and sat beside her. "I'm here as your fiancé."

"Fiancé?" With a raised eyebrow, she tried to suppress her giggling, but it was too much. She tipped her head back against the sofa and let the laughter burst through until tears rolled down her cheeks. "You've...you've got to be joking. Who put you up to this? Jenna?"

"Jase."

The amusement died away at the mention of her brother's name. Jase was the only one she kept in touch with in Crimson Hollow and mentioning him sent a wave of homesickness rushing through her. They had always been close, so much that their other brother had tried to drive a wedge between them. That wasn't a memory she was interested in reliving at the moment, so she focused on trying to figure out Jase's plan. What was he thinking? A fake fiancé—how was that going to help anything? The better question was, where did he get this guy? *I'll kill him if he put an ad online seeking a fiancé for me.*

"He asked me to escort you home."

"What the hell was he thinking?" she voiced aloud this time. "Granddad will never believe it." She pulled her legs up against her chest, hugging them to her.

"It's only a week. I'm certain we can make sure he doesn't question things too much. Jase seems to believe we can make it work." He dragged his hand through his thick hair, leaving finger tracks between ebony locks. "I'm under strict orders not to let you return without an escort."

"Orders…" She looked at him and tried to see through the haze of alcohol in her system. "You're not part of the tribe, otherwise this act of posing as my fiancé wouldn't work. So what does my brother have on you? And don't lie to me; you wouldn't be here if he wasn't offering you something. I know how persuasive he can be."

"What does it matter? We're both going to get something from this. You're going to get your family off your back." He glanced at the wine bottle sitting on the coffee table and back at her. "From the looks of it, you were dreading this visit."

"Don't you dare think you know anything about me!" She rose from the sofa, then swayed on her feet for a moment before catching her balance. "I live my life on my terms. I don't have a man in my life at the moment because I'm very busy with my career. I shouldn't have to justify my reasons to anyone, not even my family." She caught a glimpse of herself in the mirror above the fireplace. Her chestnut red hair stood wild and unruly as she had raked her hands through it multiple times over the last hour. Her face was flushed and dark circles were starting to form under her eyes. She was a mess and in a few hours she had to face her family. Fighting was no way to start the visit.

Just like lying wasn't helping this situation—but she could barely admit this to herself while she was alone; she surely didn't want to come clean to a stranger. Her career…that was just an excuse to explain why she hadn't mated yet. Jase knew it as well as she did.

"Sinopa, I'm not judging you." His tone remained soft and compassionate, as if he truly understood what she was going through. "Your reasons are your own. I'm only here at your brother's request. If you wish to refuse…my company…than please feel free to call Jase and explain it to him, and I'll leave."

"Sin."

"Excuse me?"

She plopped back down onto the sofa and met his gaze. "No one calls me Sinopa except Granddad. It's just Sin."

"Sin…that seems to fit you." His lips curled up into a smirk. "So what are you going to do?"

"Kill Jase." She meant it as a joke but images of her hands wrapped around her brother's throat raced across her thoughts. "I don't know what he was thinking, but I need to have a few words with him." She grabbed her cell phone off the coffee table and pressed her brother's number.

"I doubt he's going to answer. He'd expect you to be upset and call him to bitch."

She didn't bother to reply, even as ring after ring echoed in her ear. *Damn it, Jase. Pick up.* The ringing continued until his voicemail activated. "Shit!" She hung up without leaving a message and tossed her cell phone onto the sofa.

"I told you."

She glared at him and let the anger override the alcohol still coursing through her. She really didn't care what kind of deal Jase made with Garret because it wasn't going to happen. There was no chance she was going to show up at Crimson Hollow with a wolf by her side. Other wolves lived within the tribe, but they were not her type. Wolves were too high maintenance and their alpha personalities proved more than she could deal with. Was it too much to want a quiet life with someone who thought about her needs for once?

"So…" He folded his hands in his lap and watched her. "If we're going to pull this off, we'll need to get our story straight."

"There's nothing to pull off. I'm not going anywhere with you. Jase was out of his mind to even consider I would go for this."

"Jase told me you'd say that and he told me I would need to say…" He paused as if he was trying to remember what the exact wording was. "Much has happened since you've left and there's soon to be a new commander. Swift needs you, and so do I. Come home, Sin, and see what can be."

"What the hell?" She sank down onto the arm of the chair across from him.

"There's something more—not in his words, but the meaning is still the same. He's sent me as your escort because until changes are complete, he cannot guarantee your safety. It would be up to your Granddad and well, you know how that is."

"You mean the fact he's never done much to protect me." Anger tightened every muscle in her body as she fought to leave the past where it was. "Oh yeah, I know all about that. Jase was the only one who stood up for me. If there's to be a change of Chief for the tribe and Jase wants you to protect me, that means he's about to take over. But Swift, how does she play into this?" She thought about the only true friend she'd ever had. They had been inseparable until Sin left their land.

"I wasn't told that." He leaned forward, his elbows resting on his thighs. "Your brother cares deeply for you. He wants you home, and he wants you safe."

"I don't understand his plan." Once again, she took in the man before her and tried to figure out how he had become indebted to Jase in the first place.

"As your fiancé, I would be able to protect you, where Jase could not."

"But if this was to be long term…if Jase is taking over the tribe and wants me to come home permanently, then this charade would only make a mess of things. We might marry like humans do, so that things are legal for the rest of the world, but when shifters find the one they're supposed to be with, they mate. Anyone that got near us would be able to smell that we've not mated."

"He's thought of that as well." He leaned back against the sofa and smirked. "A bite will mark you as mine, but will wear off without us completing the mating. You've spent so much time among the humans, it wouldn't be considered unbelievable that you'd want to wait for the wedding night to complete the mating. It will also make sense that we're still getting to know one another, as we met not long ago, and our wedding will be soon because our animals will not wait long to be satisfied."

"It seems that you and my brother have considered almost everything." She glanced around her house, and while it might be small, it was hers. "But there's one thing Jase didn't consider. Maybe I don't want to return to Crimson Hollow. That I won't want to be under someone's rule or deal with the crap I went through before. Out here among the humans and maybe against all odds, I've come into my own. I have a life, a good job, and my own home. I don't want to go back to being the tribe's outcast."

"I don't know what happened to you back then, but the choice will still be yours. You can return here and back to your life. This arrangement will at least allow you to be among your tribe for a short time while you consider what your options might be."

She dragged a hand through her hair, pushing the reddish strands away from her face. "I need to think…I need a clear head before I make any decisions. The guest room is the second door on the right just down the hall. The bathroom is the first door on the right." Without further comment, she strolled away from him and toward her bedroom. She needed a hot bath to clear her head and think things through. Leaving a stranger alone in her house wasn't nearly as insane as going home with him as her fiancé.

Alone in the guest bedroom, Garret unlaced his boots and tossed them aside. Sinopa was nothing like he'd expected. The sexy as sin fox looked delicious even when she stumbled away from him drunk. Flecks of her temper had shined through tonight, making it clear that her fury was as fiery as her hair. She was going to be a challenge but one that he was up for, as long as it got him what he so desperately needed.

He unclipped his phone from his jeans and unlocked the screen to send a quick text message to Jase. *Things are going as planned. I'll let you know once we're on our way.* It wasn't a complete lie. After all, she hadn't kicked him out of her house.

He was there for one reason, and that was to get out of Jase's debt. This was a small price to pay after what Jase had done for him months before. There weren't nearly as many risks or danger now as there had been the last time they worked together. The only danger that concerned him was this attraction to Sin. He couldn't afford to let himself get distracted by her.

One week—that was all he had to get through, and then everything would go back to the way things were. Surely, he could keep a lid on his attraction to her while pretending to be her fiancé.

Who am I kidding? She's mine.

Chapter Two

Early morning sunlight streamed through the kitchen window as Sin poured a mug of coffee. With her guest still asleep, she had a few minutes to enjoy her brew in peace. It had been a rough night and she needed to get at least one cup of coffee into her system before she could even try to make civilized conversation. She had never been a morning person but add in the lack of sleep and splitting headache, it turned into a mixture for disaster and she had no desire to take her bad mood out on Garret. He didn't deserve that.

Sitting down at the table, she wrapped her hands around the mug and tried her best to chase away the chill that had settled over her. It had nothing to do with the wet hair that hung around her shoulders. The chill settled over her every time she thought about going home. While Crimson Hollow had some great memories for her, especially ones of Jase, it also held dark ones.

No matter how hard she tried, she had never been an accepted part of the tribe. She had always felt like an outsider. Jase and Swift were her only companions while growing up and Jase had done his best to protect them. *Swift needs you and so do I.* After all he had done for her, she wasn't about to turn her back on him when he needed her. Swift...well, she wasn't sure how things were going to be between them. When she'd left, their friendship had taken a hit, one that she hadn't been able to fix over the years.

"You're just going to turn your back on all of us?" Swift sat on a log near the fire pit, staring into the flames.

"Come with me. We can do this. I've got everything in order—a job and an apartment. There's nothing I'd like more than to have you come with me." Sin pulled the sweater tighter around her and swallowed back the tears that tightened her throat. She didn't want to leave Swift and Jase behind, but she knew her brother would never leave their tribe. With Swift, there was a possibility, because she was as much of an outcast as Sin. That was what made their bond so strong. "Please."

"We'll be eaten alive out there. I just can't." Swift shook her head, sending her wild red curls through the wind. "Don't do this. Sin, you're like a sister to me. Please, I don't want to lose you. Without Jase's protection, we'd never survive out there."

Sin sank down onto the log next to her friend. "I thought that once too, but now…"

"Now what?" Swift pushed.

"There's so much out there, so much I want to experience. I'd rather end up dead than live like this any longer. I'm tired of having to defend what I am. This tribe has more different species than any other group, yet they choose us as targets. Well, I'm done." With a deep breath, she rose and looked back at the woman she considered a sister. "I have to do this and I wish you'd come with me, but I understand you're scared. If you change your mind, my door will always be open to you. I will miss you."

"If you leave, there won't be a door to open. You'll be dead within the year." Tears rolled down Swift's cheeks.

She shrugged. "Then so be it. At least I'll have a chance to live before I meet my demise." She strolled away, her heart breaking into pieces with each step. "I wish you luck because you're going to need it." Without her there, the tribe's hatred would be focused on Swift.

"Morning," Garret's deep voice pulled her from her memory.

She glanced up to see him standing before the table in jeans and a shirt that molded to his body, showing off the deep contours of muscles hidden beneath the thin material. He was a fine specimen of manhood, but she had to remind herself that he was off limits. Wolves were not for her, no matter how attractive. "Morning. There's coffee in the pot. I have sugar and milk, but no creamer. I wasn't expecting company."

"Do I look like a man who takes fancy creamers in my coffee?" he teased, making his way toward the coffee pot. "I take it just how it was intended, black and piping hot."

"Typical wolf," she muttered under her breath. She hovered over her mug, letting the heat seep into her body. She refused to acknowledge the demands of her fox. He was here to do a favor for her brother; he was not hers. No matter how much her body called to him, she had to remind herself he was off limits. *He's not the mate for me.*

"I'm going to pretend I didn't hear that." He poured himself a mug and came over to the table to sit across from her.

Guilt tugged at her as she glanced up to meet his gaze. "I'm sorry. I'm not a morning person and well, with everything that's going on, it doesn't have me in the best of moods." She took a drink and leaned back against the chair. "I'm positive this is a bad idea, but if you're still willing to accompany me, then I guess I'm willing to do this. It's insanity, but I think you might be the more foolish one. I have to go, but you made the choice to go. I'm not sure anything is worth the hell I know awaits me there."

"I'm sure it won't be as bad as you think it will be. We have a tendency of making things worse in our mind the longer we push them off. Jase assured me it wouldn't be a dangerous situation, so I don't believe any harm will come to you."

One corner of her mouth twitched up into what she guessed was somewhat of a smirk. "Harm comes in more ways than just physical." While she didn't doubt there could be physical confrontations, she was more worried about the emotional and mental aspects of this trip. "How well do you know my brother?"

He sat his mug aside and leaned forward, resting his elbows on the table. "Well enough to know that he cares for you and wants you protected."

"I'm going to assume that you're aware he's a bear shifter, but did he make you aware of our tribe's dynamics?" When he shook his head, she continued. "Unlike wolves who live in a pack of their own species, we are open to anyone. There are bears, lions, tigers, panthers, and leopards. However, Swift and I were the only foxes within the tribe. We were taken in by the Crimson Hollow tribe when our skulk—group of foxes—were killed off. We were young and had no one else. Granddad knew that we couldn't be dropped into the state's care without someone finding out what we were, so he took us home."

"Then, Swift and you are siblings?"

She shook her head, sending a strand of her wet hair into her face. "No, cousins, but we stuck together because we were the only ones left."

"But you're Jase's sister." He stated it as if he couldn't believe what she was saying.

"I am." She paused as she remembered arriving at the tribe's land and how utterly terrified she had been. Jase and his mother had been the first people they met and she and Jase had instantly taken a shine to one another. While the adults talked, she and Jase played in their animal forms. She'd slip into places he couldn't fit and would taunt him by flicking her tail at his face, teasing him because his big cub body wouldn't shrink small enough to fit. Swift had sat in the corner, silent tears streaming down her face and her thumb in her mouth. *Another wedge between us.* "His family took me in because we bonded together and Mom couldn't bear more children. They raised me as their own."

"They are in control of the tribe so that should have kept you safe."

"Oh, they kept me safe from harm as much as they could, especially Jase. It was the teasing and horrible things people said that made me want to leave. No matter what I did, I always felt like an outcast. For centuries, there had been multiple species living within the tribe, but never before had there been foxes. Foxes had always kept to themselves, staying in their skulks. It was hard for the tribe to adjust to the new animals."

For years, she had tried to do whatever she could to earn acceptance, but nothing worked. When Jase, her parents, or Granddad weren't around, the torment she suffered proved too much. At nineteen, she decided she'd had enough and left. It was a decision she hadn't really regretted but at the same time, she missed being around others of her own kind. Even if they weren't foxes, they understood the shifter lifestyle. Out here in the world, she had to keep that side of herself boxed up.

"Jase was the one hurt the most when I told him I was leaving. We were best friends, but this was something I had to do for myself. I knew he wouldn't leave, but I did try to get Swift to come with me. I thought she would because she had it even rougher than I did, but she was too scared of the world outside of Crimson Hollow. Afraid of what it would be like without Jase to protect us. I've always wondered what her life has been like since I left. I hope she found a way to be accepted."

"Well, we've got a few hours' drive ahead of us but you'll know soon enough." He polished off his coffee and leaned back.

"The bite?" Heat rushed toward her cheeks. Her stomach churned with the thought but if they were going to leave, it had to be done. Mating was supposed to be something special and intimate, and yet they were about to deceive her tribe by using it to their advantage. She just hoped the act wouldn't come back to haunt her later.

Nodding, his gaze sharpened on her. "We should do it before we leave. It will be easier than on the side of the road somewhere and it will allow time for my mark to circulate through your body. If we stop on the way, it might appear too fresh and raise questions we don't want."

"Then let's do this." She polished off the rest of her coffee and pushed back from the table. During the night, she had made her decision and there was no going back from it now. She'd return home to Crimson Hollow, at least for a few days, and if he was willing to deal with the shit that was waiting for her, then she'd gladly have him by her side. Right then, it didn't matter if he was a wolf or not; she needed that extra support to deal with the coming days.

Jase, you better be right about this and about him.

Garret sat on the sofa, waiting as if he had all the time in the world while his wolf clawed at him, wanting so much more than he was about to get. The idea of marking a woman as his mate excited the wolf, because normally the act happened in the middle of or following sex, making the claim absolute. Only this time, the wolf would be denied. There would be no sex, and no mating union. No matter how drawn to this woman he found himself, this was just for show—a precaution to get them through their time in Crimson Hollow.

"You can't be serious." She stood before him with her hands on her hips, looking at him as if he had lost his mind.

"I need you to sit on my lap and straddle me," he repeated. "It needs to be an intimate position so that my wolf musk will tease along your skin. It will also give me a good position to access your neck, while holding you close so you won't squirm away."

"Why would I squirm away?"

"Fighting me will be a natural instinct. Most times the bite happens in the middle of sex, because the ecstasy makes it easier to take and the endorphins mute the pain. We're doing it this way for our own reasons." He patted his thighs. "Why don't you climb onto my lap and we can get this done? Jase needs us there before five this evening."

She stared at him long enough that he questioned whether she was going to go through with it, before finally closing the distance between them. "Don't try anything, wolf." She placed her legs on either side of him and straddled his thighs.

"I wouldn't think of it." He slid his arms around her, rubbing his hands slowly up her back until his fingertips touched the ends of her hair. "Could you push your hair to one side? I wouldn't want to accidently tug on it."

She reached up and coaxed the long strands to the side, tipping her head to arch her neck toward him. "I know it's going to hurt, so just do it."

"If you'd like I can make it so it doesn't hurt." He shot her his best cocky smile. It was doubtful she'd take him up on the offer, but he could make sure they both enjoyed it.

Don't get involved. One week and she'll be out of my life. You'll find another woman who excites your wolf.

Even as he reasoned within himself, his wolf growled. He wanted the woman before him. Her scent called to him but more importantly, it called to his wolf.

"I'm not a human who has no clue of our ways. You're not going to convince me sex will make all the pain go away. I know if we join in that way, the mating would be complete and that's not happening. You don't know me so trust me when I say you don't want to be saddled with me for the rest of your life."

"You have no idea what I want," he murmured. He caressed along her back, gently pulling her closer to him. "Don't put yourself down because of your tribe's belief. You're not worth less because you're a fox instead of something bigger. Foxes have advantages that larger shifters don't have. It's much harder for me to crouch down to camouflage myself in the terrain than it is for you. That gives you an advantage when it comes to hunting."

"Hunting small game, that's it. When it comes to protecting ourselves, we are easy prey."

"Not any longer." He leaned forward, nuzzling his face against the curve of her neck.

"Don't make promises you can't keep."

His tongue flicked across her cool skin, causing a soft moan to escape her throat, and she pressed into him. Licking small circles, he drew out the process to keep her in his arms a little longer. After a night of her in his thoughts, to now feel her against him was better than anything he could have dreamed of. Giving into his wolf, he bit down just below her collarbone until the metallic taste of blood filled his mouth. His wolf howled both in victory and in frustration for being denied the rest.

"Ahh!" Her voice held pain as he pulled his teeth back and licked the wound.

She tasted so sweet and felt so right in his arms that he didn't want the moment to end. His wolf demanded he pick her up and carry her into the bedroom to complete what they'd started. Rather than do that, though, he pulled back enough to look at her. "Well, my fiancé, I hope that was good for you, but I promise if you let me do it again, it will be so much better."

She blinked at him as if trying to focus. "In your dreams, wolf." Even as she said it, her voice sounded soft and dreamy.

"In my dreams and soon, it will be reality," he whispered more to himself as she slipped from his embrace. This had started out as a way to clear a debt, but now he didn't care about it. He'd rather have her and still be indebted to Jase than be without her. There was something he knew from the moment she opened the door and he could no longer deny it.

My mate.

Chapter Three

The long car ride served them well by allowing them to get to know each other, but in the last fifteen minutes, no matter the topic, Sin couldn't keep focused. They were nearing the tribe's land and dread settled over her shoulders. She wanted to demand that Garret turn his truck around and take her anywhere but where they were going. *You can't turn your back on Jase when he needs you.*

"You ready for this?" He reached over and took her hand in his. "It's going to be okay."

She glanced over at him, and her body heated with desire. She tried to blame it on the bite, but she knew it was more than that. All night she'd tossed and turned, thinking about him. There was a connection between them, tugging them toward each other. *I can't believe I'm trusting a wolf.* He turned right, taking the dirt road back to her tribe's land, and her heart pounded against her chest. "We should…"

"I'll be by your side. You can do this, and if you want to leave early, we can. But we've come all this way, you should at least find out what Jase needs from you."

"Leave early?" Instead of thinking about why Jase wanted her, she focused instead on the thought of making an early escape. "If we did that, Jase won't forgive whatever debt you owe him. I couldn't put you through all of this, and then leave early. It's not fair to you."

"Screw Jase. Forget what brought us together, and remember I'm here for you.

I'll support and protect you in any way I can, and if that means leaving, even tonight, that's what we'll do. You're not a prisoner here, and you're not alone."

"I'll try to remember that," she whispered as they drove closer toward the houses. Granddad's house stood straight ahead, with her parents' house on one side, and Jase's on the other. Seeing them brought memories flooding back, but it was Jase, who stepped out as they neared, that stole her breath.

Her big brother, her protector, had changed so much since she'd left. He filled out more than she could have believed. Standing in front of the truck was a man twice her size, all toned and muscular. He had always been sculpted but she could have sworn he hadn't been that big before. His deep brown hair was cut shorter now, nearly hiding the natural highlights within it from his bear's fur.

Garret shoved the truck into park and shut off the engine. "Wait in the cab until I come around." Before she could reply, he was out of the truck and came around to her side.

It's just Jase. You can do this. He sent Garret for protection. Obviously he's not going to hurt me. She couldn't tear her gaze away from her brother, even as she caught new movement out of the corner of her gaze.

Her door opened and Garret held out his hand to her. "Shall we, darling?"

She took his hand and stepped down from the cab. After all, what was she going to do? Stay in the truck after they'd driven all that way? Once she was standing next to the truck with the door shut, she kept Garret's hand.

"I'm glad you came." Jase approached her.

"We need to talk." She kept her voice low as people appeared out of doorways. Some members were setting up for the night's celebration, while others were eying her. No one seemed to be angry that she had arrived back home after all this time. Had Granddad announced it? Still, with everyone moving about, she felt uneasy. She needed to get Jase alone, gather more information, and pull herself together before the gathering.

"Inside." He nodded before glancing toward Granddad's place where the old man stood on his porch with their parents. "If you'll excuse us a moment."

Before she could make it into the safety of Jase's house, their mother stepped in front of her. Tears streamed down her face. "I didn't think you'd come. Oh Sin, I've missed you."

"Mom…" She let go of Garret's hand and wrapped her arms around her mother. "I've missed you too." She let the tears roll down her cheeks without trying to wipe them away. Since the day she had left, there had been a hole in her chest where her family had once been. The terror of possibly never seeing them again had been a sore spot within her gut for years. They had their issues but what family didn't? In the end they had a bond and they stuck together.

Before her mother let her escape the embrace, she tipped her head close to Sin's ear. "Take your brother up on his offer. We need you. He needs you."

She didn't know what to say. Thankfully, she didn't have to because Garret came to her side and escorted her through the door Jase was holding open. What the hell was going on? She was tired of being kept in the dark. She barely noticed that nothing had changed in the living area since the last time she'd been there. The room was still mostly bare, a sofa and recliner the only furniture besides the flat screen television mounted on the wall. Even the dining room was empty of furniture.

"You still don't have a dining room table." She shook her head.

"You didn't come all this way to criticize my home." Jase sat on the recliner, leaving the sofa for her and Garret. "Plus, you know I prefer to have a quick bite at the kitchen bar or with the family."

"You're right, I didn't come to criticize your décor. Why don't you tell me what Mom meant? What do you want from me?"

"Maybe you should have a seat and Garret…if you'll excuse us."

"Oh no." She cut her brother off and Garret gave her a hand a gentle squeeze. She wasn't sure if it was to let her know he didn't mind or that he was there for her. Either way, she kept her attention on her brother. "My fiancé will stay." As she said 'fiancé', she glared at Jase, letting the heat show in her eyes.

"Have it your way." He nodded for them to sit. "I asked you here because I want you to return home."

"Absolutely not." She rose from the sofa nearly as quickly as she'd sat down, pulling Garret's hand up with her. "I love you, Mom, Dad, even Granddad, but I can't come back to being an outcast. I have a career and a good life now."

"You're still as hard headed as ever." Jase leaned down to the pile of folders sitting on the floor next to the chair. "Tonight, I'll be named the new Chief of this tribe and I want you as my Deputy. I wouldn't want anyone else by my side but I also need you because of this." He held out the folder he picked up, waiting for her to take it.

She shook her head, her mind reeling from what he'd said. "Jase…"

"Just look inside. If you still don't want the job, I only ask that you wait until after the ceremony to leave. I'd really like to have you there as I begin my reign."

Taking the folder, she sat, and opened it. Images of dead bodies lying on the ground stared up at her. Blood tainted the ground but the worst part was that their bodies had been torn apart. Just like that incident long ago…

Her hands shook as flashbacks poured through her mind.

Huddled under a table, terror filled her, leaving her unable to move. Wind came through the opened front door, blowing the thin tablecloth, and she shivered against the chill it brought. The scent of blood filled the air, turning her stomach at the stench, but what she saw was worse. Through the thin material of the tablecloth, her mother's dead body lay a few feet away, her eyes wide, staring toward Sin, but they were vacant. There was nothing left, none of the joy that always seemed to be there. No smile that had stretched across her face anytime she looked at Sin. Now there was only blood. Blood everywhere, until the air was thick with it. She wanted to cry out for her mother, or anyone, but terror kept her from doing so. Whoever had hurt her mother might still be there.

Where was her father? Was he okay? She pulled her gaze from her mother's body and turned toward the door, silently hoping she'd see him out there, somewhere. In the distance, she caught a glimpse of Swift and opened the mental communication between them. "Swift, can you see anyone?"

"Dead…they're all dead. We're alone. What's going to happen to us?"

They weren't alone, they had each other, but she had no idea what to tell her cousin.

"Sin…" Garret shook her hard enough to pull her back from that bloody night.

She blinked at him and realized he was kneeling in front of her. "Gar…" Her voice broke.

"Drink this." He held a glass to her lips, forcing her to take a drink.

Alcohol met her lips and she wanted to spit it out but instead swallowed the burning liquid. "Whiskey?"

"Comfort drink." He cupped the side of her face, wiping her tears away. "You okay?"

She nodded, not trusting her voice yet, and he rose to sit next to her. She glanced at Jase and wanted to rant and rave. If he was going to show her something like that, a little warning would have been nice.

"What the hell were you thinking, pulling a stunt like that?" Garret growled at him. "You wanted her here so you could show her dead bodies? What will that solve? She was safer before you called her home."

"You know nothing, wolf," Jase growled.

"I know that you brought back memories that were better left buried. The bond that you had us establish gave me a clean connection to what just happened. So unless you want me to shove her back in my truck and get her out of here, you better start explaining and quickly."

Jase darted forward, coming to stand before them, his hands in fists at his sides. "You're nothing, wolf. That connection is short term and then there will be nothing protecting you. I'd suggest you remember that before you open your mouth. I can make your life hell because if you don't complete this, your debt won't be wiped out."

"Screw you." Garret rose to his feet to stand face to face with Jase. "I won't let you torment her just to clear the slate."

"If I didn't know better, I'd think she really meant something to you." Jase glanced at her and then back to him. "She's not stupid enough to fall for a wolf."

"Stop it!" she hollered, causing both men to look at her. "Jase, you do have some explaining to do, and no matter my decision, you will wipe this slate clean. Garret will be free of you. Do you understand me?"

"You really do care for him." Jase shook his head as if he was unable to believe what he was hearing.

"If you even want me to consider helping you, then you'll agree to do as I ask and erase Garret's debt."

Garret laid his hand on her arm. "Don't, Sin. I'll deal with him later. It's not worth it."

"It is to me." She placed her hand over his before turning back to her brother. "Jase?"

"Fine." Her brother stepped back to his chair. "Wolf, you're free, but next time you need help, don't call me."

She let out a deep sigh. Jase hadn't changed. His attitude and temper were his biggest issues. He needed a Deputy that would keep him grounded; she just wasn't sure she wanted to come back home to be that person. Instead of worrying about that at the moment, she stepped closer to Garret, hoping he'd wrap his arms around her again. When he did, she stared at her brother. "Who the hell was in those pictures?"

"Littleton's tribe." Jase glanced at Garret. "It was a tribe a few miles down the road."

"They're all dead?" Focusing on the tribe and its members, she tried to keep more of her memories at bay.

"The sole survivor, Zoe, a fourteen year old girl, is here with us. She's terrified and was staying with Swift but now she's in your old room. I didn't know what else to do with her once Swift freaked."

She shivered not from the cold but when the horrid memories of the weeks after joining her tribe flooded back to her. She had been terrified, too, but then she had Jase and Swift. This little girl had no one. But to put her with Swift when she first came and then move her again—that was no doubt making this harder for the young teen. "What were you thinking putting her with Swift?"

"She wanted to help the child. I was hesitant but accepted because I didn't know what else to do with her. Mom and Dad don't need to be raising another child, and most of the tribe have their own stuff to deal with. I couldn't just drop a kid on them, especially one with the issues that she has." He leaned back in the recliner. "Maybe you could talk to her?"

She ignored his question, not willing to commit to anything until she got more answers. "How's Swift?"

"Unstable is what Granddad would say, but I think she'll come around. Having this happen again has brought back all of those memories of what the two of you witnessed."

Garret squeezed her tighter against him. "I can't believe you brought her back here because of this. You'd risk Sin's mental health to help you with a child that isn't even one of your own?"

"Sin is strong. I had no doubt that she could handle this or I wouldn't have risked her." Jase glared at the other man for a moment before returning his gaze to her. "Even though our blood and animal are different, you're my sister. I wouldn't risk you for anything. I love you, little sister. That and the fact I know you can handle shit is why I asked you to be my Deputy. There's going to be more coming and I need you by my side."

"What do you mean there's more coming?"

"Another tribe was attacked but more survived. Their leader was killed so, since they have small numbers, they're joining us instead of rebuilding. They are a mixed tribe like us. Granddad is tired and doesn't have the strength to deal with the adjustment that will happen with new members. So he's turning the tribe over tonight and I will take the reins."

"Two tribes attacked recently, but it hasn't made the news. How is that possible?" Garret's fingertips caressed along her skin.

"So far we've been able to keep it under wraps, but if it continues, things for our kind could get desperate."

"You'd risk your sister's life with maniacs still on the loose?" Garret snapped. "She'd have been safer in the human world where no one knew what she was."

"I'm saving her life." Jase rose to his feet and stepped forward before gaining control over his anger. "They've been killing foxes. Any other casualties have been because someone got in their way. Liam, Noah, and I killed the ones who attacked Littleton's tribe. Those who were involved in the second attack are dead as well. We're not sure if there are more involved but at this time, we believe we might have killed all of them. With some luck we have, but if not, Sin could be in danger if she doesn't come home."

Sin shot him a glare. "I've protected myself this long, I can continue to do it. Unless they are a shifter or knew us, they wouldn't be able to tell what I was." She had been living a peaceful life, not overly happy but at least without drama and people trying to gun her down because of what she was. Now, one trip home and everything changed. "If you haven't got them all, then you've made this tribe a target by taking in the survivors."

"I've got that handled. Once I begin my reign tonight, the new guards will go into effect." Jase's tone remained natural as if he didn't have a care in the world, while she tried to keep her fox from forcing a shift from the panic running through her veins.

"The killers…were they shifters?" She couldn't remember any unfamiliar scents from the night her tribe was attacked. Just screams and blood…so much blood.

"The ones we've killed were humans." Jase sighed. "We haven't figured out how they know. There must be a shifter working with them, or they are stalking the tribes before they kill them."

"Didn't you question them before you killed them?" she snapped, needing the information.

"Oh yeah, questioning them was at the top of our to-do list, right after saving our own asses." He shook his head. "Damn it Sin we were fighting for our lives and trying to protect those that were still alive. Questioning them didn't come into play."

"How many others are joining the tribe? And will they arrive while we're here?" Garret questioned.

"That's not really your concern, now is it, lone wolf?" Jase glared at the other man, teeth bared.

"She's my responsibility." Garret's words came out clipped. He squared his shoulders as if ready for a fight. "If you have unknowns coming into your tribe, it increases the danger she might be in. So yeah, it is my concern when you are putting both of our lives in danger."

"What do you want? Money?" She caught the change in Jase's tone and his stiff body language. Whatever had happened between the two of them had left some hard feelings.

"Stop it." Needing to think, she slipped out of Garret's embrace and stepped away. "We're talking about people being murdered, children who have lost everything, and what do the two of you do? You bicker about whatever bad blood is between you two. Well, Jase, you obviously trusted Garret enough to protect me or you wouldn't have sent him to me. So whatever bullshit is going on with you two, put it aside. We've got shit to deal with."

Silence stretched out until it became uncomfortable and Jase nodded. "My dear sister, you're right. I'm letting the fact that you two appear to be closer than I expected get my bear worked up. He's by your side at my own doing and I must remember that."

Sin let loose a sigh of relief. "How many new members will be joining the ranks? Have you checked them out? Just because they are from a friendly tribe doesn't mean that they are true to what this tribe stands for." She dragged a hand through her hair and sank down onto the sofa. "What the hell do I even know about what this tribe stands for any longer? It's been years since I've been home. Everything could have changed. Wanting me at your side is a mistake. You need someone who has been a part of the tribe."

"No, I need you, Sin." He stepped toward her. "There are seven joining us and they will be here the day after tomorrow. I met with them two days ago. There's a mixed species, mated couple—leopard and fox—with two children. The other three are unmated male shifters, a bear and two lions. The female and one of the children were the only foxes within the tribe and fortunately, they were uninjured. The Chief and some of the other men caught the attackers before they had a chance to kill any of them. Some that got in the way were killed and a few have decided they are not interested in joining us. Do you see why I need you here?"

She thought about what he said for a moment, taking in the new information, but she still wasn't sure why he thought she was a better fit than someone else from within the tribe. "No. If you were going to name anyone as your Deputy, I would have expected it to be Noah, or at least Liam. Not me. So just lay it out on the table. Why me and not them?"

"There are multiple reasons why I feel you would be the best fit. But here's a few. I believe that humans might change their views on us. While over the years we have proved that we are not a danger to them, once these attacks leak to the media, this could change. It could become a dangerous time for all shifters. I'd rather you be here where you're safe. Also, your time away from our land has made you stronger, more sure of yourself, and that will make you a better Deputy than anyone else."

"How do you know?" she interrupted before he could continue.

He arched an eyebrow. "Do you think I haven't kept tabs on you? Though we talk on the phone occasionally, it wasn't enough. I've made trips to check on you, always staying out of sight, so no one would know I was near you. I couldn't risk coming back and them catching your scent on me. It could have made trouble for you and I know you wanted a life away from all of this." He tipped his head toward Garret. "It's how I met your friend here, but that's his story to tell you."

"It's also off topic at the moment," she reminded him. "The clan would never accept me as your Deputy…" Until the words left her mouth, she hadn't realized how much she wanted to come back home. Being his Deputy would give her a certain status within the tribe, and the woman she had grown into while she was away wouldn't allow her to put up with the crap she had before. She hated to admit it, even to herself, but she was considering his offer.

"They will accept you, because they'll realize we need you." He leaned forward, resting his elbows on his thighs. "Things have changed since you've left. Besides Swift, Zoe, and the foxes that will soon be joining us, there is one other male fox within the clan. Since I've begun to take over the tribe, I've made changes. The stuff that went on before doesn't happen any longer."

"Then why is Swift unstable?"

"Because of all the memories of the attacks on your families that Zoe brought to the surface. Before the teen came here, things were great with Swift. Talk to her if you don't believe me, things have changed here. I won't allow the members to pull the crap they did under Granddad." Jase let out a deep sigh and rubbed a hand over his face. "Sin, there's no one else I want by my side as I lead this tribe. We used to talk about the day that I'd take over. The plans we made…they can still come true. I know it's a leap for you and you have to give up a lot to come home, but you won't regret it."

And if I do, then what? If I can't cut it, there might be a challenge for my position and I'd have to fight to the death. Can I defend myself well enough to survive against one of the other bigger shifters? She had kept up with her training and workout routine, but she wasn't sure she'd be a worthy opponent, and if she wasn't, Jase would be burying her. She needed to think without him sitting across from her waiting for an answer. "I need a few minutes. Can you give me some time to think? When is the ceremony?"

"You have a little more than an hour. I know it's not fair but I need an answer before it starts. Meanwhile, I have a few things to take care of. I know Mom is waiting to speak with you, but I'll tell her you need a few." Jase rose and looked at Garret. "I can show you to the guest cabin. I've put you in one of the two bedroom ones, so no one will question you being in separate cabins."

"Actually, Jase, I'd like him to stay. I mean if you don't mind Garret? We'll find the cabin later."

"I'm not going anywhere." Garret's lips curled up, giving her one of his devilish smiles that she hadn't seen since they'd left her house.

"Fine." Jase tried to hide his surprise but the growl gave him away. "Make yourself at home. I'll be back for you before things get started."

"Thank you." She watched him walk toward the door and wanted to be able to tell him that she'd do it. "Jase…I'll see what I can do about Zoe after the ceremony. I might be able to help her."

With a nod, he was gone, leaving her alone with Garret, and the biggest decision of her life hanging in the balance.

What am I going to do?

Chapter Four

Sin sank back against the worn sofa cushions and let out a deep breath. Every time she thought she could handle things, something else was tossed at her. Now Jase wanted her to commit to him and the clan, and when they were children—although she never truly expected him to ask her—she had always dreamed about being his second. Now she was faced with the opportunity and it scared her. She wasn't sure if she wanted to jump at it or dive back into Garret's truck and speed off in the opposite direction. Tugged in different directions, she didn't know what she actually wanted anymore.

"Maybe now would be a good time to tell me what's between you and Jase." She opened her eyelids to look at him. "I didn't really care before. I figured it was your business and that he must have trusted you to send you to me, but this tension between the two of you…well, it leaves me wondering what I'm missing."

"I have nothing to hide." Garret leaned against the wall, his thumbs laced through two belt loops of his jeans. "My sister managed a bar and when it was bought out by a bear, things got hairy. He was an abusive ass and he thought he owned her because she wasn't a member of the local wolf pack. He cut her off from her family and friends, growing more paranoid and abusive with each passing day, until he locked her in the apartment above his bar. I was staking out the place when I met Jase. I took him up on his offer to help get her out of there. My sister's life means more to me than being in debt to him, just as yours does. So I'm serious—if you want to leave,

I'll work things out with Jase. Don't concern yourself with that."

"He forgave the debt," she reminded him.

"Yeah." His chest rumbled with a light chuckle. "Just don't worry about your brother and me. We'll deal with it."

She made a mental note to make sure Jase understood the slate was clear with Garret. He dealt with enough on this trip. He didn't need a debt still hanging over his head because of whatever decision she made. "What happened to your sister?"

"We got her out of there and she's safe. But…well, I killed the bear and as you can guess, that pissed Jase off. I imagine he wanted to reform him or some shit." Garret pushed off the wall and strolled toward her. "But it doesn't matter if he was a shifter or not; a man like that can't be reformed. I did what I had to do to protect my sister and others. I have no regrets. Does that change what you think of me?"

"No." She reached out to touch him. "You did what you had to and your sister will always be safe because of that."

"Come here." He tugged her hand until she was standing and he wrapped his arms around her waist, pulling her tight against his body. "You're an amazing woman. I wish I met you under different circumstances."

"What does it matter what brought us together as long as we met?" She pressed her head against his chest and his heartbeat thundered in her ear. "I know the bear you're talking about. His bar was a few blocks from my place. When they found him…"

"I know he was in bad shape." Even as he said it, there wasn't a drop of remorse in his voice.

She had been honest before when she said it didn't bother her to know that he killed that bastard. In her heart she didn't believe Garret would kill like that. His wolf must have gained control. "I wasn't referring to the condition of the body. The news said they'd found a woman's body in the basement. He'd killed a woman a few months before and her body was in the freezer."

Garret's body was tense against her. "My sister wasn't the first he kept prisoner and wouldn't have been the last."

"Jase always wants to believe he can save everyone. Since it was a bear, he most likely felt obligated to at least try to save the asshole from himself." She tipped her head back enough to look up at him without stepping out of his embrace. "Don't get me wrong, Jase is a good man and he'll make a good Chief, but he wants to save the world. At some point, he's going to have to realize he can't save everyone."

"No one can save the world, but we can all save those we care about." His arms tightened around her, as if he didn't want to let her go. "Your brother has a big heart. He's seen the worst of the world, so he wants to give others a chance. There's a time and a place for second chances. He might disagree but that bear didn't deserve one, not after the condition he left my sister in."

"Second chances…" Her words came out breathy and her heart hammered against her chest.

"You're going to do it, aren't you?"

Before she could answer, a knock sounded from the door before it was pushed open. "May we come in?" Her mother peeked in the crack of the door.

"Sure." She leaned back and mouthed *I'm sorry* to Garret, even though she was somewhat thankful for the interruption. How was he going to take it when she told him she was going to accept the position? Would he leave? As Deputy she wouldn't need his protection, because the only way there'd be an attack on her was if someone wanted to challenge for her position. He wouldn't be able to do anything for her in that case. Mentally, she cursed herself for worrying about him when he'd be leaving her life in a matter of days, anyways. The connection between them would fade and she'd be alone just like she'd always been. Only this time she'd be alone while still being in the clan. She wanted a mate, craved the connection she was feeling now, but this wasn't how she was supposed to find the man she was to be with. She shouldn't be tied to him because her brother wanted to make sure she was safe. *It's not just the connection of his bite. I wanted him before…* She pushed those thoughts away and focused on the next few hours.

Accepting this position also meant she had another big problem to deal with, and that was how she was going to explain to the tribe who Garret was and why she smelled like his mate. They couldn't stick to the mating lie. Mates didn't leave, no matter what obstacles life threw at them. *But we're not mates, we're just pretending. One day I'll find my true mate…*

Her fox barked within her. *He's my mate.*

"Sin…my little girl." Her mother wrapped her arms around her, catching her off guard. "I didn't think you'd ever come back home."

Not sure what to say, she decided to go with the truth. "Me either, Mom."

When her mother finally let her go, she found her father standing directly behind them waiting for his own hug. "Dad…"

"Give your old man a hug." He held out his arms and when she neared, he wrapped them around her. Just like when she was young, she felt warm and safe in his embrace. With a grumpy old bear as a father, she was safe as long as he was around. The teasing might have always been there, but kids were ignorant. "We've missed you, Sin."

"I've missed you too, all of you." She had been homesick, missing them, Jase, and Swift, but as she stood there, all of the loneliness came rushing toward her. Even though some thought she didn't belong because of the animal she shifted into, this was her home. The tribe she had been born into had never been home because she was too young to understand what was happening around her. Family and friends had been killed and her heart broken, but the loss had been replaced with Jase and their parents—a double edged sword that would always be wedged in her heart.

"Are you going to take Jase up on his offer?" Dad kept his voice low but there was a hopefulness to his tone.

Surprised, she stepped back from him and took a deep breath. "I can't believe he told you about that."

"Granddad and I asked who he'd name. We needed to make sure he was ready to lead this tribe. If Granddad would announce him as Chief and he wasn't ready, it could be the demise of all of us."

"Who's your friend?" her mother interrupted their conversation.

"Mrs. Locklear." Garret held out his hand to her. "I'm her mate."

Her father took a deep breath, looking between the two of them, and shook his head. His eyebrows furrowed. "I smell her on you but the connection is not complete."

"Dad, we just met recently and…" So much for coming clean. With Garret sticking to the plan, she had no option but to continue with the lie or let them know that Jase had planned to deceive everyone. Protecting her brother, she stepped toward Garret and slipped her hand in his. "When Jase called and asked me to be here today instead of tomorrow like I had planned, we got interrupted."

"Sir, living in the human world, we had planned to marry and be mated the same day," Garret added.

"That is a human tradition," her mother spat out, disgust deepening her tone.

"My former tribe made that *human tradition* a part of their mating ritual." She took comfort in Garret's touch as memories of her biological parents flashed before her eyes. "It was something that my birth mother valued."

"How do you know that?" Her mother crossed her arms over her chest, disbelief clear.

"She told me. I remember sitting on her lap looking at the photo album from their wedding. It was done in front of the justice of the peace, days after they'd met, but it was special to her. I wanted that as well." She turned slightly to glance at him. "Garret was kind enough to understand and indulge me on this."

Her mother shook her head. "A daughter of mine and such human nonsense."

She arched her back and for the first time in her life, she stood up to her parents. "When you took me into your home, I had to adjust to your bear customs. I've accepted those, merged them with the beliefs that were already instilled in me, and have found some of my own along the way. I'm sure you realized over the years I've never been one to follow the straight line. I like to make my own, one that works for me."

"That's why, unlike your father and Granddad I don't believe Jase is making the right decision bringing you on as his Deputy."

Sin stared at her mother, too shocked to speak. The woman who had stood up for her countless times, who told her that she could do anything she wanted, now sliced a deep wound in Sin's chest. She swallowed the lump forming in her throat and refused to let the tears shine in her eyes.

"Why's that?" Garret slipped his hand from hers and wrapped his arm around her waist, holding her tight.

"He needs someone by his side who will do what our tribe needs, keep our tradition alive, and not bring human ones in."

The door behind her opened. Jase's large figure appeared in the doorway before stepping in and shutting it behind him. "Mother, we've had this conversation. Shifters are mixing with humans now more than ever and we need to accept that. Also, this tribe is no longer a bear majority one, as it once was. We must accept that. Our values and beliefs need to merge to create a stronger tribe. While Granddad is not interested in making the change, he understands this. It's why there will be a new Chief tonight."

Sin tightened her grip on Garret's hand. "And a new Deputy."

Sin's announcement came as no surprise to Garret, but from the collective gasps of the rest of her family, it seemed that none of them had expected her to take the position. It became clear to him that those she considered family didn't know her as well as he did. It was somewhat surprising since they'd just met but the connection between them gave him an extra insight into her.

"Are you serious?" Jase stepped passed his parents and eyed her with suspicion.

"I am."

"Jase, I think we have a bit to talk about." Garret's fingers teased over the curve of her hip as he pressed her tight against the side of his body. He hoped Jase and Sin understood just what he was getting at.

"He's right. Mom, Dad, if you could give us a few minutes."

"This is a family run tribe," the older woman complained as her husband touched her shoulder.

"It is to a point." Jase's words grew clipped. "Granddad didn't include you in all of the decisions and as much as I love you, I won't either. This will be our tribe and you must trust that we will do what's right for it. You've taught us the difference between what's right and wrong, instilled beliefs and morals in us. Now it's time to let us lead."

"Obviously, we didn't do enough." Mrs. Locklear gave Sin a pointed glance before strolling out of the room.

"It's good to have you back home," Mr. Locklear added with a soft smile before following his mate.

"Actually Jase, I need a minute with Garret." She stilled under his touch, her body tense.

"I'll be in my office upstairs. That's the best I can do after kicking our parents out." Jase crossed the distance to the steps before glancing back to them. "There's a lot to life and one of the most cherished gifts is mating."

Garret wasn't sure what to make of the comment. Did Jase know what he already knew in his gut, that Sin was his mate? Why send him after her under false pretenses? Did the bear think this was all some kind of game, that he could move everyone around like chess pieces to get his desired results? This was why Garret wasn't part of a wolf pack. He didn't have the patience for the games that went along with it.

"I'll understand if you want to leave." She didn't move away from him but he could feel the distance she was trying to put between them.

"Don't close yourself off from me." He turned her around so she was facing him. "I know we came together under questionable circumstances, but I think there's more here between us."

"What do you mean?" Her fox howled softly, tantalizing him.

"From the moment you opened that door, I was drawn to you. I wanted to press you up against the wall and run my hands over the curves of your body. I knew in that moment that you were my mate—not because Jase wanted me to protect you, but because our destinies were intertwined. We are supposed to be together." He placed his hands on her hips, keeping her there in front of him.

"It's just this bite." She tugged her hair to the side and tipped her head to show him the bite mark. "This is what you're feeling. It's making you believe in things that didn't happen. You don't want me; you want a nice little wolf of your own."

"You're my mate," he growled. "It's not the bite, it's you. My foxy red-head with a temper to match. I want you."

"You don't know me." Her jaw tightened as she blinked away the tears that glistened in her eyes.

"I know enough and we'll have the rest of our lives to get to know each other."

"Say just for one minute I believe you. I'm to be Deputy to the tribe. I can't go back to the life I had. What kind of life is that for you? You are a lone wolf but you'd be stuck here by my side."

"I'm a lone wolf because I don't believe in the wolf pack's beliefs or structure. When I reached the age when I could choose my own path, I chose to go on alone. Multispecies tribes or clans are different than an all wolf one." He reached up and cupped the side of her face. "Plus, it doesn't matter where we are, as long as you're by my side. I want you, here or back at your house—location doesn't matter. I'm a virtual tech expert. I can work anywhere."

She shook her head. "This is insane."

"No, darling, this is mating." He pulled her against him and kissed the top of her head. "We'll get through this and you're going to do this tribe proud."

She wrapped her arms around his waist. "I was being honest when I said that I want marriage. It meant something to my biological parents, so it means something to me. The tribe, even my parents, don't get it…"

"Shh, darling. We'll do it however you want, but my wolf wants you now, so we'll have to get married soon."

"Is tomorrow too soon?"

Garret's gaze shot to the stairs. He hadn't heard Jase come down.

He was watching them and when they turned to look at him, he said, "What? I knew this was wrapping up so I came down to explain."

"Explain what?"

"Dear sister, haven't you wondered whether I knew you two were destined for each other? I know Garret has." He continued down the steps. "I have the ability to know who will be mated together. When I met Garret, I figured it out instantly. I sent him to you because I knew that if you came back with your mate, you'd be more confident and would be able to lead this tribe with me better than if you were alone. We have new members arriving and we'll need to be at our strongest. The three of us can be what the members need."

"Three?" Garret's eyebrow rose at that.

"You are my sister's mate. That means you're just as important to this leadership as she is. As my mother said, this is a family tribe, which means someday we will give over the reins to one of our children. As I haven't found my mate yet, that could mean your child."

"Jase!" Sin hollered at her brother, a blush staining her cheeks. "Could we not rush things? The mating isn't even complete."

Jase smirked. "Fine, but you didn't answer me. Is tomorrow too soon? I have a friend who can marry you?"

Sin gave him a glare. "You've thought of everything, haven't you?"

"Tomorrow's fine," Garret answered before Jase had a chance to give a reply to her question. "Though I have to say for someone who doesn't even like me, you're sure eager for your sister to mate with me."

"I don't agree with your practices…" Jase eyed him, as if not sure how much to say.

Garret waved his hand. "Don't worry, I've already told her about the bear I killed."

Jase nodded. "Good, she deserved to know. Nonetheless, I know you will keep her safe at all costs. You've met my parents, so you know what you're getting into. Mom runs hot or cold, there's no in-between with her. She is Granddad's daughter, so she believes in the old ways, and doesn't like change. Sin had a way of getting under Mom's skin, but she's always been a daddy's girl. They are more alike than you can tell at first glance."

The door behind them swung open to reveal a woman with the same red hair as

Sin, only cut into a stylish short bob, but her green eyes were dark and haunted. He had no doubt he was looking at Swift.

"I didn't believe them when they said you were coming home." Swift entered, but didn't move farther into the room. "It's been years." Her arms crossed over her chest as she glared at Sin.

"You had the chance to come with me." Sin turned inside his embrace, to face her cousin.

"I don't understand why you'd come home only to leave again." Swift leaned back against the wall. "We were getting along fine without you. Why did you come back? Just to rip open the wounds again?"

"I'm not leaving." She touched Garret's chest. "This is Garret, my mate, and we'll be making our residence here."

"You think you can just stroll back into the tribe and pick up where you left off? Well, the Locklears might be willing to welcome you back but not me." Swift reached for the door handle but didn't pull it open, seeming to hesitate.

"She has come home because we need her." Jase's voice was soft but there was a heat in his gaze. "Swift, I know you're dealing with your own personal demons but tonight there will be an announcement naming me the new Chief, and Sin, my Deputy. I expect you to show her the respect that she deserves. This isn't easy for her."

"I'd never thought I'd see the day a Locklear would allow an outsider to take a leadership role. Figured you'd choose a cousin for that position. But you chose her? I bet that really pissed off your mother."

"She's not an outsider." Jase's voice held a hint of a growl, warning Swift to watch what she said. "She's my sister, a part of *my* family."

"Whatever." Swift left without another look in Sin's direction.

Jase wiped a hand across his face. "Give her a few days and she'll come around. Right now she's angry and is struggling to deal with the memories."

"We're all struggling with something." Garret nuzzled the side of his mate's face. "An adjustment period is going to be needed for everyone. I haven't lived a pack lifestyle for years but I know you're going to have more people testing you than normal because they need to see how Sin's grown and how she's going to handle the new role. I hope you're both ready for it."

"I hope you are ready for it as well." Jase stared at Garret. "You're going to have your own battles being accepted within the tribe."

"To be with her I'd go anywhere and deal with any obstacle." He kissed her temple. "We're destined to be together, just as you were destined to take over the tribe. Everything happens for a reason."

Chapter Five

After legally becoming Mrs. Garret Fox, Sin stood staring down at the wedding ring on her finger. There was nothing standing in the way of completing their mating ritual except for her nerves. How he ever managed to pull off finding wedding bands that fit in the time frame they had and without even leaving her side was beyond her. The ceremony had been a quiet one, with only Jase in attendance. She had wanted Swift to come, but her cousin had declined and Garret's sister lived too far away to make it. While it wasn't the wedding of some girls' dreams, it was good enough for her. They were legally married in the human world and by morning, they'd be joined in the shifter world as mates.

There were things she should be doing—claiming her new role as the Deputy of Crimson Hollow Tribe, but Jase had made the mating a priority over all else. He wanted it completed before the new shifters arrived the next day. Still, she wasn't sure how she felt about her leadership roles controlling her personal life. But that was a problem for a different day.

"My darling wife..." Garret came up behind her, wrapping his arms around her waist. "I thought we weren't going to worry about work tonight."

"I'm not."

"Sure." Sarcasm dripped from that single word.

"I was thinking about the stuff I need from my house. About selling my place, quitting my job, and everything else I have to do because life threw me another curve ball." She'd been thinking about it to try to keep her mind off of what was coming. She wasn't a virgin, there had been a few men over the years, but she felt like one, all nervous and giddy.

"Worry tomorrow. Right now, I want you." He slipped his hands under her sweater, tugging the thin material up. "It's time to claim my mate."

"My lone wolf is demanding." She spun around to look at him.

"Not a lone wolf any longer. I found myself a mate and a whole tribe depending on us. Now, although I enjoy talking with you, I want you naked." He tugged the sweater over her head.

"Shouldn't we go upstairs first?"

"Why?" He wiggled out of his long sleeve shirt and let it fall to the floor. "I'm going to have you in every room and then some."

The fox within her trotted forward, howling in agreement. She wanted the man before her like nothing she'd ever experienced. Her desire soared like a fire burning within her and the only thing easing back the flames was his touch. The more he touched, the less overwhelming the fire, though his touches heated other parts of her. There was more than just the mating bond fanning the flames between them. She wanted Garret. This was her mate.

Her skin grew hot and her breaths came in short gasps, she let her hands travel down his chest until she reached the button of his slacks. "You're not a lone wolf any longer, but you're *my* wolf." She glared up at him and unzipped his pants before sliding her hand under the thin material of his boxers until she found his shaft. Hard and ready for action, she wrapped her hand around it, sliding up and down the length. With each stroke she sped her pace, until a growl vibrated through his chest.

He crushed his mouth to hers, while his hands slid under her skirt and grabbed her upper thighs, forcing her to lose contact with his shaft. The growls intensified as skin met skin and he realized she had nothing on under the skirt. He lifted her onto the counter before breaking the kiss. "My mate the tease. All afternoon I've fantasized about what you might have on under this short skirt and now I find out it was…nothing." The last word was bitten out as he slid a finger between her legs, finding her core in one smooth motion.

"I knew we'd be anxious and I didn't want any of the beautiful panties I brought ruined. They'll have their uses *later*." She drew that last word out, teasing him.

"I wouldn't want to rip anything you could tease me with later," he teased and slid his finger over her clit, making her arch into him.

A moan escaped her lips and she wrapped her arms around his neck. "I need you now."

"But darling, all this talk about teasing…" He caressed her clit once more before sliding a finger into her passage.

Fierce desire rose within her like a tidal wave smashing through a dam.

"I thought we'd draw this out for a bit. Make you scream my name before I even entered you."

"There's a time for teasing and a time for mating. Now it's time for mating." When he continued to push his fingers in and out of her core, she gasped, "Please, Garret."

He slipped his fingers from within her and spread her legs farther apart. He kissed along her shoulder, up her collarbone, and along her neck. Even as she cried out in frustration, he ignored her demands.

"Garret…" she murmured as his mouth found hers. "I need you."

Without further delay, he gripped her hips, pulling her toward the edge of the counter, and drove into her with one powerful thrust, a growl echoing through the house. "So tight," he rasped as he worked his way further into her channel. When he was buried deep within her, he gripped her hips and began rocking in and out of her, each stroke faster than the last one.

"Oh, Garret!" Digging her nails into his shoulders, she pushed herself toward him, meeting each thrust with one of her own, drawing them together faster and harder than before. She needed this as much as her beast did.

Lifting her off the counter, he stumbled back until he could press her against the wall. The angle gave him a better reach, allowing him to bury himself deeper. She held on as every pump of his hips sent pulses of pleasure exploding through her. She came apart at the seams, her inner muscles clenching around him as he continued to drive into her.

"Yes darling, squeeze those muscles around my dick." He slammed home in a frenzy as his climax burst through, and a second orgasm shattered her world. She shook with the force of it, clinging to him to keep herself upright. He leaned forward, pressing his body against hers, holding her against the wall, and howled.

"Mated to a wolf." She chuckled but tightened her arms around his neck. "I wouldn't have it any other way."

"I wouldn't want this any other way, either." He slipped out of her but kept her in his arms. "Now, I think we shall test out the bed."

After spending most of the day having sex in every room of the cabin, Sin leaned against the kitchen counter in one of Garret's shirts, eating cold pasta left over from the celebration the night before. She was exhausted and blissfully happy at the same time. Sex had been enjoyable before but with Garret, it was unbelievable. When she was young, she overheard one of the other tribe women mention intimacy with their mate was unlike anything they'd ever experienced before. She didn't understand it then but now she did. It wasn't just sex; there was a bond between her and her mate that could not be matched.

"Darling…" He came up behind her, wrapping his arms around her waist, and nuzzling her neck. "I'd have cooked you something."

"A man with skills in the bedroom and in the kitchen. How did I get so lucky?"

"I'm pretty sure I'm the lucky one." He nipped her neck. "How about I cook you something delicious? It will be better than leftover cold pasta."

"I have better use for your skills." She dropped the fork into the bowl and wiggled around to face him.

"A woman after my own heart." He cupped her butt, lifting her off the floor, only to be interrupted by a knock at the door. "Your damn brother." Growling, he let her slide back down to her feet.

"Come in, Jase." She didn't even raise her voice because there was no doubt he could hear her even across the house. "And this better be good."

"It is." The front door shut and a moment later Jase stood next to the counter. "It's Zoe."

"I told you I'd speak with her in the morning. Tonight is about…other things." She rubbed a hand up Garret's chest.

"She overheard Mom talking about the new members arriving tomorrow and she's locked herself in your old room, scared out of her mind. I tried to go to her but that only scared her more. I wouldn't ask but I don't have anyone else who can help her. Swift is in no frame of mind to help."

"Go ahead," Garret urged. "She needs you."

She looked at her mate and let out a deep sigh. This was part of her job but right now she just wanted to strip off the shirt she had on and climb back in bed with Garret. "Fine. I need to get dressed and I'll meet you over there."

"I'll wait for you and fill you in as we go."

Instead of arguing, she headed to the bedroom to throw on a pair of pants and shoes. Fighting with Jase would have taken time—time she didn't want to spend that way because it would delay her from getting back into bed with Garret. *Selfish…all I can think about is sex when there's a terrified little girl who needs my help.*

"By the way, Sin," he called through the door. "The house next to mine is yours. You can move in whenever you like. I figured you'd want to bring your stuff or buy new things so I haven't had it furnished but give the word and it will be done."

"The house next to yours? Why?" She tugged a pair of jeans out of the suitcase and slid them on.

"As Deputy, you should be close to me. Granddad is moving to one of the smaller cabins now that he doesn't need the room for tribe members coming in and out. I'm planning on using it to house the guards because I don't wish to move into it."

"Thank you. Better get some furniture yourself. Members will be in and out of your place often now." She buttoned her jeans, slipped into a pair of sandals she had sitting next to the suitcase, and stepped back into the kitchen. "Garret and I will deal with our place. After we get the new members settled, we'll see what we want to keep from our places and go from there."

"Whatever you want." Jase shrugged. "Ready?"

With a nod, she came around the counter and kissed Garret. "I'll be back soon."

"I have no doubt." He glanced to Jase. "Keep my mate safe."

"I can keep myself safe," she reminded him as they strolled toward the front door. After years of being on her own, doing what she liked whenever she wanted, she wasn't used to having so many alpha males around her. Garret was an alpha in his own right, even if he didn't have a wolf pack to command. Then there was Jase; he had changed since she'd last seen him. Not just by looks but his attitude. He was more confident now. Authority poured off him.

"Zoe hasn't spoken much since she arrived, but she likes to read. She devoured the books you had in your room and Mom gave her some new ones yesterday. Books seem to be her escape." Jase stopped her outside of their parents' house. "I'm telling you this because you might be able to use that as a way to connect with her. You used to love reading, escaping reality through the pages of whatever novel you were reading. Well, she's doing the same thing."

"Yeah, but I grew up. I realized that I'd never get the happy ever after the characters in books do." Her wedding ring glistened in the moonlight.

He arched a brow. "You might want to rethink that because I'm pretty sure you just did. Maybe it didn't arrive the way you envisioned it, but it happened for you. Just as one day Zoe will find her happy ending."

"Maybe you're right." She touched her ring, gliding her finger over it. "He found me, maybe against all odds, but he found me thanks to a little help from you."

"He'd have found you even if I hadn't sent him your way. Mates always find a way." He pushed open the door to their parents' house. "I figured we'd need some space so Mom and Dad are over at Granddad's. I'll be down here if you need me."

She nodded and headed for the stairs. "I'll see what I can do but she might just need time. She's afraid of everything that's happened so far and now that there are more new people coming, she's worried it will happen again."

She made her way up the stairs, glancing at the pictures as she did, but it was one picture that caught her attention more than the others. It was one of her parents, Jase, and her sitting near a campfire. They looked like a normal family and she remembered that night vibrantly. It happened a few months after she had come to the tribe. The nightmares of what had happened still haunted her, but she had finally started to not fear every bump in the night. More memorable about that night was the happiness she'd felt. For that one night, her grief didn't control her and she could be happy without guilt. It was the first time she'd felt like she was a part of the Locklear family.

She had been a part of this family but never truly a part of the tribe. There had always been a discord between them because of her animal nature. She had left because of it and now they brought her back because of it. It was crazy how things worked out. Standing outside of her old bedroom door, she paused, letting the memories of that time, when she'd first arrived, flood back. If she could connect with those emotions, she might have a better chance of bonding with Zoe. Memories of a conversation she'd overheard long ago ripped through her.

She sat on the steps, peering down at her father and Granddad, watching them as they stood in the middle of the room. Their voices were hushed but she could hear every word. "They weren't the only tribe. There's been two more, further east. Foxes killed but other members left alive."

"Why foxes? What are we going to do about it?" Her father kept his voice low, but there was concern hidden in the hushed words.

"I don't know but a bear sleuth has killed the attackers from the latest scene. If it happens again, we'll have to go after them. If not, and they realize Sin and Swift survived, they'll come back to kill them off."

This had happened before but the question was, why was it happening again? Why no activity over all these years and now people were hunting fox shifters once more? It was a question she'd have to bring up to Jase and Garret when she was done dealing with Zoe.

She knocked lightly on the door. "Zoe..." She paused, waiting to hear if there was a response. "My name is Sin. I'm Jase's sister, and I'm here to help. Do you mind if I come in?" While she didn't need the girl's permission, she was hoping to put her at ease. When Zoe didn't answer, Sin tried the door. Locked. Still, that didn't stop her. Jase had taught her how to pick any lock in a matter of seconds.

She slipped a bobby pin from the pocket of her jeans, where she always carried one, and went to work on the lock. Bobby pins were something a lot of people had stopped using but she always shoved at least one in her hair or her pocket, in case she needed it. The lock clicked. She pushed it open and stepped into her old room to find Zoe sitting on the bed with a book in hand. The room hadn't changed since she had last seen it. The same blue and gray deco decorated the room.

"Zoe…" She said the girl's name again as she neared the bed, her hands held out before her. "I just want to talk." She sat down at the edge of the mattress, far away from Zoe, and tried to stay focused even as the pictures scattered across the wall behind the bed caught her attention. The best memories of her life all surrounding two large pictures in the middle. One of her with her biological parents, just days before her life changed, and the second with her Locklear family. Arranging them that way had been her way of bringing two halves together.

"I was just like you when I arrived. Terrified and thought I was alone, but Jase was there for me and he helped me through the pain. I was younger than you are so some might say it was an easier transition for me, but we're all here for you." Her gaze fell on a picture of her, Jase, and Swift. "Swift isn't mad at you, she's angry at the world, so please don't take it personally. Instead of dealing with her grief, she bottled it up inside of her and to see what happened to our families happen to another group is just too much for her."

She sat there, hoping the teen would say something but got nothing. Rather, Zoe continued to keep her nose in the book, even though the page hadn't changed. It was a front for the moment, but she knew books could be an escape. They had been for her when she was in the girl's shoes. *What am I doing? I barely handled my own shit and now I'm trying to give advice to someone else. Jase is ridiculous. I can't do this.*

"She left me, just like everyone else does." Zoe's voice was whisper quiet and if Sin had been human, she doubted she would have heard it.

"She didn't leave you. She's still here with us, just distant. I know it's not what you want to hear but she needs time. It's like she lost her parents all over again and she can't deal with it, let alone help you deal with your loss. But I'm here and if you'll let me, I can help you."

"You'll leave, too."

"I won't because as Jase's Deputy, this is my tribe now. I'm going to make it strong and do what's right by all members. Just as I'm here to help you, I'm going to make sure Swift works through her grief this time. Otherwise, she's not going to be a valuable, contributing member here, and we all have to be held responsible." She wasn't sure how she was going to handle Swift, but she'd deal with that later. Maybe Jase or Garret would have some ideas. She put the issues with Swift aside for the moment and focused on Zoe. "Now I know you overheard my parents discussing new members joining us, but I don't want you to worry about that."

"How can I not?" She slammed the book closed and tossed it on the bed. "Right before my family was murdered, we allowed an outsider into our walls. He…he was…responsible." Tears rolled down her face.

Without thinking, she closed the distance between them and wrapped her arms around the young girl. "I'm very sorry." But sorry didn't begin to cover it. A new member…it took her a moment to realize why that tugged at her stomach. It had been the same with her tribe. It was too much of a coincidence for her to ignore. *It can't be the same man…*

"We need to know everything you can tell us about that man."

She glanced at Jase who was standing in the doorway, his expression so taut and dark, he was frightening the girl. She wasn't happy about his interfering. She had felt his presence near the steps, but she had been so preoccupied with Zoe, she hadn't realized he'd come up. Their connection had always been there but felt stronger since they'd undergone the ritual making them Chief and Deputy of the tribe.

"I have this." She kept her voice low as Zoe clung to her.

"It's information I need now. I need to confirm if they have the man." Tension brimmed in his tone, making her raise an eyebrow.

"What?" She rubbed a hand along Zoe's back.

"Outside, now." He tipped his head to the hallway.

"Sweetie, can you give us a minute?" She tucked a strand of the girl's hair behind her ear. "I'm going to find out what's going on." With a nod, Sin rose from the bed and stalked toward the hallway. "I was just making progress. Give me some time and I'll have the information. But coming up here all alpha isn't going to help anything."

He held out a pad to her, his handwriting scribbled over the page. *Another tribe was attacked tonight but the Chief has what appeared to be the leader responsible for these attacks in his grasp. The others are dead. The leader had joined the tribe three days before.*

Through their connection, she could feel Jase's bear growling in frustration. He had wanted to be part of the take down. To bring justice to her, Swift, Zoe, and all of the others that had suffered because of these assholes. She held onto the doorframe and tried to keep her legs solid underneath her. "It happened to mine as well, right before…"

"We need this information and we need it now," Jase pressed. "We have to know if he's behind all of these attacks or if there's anyone else we should be worried about. If someone else is leading this crusade, then it's not over yet."

"I'll tell you what I know," Zoe called to them. "But in return, I want to live somewhere else. I know they are your parents but they don't want me here. I've heard them talking. They don't want you to bring these new people here either. They long for the way things were."

"I know." Jase sighed. "I'm Chief now and I will choose how to lead this tribe—"

"Jase," Sin cut him off. "Another time, maybe."

"Very well." He nodded. "But I don't have anywhere else to put her where she'll be safe. You know this, Sin."

"She'll come stay with me," Sin blurted out without giving a thought to it before she spoke.

"You're newly mated." He shook his head. "I'm not sure Garret would approve and I don't think Zoe wants to be kept up all hours of the night with your…activities."

"Garret will be fine with it and will welcome her into our home. I suspect that you've soundproofed the master bedroom and the office at the new place just like yours is. Correct?"

"Yeah."

"Then it won't be a problem. The insulation is done well enough that even shifters can't hear noises through the walls."

"I didn't have it installed for the reasons you're claiming but for tribe business."

"What works for one thing will work for another."

"Hey." Zoe waved to them. "I'm right here and I really don't want to think about her sexual activities. So could you…stop talking about it? And even if I had to listen to it all night, that would be better than living here."

"We'll have the place furnished tomorrow and you can move in then." Sin resumed her seat on the edge of the bed. She'd have some explaining to do when it came to Garret and a ton of work to get the new house livable, but somehow, they'd make it work. They had to…

Chapter Six

With the fire crackling before him, Garret sat trying to focus on a tech job that had the deadline creeping up, but his thoughts kept turning back to Sin. He had only known her a few days and already they were married and mated. For a man who had never believed in love, he sure couldn't believe what was happening. His sister had told him that one day his mate would sneak up on him and he'd believe in the happy ever after that she'd always dreamed about. He hadn't believed her until now. He just hoped she'd find the same joy he had.

The front door opened and Sin called out to him. "Garret?"

"I'm in here." He shut the laptop and turned to see his mate stroll toward him. "How did things go?"

"Your mate just took in an orphan teen." Jase sounded disgusted as he plopped down on one of the chairs. "She didn't bother to talk to either one of us before she opened her mouth and issued the invitation. What the hell does she know about raising a teenager?"

"What does any parent know?" Garret countered as he glanced toward his mate. "Where is she?"

"You're not mad then?" She sat down beside him, angled to face Jase, too.

"No. I'm sure you had good motives, but I would like to know what you've gotten us into." He ran a hand along her thigh.

"Zoe's terrified and well, Mom is constantly bitching about letting outsiders in.

Zoe feels unwelcome there. What could I do?"

"It sounds like you did the right thing. Where is she?" Garret gave her thigh a gentle squeeze. "You didn't leave her outside, did you?"

"She'll stay with my parents tonight and tomorrow we'll furnish the place with whatever we can and stay there." She gave him a waggle of her eyebrows. "By the way, the bedroom is soundproofed. Just like the home office, it will be better to just move there tomorrow instead of bringing her here."

"We don't want you to taint her with your mating growls," Jase joked, a smile curving one corner of his mouth.

"I'm sure Sin didn't need you here to tell me about Zoe, so why are you hanging around?"

"We're stuck with him until we get a call." She slid closer, cuddling against the side of his body. "There was another attack on a tribe tonight but they caught the person they believe is the leader of the perpetrators."

"Okay, but what's this call about?" Instead of pulling her into his lap like he wanted to do, he wrapped his arm around her shoulders, keeping her close.

"Zoe mentioned that a new member joined her tribe three days before the attack. She described him and we're waiting for the Chief to call us back and confirm the identity. If it's the same person, we'll know the attacks were connected. Maybe it will be over." She rubbed her hand over his chest, tracing the outline of his muscles, and refused to meet his gaze.

"An inside job would be easier to pull off." He frowned. "It makes sense to send someone ahead of the others to infiltrate."

"What doesn't make sense is the gap between these attacks and the one on your tribe." Jase leaned forward, placing his elbows on his knees. "Why has nothing happened for all these years and now, in the last week there have been four different attacks?"

"Your tribe?" Garret hooked his forefinger under her chin to force her to look up at him.

She swallowed, but met his gaze. Her eyes shimmered with tears. "We had someone join a few days before the attack. It's too much of a coincidence for it not to be related. It's happening all over again…"

"We'll get to the bottom of this and I'll keep you safe. I promise." He kissed the top of her head and glanced over at Jase. He needed to get a few minutes alone with the bear and see what else he knew.

Jase's cell rang. He rose from the chair and headed toward the kitchen. "I've got to take this."

Garret took the opportunity to bring her closer. "You know that no matter what happens, I'll protect you and we'll put an end to this." He squeezed her tight against him, the pain of seeing the hurt in his mate's eyes tightening his chest.

"How many more will die before we do? How many children will be orphaned before this ends?"

He didn't know what to say to that because he didn't know, so he just held her. If he knew who was responsible, he wouldn't be sitting there in front of the fire with his mate. He'd have gone after them himself. The bastards wouldn't be walking the earth any longer, planning their next targets. They'd be dead. His wolf paced restlessly inside him, ready for a fight.

They sat there in silence until Jase returned a few minutes later. Garret couldn't make out the other man's expression but from the twinkle in his eyes, it appeared he might have found out something worth the wait. "So?" he pressed when Jase continued to lean against the archway, watching them.

"It's the same man from Zoe's tribe. The son of the one who attacked your tribe, Sin."

"What?" She pulled away from Garret.

"His father was on a mission to eliminate foxes but he was killed. Now that the son is of age, he decided to continue his father's work. But he won't be an issue any longer. Everyone that was working with him is dead." Jase shoved his phone into his pocket. "They're done."

"How do you know this?"

"The Chief and his guards took matters into their own hands." He shook his head at his sister. "I didn't know they had planned that but they were able to get the information we needed out of him. Now we know why there was a gap from the first attack to what's happening now. The kid was too young, but now he picked up where his father left off."

"How did the father die? Why does he hate foxes?" Sin questioned.

"Someone from your tribe got a few good shots in and he ended up succumbing to his injuries. As for his hatred of foxes he told some rambling story of his father falling in love with a fox but she wouldn't accept him because he wasn't her mate." Jase rubbed a hand over his face and shook his head. "He went on and on, adding to the story, they're not even sure if that's the truth."

"How can you be sure there aren't others involved with him?" Garret asked.

"He bitched that the last few attacks hadn't gone as planned and his people were killed. That the last two were with him and now they're dead. We're going to have to believe that for now because we have no other leads but until we know for sure, we'll have to be careful."

"What about the new members? They arrive tomorrow. Could any of his group be among them?" Sin shivered against Garret and he ran his hand down her arm.

"None of them are new to the tribe that was attacked, so we'll have to assume that they are no threat. Until we are positive, we'll have to be careful. You'll need to keep a close eye on Zoe without scaring her more than she is already. She hasn't been out of the house much but we don't need her to be more afraid."

"We'll deal with her," Garret assured him, though his bigger concern was for his mate.

"Very well." Jase headed for the door before glancing back at them. "Let me know what you need me to do for the house. If you want I can send some guys to get whatever you need from your houses, or into town for new stuff. Hell, you can take whatever you want from here." Before they could say anything, he opened the door and left.

With Jase gone, he turned to his mate. "Are you okay?"

"I remember him…the father, I guess. He came to us with this story that his mate was missing and he was seeking a place to stay while he combed the area. Dad was a guard and he said something rubbed him the wrong way about the guy, but he couldn't put his finger on it. Mom thought it was how he spoke of this mate, the anger that sparked in his eyes."

"Are you sure?" He took her hand into his, squeezing it gently.

She nodded as a tear fell from her eye. "I overheard them discussing it just before the commotion. That's when Dad sent Mom to me and he went outside. It was the last time I saw him."

"How did…darling, it's a sensitive question, but from what I've gathered, they try to eliminate the whole tribe, leaving behind no witnesses. How did you and Swift survive?"

"I was hiding…after Dad took off to see what was going on, Mom must have known something was wrong. She forced me to hide under the table. She tried to tell me we were only playing a game but I knew something was wrong. I begged her to leave but she wouldn't leave without Dad." She ran her hand through her hair. "I sat under the table as the humans killed her."

He pulled her into his lap and hugged her tight against him. "Darling, there was nothing you could do. You were just a child."

"What if this isn't over?" She laid her head against the curve of his shoulder.

"We'll make sure it is. Jase has extra guards on duty and we'll keep our guard up." He ran his hand down her arm. "I have a friend—he's a security expert, and I'd like to bring him here."

"Why?"

"There are things we can do to make this tribe safe and he can help with that. Precautions are not a bad thing to have. We can make the homes safer for each member so if there was ever a breach of the perimeter, they'd still be safe in their homes."

"Tomorrow. You'll make the arrangements and I'll let Jase know."

"Anything for my mate." He slid his hand underneath his shirt that she was still wearing. "Now I seem to remember the idea of a shower before Jase arrived. Why don’t we get one and you let me wash these memories away?”

A smile stretched across her mouth. “You just want me naked again.”

He rose, lifting her up in his arms as he did. “Naked, now and always.”

Epilogue

Two weeks and Sin's life did a complete turnaround. If someone would have told her that she'd be back home as Deputy to the tribe and mated, she'd have never believed them. Even half of that she'd have said was out of the question. Now she lived in their new home, trying to find her way through raising a teenager too. A few curve balls but she wasn't sure she'd have had it any other way.

She slid the casserole into the oven just as the teenager in question came into the kitchen. "Zoe, I know you've been burying your nose in a book since coming here, but do you think you could actually spend some time with us tonight? Ari is a good friend of Garret's so it would mean a lot to us."

She plopped down on one of the bar stools and slid a paper toward her. "I will if you'll pick up a few of the books I have on my list."

"We're going into town tomorrow, put the list on the fridge and I'll get them." She leaned against the counter and looked at the young girl. Who'd have ever thought she'd be raising a teenager, especially one that had a reading addiction like she did? "If you need something to read in the meantime, check my bookshelf in the office. I'm sure you'll find something. There are also two boxes of books next to it that I haven't put away yet."

The stuff from their houses had arrived the week before and while most of it Garret had dealt with while she was dealing with everything else, she hadn't had a chance to organize their office or put the books away. The first goal had been just to make the home livable for them and Zoe.

"Thanks. I might once I finish this one." Her hand caressed a paperback that she had laid on the bar.

"We need to talk about school…" Sin crossed to the bar to stand next to her. "Garret, Jase, and I had a lengthy discussion about this."

"And?" Zoe bit her lip anxiously.

"Your tribe was strong on homeschooling, making education the responsibility of the parents. It's different than what we do here. We have a school house with two teachers and the children are divided into grades. We have elementary students attend in the morning and high school students in the afternoon. It makes it easier on the teachers and the kids only go half a day but year round. The parents work with them if there needs to be extra help and the teachers make themselves available."

"You're going to put me in this school?" Zoe's forehead furrowed.

"Actually, we've decided that you've had enough changes lately. So I've worked it out with one of the teachers and for the time being she'll come here to work with you. It will help her determine where you are compared to the others your age." She glanced up as Garret stepped out of the office where he had been working.

"That being said, Sin and I want you to start taking part in the tribe's activities. There are others your age here and you need to interact with them and everyone else." He came to stand next to Sin, his hand resting gently on her back.

"What is this, punishment for being homeschooled?" Zoe complained.

"No, it's about giving you a healthy life." Sin glanced at the book on the counter. "You can't spend all of your time reading."

"You did and look how you turned out."

She smirked at the girl. "I had Swift and Jase, but I also had to attend school. It was different for me…the others weren't as accepting of my animal as they are now. What I had to deal with in my life is what made me love reading. But I want you to have friends and real life happiness, not only the stuff you read about."

"It's a fair compromise," Garret said gently. "We can't have the Deputy's charge hidden away from the rest of the tribe. Like it or not, you're part of the leadership of this tribe and you have to do your part."

"Hey." Sin hit his chest lightly. "You're not supposed to be giving her more to worry about."

"I'm part of this?" Zoe's eyes glistened. "I've never been a part of something like this."

"You're a part of everything that happens here." Sin leaned into Garret's embrace. "It's why we want you to grab hold of everything we can offer you with both hands."

"I'll try." Zoe hopped off the bar stool. "Can I go check out those books now? I promise I won't stay buried in a book while Ari's here."

"Go." Sin nodded and glanced up at her mate. Grab life with both hands…that's what she was doing. "Think we can get a few minutes alone before…" Her words were cut off as the doorbell rang, announcing Ari's arrival. "Guess not."

Loving the Bears

Ari Alexander and Kaden O'Malley knew from a young age that they'd share one mate who would complete their unique bond. The problem was they couldn't find a woman who satisfied both them and their bears. Their thriving security business has kept them both busy, but as their beasts grow more and more impatient, they must find a mate.

After escaping a past she wanted to forget Camellia stayed hidden away in the forest. Working with the children of Crimson Hollow, has given her life new meaning. Until the bears came into her life, she thought she had everything she wanted.

When Ari and Kaden meet the beautiful but reserved Camellia, they know she's the one. It's clear she feels the connection too, but she's fighting it. Can they help their mate fight the demons from her past or will she slip from their grasp before they get the chance?

Chapter One

Crimson Hollow was off the beaten path, making it difficult to locate. So when Ari arrived in the late afternoon, he was surprised to find that the community was like its own little town, hidden in the middle of the forest. Log homes were scattered in a clearing, all situated around a large meeting place—an open field with a fire pit. Across the fire pit, on the far side of the grassy expanse, was a road where Garret had told him he'd find his new home. Garret and Sin had the house at the end of the road, next to Jase's, who was the tribe's Chief and Sin's brother.

His best friend Kaden leaned forward to stare through the dirty windshield of Ari's pickup. "Well this is unexpected."

He gave a halfhearted grunt and continued to drive down the dirt road into the compound. He couldn't help but wonder how Garret expected him to make this place safe. He could secure the homes individually, but to keep the whole compound safe there needed to be a perimeter and a gate blocking trespassers from wandering onto this road. Ari ticked through his mind the few issues that were readily apparent. These issues would need to be addressed immediately, even before he provided recommendations for each home's individual security measures. The question was how much expense did the Chief and his Deputy want to get into?

He pulled the truck in front of Garret's house, shut off the engine, and took in the area. There were guards sporadically placed, but none of them seemed prepared for an attack on the tribe. Two stood off in the distance chatting, another leaned against a tree, and most shockingly, one fiddled with his phone. Only a few of them looked to be armed and paying attention to the surroundings. One, in particular, watched them closely. "Looks like we've got our work cut out for us." Shaking his head he reached behind the seats for his bag, also grabbing Kaden's and tossing it to him.

Kaden gave a low whistle. "It's more work than I thought. Are you sure you've got our upcoming jobs covered?" He dragged a hand through his nearly chin length hair, pushing it away from his face, only to have it fall back to where it had been. His work boots, worn jeans, and T-shirt made him look like an average blue collar worker, no one would suspect he was the financial genius behind getting their security business off the ground. Even to this day he was the one handling that side of things, and investing it wisely, so they'd always be comfortable. Unlike Ari, who did his best work with his hands, Kaden had a business mindset.

"Our crew can handle the work for the next two weeks. After that, if we're not back home, I'll have to see what I can juggle." He shrugged because he'd find a way to make it work. They'd committed to helping Garret and that's what they'd do. After Garret's call, Ari dropped what he was doing, passed the work that needed handled onto his crew, and headed out.

Friends helped friends when they needed it. That's just what they did, especially their kind. But if he was honest with himself, he was curious to check out the woman that convinced his friend Garret and his wolf to settle down. He wondered what Garret's feisty sister thought of him moving across the state and joining a tribe instead of a wolf pack.

"Who knows what we might find here." Kaden pushed open the passenger door and hopped out. "Maybe *she'll* be here."

Ari climbed down from the truck and slung his bag over his shoulder. While they might have seemed so different from each other, Kaden was his best friend, and since childhood they both knew they'd share a mate. They just needed the right one to satisfy both of their needs, and the one that both of their inner beasts could desire.

That last requirement had proven the hardest to fulfill. Their beasts were demanding in different ways. But soon, they'd have to settle on one mate because their animals were getting impatient. Though Kaden might have hopes they'd find the one here, he didn't. They had looked far and wide, and had yet to find one who sparked their interest.

Instead of voicing his doubts, he made his way around the truck and toward Garret's house. They were here to do a job not find their illusive mate, and it was time they found out what exactly was expected of them. They were security experts not miracle workers. Hopefully Garret was realistic about what could be done here.

"Where is everyone?" Kaden asked as Ari pressed the doorbell. "Besides the guards standing out like sore thumbs there's no one around, no children playing outside. It's weird not to see anyone moving about."

He hadn't realized it until Kaden spoke, but as his gaze scanned the grounds an unease settled into his shoulders. A group of shifters this size should have had people moving about. People gathered outside enjoying the cool weather while children ran around. There was nothing but an eerie silence.

"You've noticed it too."

Ari turned around to find Garret standing in the doorway.

"What's going on here?" Kaden asked.

Garret stepped back, allowing them to enter, and shut the door behind them before answering. "The attackers have been captured and dealt with, yet the tribe remains uneasy. Parents are keeping their children inside for fear of what might happen. They're apprehensive and don't trust our new members. Jase and Sin are doing what they can to allay fears, but added security might give them the peace they need."

Ari nodded. "The first thing that needs to be done is establishing a defensible perimeter. Otherwise, anyone could stumble upon you. You're pretty much hidden in the forest, but that same isolation also puts you at more of a risk because you are all alone. Anyone could come across the houses here and decide to cause some problems. In the winter, the smoke from your fireplaces would attract people."

"I've already discussed that with Jase." A beautiful red head strolled into the living room. "You must be Ari. I'm Sin. Please come in and make yourself at home."

They sat their bags near the door and took a seat on the sofa before Ari got back to what he was saying. "So, you're not against a fence?" he said, directing his question to the woman, since she was the Deputy of the tribe.

"No, we have a crew ready to begin work, but Garret talked us into waiting until you arrived. He thought you might have some suggestions for improving the design of the perimeter fence." Her words were brusque and businesslike, but Ari couldn't hide a smile as Garret reached out and pulled her onto his lap.

Garret gave Sin's supple thigh a pat. "We're open to whatever suggestions you might have. Our goal is to protect the tribe, and we're aware changes need to be made." Garret ran his hand down his mate's arm. "Since humans became aware of us there have always been issues, but recently the growing numbers of hunters looking for shifter skins have increased."

"When will they learn that even if we're killed in our animal form we'll revert to our human skin when we die?" Ari growled.

"I don't think they will until someone catches it on video," Kaden muttered.

"Even then someone will say the footage is a hoax." Sin shook her head. "I just don't want it to be one of my people killed because of some stupid hunter."

The front door opened and a man stepped through. His wide shoulders and the authority that poured off him left little doubt in Ari's mind that it was the tribe's Chief, Jase. "So they're here. What are their suggestions?"

"Jase," Sin scolded.

"I'm busy dealing with another issue. One my Deputy couldn't be bothered with." Jase said, his gaze narrowing on her.

Sin's mouth thinned. "I know you mean Swift, and this is not the time."

"We can—" Kaden's words were cut off when Jase turned to him.

"Who the hell are you anyway?" Jase snapped.

"The name's Kaden."

Jase turned toward Garret, his dark eyebrows lowering. "I thought you invited one person, not two?"

Sin stiffened on Garret's knee. "I swear to you that my brother isn't always a grumpy bear." She gave Ari a quick, tight smile. "He really is a kind guy. He's just dealing with a lot right now." Her gaze swung back to her brother. "Jase, could you please be hospitable?"

Ari waved a hand, not the least put off by the growling bear. "That's why we're here. We'll take some of the weight off your shoulders, and do what we can to make sure that you can provide a safe place for your tribal members." Ari hoped that knowing someone was working on the problem would ease the tension the leaders were feeling. "I had hoped to get here earlier to get started right away, but darkness is already falling."

"We'll start with the perimeter in the morning." Kaden leaned forward, clasping his hands in front of him and resting his elbows on his knees. "We'll go over it with a fine tooth comb, looking for places for access points and mark your most vulnerable areas."

Jase sank down into a chair across from the sofa. He rubbed a hand over his face before meeting Ari's gaze. "Sin will show you around and get you anything you need. How long do you think it will take before you can give me a list of your suggestions?"

"We should be able to meet with the crew you have ready to build the fence tomorrow evening. The rest will take more time. We'll have to inspect each house—" His words were cut off as Jase rose abruptly and moved toward the window.

"After the perimeter, I want you to focus on this house first."

"What?" Sin's voice held surprise. "If anything, they should focus first on yours."

"The attacks have been against foxes." Jase pinned her with a steady glance. "I want to make sure you and Zoe are safe. Once these guys are done here, they can look at my place."

"We can go over the house tonight," Kaden offered.

"Whatever you'd like." Jase turned back to them. "Sin's right. I was an ass, and I apologize. I'm sure Sin and Garret will be excellent hosts tonight. I won't be able to join you, but I'll catch up with you sometime tomorrow."

"Jase…" Sin called to him as he strolled toward the door. "Is something happening?"

"Just the normal…Swift, the parents…I've got it under control." With that Jase was gone.

"Why do I suspect there's more?" She rose from Garret's lap and went after her brother.

"Why didn't you tell them there'd be two of us?" Ari eyed Garret, watching his friend's reaction.

"I told Sin, but as for Jase, he's been dealing with…" Garret paused and glanced behind him. "Swift. She's Sin's cousin, and when their tribe was attacked years ago, she came here too. But lately, she's been having a harder time."

"Because of me." A soft voice announced as a teenager stepped out of another room, hugging books to her chest. Her long reddish-brown hair was pulled back from her face in a ponytail and her forest green eyes held sadness. She met Ari's gaze. "I brought back all the memories she buried, and now she hates me."

"Zoe," Garret said softly. "This isn't your fault, and she doesn't hate you. She just needs time to process the grief she bottled up over the years."

"She won't even talk to Sin," Zoe whispered. "If only Jase hadn't brought me here…" Tears rolled down her face as she turned and dashed up the steps.

"Excuse me." Garret rose from the chair and followed her.

Left alone, Ari and Kaden shared a glance.

Kaden leaned back against the sofa. "Why do I feel like we've stumbled into family drama and we should leave?"

"Because we did." Ari shook his head and let out a light chuckle. "And you're the one desperate to find our mate."

Chapter Two

With both Garret and Sin taking care of different business, Kaden made himself useful in the kitchen. He checked on the casserole that was in the oven and pulled out the stuff Sin had obviously planned on using to make a salad. He moved around the space with ease, finding what he needed, and made quick work of the preparations.

"If I'm not careful someone else is going to sweep you off your feet." Ari teased, snatching a piece of bell pepper from the cutting board and popping it into his mouth. "Then how am I going to eat?"

"I guess you should focus on finding us a mate to cement things then." He lifted the cutting board to the salad bowl and let the cut vegetables slide onto the lettuce.

Ari leaned against the counter. "We've been looking for years now and haven't found anyone that either of us can agree on."

Kaden eyed Ari with irritation. Ari leaned against the counter like he didn't have a care in the world, all the while his beast was growing impatient within. Kaden knew because he could feel it. They were connected on a deeper level than just friendship, their bears were linked together. Ari was the more dominating of the two, so his bear was more actively protesting the lack of their mate, and while doing so, made Kaden's beast more edgy. "We haven't explored any possibilities outside our own area. We're hours away, and we have a whole community of shifters to consider…" His words died off as the front door opened. Sin's scent drifted toward them even before she made her way into the kitchen.

Sin's scent of fox and wolf together, mingling in a harmony to create a unique scent that surrounded Sin and Garret. He couldn't stop his thoughts from drifting to what his mate might smell like. To have the scents of the three of them mixing together to make a new one excited him. Now if they could only find her. He glanced up at Ari, their gazes locked and it was clear that his thoughts had followed along a similar path. A quick nod let him know that he understood, they needed to expand their hunting grounds.

Sin's eyes widened as she glanced around the kitchen. "Oh guys, I'm sorry. You didn't have to do this. Where's Garret?"

"It's no big deal, and he's upstairs with Zoe." Kaden grabbed the radishes he had drying on a paper towel and placed them on the cutting board.

Her eyebrows drew together. "Your guests—he should be down here."

"Your…umm I'm not sure what to call her…Zoe." Ari looked at Kaden for help.

"Her name or ward would do fine," Kaden said. "What he's trying to say is Zoe had a bit of a meltdown. She blames herself for whatever is going on with Swift. I believe she overheard Jase and thinks his short temper is because he's dealing with Swift, and therefore his frustration is her fault."

"It's not her fault. The whole issue with Swift is something she brought onto herself. But that's not really why Jase was a grumpy bear." She dragged a hand through her hair. "Our parents left the tribe. Granddad—who recently turned the tribe over to Jase—went with them. Jase tried to talk them out of it, but they refused to listen. They didn't even say goodbye. Maybe part of it's my fault, coming back here, but the majority of it is they don't want the changes that are happening. They're going to find somewhere they can be alone and stay set in their ways." She let out a deep sigh and looked to the ceiling. "I guess I should see what I can do about Zoe."

Kaden began slicing the radishes. "Go ahead. I've got this."

"Please help yourself to a beer or whatever you'd like. Just make yourselves at home." Sin glanced between the two men, finally settling her gaze on Kaden.

"Thanks."

"Don't worry about it. I enjoy cooking." He tossed the radishes into the bowl and wiped his hands on a dishrag. "And for what it's worth, I'm sorry about your family. Maybe some time away will give them a better outlook. It won't hurt for you and Jase to have some time to rule the tribe without their interference."

As she left Ari moved to the refrigerator and grabbed two beers. After popping the caps, he handed one to Kaden. "See? We make a good team. You knew just what to say to her."

Kaden grinned. "Yeah, a great team." He stepped toward the pantry, looking for the ingredients he'd need to make his signature salad dressing and considered Ari's words. They were the perfect pair. Where Ari was a protector, fierce, and all business, Kaden was the emotional rock, and while they worked together on the occasional job, he preferred the numbers side of the business. Or being in the kitchen, which was good because Ari wouldn't know a paring knife from a filet knife. They balanced each other out, making each other whole, and their mate would only connect them further. "I've never doubted that we're good together. If I did, I wouldn't be waiting for your bear to take control and demand a mate."

"I never said I didn't want a mate. It's disappointing never finding a woman that works for both of us." Ari took a long drink from his beer. "But I haven't given up that somewhere out there we'll find our mate. I'm just not as impatient as you are."

Kaden leaned back against the counter, took a drink of his own beer, and watched his friend. "I say, if we don't find her here, let's do some traveling. The business is doing fine, and Jack can handle things for a while."

"We'll see." Ari sat the beer bottle on the counter with a thump. "We're going to be here at least a couple of weeks. I don't know about leaving again right away."

"Fine," he said, adding the salad dressing ingredients together into a small mixing bowl. While he frowned at Ari, he stirred. "We'll wait a little while, until you feel comfortable leaving him in charge again. But you've got to admit that we need this." He paused stirring and tasted the mixture he'd created, and then added some red pepper flakes to heat it up some. "Your bear is clawing at you, demanding that she be found. It's our time, and it can't be put off much longer."

Ari's eyebrows rose. "I'm going to walk around the outside of the house. Search for possible intruder entrances." He grabbed his beer and headed for the door.

"You know I'm right," Kaden called after him as he left.

Alone in the kitchen, he set the dressing aside, then quickly checked the casserole in the oven, determining that everything was ready whenever Garret and Sin returned. He turned off the oven and blew out a deep breath.

Not knowing what else to do, he wondered over to the table with his beer and sat down. He pondered why Ari was so hesitant to venture outside of their comfort zone to find a mate. It wasn't like they had a sleuth that they'd have to justify their decision to. They were lone bears, choosing this path because it fit their needs and wants better.

Ari's hesitation was putting Kaden in a tough spot. He wanted a mate, his bear growled in agreement, but he couldn't do it without Ari being onboard. *If only she'd find us and then Ari would have to accept her. His bear wouldn't give him any choice.*

"Where's Ari?" Garret strolled toward the table.

"Checking the outside." *And avoiding our conversation.* "He's already thinking about the security measures he wants to put in place. How's Zoe?"

"She's upset, but she'll be okay. She has had a lot thrown at her lately. She's still adjusting." Garret grabbed a beer from the fridge and leaned against the counter. "There seems to be some kind of tension between you and Ari. On the verge of sounding unmanly, anything you want to share?"

"What, mating make you soft?" Kaden smirked. "Naw, we're fine. He's got a bit of the grumpy bear syndrome that Jase has."

"You bears must need to be in hibernation. The rest of us don't go through stages of irritability like you guys do."

Kaden arched an eyebrow. "Oh yeah, wolves are so even tempered. I remember the time you nearly broke a guy's spine for barking at you."

"I'm not a dog," he growled.

"Did I miss something?" Sin came up to her mate's side.

Garret wrapped his arm around her, and she snuggled in closer.

That was what Kaden wanted for him and Ari. A woman to hold tight in the coming cold months. Someone who would love them despite their cranky asses. But more importantly, someone who could bear their cubs. Family had always been important to him, but since his sister had her first set of cubs, he found himself wanting a dozen of his own. His bear roared within him, demanding that Ari and he find their mate. *Soon…*

Chapter Three

Shifting from foot to foot, Camellia Clarkson tried to ease the tension that settled into her shoulders. There was a scent in the air, unlike anything she smelled before. Honeyed and woodsy, mixing together to create an undeniable smell. She wanted to find it. Unable to place its source, the unease increased as the aroma heated her blood and set her lioness on edge. She was supposed to be there as a teacher, giving the daily lesson to the Deputy's ward, Zoe, and she couldn't keep her mind from wondering away from the task at hand.

"I've finished." Zoe dropped her pen and slid the paper across the kitchen table.

"Very well." She slid the paper inside her folder and pulled out the worksheets she had stapled together earlier. "I'll look it over tonight. In the meantime, I want you to complete these worksheets and have them ready to turn in tomorrow when I arrive." She pushed back from the table and rose, grabbing her sweater from the back of the chair as she did.

Zoe scrunched her nose in disgust. "This stuff is too easy."

"The package you just finished will allow me to see where you stand on all your subjects. Once I know what concepts you already know, we can go from there. From what I can see so far, you are beyond what the ninth graders are doing now. I just need to know how far beyond you are. Everyone has subjects they are better at, I expect you are more advanced in some than others. Once I've gone over the worksheets, I'll have a better understanding and will bring you your schoolbooks." The front door opened, but from where she was standing she couldn't see whether it was Sin returning or someone else. "In the meantime do those new sheets. The further you get in the package, the more advanced they are. Look through and skip over what's too easy. Don't be afraid to challenge yourself."

"Yes, Miss Camellia."

Two men strolled into the kitchen, stealing her attention. Their tight shirts contoured to their toned stomachs, while faded jeans and work boots completed the picture. Her gaze traveled over each of them, and her breath caught. Just standing a few feet away they made her legs weak. Both were roughly the same height and build, and for a moment, she thought they might be brothers. But when she looked up at their faces that idea was blown out of the water. They looked nothing alike. Where one had his hair cut short, almost military-style, the other's was long and shaggy, coming to just below his ear. The one with the longer hair had more pronounced cheekbones, his brown gaze seemed to devour her. Her gaze left him and traveled over to the one with shorter hair. His eyes where harder, his body a little wider and more muscular, overall he appeared the more dangerous of the two.

He smiled at her, and there was a twinkle in his eyes. "We didn't mean to interrupt."

"It's okay Kaden," Zoe said. "This is my teacher, Miss Camellia Clarkson."

Kaden. Her lioness purred at the way his name rolled off her tongue. With the hopes of pushing her lioness aside, she took a deep breath, but that only brought her animal closer to the surface, growling as it leapt forward. *Oh shit!*

She grabbed her bag from the chair, scooping up her folder as she did so. "I've got to go. Do your work, Zoe. I'll see you tomorrow." Needing to get away, she practically ran from the kitchen, slipping past the two men and out the door before anyone could stop her.

Outside, she jogged toward her house, ignoring the comments from those who were out in the common area. Bears…new bears. Fear sped her heartbeat until she thought it would beat right out of her chest. *This can't be happening.*

Inside, she slammed the door and quickly clicked the lock home. It was rare for anyone in Crimson Hollow to lock their doors, but she couldn't help it. She needed the idea of a barricade between her and the unknown bears. What were they doing here? Were they here for her? From the look in their eyes, they didn't seem to recognize her. Their look reflected desire, not hatred.

Maybe they desired to bathe in her blood. Turning, she let her stuff fall to the ground and let her body slide down the wall. "Damn it, Camellia. You need to get hold of yourself."

Her living room faded from view, and she was back in Boston. The stench of the alley filled her nostrils and her lioness trotted forward, warning her something was wrong. She scanned the alley, looking for whatever had her beast on edge. Not seeing anything, she forced herself to take a deep breath and smell beyond the rotting food in the trash and the piss from the homeless who used this alley as a bathroom. She had almost convinced herself she was overreacting when the scent hit her full force. A bear shifter on the other side of the…

He peaked around the boxes, his gaze landing directly on her, and blood oozed from between his lips as he chewed whatever he had in his mouth. Fuck! She backed away slowly, her heels clicking on the cement, but it was too late. He'd already seen her. With the heels and the slick cement from the earlier rainfall she'd never reach the door or the street before he was on top of her. She'd have to make a stand and hope to scare him off.

Scurrying backwards, she reached into her purse, trying to feel for the hidden compartment for her gun. A shifter with a gun—that was irony. Her lioness was deadlier, but the risk of exposure was too great this close to work, and if her boss found out, she'd be out of a job. If only she had gone out the front door of her office building instead of using the back staircase. She had wanted to get home quicker and this cut five minutes off her walk to her apartment, but the cost might have been her death.

"Come here, bitch." He had shifted back to human form while she was searching for her gun. He glided toward her like he had something on his mind besides murder, not the least bit concerned that he was naked.

Her fingers wrapped around the gun, and she tugged it out of the pocket, ready to shoot. "I'm armed. Stay away!"

"Stupid bitch, your bullets won't hurt me." He pounced on her, pushing her to the ground, with him landing on top of her.

She pulled the trigger…

A fist pounded against her door, and the memory faded like the end of a movie, leaving her raw. She wiped a hand down her pants and forced herself off the floor. She debated pretending that she wasn't home. Maybe they'd go away.

It was the bears, she could smell them. The sweet honey and woodsy scents that she'd smelled earlier teased in the air—both tempting and terrifying.

"We know you're there." A deep voice called from the other side of the door. *Kaden.* "Just open up."

"I'm busy." She couldn't breathe. Her heart pounded against her chest until it ached.

"We're staying here until you open this door," a second voice called. It had to be the other big bear.

"What the hell is going on?" Jase's voice came from outside, mixed with the bears.

"Stay out of this," one of them growled.

"You're a guest here," Jase said, his voice deepening in warning. "This is my tribe and my business."

Shit. She tugged open the door to find Jase and the two bears faced off. "It's…" She took a deep breath and forced the words out. "It's fine, Jase."

"What the hell are they doing pounding on your door?" he asked without looking away from the other two men.

"Jase—" Her words were cut off as the bear whose name she didn't know advanced on Jase and growled.

"She's our mate."

Oh, hell, no! Darkness closed in around her, and she felt herself falling with no way to stop herself.

Chapter Four

Camellia's eyes fluttered open to find three faces leaning over her, watching her. Not ready to face them yet, she let her eyelids drift shut again. Surprisingly, her body didn't feel bruised from her fall. Had she hit the ground? She couldn't remember. All she knew was that she woke up on the sofa. *Mate*…that one word sent fresh anxiety through her.

"Camellia?" Someone called but she couldn't make out who said it.

Panic rushed through her, setting her blood on fire, burning her from the inside out. While her lioness charged forward, wanting to smell them more deeply to confirm that what they had said was true, she wasn't ready to know. She tried to shove her beast down, but it was too powerful. She hadn't regained full strength after passing out.

Please, let them be wrong.

Her lioness took a deep breath, filling her lungs with the sweet undeniable smell and purred, begging her to be set free so she could rub her fur all over her mates.

"Camellia." Jase's voice pulled her from her thoughts.

"Huh?" She tried to focus on hearing him over the purring within her. *Could they hear it?*

"Are you okay?"

Okay? The lioness within wanted to scream she was better than okay, but her brain knew that she was far from it. If they found out what she'd done before she came here, they'd kill her. A bear. Just like the three of them standing above her. Even Jase didn't know. She had come here seeking a new start, and because they'd needed a second teacher, they'd gladly welcomed her into their tribe. But she'd never admitted to anyone other than Granddad why she needed that fresh start.

"I'm calling the doctor." Jase tugged his cell phone out of his pants pocket.

"No…" She forced herself to focus on him. "I'm fine. Really, Jase."

"She said she's fine. Now, leave us alone." The short-haired man glared at Jase.

"Drink this." Kaden held out a mug to her. "It's tea. If you don't trust me, ask Jase. He saw me make it."

Jase nodded. "It will be good for you, and I made sure he didn't sweeten it with too much honey."

She took the mug, but didn't bring it to her lips. "Bears and their taste for honey," she muttered.

"It's like kittens and milk." She looked at her other mate, unsure what to say to that, when Jase interrupted.

"You are a member of my tribe, and if you need me to stay, I will. But I feel this might be something the three of you need to work out. Mating…well it has little to do with me."

"We'll be fine." The same man spoke, while Kaden nodded toward the tea.

"Camellia?" Jase pressed.

She drew a calming breath and forced a small smile. "Go ahead. I'll be fine." She wasn't sure that she would be, but she didn't want to have to explain to him why not, either. She'd let him leave, and then she'd face the two bears left in front of her. It didn't matter what her lioness wanted; she couldn't be their mate.

As Jase left, she brought the mug to her lips and inhaled the aroma, trying to focus on that instead of their scents. But the hint of honey only reminded her of them. Purrs vibrated through her body until her hand shook, nearly spilling the tea. Her lioness wanted them.

"Camellia…" The other bear leaned in closer. "Why did you run from us when you knew you are ours?"

"I'm no one's mate." Unable to drink the tea she set it aside and pulled herself up into a sitting position. "I don't know who you think you are, but you cannot come into my home with some claim of ownership over me. Get out!"

"Let's wait a moment here." Kaden, who still knelt by the sofa, eyed the other man. "He's being an ass. I get it, but we do need to talk about this."

She shook her head, trying her best to hide the fear trembling through her. "I don't think we do. I won't have anyone expecting that just because I'm their mate, that I'm theirs. I'm my own person, and I won't be anyone's property, especially not some bears'."

"Ari's being an ass, but he's not normally like this. I'll admit he can be a grumpy bear…hell more times than not he's a pain in the ass, but he's a good man." He eyed Ari as if waiting for an objection before turning back to her. "We've searched for our mate for years, and now that we've finally found you, he's unable to control his beast."

She looked from one to the other, trying to take them both in. Now that she knew the other man's name, she realized they were friends of Garret's. Ari was the security expert he'd brought in to keep the tribe safe. If he'd only known about her past, he might have thought twice before bringing unknown bears into their land. *Bears…why do I have to be mated to bears?*

Without letting her fear gain control of her again, she frowned as she eyed the men. Both were handsome. Just looking at them stoked a fire within her. Their wide chests were toned, making images of them shirtless pop into her thoughts. There was no doubting that they were fine specimens of manhood. Yet there was more to them than what met her eyes. Kaden seemed to have a caring side to him, and Ari seemed to have a solid steel core, a quiet strength that that was more than just the surly attitude she had seen so far. "Why would the two of you want to share a mate?"

"It's not about what we want," Ari rumbled.

"Damn it Ari," Kaden said, his voice clipped. "Keep your mouth shut. Every time you say something you push her further from our grasp."

Camellia deepened her frown. "What do you mean it's not about what you want? If you don't want to share a mate, why would you be searching for one together?"

Kaden held a hand out to Ari, silencing him, before turning to her. "It's our destiny. Something we've known all our lives, and trust me, it's for the best. You wouldn't want one of us without the other. We give each other balance."

"And you will unite us more firmly," Ari added, coming back to stand near the sofa. "I'm an overbearing, stubborn bear that is used to getting his own way, while Kaden's gentle, and well, downright annoying when he tries to take care of everything for you. He tries to fix things before you've even admitted they're broken." He shrugged and gave her a one-sided smile. "But he's one damn good cook—so he does have his uses."

Kaden raised an eyebrow. "Thanks for the support."

"Well, good luck." She twisted to the side so she could put her feet on the floor. "I can't be mated to bears."

Just as she rose to her feet, Ari came around the sofa, faster than she could blink, and stood in front of her. Their bodies barely touched, but his heat radiated onto her. "Got something against interspecies relationships, kitten?"

"No, ah…" she stuttered. What was she supposed to say? Anything she could think of would give away a past she wanted to keep hidden.

Chapter Five

Kaden's bear arched up as the stench of fear flooded the room. What caused the sudden rush? When they'd shown up at her door, she'd been terrified. But this was new…and different. She was shielding herself from them. What was she hiding? If she didn't have something against interspecies relationships, than it had to be something specifically against bears. Which didn't make sense when the Chief of the tribe was a bear.

"Just leave." Her voice wavered and she couldn't meet their gazes.

"Camellia, what's wrong?" he asked softly.

"What's wrong, kitten? Don't think us bears can make you purr?" Ari kept his voice husky as he leaned in to her neck.

"Stop…" The word came out as a moan as he kissed her neck. "I can't…"

"Precious, what's wrong?" Kaden placed his hand on the small of her back. "Talk to us."

"I just can't…not bears."

She met his gaze, and there was a sadness there, deep in her green depths that pierced Kaden's heart.

"Please…"

"How about this?" Kaden rubbed his hand along the curve of her back, soothing her. "We'll leave for tonight. You can have some time to think about this and let your lioness adjust to us as bears. Tomorrow between your classes, we'll meet for lunch."

"We're mates, kitten. You'll have to accept that." Ari ran his hand through her long brown hair, tipping her head up as he did, so she had no choice but to look at him. "Bears might be moody, but I can assure you that once you've allowed us to claim you, you won't have any regrets."

"I'm sorry, but I can't." Her voice broke as she backed away from them.

Everything within him told him to go to her, to wrap her in his arms and take away whatever weight was on her shoulders. Instead, he fought against the urge and took a step toward the door. "Ari…"

Ari's jaw tensed, but he nodded. "If you change your mind and want to come to us tonight, we're in cabin four." With a final, searing glance, he left.

"Tomorrow will look brighter." Kaden shut the door behind them and hoped he was right. "Tomorrow, we'll convince her she's ours." He wasn't sure if he was saying that to convince himself, his bear, or Ari.

Ari rolled his shoulders. "Why the hell are we leaving her tonight? She's ours, and if we have to fight to prove it to her than we must." Ari stalked further away from her home before turning toward him. "Damn it, Kaden, you better have a fucking good reason for this!"

"She's hiding something," he said, keeping his voice even to keep from further inciting Ari's temper.

"No shit," Ari roared.

"She's not going to let us claim her until she lets go of whatever she's hiding. Once the bond is in place, there will be no holding back. She has to let it go, or tell us about it before then, but she doesn't seem ready to do either. So I'm going to have to find out what it is."

"How do you expect to go about that?"

Kaden continued walking toward their cabin, his thoughts scattering. She could be hiding anything, and that made his job harder. He didn't have a clue where to start, which meant he'd have to start with a background check like he'd run on one of their employees and work his way from there. They arrived back at the cabin, and he headed for the laptop he'd left on the coffee table.

"I'm grabbing beers, and then maybe you can enlighten me regarding your plan," Ari called over his shoulder as he headed toward the small kitchen at the back of the cabin. "I doubt I'll be much help, but you know I'm here."

"You've got enough on your plate dealing with on the community's security. Let me worry about the past our mate is trying to keep buried." His laptop chirped as it powered on, and he took the beer Ari handed him. "I'm going to dig into her past until I find whatever it is she's trying to hide. And when I do, I'm not going to let it stop us from claiming her."

"She seems pretty adamant that she doesn't want bears in her life." Ari leaned against the wall and took a long swig from his beer. "How's that work with Jase and the other bears in the tribe? Or is it just that our kitten doesn't want us?"

"I think it's because we're outsiders, and she doesn't know anything about us. She trusts Jase. Maybe he had to earn it." With the laptop powered up, he set the beer aside and went to work. "I've got this, Ari. Go draw up the perimeter plans for Jase and the construction crew. I'll get you when I find something." And he'd find something. There wasn't anyone better at digging up the dirt on people than him.

He was the guy who ran the background checks for all the men they hired—scanning every inch of their lives. They wouldn't have anyone with a criminal past working as part of their security operations. Too many people trusted their company for them to allow even one person with a sketchy past to slip through the cracks. They didn't just provide security to shifters, but to some very wealthy and high-placed humans.

Whatever Camellia feared, he'd find it, then make damn sure they protected her. His bear growled, wanting his mate and wanting her safe. *Tomorrow…*

The moon hung high in the sky, telling Camellia that the time was right. If she was going to leave Crimson Hollow, she needed to do it while everyone slept. Sneaking out in the middle of the night was the cowards' way out, but she couldn't face Jase.

He'd want to know why, and what was she supposed to tell him? She made commitments within the tribe, but if they found out what she'd done, she'd be removed from her position anyway. She'd rather leave before they could learn the truth. The embarrassment of them finding out was the least of her problems, it was death she fought to avoid.

This small, isolated community that had been her haven, no longer made her feel safe. She grabbed the backpack she'd packed, slipped it over her shoulder, and tipped the letter to Jase she'd written against the candle centerpiece on her table. It didn't explain everything, simply apologized for running out on them. She glanced around her house and tears prickled her eyes. The memories she'd made here would be carried with her for all of her days. There had been times of joy and times of grief. But there had been more happy moments than sad ones. She had made some of the best friends she could have ever asked for. While they all knew she had something in her past that had brought her there, none of them had pressed. The only person who knew her story had been Granddad. As the Chief, she'd been forced to tell him in order to join his tribe, and even then she'd told him as little as she could. In fact, she'd left out the fact that the man she'd shot had been a bear. True to his word, as far as she knew he'd never told anyone, not even Jase.

She stepped out into the cold night air, shut the door behind her, and stood there for a moment. Taking a deep breath she opened up her senses. No one was about, so she stepped off her porch and headed away from the town, toward the road. She couldn't take her car because starting the engine would wake the entire tribe. But that meant she'd have to hoof it to the road and hope that someone passing through in the middle of the night would pick her up. If not, she'd have to make her way nearly twenty miles to the next small town before she could hitch a ride. Truckers would be her best bet to put some miles between herself and the bears.

In case anyone might have been moving about inside one of the houses and happened to look out the window, she kept to the trees. A branch cracked nearby, and she scanned the grounds. It was doubtful any animal would venture this close to the compound, not with all their scents lingering. They were predators and any creature that strayed near was fair game.

"Going somewhere, precious?"

She spun toward the voice with such force that she nearly dropped the bag slung over her shoulder. "Ahh…"

Kaden stood steps in front of her, blocking her path. "You weren't running out on us, were you?"

"No, ahh…" She couldn't think as he closed the distance between them. Her lioness darted forward, purring with great excitement. *Mate.* She shook her head at her lion. *He can't be.*

"Than what were you doing out here at this time of night?" He pulled the bag off her shoulder and unzipped it. "Couldn't sleep so you thought you'd take your clothes for a walk?"

"I ahh…" She was beginning to sound like a broken record, but she didn't know what to say to him. Her lioness just wanted him naked, and that made it harder to think straight. "Kaden, please."

"Please what, precious? Press you against that tree and have my way with you until you're screaming my name for the whole tribe to hear? Or maybe you'd prefer to be naked, riding me, as the moonlight shines down on us like a spotlight?" He pulled her close to him, pressing her against his body so that she could feel how ready he was for her. "Your lioness wouldn't be growling like that if you'd only give in to her."

"I just can't." She forced herself to back away from him.

"Because of your secret." He advanced on her, closing the distance that she had just created between them.

"I have no secret."

"Oh, precious," he said silkily. "There's no need to lie to me, I know all about it." He took her hand in his.

"I don't know what you're talking about." A shiver of fear ran up her back. If she screamed for help would Jase or one of the guards get to her before he had a chance to kill her? Even if so would Jase order her death to revenge one of his species?

Which would be quicker and painless?

"Kitten, we know about the man you killed." Ari strolled from the shadows. "The bear."

Kaden's gaze locked with hers. "That's what you're hiding, isn't it?"

Shock quivered through her. "How?" She tried to keep them both in view as she braced herself for the attack. At that moment, she didn't believe it mattered they were mates. Bears stood up for each other, no matter what. She'd killed one of their kind, and to honor him they had to kill her in return.

"Kaden's the best there is." Ari's voice held a hint of pride. "He can find dirt on anyone, and he knew you were hiding something. After we left, he went to work finding yours."

She squared her shoulders. "Go ahead."

The guys shared a look before Kaden asked. "Go ahead with what?"

"Aren't you going to kill me?" She forced herself to keep her eyes open. If they were going to kill her, she refused to cower in fear. She had always suspected that one day someone would find her and end her, just as she had ended that man's life. As time went by, she'd gradually stopped looking over her shoulder, waiting for someone to jump out of the trees. But now that they were here, she was both scared and somewhat relieved. She'd no longer be living in fear that someone would find out.

Ari's gaze narrowed. "Kitten, why would we kill you?"

She glanced at Ari to see if he was being serious or if he was just provoking her. "It's what bears do."

"Who told you that? Jase is a bear, but he didn't hurt you when you told him, did he?" The last question came out more as a growl, as if Kaden thought Jase might have hurt her.

It only served to confuse her more. It was almost like he cared for her, but he couldn't. Could he?

"Jase doesn't know, does he?" Ari touched her shoulder, but she still remained silent. "Fuck."

Camellia's gaze slid away. "I told no one except the police officer who questioned me after…" As the emotions ran through her from that night, she sank down onto the cold ground. "He told me to run, to leave Boston and never look back. That if the bears ever found me, they'd tear me limb from limb for what I did. So please…just get it over with."

"Kitten…" Ari squatted next to her. "We're not going to hurt you."

"But I killed one of your kind." She looked at Ari, unable to believe he wasn't about to rip her head off. All these years she lived in fear of this moment. She didn't want to draw it out any longer than necessary, and she sure didn't want them to lie to her just to keep her guard down. She wasn't going to fight them. She had killed one man and that was enough of a burden to live with. She couldn't do it again, even if it meant her own demise.

Chapter Six

The grief and pain that poured off his mate tore at Kaden's soul. He wanted to ease her pain and convince her that they were not going to harm her. No one would ever hurt her as long as they were alive. She was theirs, and now that they knew why she'd rejected them, they'd be able to claim her.

He sat on the ground and pulled her into his lap. "I read the police reports. It was self-defense."

"I was leaving work…" She stared out into the forest, refusing to meet either of their gazes. "It was late, and I went out the backdoor because it shaved a few minutes off my walk to my apartment. He was there in the alley."

"You don't have to do this." Ari took her hand into his.

She ruthlessly wiped away the tears that began to flow. "There were boxes and trash on the side of the building, but my lioness was on edge. She knew something wasn't right. That's when the bear looked over the top of the boxes. Blood dripped from his mouth as he chewed on…"

"He ripped out the throat of a hooker," Kaden said quietly, supplying the information he'd found in the police report.

"I had started to back up, trying to get into the building, but I didn't make it." Her body shook, and he held onto her tighter. "The gun…I finally got it out of my purse, and I didn't think. I just shot. I couldn't shift…I couldn't make it a fair fight.

Someone might have seen. He was on something, I don't know what, but I could see it in his eyes. He wasn't right. It was like he was drunk, his eyes were glazed, but I didn't smell alcohol."

"The toxicology report listed meth in his system." Kaden smoothed his hand down her arm. "Even in your lioness form, you wouldn't have stood a chance against a bear screwed up on meth. You kept yourself alive, that's what matters."

"Alive for us." Ari brought her hand to his lips. "We won't let anyone hurt you."

The corners of her mouth turned downward. "I deserve—"

"Don't even say it." Kaden cut her off. "What you deserve is to be happy, to live the life you have, and to have mates who will cherish you. You don't deserve to live in fear."

Ari sighed. "You know that Jase needs to know."

"No!" She shook her head as the Chief stepped into the light.

"I already know." Jase stayed back from their gathering on the ground.

"You were listening," Ari bit out.

"I followed after her when my bear alerted me." Jase nodded. "But I've known about her past since she arrived here. You told Granddad, but when he told me it didn't matter. I looked into your past. I was his unofficial Deputy while he prepared me for taking over the tribe. I couldn't let someone come into our tribe without knowing their past. Especially someone who was going to teach our children. After I found out, I went to Granddad with the information. He confirmed it, but we never told anyone else."

"Why didn't you tell me?" There was a hint of anger in her voice, but there was more relief than anything. "I was always careful around you, so you wouldn't find out."

"I knew that when you were ready, you'd tell me." Jase shoved his hands into the front pockets of his jeans. "While the bears here were never a threat to you, I wasn't sure that the one you killed wasn't a part of a tribe or a sleuth. I watched to see whether anyone came after you, if there was any hint of danger. But there's been nothing. I believe he was a lone bear. No one is looking for you."

"Will you tell Sin?" Ari looked back at the other man.

"I guess that depends on the three of you."

"What do you mean?" she asked when he started to walk away from them.

"They are your mates." Jase paused just before the tree line and turned back to them. "You must decide if you're leaving us, or if the three of you will be staying. For this to work, you must all be willing to compromise because something will have to give. Camellia, are you willing to give up your position here? Leaving, you'd give up all the work you've done with the children. Ari and Kaden, are you willing to take a less hands-on approach to your business? Maybe it's time to open up a second branch here. Those are just some of the questions that you will have to answer. But if you're going to stay, then yes, Sin will need to know. She's my Deputy, and I don't keep tribe business from her. But like with Granddad, it will go no further."

"Why the hell does mating have to be so complicated?" She pushed out of Kaden's lap and rose.

"It's not." Ari rose and wrapped his arms around her waist. "Do you want to stay? Because a few minutes ago you were running off under the cover of darkness."

"I thought I didn't have a choice. But this is my home."

"Then we'll make it work." Kaden pressed his body against her back and nuzzled her neck.

"Hell yeah, we will." Ari agreed. "If you want to stay, we'll stay."

Without moving away Kaden, glanced at Ari. "That's a bit of a change. What about the business?"

Ari shrugged. "Jack can handle things there. We'll promote him to manager. This job will take weeks anyway, and then we'll take some time off to spend with our mate. After that we can open up a branch here, just like Jase said. Maybe we can hire new crews from right here. There are always jobs coming in, and most of the work already requires that we travel. We'll make it work." Ari dropped his gaze to Camellia. "That's if you're willing to put up with two grumpy bears all the time?"

"This is all happening so fast." She leaned back against Kaden. "A few hours ago, you strolled into Sin's kitchen and pulled the rug out from under me. Now I've shared my past with you, and I am about to commit to two bears. My lioness pushes for me to say yes and for us to dash back to my place, but my fears are still there. What if Jase is wrong?"

"What do you mean, kitten?"

"What if there's a sleuth out there looking for revenge? I can't put you two in the middle of that."

Kaden kissed the curve of her neck before spinning her around to look at him. "We're in this together. No matter what. You're our mate, and if it takes time to convince you of that, then we'll take the time. But your lioness will grow more impatient than she already is."

"He's right, we'll take on the world to keep you safe," Ari said, nuzzling the side of her face. "You're ours. Now and always."

"Screw it." Her mouth slowly stretched into a radiant smile. "My place or yours?"

"Why wait?" Kaden dug into her bag, looking for whatever he could lay on the ground to make a bed as Ari lifted her into his arms. "We want you now."

Chapter Seven

Moonlight sparkled through the trees as Ari carried Camellia to where Kaden had made a makeshift bed, just off of the path. She leaned into Ari's warmth and slid her hands under his shirt. She wanted them, and the more she touched Ari's hot skin, the stronger that desire became. Her lioness purred, vibrating her from the inside out, urging her to move forward and past her doubts. It didn't matter that they were bears, or that she hadn't been looking for a mate.

All that mattered was having them claim her. She needed this as much as she needed her next breath. Mating was vital for shifters. Otherwise, over time, they'd die without the contact. They needed that bond to live a long shifter life.

Ari stopped in front of Kaden whose gaze gleamed in the moonlight.

Kaden reached out a hand and smoothed it over her arm. "I feel the tension seeping back into your muscles." He brushed her hair away from her face. "Don't think—just relax and feel."

His touch caused her skin to tingle and she glanced at Ari. "Put me down." When Ari did as she asked, she stood between them, her hands on each of their chests. "I don't know if it's my beast driving my desire or not, but I want you. I just hope I don't regret it in the morning."

"We'll do whatever we can to please you." Kaden laid his hand over hers. "Your happiness means everything to us. Our Mate—"

"But bears…" She shook her head and tried not to think about what they shifted into. "Seems to me it's a cruel twist of fate."

"Kitten." Ari leaned toward her and nuzzled her neck. "There's nothing cruel about this. Now stop delaying. I want you."

"Oh, really?" She arched an eyebrow at him. "Grumpy bear has decided to play nice so he can get a prize?" she teased as she grabbed his belt and began to unbuckle it.

"I want to bury my cock in your pussy and have you screaming my name."

There was more of a growl in his voice as she made her way into his pants. No boxers—her bear was commando under his jeans. Smirking, she cupped her hand around his already hard shaft. When she stroked her hand down the length of him, he released more growls.

"She has too many clothes on." Kaden tugged her sweater upward; his fingers brushed along the curves of her body as he did.

"Kitten, clothes off…" Ari's bear deepened his voice. "Now!"

"You're not only a grumpy bear, you're also very demanding." She released his shaft and let Kaden pull the sweater over her head. "But gentleman, I'm not the only one who's getting naked."

"Don't worry, precious. Our clothes will be gone in a blink of an eye." Kaden tossed the sweater aside. His hands came around her waist, quickly finding the button of her jeans, and he worked them off her as well.

Before she could protest, she was standing in the middle of the forest naked, sandwiched between them. Her heart pounded against her chest, and butterflies danced in her stomach from a mixture of nerves and unease. The coolness of the night's air blowing against her warm skin sent goosebumps rushing down her arms.

Kaden leaned down, nuzzling her neck, kissing a path down her collarbone, as Ari stripped out of his clothes. Since he was standing before her, she watched his body as the clothes came off one by one. Ari was built for his bear nature, wide and tall, but every aspect was toned and muscular. She wanted to reach out and touch him, but he stayed just out of reach.

"The scent of your desire is making my bear anxious. He's demanding we claim you and soon." Kaden spun her around to look at him. "The question is: will you be as turned on when you watch me undress?"

"Kaden…" Wanting to reassure him, she reached out for him, but he stepped just out of her grasp. Now, Ari was behind her, his shaft pressed against her back.

"Watch, kitten." There was something in his voice that made her wonder if he was hoping she'd reassure Kaden.

Did Ari think she'd only want one of them? They might have believed they'd share one mate, but were they concerned that she'd reject one of them? Did she have a choice in accepting both of them as mates? It didn't feel like it. Her lioness didn't want to choose. She wanted both of them, and she wanted them now.

Kaden tugged off his shirt. He wasn't as muscular as Ari, but his body was still toned enough that even in the dark she could make out the contours of his abs. He had a trail of light chest hair that started between his pecs, creating a path straight down his chest. As if leading the way to where she really wanted to be. The hair was thin and a lighter brown than the hair on his head, it almost blended into the tanned skin.

Her gaze fell lower, until she reached the curves of his hips. Her breath hitched in anticipation. She wanted him naked so she could run her fingers over his body until she memorized every inch of his body. His fingers were already working on the button of his jeans. She could feel his gaze on her as he slowly worked the zipper down, but she couldn't look away. She knew what was coming, and she wanted to give his reveal her complete attention. In one quick movement, he pushed down his jeans, sending his boxers with them. As quick as they were off, he was there in front of her, his hands running up the front of her body.

"I love that look in your eyes." He cupped her breast, sliding his thumbs over her nipple. "The one that screams your desire."

Needing more of his touch her body arched toward him. "I want you. Both of you." It came out more like a moan than she had anticipated. "Fear filled me before to the point I wanted to run. Now…" She tipped her head to look back at Ari. "I guess the fear is still there. I'm still waiting for you to decide that revenge is worth more than a mate, but screw it. I want this." *Even if it's only in my dying moments.*

"If I find the bastard who told you bears would care more about a murderous bear than an innocent he'd be the one torn limb from limb." Ari growled. "Bears are like any other shifter group. We'll protect our own, but we wouldn't seek revenge on someone defending herself."

Her bottom lip trembled. "Years of fear are hard to give up. You're asking me to trust what you say is true, but we barely know each other."

"Then let us prove you can place your trust in us." Kaden tweaked her nipple, sending a ripple of pleasure and pain through her. "The connection between mates will help you see that we speak the truth and that we'd die protecting you."

Ari nipped her neck. "Mate with us, kitten."

She couldn't force words past her closed throat. Instead, she reached backward and hooked her hand behind Ari's neck and leaned against his nude body while she locked her gaze with Kaden's.

With a quick nod, he picked up her hand and pulled her toward the makeshift bed placing her in the center. They lay on each side of her. While Kaden's thumb resumed teasing over her nipple, Ari's hands slid down her body.

She moved restlessly between them. "Please, I want this."

"We know, kitten." Ari pressed his hand against her inner thigh, gently pulling her leg toward him, opening her up so he could slide his fingers between her folds. "I could smell your desire, but I didn't realize how wet you were for us." He worked his finger into her channel, and his thumb caressed her clit, gently teasing the nerve buds until she pushed against his hand.

"Someone is eager." Kaden leaned down and captured her nipple between his teeth.

"Please…" she moaned, pressing into Ari's touch and arching her back.

Ari removed his hand from between her legs, and the men shared a quick look before Kaden nodded and moved away. She held no further reservations when Ari moved over her. His shaft teased along her entrance. "We're going to show you the best night of your life." He kissed her, a long, slow deliberate kiss that gave and demanded. He cupped her breasts and teased the nipples, gently rasping his thumbs over the hard buds, and then pinching them. Pain mingled with pleasure, and her back arched.

His warm laughter washed over her, and he abandoned her mouth, moving downward to suck one nipple against his teeth. The warmth of this breath and the coolness of the night's air had the nubs hardening, arching toward him.

Sparks of pleasure fired inside of her. He slid his hand between her thighs, urging them apart, and just when she thought he would take her, he teased her clit again and wrenched an orgasm from her. She cried out at the unexpected climax as the air sizzled. She wanted them both inside her. It was the only way to bring the connection between them alive. Only then could they bite her, claiming her as their mate.

Turning her head, her gaze found Kaden. He was on his knees, just far enough back that he wasn't in the way of Ari's touches, but his fingers dragged along her arm as if he still needed to feel her.

With Ari working his fingers in and out of her core, she was too far gone for words. Instead, she wrapped her hand around Kaden's cock and gave a slight tug, letting him know she wanted him closer. She needed to taste him.

She watched as his control slipped away, and he inched toward her. His shaft hard and swollen, ready for her. Heat melted through her as she caressed his length.

Aware that Ari watched while his fingers glided back and forth against her wet folds, she never took her gaze away from Kaden. "Don't make me beg. I want both of you. Now." She didn't wait to see what Ari would do; instead she leaned sideways and took Kaden's cock into her mouth.

A sharp intake of breath shook through him as she swirled her tongue around the tip, sucking it hard. Drunk on the need to have them both, she sped her pace, hoping that Ari would join them.

Kaden groaned, and his hand reached down to tentatively cup the back of her head. He didn't try to urge her to go faster. He allowed her to set the pace.

Needing Ari inside of her she reached out to him, her hand landing solidly on his chest. Her nails raked against his skin as she silently pleaded for him to realize what she so desperately needed. She wanted him buried deep within her channel.

Out of the corner of her gaze, she could see him watching them, braced above her with his shaft hard and thick, eagerly straining toward her. She let Kaden slip from between her lips but kept her hand at the base of his cock, holding him close.

"Ari…" She called his name, the desire dripping off the single word. "Take me."

"Turn over." He waited while she released Kaden's cock, then gripped her hips and helped her turn, until she was on her knees before him. "It will be easier."

"For the bite." Kaden moved to kneel in front of her, his shaft bouncing in front of her face.

With one powerful thrust, Ari slid into her. She moaned as he worked his way inside, inch by inch as her body accepted him. With Ari working his way in and out of her, she let her attention go back to Kaden's shaft. She pulled it into her mouth again, and then slowly worked up and down his shaft, until the three of them fell into a rhythm together. As they synced, their speed quickened, allowing them to find pleasure as one, rocking together in perfect harmony. She cupped Kaden's hip keeping him close as Ari slammed into her, their bodies slapping together with every stroke.

Kaden pulled out of her mouth. "I'm not going to finish in your mouth. I want to be buried deep within you when I finally let go."

She wanted to fight him, to pull him back and have him filling her mouth, but she didn't. She pulsed backward, meeting Ari's thrusts as Kaden's fingers found her nipples. She was too close to the edge to stop. Waves of ecstasy engulfed her, and she arched up until her back was pressed against his chest.

Ari slammed home, burying himself deep within her. He leaned forward, biting into her shoulder, his teeth breaking the skin. At the same time Kaden bit her on the left just above her collarbone. She clawed her nails against Kaden's body. *Mated for life to bears…*

Chapter Eight

Camellia would have collapsed into a heap on the makeshift bed if it wasn't for Kaden and Ari holding her up on her knees. With the mating bond cemented, what she felt for them was taken to a whole new level. She had never felt this connection with anyone else, ever. It didn't even come close to the bond she had with the tribe or the Chief. It was unlike anything she could have hoped for.

"Our beautiful mate." Kaden smiled at her as he smoothed her hair away from her face.

"Wow." She wasn't sure what else to say. It was unbelievable what was happening within her and the bond; her body was overloaded with sensations. Everything seemed to smell stronger, emotions were clearer, and her body crackled with electricity. She tipped her head forward and nuzzled against the curve of his neck. The scent of honey and woods filled her, but for once it didn't make her want to scurry away. She wanted to snuggle against Kaden and wrap herself in his scent.

"Take her back to the cabin. I'll grab the clothes." Ari kissed her shoulder just above where he'd bitten her. "We're not nearly done with you, kitten."

Kitten, she liked the way it sounded coming from him. The deep voice was like a direct line to her core, sparking the fire within her.

Kaden slipped his shirt around her shoulders, lifted her into her arms, and still naked, he rose from the makeshift bed. "Back at your cabin, you're mine."

She wrapped her arms around his neck. "There's nothing I want more." How things had changed. Just hours ago, she'd run in fear of her life. Now, the lion inside her was ready to surrender to her mate.

They were her mates. Their species didn't matter. She ran her hand along the curve of his jaw, and her fingers were met with the roughness of his stubbles from where he hadn't shaved. Something she found wildly attractive. The coarseness fit perfectly with his longer hair and his beast.

A sudden burst of fury blazed against her skin. Not hers. Not Kaden's. Someone was hiding in the darkness. Her body went ridged and her chest tightened.

She stiffened and held her breath, tuning her sense to seek out whoever was out there. Her lioness trotted forward, head tipped toward the sky, sniffing the air. Her hand stilled as she glanced around the compound, searching in the direction her lioness urged her to.

There, not ten feet away from her cabin, stood Swift. Her red hair billowed in the wind, but it was the anger rippling off her that made Camellia take notice. What had her in such a twist? They had become friends over the last few years. But since Zoe had arrived, something had changed. Swift had hidden away in her cabin, avoiding everyone. Even when Camellia had tried to comfort her friend, Swift had pushed her away.

"Put me down," she whispered.

He did as she asked, but kept his hand on her back. She could feel the tension vibrating through him as he evaluated the situation. Whatever he sensed had his bear on guard, too. Instead of listening to her better judgement, she continued toward Swift, buttoning the shirt Kaden had wrapped around her as she did.

"You fucked them!" Swift's accusing glare drifted between Camellia and Kaden's naked body. "Outsiders in our tribe and you bring them to your bed. What if they are part of the attacks on the foxes?"

Camellia took a deep breath and tried not to let her anger get the best of her. Swift was her friend, and she was hurting. This wasn't her, but her anger and fear taking control. "They're bears, not humans like the ones that have attacked—"

"Don't give me that shit." Swift marched toward them. "You don't know anything about them. They could be part of it."

"Swift…" She tried to keep her voice calm, even when she wanted to fight. They were her mates, and while she hadn't known them but a few hours, she knew they didn't deserve Swift's accusations.

"How could you jeopardize this tribe? Our friendship? Do you care so little about me that you'd allow them to come here and kill off the foxes that remain?"

"Damn it, Swift." Camellia could no longer keep her anger in check, but it was Kaden who growled behind her.

"You know nothing about us, or how much she cares for you. Yet you stand there and curse the one person who's been by your side, trying to help you through this turmoil."

"Bear, you know nothing." Swift swung at him, missing, but giving Camellia time to step between them before Kaden could retaliate.

"Stop this!" she hollered over his growls. "Kaden please," she said, darting a glance over her shoulder. "I'll meet you at the cabin."

"I'm not leaving you."

"Fine. But back up a few paces." She wasn't going to argue with him. Swift was angry, but Camellia could easily take down her friend if she needed to. When he took a step back and stopped, she realized that was the best she was going to get from him.

Swift tried to sidestep Camellia as if she was going to go after Kaden again. Camellia grabbed her wrist. "Stop this. I'm trying to give you the benefit of the doubt because I know you're letting your emotions get the best of you, but if you go after him again I'm not going to intercede."

Swift's upper lip lifted in a snarl. "Since you're so willing to welcome my executioner, maybe it's for the best. Maybe I can eliminate him before he can wipe out the rest of the foxes."

"Damn it, Swift. I'm at the end of my rope tonight." She let go of the other woman's wrist and took a deep breath. "Why were you waiting out here for me?"

"I know Jase approved them, but I don't trust them." Swift paused for a moment as Ari came up behind them.

Camellia held up a hand to halt him. "Just stay back. I've got this."

Swift's body shivered with outrage. "I've been watching them. Waiting for them to attack."

"They're not here for foxes. They're security experts, and are giving Jase and Sin assistance to keep everyone safe." Even as Camellia said it she knew her friend wouldn't believe her. She was convinced they were here to kill her and the other foxes. Nothing anyone said would change that.

"I felt your fear when they showed up at your door, and you were still terrified when they left." Swift crossed her arms over her chest. "You've always been cautious around bears, and while I've never pried I know you were hiding something. Now, instead of being afraid of them you're welcoming them into your bed. That doesn't seem like the friend I've known for years. Maybe you're a part of all of it, too?"

Her chest tightened as Swift accused her of being part of the attacks on their neighboring tribes. Their friendship was falling apart before her eyes and she didn't know how to fix it. "The attacks are over and those responsible have met their demise."

"Only time will prove that." Swift glanced toward the men. "Or when they kill one of us."

"That's enough!" Camellia howled. "Everyone except you is working together to keep this place safe, and they are here doing us a favor."

"It would seem they're here doing you." With one last cold glare, Swift turned on her heel and headed back to her home.

Kaden and Ari came closer, their hands touching her shoulders before she could react. Anger, hurt, and insult raced through her. In a matter of moments, Swift had sliced apart their friendship. Part of her wanted to go after Swift and beat some sense into her, while the other part that was hurt and betrayed wanted to forget the whole mess and seek comfort in her mates.

Chapter Nine

Kaden snuggled into Camellia's body, nuzzling her neck, as Ari showered. The night had not gone as he had planned. Instead of mad, passionate sex with her screaming their names until the sun rose, they had collapsed with exhaustion after spending the last few hours talking and cuddling. She was upset with Swift's outburst, and while he wanted to ease the tension between the two women, he wasn't sure how to do it.

"I need a pot of coffee." She rolled to face him. "I'm sorry."

"For what, precious?" He lazily teased his finger down her arm.

"Last night…I guess that would be this morning. Swift. This…" She slid her hand down his body until she brushed against his shaft. "I do want you."

Her hand caressed his length, instantly bringing a response. His heartbeat sped. Heat pooled in his groin. He wanted her too, more than anything else. "We can wait."

"Wait?" She rose and straddled him, never letting go of his cock. "I think I've let her get to me enough, and I think your bear would agree." Her gaze went to his hardening flesh. "You seem like you want this as much as I do."

"Oh mate, you have no idea how badly I want you. I get hard just thinking about your sweet body and the way you looked with your lips wrapped around my dick." His hands slid up her thighs then gripped her hips. "You're so fucking beautiful."

"Should we wait for Ari?"

"If he hurries he can join us; if not, he'll have to wait until later." He cupped her breast, his thumb teasing over the nipple. "I'm tired of waiting."

"Me too." She hovered over his shaft. "Don't make us wait any longer. I need you inside of me."

Without hesitation, he guided her down his shaft. Their gazes met as he worked himself into her tight passage.

She tossed back her head and a soft moan escaped.

"That's it," he groaned. "Let me in."

Working in and out of her, his beast growled within him, urging him to speed the pace. He wanted her hard and fast. There'd be a time for gentle lovemaking, but that time wasn't now.

She began to set her own pace, urging them faster. Her hips rocked up and down, slamming against him. Her head tipped back, and the morning sunlight fell across her. Her bouncing breasts taunted him. She was beautiful, and she was his. *Theirs,* he corrected. He leaned up to claim her nipple between his teeth. Gently, he bit and tugged, letting his tongue swirl around the bud.

"Oh, Kaden." Her nails scraped his chest.

Gaining control, he let her nipple slip out and rolled her over. He slammed into her, sliding his full length home, in and out, as her muscles tightened around him, warning him that she was close.

He bent and claimed lips full of need and desire, and held there enthralled as her climax spiraled through her. Her moans stifled as his tongue slid into her mouth. Her core muscles tightened around him, and he surrendered to the pleasure. He tipped his head back and roared as he slammed home one final time, filling her with his seed.

Kaden slipped out of her and collapsed onto the bed beside her, pulling her tight against his body. While his breaths slowed, he reveled in the joy of simply holding her soft, warm body.

The sound of a door opening drew his gaze to Ari who leaned against the doorframe, a towel slung around his waist and droplets of water still trailing down his chest. "Seems I showered at the wrong time."

Camellia laughed softly. "There's no reason it needs to end." She patted the mattress, beckoning him.

"Our mate the temptress." Ari smirked. "I wish I could, kitten, but I have a meeting with Jase, Sin, and Garret this morning."

"All work and no play makes for a grumpy bear." Slipping from the bed, she crossed over to him and ran a hand along his chest. "I could use a shower. Why don't you come wash my back? Surely you have enough time for that?"

"You're already naked." Kaden yawned and watched them from the bed. "We can't let our mate shower alone, and I'm pretty comfortable here."

"If I must…" Ari slung his arm around his mate. "Come on, kitten. Let me give you a shower you won't forget."

Ari leaned back in the chair and waited. He'd laid out his ideas, making sure he highlighted what he would do if he were Chief, and also providing lesser, minimal alternatives that needed to be taken to ensure the tribe's safety. There were weeks, if not months, of work to make this place completely secure. However, unlike when he had arrived, he had plenty of time. He wasn't planning on going anywhere.

"You've mated with one of our members." Sin didn't look up from the packet he had printed off for each of them.

"Umm, yes." He fought the urge to shift with unease. Kaden and he were lone bears, and they were very private. They didn't belong to a sleuth, and they weren't used to anyone prying into their personal lives.

"Camellia is very dear to this tribe. She's an amazing teacher, and if we are going to lose her because of this we need to know. She would be a great loss." Sin's gaze was on him now, her hands folded over the papers.

"We told her last night that we would stay. She cares for this tribe, and unlike our jobs, hers is here. We can work from anywhere, and our foreman, Jack, can handle our crew. We'll promote him to manager and things will be fine. We'll take some jobs out of the area, and possibly open up another branch here. Maybe some of the tribe can work for us."

"That will be their choice." Jase raised an eyebrow at him. "I made the three of you aware that I would have to fill in Sin and Garret concerning Camellia's past."

Ari drew a deep breath and nodded. "We know. Camellia's only request is that it doesn't go any further. I would add that, if this news got out, it could jeopardize her safety. There could also be some backlash from some of the children and parents."

"It will go no further than us." Jase nodded. "We'll discuss that along with these suggestions and get back to you this afternoon. Meanwhile, I believe you had a meeting with the crew installing the perimeter fence."

"I do." Ari pushed back his chair and rose. "While you're discussing that, I suggest you consider what options might be open for Swift. She's unstable."

Sin frowned. "Why do you say she's unstable?"

"She's been following Kaden and me since we arrived. We knew about it, but left it be. She was no threat to us." His bear edged forward, the anger over last night's confrontation returning. "She was waiting for us when we came back from the woods." He eyed Jase, knowing that he understood what they'd been doing out there.

Jase's gaze narrowed. "And?"

"She accused Camellia of harboring the enemy. It seems she believes Kaden and I are here to murder her and some of the other members. If you don't do something about her, you might not have to worry about outsiders destroying the tribe. It's going to happen from within. She'll cause a panic."

Sin reached for her mate's hand. "We knew she was upset, but we didn't realize that she was growing paranoid. We'll do something."

"We'll find a way to help her," Garret assured her.

Ari paused in the doorway. "I hope so, because I'd hate for the work we're going to do to make this place safe be a complete waste. She's terrified, and even if she doesn't start trying to convince others we're here to murder her in her sleep, they'll feel her terror." He strolled out of Jase's house and headed back to where he knew Camellia and Kaden were waiting for him. He had twenty minutes before he had to meet with the fence crew, and he planned to put that time to good use.

Epilogue

In the weeks since Ari and Kaden had arrived in Camellia's life, she'd never been happier. The men were busy with the security of the tribe and she had her teaching duties, but they made time for themselves. Their mating had been quick, and she was still coming to terms with it all, but already she was falling in love with them. It wasn't just the amazing sex, though that was a huge benefit—it was them. Ari and Kaden made her feel cherished and special. The cute names they called her and the way they were always sharing an intimate touch were endearing. Never before had she felt like the center of someone's world.

While no out of town job had yet arisen because they were busy with the tribe's needs, she knew there would come a time when it happened, and she hated to think of them being away even for a night. She couldn't image sleeping in bed without their warm bodies pressed against hers, or waking next to them.

"You seem lost in thought," Kaden said as he stacked the dishwasher with their dinner dishes.

She leaned against the counter, watching him for a moment. "I was thinking about how much my life has changed since you two stumbled into my life and moved into my bed."

"Kitten, you know you wouldn't want it any other way." Ari snagged her from behind, tugging her close to him.

"I only wish Swift could…" She brushed off the longing and tipped her head back to Ari. "You're right. I wouldn't want it any other way. You guys are more than any girl could ask for."

Kaden closed the dishwasher and took her hand. "Swift will come around."

"Maybe." She tried not to let it bother her, but it did. They had been friends since she'd come to the tribe, and now Swift wouldn't even look at her.

"Garret's sister, Ginger, is arriving next week. Maybe she can help." Kaden brought her hand to his lips and kissed her knuckles. "Ginger's been through some rough shit in her life. Garret was there to save her, but the horrors she witnessed will always be with her. Because she has her own hidden scars, she might be able to get through to Swift and help her deal with the demons that are haunting her."

"What if she can't?"

"I don't know." Ari finally said when Kaden remained quiet. "No one is going to give up on her without a fight. We're all trying to help her through this, but she's letting her fear get the best of her."

"We've put up with her comments and have tried to prove to her that we don't mean her or anyone else here any harm. We've committed to the tribe, and Jase wouldn't let us remain here if he wasn't sure of our intentions."

"But if we can't get through to her…" She paused, hating the very thought. "Jase will have no choice but to ask her to leave. She'll cause panic if she keeps this up."

"It's not going to come to that." Ari nuzzled her neck. "There are people around here who care about her. They'll find a way to get through to her."

Kaden tugged her hand. "Let's get away for the weekend."

"What?" She opened her eyes to look at him.

"It would be good for you to get away from here for a few days and stop worrying about Swift. The school's closed on Friday so let's take a trip. A nice romantic weekend—just the three of us."

Her heart beat against her chest as she grew excited about the idea of spending a few days with just them and no interruptions. Sure, she had them in her bed every night, but during the day they were both busy with their work.

"I know of this cute cabin. It has spectacular views of a lake, and the best part is no one will be around." Ari said, waggling his eyebrows. "Just think, kitten, no one to hear your screams of pleasure."

Once upon a time, being alone with them had scared her, but now it tugged the muscles in her stomach and made her heart flutter. Her mates…the best things that had ever happened to her. "What about work?"

"Things will be fine for a few days. The team is almost finished with the fencing and the guard house at the gate. When we get back, we can install the security measures there, and have someone on duty around the clock." Ari slid his hands down her stomach, until he brushed against the top of her jeans. His fingers opened the button at her waistband before sliding underneath the denim. "Say yes, kitten. We need this."

She reached forward, her hand seeking Kaden's shaft cloaked within his jeans. Hard and ready for her. "Yes," she purred. She'd say yes to anything just to keep their hands on her.

A Lion's Chance

After a near death experience, Ginger Fox wonders if there is more to life. In search of answers, she takes off to visit her brother, who recently mated with the Deputy of the Crimson Hollow Tribe. Maybe finding out what made her free-range brother settle down will allow her to put the past behind her and do the same. If not, it will give her time with her brother and maybe she could find a way to thank him for saving her life.

Liam O'Neil has never wanted a mate to get in the way of his desire to climb the ranks of the tribe's guards, but when his lion catches Ginger's scent, he can't stop himself. Trying to play the friendly host allows him to spend time with her but she continues to shut him out every time he tries to get close to her.

With the help of a little boy, who needs the pair's help, Ginger soon realizes there's more to life than touring the country, but is she ready to be stuck with a lion? More to the point, is she ready to settle down and live life within a tribe after she left her own wolf pack?

Chapter One

After growing up in a wolf pack, Ginger Fox was surprised to find Crimson Hollow unlike what she had expected. The wolf pack had structure and the Alpha had control over everything. Under her former Alpha, they could barely sneeze without seeking his approval first. He controlled their environment with an iron fist; a brief look from him made the members fall in line, doing whatever they thought he wanted from them. The reactions weren't out of respect but out of fear.

Even though the pack lived in their own houses, they came together for every meal, so there were no kitchens in the individual homes. A small micro fridge for drinks and a few snacks, but that was it. Their Alpha had controlled every aspect of their lives and when given the chance, Ginger turned her back on them and went her own way, following in her brother's footsteps. In the years since they had left the pack, she and Garret had stuck together. He had been there to pull her back from some pretty dark shit and she owed him her life for that.

As far as Alphas went, Jase seemed to be top notch. From what she had gathered since she arrived in Crimson Hollow, he cared for his members, taking precautions to make them safe, and actually listening to what the tribe wanted. Her only reservation with him was, he happened to be a bear and she had been down that road before. Bears were bad news and, though Garret told her Jase was different, she couldn't wrap her mind around it. She had been on the wrong side of a bear's claws before and she had no intention of letting that happen again.

"Hey there...Ginger, isn't it? You're Garret's baby sister." A man strolled toward her. His black hair brushed against the collar of his shirt and glistened under the last rays of sun, while his warm, yellow-brown eyes honed in on her.

"Yeah." She set her wine glass on the step beside her and tried to keep her voice lighthearted. "I'm Garret's *only* sister." For some reason, it grated along her skin to be called his baby sister and reminded her just how often he had come to her rescue.

"No offense." He placed his hand on the railing and watched her. "I'm Liam. Has Garret made time to show you around? If not, maybe I could."

"He's dealing with stuff, but I'm fine." She didn't want to get into the fact that she hadn't actually seen her brother since she'd arrived. Garret and Sin had to handle an emergency with a neighboring tribe and left before she made it to Crimson Hollow. She had hung out on the porch in hopes of seeing them return, but night was falling and still, she saw no sign of them. She was quickly growing tired of waiting but more than that, she was tired in general. It had been a long trip and all she wanted to do was crawl into bed and sleep.

"Well, if you want to get the lay of the land, I'm just two cabins over. Garret and Sin have been busy lately, so I might be your best chance." He let go of the railing and shoved his hands in his pockets.

"Thanks, but Garret's asked me here to—" The wind shifted, sending his scent directly at her. The musk of his lion slammed into her like a freight train at full speed, sending her inner wolf dashing forward. It wasn't the urge to fight or kill, but something that terrified her even further.

"You're here to see if you can help Swift," he finished for her. "She's pretty messed up right now, and we'll all be thankful if you can do anything for her."

"I...I got to..." She shot up, knocking her wine over in the process, shattering the glass and spilling the contents over the steps, as she stumbled backwards. "Got to go..." A few more steps backwards and her hand brushed against the door handle. Without taking her gaze off him, she twisted the handle and pushed the door open. Quickly, she rushed back into the cabin and closed the door.

"Shit!" she mumbled more to herself as she pulled out her cell phone. Sliding her finger over the locked screen, she made quick work of unlocking it and pulling up her contacts. Garret's name was displayed on the screen and all she had to do was hit the call button. *I'll just tell him something came up and I have to leave. Make arrangements to see him another time. He'll understand.* Even as she tried to convince herself, she knew she couldn't do it. Her brother had helped her more times than she cared to remember and now he'd asked for her assistance, she couldn't turn her back on him. She wouldn't run out on him, even if she'd just fallen into the lion's den.

Standing next to the porch steps, puzzled over what had caused the sudden change in Ginger, Liam scratched his head. Though she pulled his lion close to the surface and he wanted to stake his claim on her as his mate, she had seemed unaffected by the mating urge as they made small talk. If she hadn't been Garret's sister and he couldn't smell her wolf, he'd have questioned if she was human because of the lack of reaction.

His inner lion urged him to climb the steps and demand to know what had changed. Why did she look afraid of him as she stumbled away from him and back into the cabin? She'd come to Crimson Hollow; what did she expect to find? Except for Garret, wolves didn't belong to their tribe. Most of their members were cats or bears, and recently a few foxes had taken refuge within their tribe.

"Liam." Jase, the Chief of the tribe, stepped off his deck and strolled toward him. "Have you seen Ari lately?"

"Yeah, he was just heading back to his cabin. Why, something up?" As Jase's personal guard, he needed to be kept abreast of any threats to the compound or Chief.

"No." Jase scanned the grounds for anyone close enough to overhear them. "I just wanted to get an update on the perimeter fence. The missing child case from our neighboring tribe is concerning. They've been searching for him for hours, but his scent disappears where he got into the car. If he was kidnapped, that makes it all the more important for us to ensure the safety of the tribe. If he took off with his friends, there is going to be hell to pay."

"We should double the guards on duty for tonight." Liam quickly ran through names of who he could add to the schedule and he came up short. "We need more—"

"Guards, I know." Jase shook his head, sending brown strands dancing in the wind. "Granddad refused to allow me to have guards training while he was in command, and now that he's gone, I'm behind the eight ball. I have members that I need to keep safe, but I don't have enough able-bodied guards. We have five new recruits in training but they're not ready to be in the guard rotation yet."

Liam went silent for a moment to consider what he'd witnessed with the new recruits training. "There's nothing better than in the field hands-on training. Let's team them up with some of the more experienced guards. It will double our numbers on patrol."

"They'll get themselves or someone else killed." Jase scanned the grounds again, his gaze lingering on the guards making their rounds. "If one of our trained guards is injured because of the recruits' inexperience, then we're in a worse situation than we are now."

"The guards know their job and they'll do it. The threat level is higher than normal but the recruits have two weeks of training under their belt. They're not going in blind."

"I don't like it."

Liam's partner, Noah, stood near the gatehouse, talking with the guard on duty, and their morning chat carried to him. "With Garret away, Noah oversaw the recruits' training session today. He'll know who can handle themselves and who would be cannon fodder. We'll handpick ones that are ready and team them with the more experienced guards. It's the best we can do with what we have. Unless you want Noah and me to take shifts on ground duty."

"Your duty is to guard the Chief and Deputy. I should have ground guards that can handle the tribe's security."

"We'll keep you and Sin safe." Unable to keep his face from revealing his thoughts, Liam looked away from Jase.

"This isn't the time."

"I didn't say anything." He kept his attention on the door, willing his mate to come back outside. There was no doubt that she could hear them; she knew they were out there, and she could feel his tension. He wanted her and his lion wasn't happy about being denied.

"I know you want Sin to have her own guards. We've had this conversation and now isn't the time to have it again. Not out here in the opening." Jase tipped his head toward the door. "And not in front of an outsider."

They had the conversation and it had gotten him nowhere. Two guards with two charges. It was impossible to keep them both safe around the clock. Then, to have Sin running off without taking a guard with her because another tribe needed assistance. Garret, her mate, was with her, this did little to comfort Liam's unease as she was in more danger outside their perimeter.

He understood Jase was hesitating to trust additional guards to protect his sister until they knew who had the skills to handle the responsibility, but having no guards was worse than having a guard that couldn't handle the situation. *Foxes have been targeted. I won't risk Sin until I know that she can be protected. Until I am certain the guard I assign to her will protect her completely, you and Noah will ensure her safety.* Liam understood Jase's need to protect his sister, but he was leaving her vulnerable without a guard that was solely responsible for her safety. Her mate, Garret, could be targeted as well for his role and would be unable to protect her.

"Chief, I'm sure you know what is best." With the knowledge weighing in his gut that if Sin was his sister he'd want her protected, he glanced at the window where he could sense Ginger watching them from behind the curtain. "I'll get with Noah about the recruits and have them assigned."

"You do that. Then I want to see you and Noah in my office." Without waiting for a reply, Jase strolled back to his cabin, leaving Liam standing outside of his mate's cabin alone.

Temptation to climb the steps and knock on Ginger's door prickled along his skin. To have her open the door and see her again wouldn't be enough. He wanted to soothe away the terror that radiated from her. He wanted to feel her in his arms and to know that she was truly his. *You're mine, Ginger. You have no reason to fear me. You'll know that soon.*

Chapter Two

Each minute ticked by slower than the last as Ginger waited for Liam to move away from her cabin. Her heart slammed against her ribs, her chest ached, and her head swam from the lack of oxygen. *A lion! The only thing that could be worse would be a bear as a mate.*

Her suitcase that she had yet to unpack sat next to the sofa, reminding her how easy it would be to leave. She could slip out before Garret came back and she could make her excuse later. She took a step toward the suitcase before she could get a grip on her emotions. The trip to Crimson Hollow wasn't just to meet her brother's mate; she was also there to see if she could help another shifter.

Years earlier, Swift had witnessed her whole leash—a group of foxes—get slaughtered. With the recent attacks on foxes, the memories of it all came flooding back and she wasn't able to handle it. Why Garret thought Ginger could help was beyond her. She was barely able to keep her own shit together, let alone help another through their turmoil. If Garret only knew what went on inside her head, he'd have never asked her to come. She wasn't good for anyone.

Her cell phone vibrated in her pocket, bringing her back to reality, and she pulled it out to see a new text from Garret on the screen. *It's going to be late before we make it back. I'll make it up to you. Breakfast? I'll cook your favorite.*

A smile tugged up the corners of her lips. Images of her brother's waffles with fresh strawberries and chocolate sauce danced through her thoughts. There was nothing like Garret's waffles. *You have responsibilities. Don't worry about me. I'm fine. I'll hold you to breakfast though.*

She slipped her phone back into her pocket, grabbed the handle of her bag, and wheeled it back toward the bedroom. The idea of Garret cooking breakfast for her was all she needed to dispel the idea of leaving. His waffles made it worth having to deal with the lion for another day. She'd meet with Swift after breakfast, and by evening she'd be back on the road, putting distance between her and Liam. *The last thing I need in my life is a lion.*

The bedroom was much like the rest of the cabin—welcoming but sparely furnished. The bed with the pale blue and white comforter dominated the small room, and a single dresser stood next to the door that led to the connected bathroom. The pale blue walls were supposed to offer comfort and put her at ease; instead, they only reminded her of her captivity. She dropped the handle of her bag and collapsed onto the bed. Soft and warm, she forgot about changing, closed her eyes tightly, and curled up on the bed. Her wolf brushed along the inside of her skin, trying to ease the emotions rising within her. Nothing helped; she had to live with the anxiety and terror that plagued her after the slightest reminders. Those reminders were why she couldn't settle down. She'd moved from town to town, trying to outrun the past that inundated her. *A lion mate doesn't help matters.* She squeezed her eyelids tight, as if that would stop the flood of memories. The room around her faded and she was back in the apartment above the bar.

"Going somewhere, dog?" He grabbed her by the back of her neck and threw her across the room. Her battered body slammed off the door hard enough that the wood splintered, and her head cracked against the handle. Stars danced in her vision, yet she forced herself to get up. This was her chance; she had to get out of there or she was going to die at his hands.

He was on her before she could get to her feet. He slammed her back against the door, his hands wrapped around her throat, squeezing the life from her body. Desperate for oxygen she clawed at his hands. She kicked at him, but he didn't seem to notice. Life was slipping away from her when they were joined by the lion.

"You said she was mine for the night." A man stepped out of the kitchen with a piece of pizza in his hand.

The bear's grip loosened but he didn't let go of her neck. As she fought to get air into her lungs, she took in the additional man. She could smell his lion, but the booze stench reeked off him. His short, spiky blond hair was wild and uncombed, but it was his glossy, angry eyes, fixed on her, that had her wolf rising within her. This man was more dangerous than the bear.

"I've got to teach her a lesson first." He grabbed her by the hair and pulled her up to her feet. "Escape is impossible."

"Make sure there's enough left of her that I can have my fun with." The lion bit off a mouthful of pizza and grinned.

That night, her will had been broken. She thought she'd never get out of there, at least not alive. Even her wolf within had begun to give up. Thoughts of Garret saving her also quickly diminished. He was states away at the time, handling a job for a company; he didn't even know about the situation she found herself in. She was alone and her fight was gone. *No one is coming to save you. You're mine now, bitch.*

Waking hours later, Ginger's body was stiff and sore from falling asleep curled into a ball with her legs pressed tightly against her chest. Fear spread through her veins, and she lay in unknown surroundings. It felt too much like her days as a prisoner and was the reason why she didn't sleep like that any longer. She slept on her side, facing the door, or on her back, ready to attack. She never wanted someone to have that kind of power over her again.

Quickly, she changed out of the day-old clothes and into a fresh outfit. The sun wasn't up yet but she needed to get out of there, to feel the fresh air on her face and watch the sunrise. It would remind her that she was free and chase the demons away, at least until night fell again. No matter how much time had passed since she regained her freedom, she needed little things like this to remind her just what was at stake if she ever fell victim to someone again.

"I'd rather be dead," she whispered to herself as she stepped out of the cabin.

"Why, when there's so much to live for?"

She stumbled back, hitting her elbow on the doorframe. "Shit!"

Liam strolled around the side of the deck and came to stand by the bottom of her steps. "You okay?"

Rubbing her elbow, she forced herself to step forward. She wasn't going to run away from him again. He wasn't going to make her miss the sunrise. "Do you have to sneak up on people?"

"I was checking the perimeter, not sneaking up on you."

As the wind picked up, she pulled the sweater she'd grabbed on the way out of the cabin tighter around her. It was chilly in the morning hours but she did it also to try to hide her unease as his lion aroma drifted toward her.

"What is it about me that puts you off? Yesterday you suddenly dashed off inside and today your discomfort thickens the air." Liam slipped his hands into the front pockets of his jeans and watched her.

"Nothing." She fiddled with a button on the sweater and wouldn't meet his gaze. "I should get ready. I'm having breakfast with Garret."

"They're not back yet." He climbed the steps and, with every step, the panic rose within her. "Answer my question. Is it because I'm a lion? Because I'm Jase's guard? Or do you just not think I'm good enough for you?"

"It's…" The button came off in her fingers as she watched him. The heat between their bodies radiated through her and it was almost enough to diminish the fear. *Almost.*

"Feel that, baby?" Catching her hands, he cupped them in his and brought them up until they were just above her breast. "This proves you're mine. You want this just as I do."

"It can't be." Even as she said the words, there was no denying the feeling that overwhelmed her just from his touch. The heat between them was unlike anything she'd experienced before. "I can't…"

"Tell me." He squeezed her hands a little tighter, offering her comfort. "What can't you do?"

"Love a lion." Garret stated as he came bounding up the steps toward her. "Hi, sis."

"Hi..." She stared at her brother and tried to figure out if he knew. *No, he couldn't.* She shook her head, trying to get rid of the idea, but it wouldn't disengage. "When did you get back?" It wasn't the question she wanted to ask but it was the one that came out.

"Twenty minutes ago. We found the boy. He went off with some friends and when he heard there was a search party out looking for him, he was too terrified to return home." Garret shook his head. "Kids...but at least he's safe."

"Can we get back to the loving a lion part?" Liam glanced between the two of them.

"Ginger had a bad experience with a lion." Garret laid his hand on her shoulder. "Did you really think I didn't know?

"How?" Looking into her brother's eyes, she could see the sorrow shining back at her, but there was also anger mixed with it. Garret was angry he hadn't been there for her when she needed him most. He blamed himself but to her, he was her savior.

"I might not be the warrior Dad was, but I know better than to go into a situation blind." He dropped his hand away from her shoulder and stepped back. "Forty-eight hours...that's how long I stood outside of that bar, watching, stalking, and waiting for my opportunity. To go in too early could have meant your life, so could waiting too long. Dad always said we'd know when the opportunity presented itself but as I stood there, for the first time in my life I doubted him."

"Did you?" She pulled her hands from Liam's grasp and stepped back to get a better look at her brother. "Did you know when the time was right? Or did you just bust down the door, without knowing?"

"I knew." He glanced over to the cabin of the tribe's Chief, Jase, as if expecting him to come out. "Jase showed up and having his help gave us a better shot of getting you out alive. I knew it was then or never."

"Jase?" Surprise had Liam's eyebrows knitted together.

Garret glanced at the other man and nodded. "Who'd have ever thought I'd work alongside of a bear, but to save my sister…" With a shake of his head, his words trailed off. "Look at me now, married to his sister, and doing what I can to assist with the tribe."

"But how did you know about the li…" She couldn't get the word out; it stuck in her throat like a hot brick.

"Lion?" Garret questioned, but didn't give her time to answer. "Hours before I found you, I bribed the cable installer to get me eyes in there. I gave him the equipment. He just had to put the bugs up, and I could see inside. He couldn't get into one room, but he put cameras in the living room and one by the door. When he killed the other man, we knew we couldn't wait any longer. I'm sorry, Ginger…I truly am. If I had known…"

She crossed the distance between them, cupped the side of his face, and forced him to look at her. "You have nothing to apologize for. You saved me. Without you, I'd be dead. For that, I will always be grateful. I owe you everything."

"You owe me nothing. I got you that job." Garret slammed his fist down onto the railing, splintering the wood.

"With the previous owner. You never knew Ken would die and his heirs would sell the bar to *him*. I should have quit, but I liked my co-workers and the customers. I stayed because of them, telling myself it would get better." She dropped her hand from his cheek, shoved them into her pockets, and glanced up at the sky. The sun began to peak over the horizon but the joy of seeing it vanished as the memories of her past surrounded her like a blanket.

"If I had been around more—"

She spun around to face Garret and shook her head. "Don't do that. None of what happened is your fault. You saved me from Hell." She dragged her hand through her hair, pulling the auburn strands out of her face, tugging just enough to fill the pressure. "That fucker had no right! No right to…" She couldn't get the words out.

"I'm confused." Liam took a step toward her but stopped before getting within reach of her. "This past…is it coming up now because of me?"

Keeping his gaze anywhere but in Liam's direction, Garret said nothing and, after a few moments of uncomfortable silence, Ginger shook her head. "No. At least not completely."

"I wouldn't have asked you here if I'd have known this would have been dragged back into the present."

"Garret, you're my big brother. You always want to take blame and protect me but this isn't your fault. All of the time I live with what happened to me. Each night it plagues my dreams—it's a part of me. I can't get rid of the memories of what happened." She leaned back against the railing, careful to avoid the spot that Garret broke.

"You can't escape your destiny and mine has led me to Sin. Yours gave you Liam. Now you have to face that and tell him." He turned to face the lion. "I'll tell Jase you'll be late. When you're done, if you want to join us, I'm making breakfast."

As her brother descended the steps and headed back to his cabin, she wasn't sure what to think. There was no denying Liam was her mate, but Garret had dropped her into it with him. She couldn't tell him that her terror was meaningless, not when her brother had just told him that she'd had a bad history with a lion. *Thanks, Garret. I'll get you back for this.*

Chapter Three

Liam stood there, feeling uneasy. Clearly, Ginger wasn't eager to tell her story, leaving him to wait her out. If they were going to make this mating work, she'd have to tell him for them to move past it; otherwise, they'd lose their opportunity at happiness. There was only one mate for each shifter. If they rejected that person, they'd be destined to spend the rest of their days alone. He wasn't eager to spend his life alone, never knowing the comfort his mate had to offer, never having a woman he could snuggle next to every night.

"Let's do this inside." She brushed past him as she hurried to the door.

Without a word, he followed her inside and shut the door behind them. She took a seat on the only chair in the room, her action was a clear statement that she didn't want him near her. So, he settled on the sofa, as far from her as he could be in that space.

"We don't have to do this now," he offered with mixed emotions. He wanted to know the complete story instead of the bits and pieces he'd gathered from her exchange with Garret. What had happened between her and this lion? If someone hurt her, he'd kill them.

"It's been nearly a year ago now but what happened stays with me every day. It was supposed to be an average day but when I arrived at the bar, I found the place deserted. All of the staff received calls that there was a water line break and the bar would be closed. I never received that call and I ended up walking in on something I shouldn't have witnessed. Tap, my boss and the owner of the bar, was bribing a private detective to hide evidence of him killing a woman." She wrapped her arms around herself, as if trying to chase a chill away, and stared at the floor. "I don't really remember but I think I dropped my bag. Next thing I knew, Tap had me up against the wall and stuck a syringe into my arm. Everything went black."

"What happened when you woke up?" he pressed when she remained silent.

"I woke up in the apartment above the bar, locked in the guest room. I had been there when the former owner, Jim, lived there. He'd been an avid photographer and because of that, he'd covered and sealed the window to use the space as his dark room when developing pictures. The only way out was the door and it was locked."

"Tap was a lion?" He tried to put the pieces together. If the man who'd kept her hostage was a lion, it would explain why she freaked when she smelled his beast.

"A bear." Her nervousness seeped from her and she rocked back and forth. "His friend was a lion. He was there when I tried to escape. Tap beat the shit out of me and chained my ankle to the floor. I was terrified and he had broken my will, but even if not, the chains were too heavy. I couldn't break them. I couldn't even lift my foot off the floor more than a couple of inches. When Tap was done with me, his friend had his chance. The lion wasn't satisfied to use me as a punching bag. He wanted…"

"Sex?" Growling, Liam shot to feet. The attack on his mate was enough for him to want the asshole dead but the thought of a man forcing himself on her made him want to torture him before ending his life. He couldn't sit there and do nothing if this asshole was out there, possibly picking another victim.

"Nothing happened. Tap had his faults and they were lengthy but he never kept me prisoner for sexual reasons. It wasn't about that." She took a deep breath and let it out again. "He knew I'd go to the police with what I heard and he didn't want to go back to prison. That's why he held me. He knew that if he killed me, he wouldn't get away with it. Garret would have never let him have a day of peace if he so much as suspected Tap was behind my murder. So he kept me locked in that room while he tried to figure out what to do with me."

"He never…it was never sexual?" Some relief set in at that but still, this man had hurt her and he couldn't stand for that.

"Never."

"I still want him dead. Both of them." He balled his fists at his sides. "Where are they?"

"Dead." As the word left her mouth, she seemed to relax a little. "I was only there a couple of days, but during that time he beat me whenever he was around. The night the lion was there and I tried to escape was the worst. When the lion attacked, Tap must have heard my screams from the other room and he came in. Tap killed him right in front of me, splattering me with the man's blood. As I watched the life drain from his eyes, I thought I was going to be next but Tap hauled the dead man out of the room without a word, leaving me alone."

"Who was this lion?"

"I never knew his name. I had never even seen him before that night."

"And Tap?" Knowing they were dead did nothing to eliminate the anger coursing through him. He wanted to kill the bastards himself.

"Jase was pissed but Garret killed him."

"How does Jase play into it?" He tried to hold back his anger until he knew. Surely, the tribe's Chief couldn't have known that Ginger was being held hostage. Jase wasn't the man to turn a blind eye if someone needed his help.

"He was there, I guess, spying on Sin to make sure she was safe, and he bumped into Garret. Somehow, Garret talked him into backing him up and he'd owe Jase for it. I don't know what happened between the two of them that night. I was in rough shape and honestly, I didn't care. I asked about it later but Garret wouldn't talk about it. I only know Jase was livid because I remember him yelling. I couldn't tell you what he said though."

"Sounds like Jase." Liam had no one to kill. All of the ones that hurt his mate had already been taken care of but he wanted to do something. Setting aside his anger, he went to her, reached down, took her hand, and pulled her up until she stood in front of him. "Evil exists everywhere but I'm sorry you had to witness it. To have a lion instill the fear in you that has you shying away from me makes me want to kill him. I want you to know that I'm nothing like him—just as Jase is not like Tap. You can't paint the whole species with the same brush because of them."

"I..." She glanced at up him, meeting his gaze for the first time. "Maybe I have done that but it's hard to separate the memories and fear from the scent of a lion."

"There are other lions throughout the tribe and none of them mean you any harm. I've known most of them all of my life. I'm not going to hurt you and neither will they." He wasn't sure how he would prove that to her but he was determined to find a way. "After breakfast, let me show you around, introduce you to some of them."

"I don't know." She tried to step back from him but she hit the chair and he wrapped his hand around her bicep before she could fall back.

"I know you're afraid, but let me prove to you that I'm nothing like the last lion you had contact with." He let go of her arm and stepped back. "Do you honestly think Garret would have left us alone if he thought I was anything like that asshole? Do you think I would be one of Jase's guards if I were like that? Garret trusts me with his mate and with you, yet you don't trust me enough to let me show you around and introduce you to some of the residents here." Her attitude against lions had started out directed at someone else but now it was becoming personal. What did he have to do to prove to her that he was different? And more importantly, how was he supposed to do it if she couldn't even stand to be alone with him?

He let out a sigh. "Tell Garret thanks for the invitation, but another time." He turned his back to her and strolled toward the door. Perhaps he was being unreasonable as he'd only known her for a short time, but already, he was tired and her attitude was more than he could handle without getting his lion edgy. Another reason why he had no doubts this woman was his mate. From the moment he set eyes on her, she'd gotten to his head.

"Liam," she called to him, but he didn't stop.

He needed to put some distance between them and think things through. How was he supposed to handle his mate's hatred toward his animal? If it continued, he'd be destined to spend the rest of his life a lonely bachelor.

The door slammed shut, leaving Ginger alone with her regret. Her wolf snarled at her, demanding to know why she let her fear get the best of her. They were better than this. Wolves fought; they didn't give in at the first sign of trouble. Her human side was weak and willing to let the terror from her past spill into the future she could have, while the wolf within grew angry at the very thought of allowing the past to control them any longer. She needed to rise above it all and fight through the horror to grab a hold of her mate. She only wondered if she could do it.

She wasn't sure how long she sat there, lost in her own thoughts, regret, and feeling sorry for herself, but when she opened her eyes again, Garret was squatting in front of her, his hands on her shoulders. He shook her.

"Ginger!" He shook her shoulder again.

"What?" Even to her own ears, her voice sounded different—weak and distant. She tried to blink away the fog that had settled around her and focus on her brother.

"Damn it! You scared the shit out of me. I knocked and you didn't respond. What the hell is wrong with you?"

"I'm…" Her voice broke, forcing her to swallow before trying again. "I'm fine."

"Where's Liam? How could he leave you like this?"

"He left before." She rubbed her hands over her face and squeezed the bridge of her nose. "He's angry that I can't trust him and you know what…I don't blame him. What hell it must be to have a mate who can't stand you because of the animal you shift into. Every time he comes near me, all I can think about is what happened. His lion scent reminds me…"

"You've known other lions before this happened to you. Focus on them." He rocked back on his heels and took her hands in his. "Focus on the happiness you can have. Finding Sin changed my life and I've never been happier than I am now. You can have that too with Liam. He's a good man, a protector."

"I already have one of those." She grinned at him. "You've always been there when I've needed you."

"And so will Liam."

Maybe he was right but it didn't ease the tension within her. The idea of being mated to a lion chilled her blood and made her want to run. Her wolf was eager to find a mate, but even the idea of a lion made her wolf's hair stand on end. She had been at the receiving end of the lion's claws and didn't want to find herself there again. Maybe spending her life alone would be the better option than finding herself stuck with an evil lion. Liam might be different when they were alone and behind closed doors. By then, it would be too late.

No, I'm not willing to do that. I'd rather be lonely than deal with that.

Chapter Four

As the night settled over them, she needed to get out of the cabin and think. For the last week, Ginger had been focused on Swift and trying to keep her thoughts away from Liam. Occasionally she'd seen him around the village but they hadn't spoken since he'd turned his back on her and walked out. She had considered going to him. Maybe if she could explain things to him, then, he'd understand.

Each time she found herself near the guards' cabin, her courage seemed to abandon her. What if he refused to see her? His anger would have had days to marinate, possibly growing strong with each hour. He wouldn't listen to her explanation but then again, she wasn't even sure what she'd say to him if he did. Everything she rehearsed sounded like an excuse. She could list the reasons why she wasn't able to do it, but, as time passed, she realized she was scared. Rather than push forward, she was letting it hold her back. She wanted to bust through it and find happiness, even if that meant living life with a lion.

Not knowing what else to do, she focused on Swift. The progress Garret had hoped she'd make with Swift was not happening. Every day, she visited with the fox, spending hours together. Mostly they used the time to get to know each other. She had hoped that if they could form a bond, it would be easy for Swift to open up, but that didn't happen. Every time she brought up the past and Swift's former tribe, the woman would shut down communication.

Not being a therapist, Ginger began to wonder if she was doing more harm than good. Sin and Garret urged her to keep trying. They needed to bond over the traumatic events they'd gone through and allow Ginger to help Swift; otherwise, they were out of options. The fear rising within Swift had begun to affect the tribe. If they didn't do something soon, Jase, Sin, and Garret would have bigger issues to attend to.

Ginger tried to use the fact they had both witnessed murders to bring them closer. This was the only common ground that would allow for her to help the fox. For the most part, Ginger had worked through what had happened to her in order to move forward with her life, but she had a reason to do it—Garret. Her brother wouldn't have let her give up. Now she needed to help Swift find the one thing that would make her fight. She deserved a life and Ginger wanted to help her get it back.

If Ginger needed further motivation, she had to look no further than Zoe. Sin and Garret had taken in a teenage fox when her tribe had suffered a similar fate to Swift and Sin's tribe when they were children. The repeat of events and Zoe's arrival at the tribe's land had brought Swift's memories back. Now, Zoe blamed herself. She reminded Ginger a lot of herself at that age and the idea of her blaming herself for Swift's mental instability didn't sit well. Zoe had witnessed enough before coming to Crimson Hollow and was still adjusting; she didn't need to deal with more.

Ginger continued along, weaving between the trees and not following any sort of path, or paying attention to where she wandered. Wherever she went, she was still safe as long as she didn't venture outside the village's perimeter fence. Off in the distance, she could see two bears engaged in a playful fight. The taller one went to tackle his companion but he ducked, sending the tall bear rolling over him into a pile of leaves. They were having a good time, which only served to remind her of happier days when she'd try to sneak up on Garret and tackle him, but somehow he was always ready for her. She'd attack from the back and they'd roll on the ground, but he always gained the upper hand and she'd end up on her back with him on top of her. Childhood had been simple. The weight of the memories Tap and the lion had left her with didn't affect her mood every day. She longed for those kinds of times.

Lost in her memories, she roamed around the tribes' land, with no idea where she was going. Her wolf pushed her forward, as if it knew something she didn't. Moments later, she stepped around a tree and found a hole in the fence. She glanced around, looking for one of the guards. Hadn't Garret said there were several of them patrolled the perimeter? Where were they? Had someone tried to come in? Boards lay splintered and tossed in from the fence, not outwards. Someone had tried to get in, not out. Anxiety rolled within her but she kept going. She needed to see if there was anyone on the other side of the fence.

"You shouldn't be here," a familiar voice called from behind her, but she couldn't place it.

She spun around to see Liam jogging toward her. "What's happening?"

"Just go back to your cabin, or at least closer to the rest of the tribe." He continued past her, without even slowing down.

"Liam," she called to him, and he turned to look at her. "Can I help?"

If there was danger, she wasn't going to run from it. The place was full of innocent people and children. She couldn't turn and walk back to them knowing she did nothing to stop whatever might happen.

"Get the fuck off me!" a deep voice yelled from the other side of the fence.

"Stay behind me and away from him. Got it?" Without waiting for the answer, he turned and headed for the opening in the fence.

Who was she supposed to stay away from? What was going on? Were they in danger? The questions tumbled through her thoughts but she didn't have a chance to voice them. Instead, she followed after him.

She stepped through the opening in the fence and there, slammed up against the tree, she saw a truck, the front end bashed in and smoke steaming from the engine. A young boy, no older than eight, leaned against the side of the vehicle, blood streaming down from a cut above his eye. Where was he going? Why were they driving a truck through the area where there was no road? Were they a threat to the tribe?

At the far side of the truck stood Jase and another, subduing a man. He screamed and fought them as they brought him to the ground. The alcohol from the man's breath tarnished the air around them as she took in the situation.

"Stay here," Liam ordered without looking at her as he made his way over to help Jase.

She listened to him for about five seconds before she refused to stand there helplessly, and made her way over to the young boy. Human. Interesting. "What's your name?" She squatted down in front of him.

"Billy." He held his dirty hand to his head, trying to keep the blood from dripping into his eyes. "My dad…is he…in trouble?"

"How about we worry about your head right now and let the guys handle your dad?" She tore the bottom of her shirt, ripping off a large portion to apply pressure to his cut. Gently, she pushed his hand away to get a better look at his wound. No glass, which was good, but the cut was long and deep enough that it bled profusely. Good thing she didn't get woozy at the sight of blood.

"My dad…he didn't mean to…"

"It's okay, Billy." Pressing the cloth to his head, she tried to soothe him. She wanted to tell him things would be okay, but how was she supposed to do that when she didn't know what Jase and the others were going to do to the man?

If drunk driving with his son in the truck wasn't bad enough, he could have killed them both. Why had he tried to drive his truck through the fence? More concerning was, why he tried to hightail it out of there afterwards? He had been in such a hurry that when he threw it in reverse, he lost control due to lack of reflex and drove head on into the tree. What kind of parent risked their child's safety like this?

"Dad drinks a lot." He glanced toward his father. "That's why Mom left him. She doesn't like me around him but I had no choice. He took me from school."

"Does your mom know?"

The boy shook his head, at least as much as he could with her applying pressure to his cut. "I wanna go home."

"Soon, sweetie, soon." She glanced over to the men and found they had managed to subdued him. Someone had located handcuffs and got his hands behind his back and his legs shackled. Interesting, but she didn't have time to consider this; she needed to talk to Liam. "Sweetie, can you stay right here and hold this to your head? I'm going to see about getting you home. Okay?"

"Promise?"

"Stay here and be a good boy. Okay?" She took his hand and placed it over the cloth. "Hold that nice and tight. I'll be right back." When he did as she asked, she stood and slowly walked toward the men. She wanted to catch Liam's attention instead of going over to them. They might have the man subdued now but the drunk had been rowdy enough that Jase needed help to get him to the ground without hurting him. There was no doubt that if Jase hadn't been concerned with hurting the human, he'd have knocked his ass on the ground in a blink of an eye.

With a comment from Jase, Liam threw a quick look in her direction before he said something to his Chief that she couldn't make out what he said over the hollers of the human. He jogged toward her, but his gaze wouldn't quite meet hers. "What's wrong?"

He stopped a couple of feet in front of her, clearly keeping his distance, and her wolf leaped forward, wanting her to do something to ease the heavy tension between them. "He's been kidnapped."

"What?"

"Billy." She nodded to the young boy but kept her gaze on Liam. "His father took him from school and his mother doesn't know. We've got to get him back to his mom. She must be worried sick."

"Take him back to your cabin and see if you can patch up his head. If you can't, maybe the nurse can, or we'll take him into town to the doctor's office. Once we get the bleeding stopped, we'll take him back to his mother."

"What's going to happen to his father?"

"You afraid we're going to kill him?" He raised an eyebrow at her in question and when she stumbled over an answer, he shook his head. "Sheriff Rogers is on his way to pick him up. We'll get a team to patch the hole in the fence and they can start repairing it tomorrow. Meanwhile, guards will be stationed here to ensure no one can use this weakness against us. Now go. I'll fill in Jase and meet you at your cabin in a few minutes."

He didn't wait for her to say anything before he turned and headed back to the others. For a moment, she just stood there. The strain between them was thick and her wolf snarled at her, demanding that she do something to fix it. How could she do that? They were supposed to be mates but she hadn't been willing to accept it. Now that she had been there for a bit, getting used to his scent that seemed to be a permanent feature to the air, she was growing used to the idea. Could she accept what existed between them? If she did, would he still be willing to accept her or had he adjusted to being denied a mate?

The thought of her having caused a rift between them deeper than she could overcome tightened her chest. Upon seeing him again, she realized that she did want to know him better. He was her mate, and while it still made her edgy, she wanted to know the man he was. Maybe she could once and for all put the memories of Tap and the lion behind her.

Chapter Five

As the miles sped past, the tension grew within the cramped quarters of Liam's truck. He'd asked for Garret or one of the other guards to take her to reunite the boy with his mother, but Jase had refused. The others had their own duties and Garret and Sin had their hands full with their ward, Zoe. This was up to him, or they could turn the boy over to Sheriff Rogers and he'd take care of it.

Sheriff Rogers would place the child in a foster home until arrangements could be made to reunite the boy with his mother, Becky Lane. That wasn't an option for Liam. Billy had been through enough and he wanted his mother. Six uncomfortable hours, round-trip, locked in his truck with Ginger was nothing when he considered how long it could take for his mother to make arrangements to come pick up Billy.

Ms. Lane cared for her own ill mother and she'd have to find someone to look after the woman in order to make the trip.

Liam sighed. What was he doing? Nothing, but sulking over the loss of his mate. He could take Billy back to his mother. There was no reason to involve Sheriff Rogers and to make sure of it, Liam had picked up Ginger and Billy before the sheriff could arrive. No doubt there'd be a few heated words over that later but for now, Jase could handle it.

Ignoring the posted speed sign, he pressed the pedal a little closer to the floorboard, speeding his old truck up. They had another forty minutes before they'd arrive in Billy's hometown and the sleeping boy could settle into his own bed instead of being curled against Ginger.

"Shouldn't you slow down?" Fear laced her voice as she held onto the boy tighter.

"This is nothing. I'm barely doing…" He glanced down at the dashboard. *Eighty-two.* Okay. Maybe he should slow down.

"Barely doing what?"

"Okay." He eased off the gas and allowed the truck to slow down. Seventy was the legal limit, and he focused on not going over it. There was no reason to frighten her. Though he had to admit that having her finally speak to him was progress. Besides talking with Billy before he fell asleep, she hadn't said a word since they left the tribe.

What the hell do I expect her to say? Hadn't she already said all she needed to? Her absence from his life in recent days had confirmed that she didn't want him. She was his mate and he wanted her, but he wouldn't push himself on her and he sure as hell wouldn't beg. *I must accept that this is how it's going to be.*

"Please, Daddy, I don't wanna! No!" Billy screamed, his little fists beating against Ginger's side.

Billy's screams startled Liam enough that he swerved. Thankfully, no other cars were around. He righted the truck so that he was in his own lane before quickly checking his mirrors again to make sure he could pull off.

"Shh, sweetie. It's okay." She tried to comfort the little boy but he didn't seem to hear her. "Billy, wake up."

Pulling onto the shoulder of the road, he put the truck in park as it came to a stop and shifted the young boy into his lap. Billy continued to pound his fists against Liam's chest but it was better for him to take them than Ginger. Even though the boy's hits weren't painful, the idea of his mate suffering the blows made his lion angry. "You're safe now, Billy. Come on, wake up for us."

"I didn't wanna go. I want Mommy!" His eyes fluttered open.

She unhooked her seatbelt and scooted across the seat. "I know, sweetie, but we're almost there." Careful to avoid the bandage over his forehead, she pushed some hair away from his face.

"Will he come back and get me? I'll be in trouble for causing problems. He'll punish me." Billy leaned against Liam's chest and looked between them.

"No one is going to hurt you," Liam told him firmly before looking at her. He wanted to ask her if Billy had told her of any abuse, but he couldn't do it verbally with the boy in his lap. Yet, she seemed to understand and shook her head.

"Will your mom punish you, or just Daddy?" she pushed and Liam knew she was concerned they were about to take the boy to an equally bad situation. Maybe they should have waited for Sheriff Rogers.

He shook his head. "Never Mommy. Daddy punishes Mommy, too. He says we're evil."

"You're not evil." She took the boy's hand in hers and squeezed it gently. "He has a problem and there are people who are going to try to help him. Don't you worry about him. Now come over here and let Liam drive so we can get you back home to your mom."

Slipping off Liam's lap, he wiped his cheeks with the backs of his hands and came back over to sit next to her. "It's going to be okay. You'll be home soon." She wrapped her arm around his shoulders and held him tight against her.

"You okay now? I'm going to get back on the road." With a nod from Billy, Liam glanced up at Ginger. Worry creased her forehead, making him want to reassure her, too. What was there to say? Was it even his place? She denied him. Not knowing what else to do, he pulled back onto the road and sped toward the Lane household. They drove alone in silence for miles before Billy spoke again, busting the bubble of stiffness that seemed to settle over them.

"Is he going back to prison? Like last time he hurt Mommy?"

Back to prison? Hurting Mommy? There was more to the story that Liam wanted to know. The boy was kidnapped from his school by his father. Was there a protection order in place? There were steps that the mother needed to take and he was going to see to it. Next time something like this happened, Billy might not be as lucky as he'd been this time.

"I don't know," she finally answered as Liam continued to question the situation unfolding around him.

The rest of the ride was quiet, passing without any further issues, and Liam stayed lost in his thoughts. Situations like this made him glad to be a shifter. There was no falling in love with the wrong person. They mated and once the mating took place, there was no leaving each other. Shifters might drink but it was nearly impossible to get drunk and they sure as hell didn't attack their spouse or children. They had problems of their own, but for him, the benefits far outweighed the disadvantages.

As he turned onto Billy's street, he sat up, nearly bouncing in his seat until he spotted the woman standing on the porch a few houses down. "Mommy!" Billy waved frantically and climbed onto Ginger's lap, taking hold of the door handle as if he was going to jump out with the truck still moving.

"Wait a minute," Liam warned, pulling the truck to the side of the road.

He had hoped Billy would be asleep by the time they arrived so he could have a conversation with Ms. Lane, but that would have to wait until the boy was reunited with his mother. He shut off the engine and opened his door, while Ginger and Billy got out of the other side.

"Billy!" Ms. Lane jogged toward them, tears rolling down her cheeks. Billy ran toward her, meeting her in the middle of the street. She dropped to her knees and wrapped her arms around him. "Oh, Billy!"

"Mommy!"

Giving the Lanes some privacy, Liam leaned back against the hood of his truck. Ginger stood off to the right of him, so he could still see her out of the corner of his gaze. Damn, she was beautiful. Beautiful and off limits. She didn't want him and he wouldn't force her to accept him. Though one thing had changed in the last bit of their trip—the tension had dissipated a little, making their closeness seem less straining. Would it stay gone, or would it return once they were alone and on their way back to Crimson Hollow?

"You were good with him." She kept her voice low as she continued to watch the family reunion.

"So were you." He wasn't sure what else to say to her, but just then Ms. Lane rose to her feet, interrupting them.

"Billy, go on inside. Grandma has been waiting up to see you. She's in her room." When the boy did what she asked, Ms. Lane stood there for a moment, watching him until the door to the house closed. Then, she came to stand next to them. "Thank you for bringing my son home."

"You're welcome." Liam straightened so that he was no longer leaning against the hood of his truck. "When Billy told us that you were caring for your mother, we knew it would take you longer to find someone to sit with her than for us to bring him home. This is where he needed to be."

"Sheriff Rogers called about an hour after we spoke. He…"

"Is livid." He finished. "Don't worry about the sheriff. I already spoke to him when we stopped to get gas. He likes to do things his way but in the end it would have been the same outcome. You have custody of Billy and allowing Sheriff Rogers to handle it would have taken longer for him to get back home. He wanted his mother and we wanted to see that happen. He's been through enough."

"For the last time."

"Ms. Lane…your son was concerned he was going to be punished by his father. Is his father abusing him? Is he abusing you?" Ginger shifted from foot to foot and shook her head. "That sounds harsh and nothing like I rehearsed in my head since he told us."

"But the question still needs to be asked," he added. "If you or Billy are in danger, maybe we can help."

Ms. Lane wrapped her arms around her chest, hugging herself, and refused to meet their gazes any longer. "Billy's father is a great man when he's not drinking but at the first sip of alcohol he's someone you don't want to be around. He's a different man when he drinks, full of anger, hate, and violence."

"Is that why he was in prison?" he pressed, wanting more answers before he could be satisfied that Billy would be safe there.

She nodded and hugged herself tighter. "I got stuck working a double and I couldn't get word to him. Our phone had been shut off because he decided to spend the money on alcohol. When I got home, he attacked me. I was still on the porch when he grabbed the bat. My neighbors called the police."

The pieces fell into place and Liam looked at Ginger, who didn't seem to understand it yet. Maybe she hadn't seen the news, so she didn't know who he was. "Mr. Lane wasn't released from prison, was he? He's the escaped convict."

"Escaped?" Ginger inhaled deeply, making him wonder if she had seen the news report after all.

Ms. Lane nodded. "He's supposed to be serving a twenty-five-year sentence. This should have never happened. Billy should have been safe!"

"You both will be now. Wait here for a minute." He went around the side of his truck, grabbed a little notepad he kept on the side of his door, and jotted down his name and number. "Ms. Lane, this is my name and number. I want you to keep it and if you need anything, and I mean anything at all, you call me." He pressed the paper into her hand.

"We're not that far and we can be here quick," Ginger added.

We? He liked the sound of that but couldn't get his hopes up. Rather, he kept his attention focused on the other woman. "My cousin is a lawyer and he'll give you a call in the morning. He's going to make sure we get years added onto Billy's father's sentence so this can never happen again."

"Thank you." She stepped forward and wrapped her arms around his neck. "Thank you both for everything. Thank you for protecting my baby."

"Everything's going to be fine now." With his gaze on Ginger, he returned the hug. The whites of his mate's eyes changed to a yellowish color. She wasn't happy about him embracing another woman. *Is my wolf jealous?*

Chapter Six

The hour was late and exhaustion clung to Ginger as the miles stretched on. They weren't even halfway back to Crimson Hollow and all she wanted to do was curl up in bed and sleep. Knowing that Billy was safe with his mother and the whole situation concerning his father, had left her feeling overwhelmed. The way she'd asked about the abuse had been tactless but all she'd rehearsed earlier flew out the window as she stood in front of Ms. Lane. She had hoped Liam would bring it up but when he didn't right away, she couldn't wait any longer. She wanted answers and she needed to know if Billy would be safe in her care.

The little boy talked so highly of his mother and was such a sweet kid, she wanted to make sure he was protected. Kids shouldn't have to worry about the things adults worried about. They were supposed to be carefree, be able to play with their friends. Being a child was supposed to be the simplest time in a person's life. Billy was forced to witness some of the horrors life offered but he was still a child and deserved to have some of his innocence saved. There was plenty of time later to learn all of the shitty aspects of this world and the people who inhabited it.

Liam yawned and glanced over at her. "We're going to have to stop for some coffee."

"We're both exhausted and we have more than two hours' drive ahead of us still. We should just find a hotel and get some rest. Jase will understand and we can head back after a few hours of sleep."

"You don't want to be alone with me. Who knows what I'd do?"

"Liam!"

"Sorry." He dragged a hand over his face. "I shouldn't have said that. I get cranky when I'm tired but that was no excuse. I'm sure you'd rather be back—"

She turned in her seat to face him. "I wouldn't have suggested it if I was worried that you'd hurt me." The words left her mouth and she wondered when she had determined that he meant her no harm. It also occurred to her that now they were alone, the tension of being locked in the truck with him was missing. Had she started to accept the fact he was a lion…and her mate? She wasn't sure but she did know he wasn't going to hurt her.

"Come on, Liam, we're both exhausted. Let's just find a hotel."

Without answering, he took the next exit and followed the signs toward the few hotels listed on the map. They'd get some rest and then they could be back on the road in a few hours. She could do it and maybe that time together would allow her to adjust to him being around. Maybe this trip with them being thrown together for Billy's sake would bring them together. *What am I thinking? He's already proven he doesn't want me. Otherwise he wouldn't have allowed the week to pass without me getting so much as a hello from him. I did this…I lost him. There's no one to blame but myself.*

Ten minutes later, they were tucked safely into a hotel room. As much as it would have been nice to have two rooms, the hotel was booked for a convention, leaving them to share a suite that had been booked for one of the members who'd missed his connecting flight. She dropped her purse on the small table by the door and looked around. The small sofa would fold out into a single bed; besides that, the only other furniture was the bar with a mini fridge and microwave. A bathroom separated that space from what she assumed would be the main bed.

"I'll take the sofa."

"Be realistic. You've got to drive, which means you need to get some sleep. We can share the bed." Her heart pounded against her ribs. Share the bed with him. What was she thinking? They were shifters, it wasn't uncommon, but that didn't mean it made her less apprehensive about being so close to him.

"I think we've pushed your boundaries enough for one day. Don't you?" He plopped down on the sofa and let out a deep sigh.

"Damn it, Liam. It's late, I'm tired, and I'm offering you a chance to get a decent night's sleep. If you want to sleep on a lumpy pull out sofa, be my guest. I've done it enough times to know you'll wake up sore and just as tired. We both know the bed is big enough and whatever is happening between us can wait until morning, but it's up to you." She snatched her purse off the table and marched into the bedroom.

If he wanted to be an asshole and sleep on the sofa, that was his call. She had done something nice, something she wasn't completely sure she was comfortable with, but she couldn't see him sleeping out there because of her. Not after he'd taken them to reunite Billy with his mother. She knew he had tried to get out of it, but Jase had refused his request. She'd heard their exchange through the living room window while she was tending to Billy's head wound. This had been another clear indication that he didn't want to be around her.

When Ginger stormed off into the bedroom part of their room, Liam sat there feeling like an ass. He wanted to go after her; his lion snarled at him, wanting him to take her up on her offer. To be close to her, even if only for a few hours, would make it worth the pain from the aloofness that would return between them when they got back to Crimson Hollow. The mixed signals coming from her proved beyond annoying. She didn't want a lion as her mate, but she would share a bed with him? She had even been willing to be alone with him for several hours as they took Billy home. What did she want? Did she even know?

He knew what he wanted—he wanted her, and not just because she was his mate. Something intrigued him about her, something that made him want to get to know her. His body ached for her, not just in a sexual way, but simply to be near her. Seeing her in passing for the last week had only made it worse, yet he kept his distance. She had come to Crimson Hollow for Swift and then she'd move on. Without her scent hanging in the air maybe he could move forward and put the fact that they were destined to be mates behind him.

"Liam."

Her voice was so soft, he wasn't sure if he heard it or not, but when he looked up to find her peeking around the wall, he knew he was a goner. She had removed her sweater, leaving on only a thin tank top that clung to her curves. Her auburn hair cascaded down her bare shoulders in soft waves, making him want to drag his fingers through the strands and pull her close. She was gorgeous.

Before he could say a word, she took a step into the room, slowly closing the distance between them. "I'm sorry I snapped. You're respecting the boundaries I set in place…" Growing more uncomfortable with every word, she shoved her hands into the pockets of her jeans. "Maybe I don't want that anymore."

He waited a moment to see if she would continue but she just stood there, uneasy. "What are you saying?"

"I was wrong." She took a couple of steps to him and sat down next to him on the sofa. "Judging you based on your animal and my past wasn't fair. I had no right to do that."

"A scent can bring back memories—"

"I know." She let out a deep sigh before continuing. "A lot of things can bring back the memories but I can't let them control my life. They're dead, but I'm alive. It's time to remember that. If I can't do that, how will I help Swift?"

"Sometimes people have to help themselves. She has to want to move past what happened when she was a child in order for anyone to be able to help her."

"This is a heavy conversation and we're both exhausted. Come to bed and we'll pick this up over breakfast." She rose off the sofa and held out her hand to him. "You're a good man. An honest, trustworthy, and compassionate one. I've seen it since I came to Crimson Hollow but tonight, with how you handled Billy, it opened my eyes to the man I'm to be mated to. I can promise you one thing: I'm a hard woman to live with. Just ask Garret. But I hope you'll find me worth the trouble."

Taking her hand into his, he replayed her words through his thoughts. It sounded like she was accepting their destiny but he didn't want to get his hopes up. If he moved too quick, she might go back into her shell and push him away. Slow and steady would get him his wolf.

As he rose to stand in front of her, he couldn't stop himself from wanting to feel her. Without making any quick movements, he looped his free arm around her back, gently pressing his hand at the small of her back, and pulled her closer to him. "I have no doubt you'll be worth it."

"You might regret that later when you find out just how bad my bite is."

"A wolf with a bite, who would have guessed?" Since she didn't pull away, he slipped his hand under the thin material of her top and caressed along the soft skin of her back. "Still, I'd rather have my wolf in my bed."

"Did I mention I'm a cover hog?"

He watched her eyes twinkle, full of mischief, but he didn't care as long as he had her. *Screw this.* Scooping her up into his arms, he headed for the bedroom. "Oh baby, I sleep nude and wouldn't want to distract from your view with covers."

Chapter Seven

Through the fog of sleep, Ginger could make out the faint sounds of a phone vibrating, but as much as she tried, she couldn't force her eyes to open. Whoever was calling would have to wait. She wasn't ready to be up. She snuggled back into the warmth of the blankets and—

Shit! Her eyes sprang open as she realized the heat wasn't coming from her blankets but from a man. Still deeply asleep, Liam lay stretched out on his back and, true to his word, he was naked as the day he was born.

She still couldn't believe he'd climbed into bed next to her completely naked. It had taken things a step further than she had planned but damn, he was a fine looking man. They had started the night on their own sides of the bed and not touching, but sometime during the night, she gravitated toward him.

Shifters liked warmth when they slept and it wasn't uncommon to find some sleeping together in a big pile. Such a sight always reminded her of a puppy pile, as they all cuddled together. The lack of someone to sleep with had her cuddling with a heating blanket instead. It wasn't a good substitute but better than a cold, empty bed. Only this morning, she woke up to not just another shifter that had shared her bed, but the man who was to be her mate. A soft moan had her tipping her head up to get a better look at him, only to find him awake and watching her.

"Morning, beautiful." With the arm he had wrapped around her, he pulled her tight against him. “I thought you’d steal the covers away and enjoy the view.”

“Maybe I was about to,” she teased and pulled the covers down, not quite revealing his manhood.

“Teasing won’t end well for you.”

“Really, lion.” She rubbed her body along his, drawing her fingers along the contours of his chest, working her way down toward his waist. “I think you might have that reversed. The woman holds the power and we tease you into the position we want you. If we let you think otherwise, it’s for your own benefit.”

“Is that so?” Without giving her time to answer, his arm tight around her, he rolled her onto her back so that he was arched over her. “Shall we see about that?”

“Liam…” His name came out on a whisper as she continued to explore his body. She didn’t want him to stop but was she ready? She wasn’t sure.

“Go with it.” He nuzzled the side of her neck, planting gentle kisses along the curve before working down her collarbone. “Stay in the moment and remember it’s me. No one else, just me and you.”

“I know it’s you.” She caressed along his sides, debating for a moment if she wanted to tell him everything or keep it to herself. “Last night, as you lay there beside me, your scent surrounded me. Instead of fearing the scent, as I did when I first met you, I noticed key differences. It’s not just a lion scent. There’s more to it. I can smell your tribe—Jase’s bear and Sin’s fox are the strongest but there are others who blend into it; even Garret’s wolf lingers within the mix. There are also hints of hickory, apples, and fall leaves. So I always know it’s you.” She cupped the side of his face, stroking her thumb along the stubble on his jaw.

“Good.” He tipped his head toward her hand and kissed her palm.

“I should have realized it before but I let my fear get the best of me. Never again.” Not waiting for him to make the first move, she arched up toward him and claimed his lips. He met her kiss with desire of his own.

As the kiss ended, he leaned back from her and watched her for a moment. “Are you sure about this?”

“Completely.” She grabbed a hold of his hips and drew him down toward her.

"Now come here."

He leaned into her, pressing his lips to hers, not allowing her a chance to deny him, and making her crave more of him. No longer would she allow the fact he was a lion to keep her from her mate. Destined mates were the perfect match for each other and she had to trust that destiny had led her to him for a reason.

With passion controlling her, she pressed into him as his fingers hooked the bottom of her tank top. "I let you sleep in the tank top and panties, even though I was naked, but now I want these gone."

"I didn't force you to get naked."

"Maybe not, but you enjoyed every minute of it." He tugged her shirt up to just below her breasts and gave her a cocky grin. "Don't think I didn't catch your glances in my direction."

"I didn't…" She could feel the blood rushing to her cheeks.

"Deny it if it makes you feel better but we both know the truth." Slowly, he pulled the tank top up over her breasts and over her head. "Soon you will be my mate and can see me naked any time your heart desires."

"You're cocky, but I like it."

"Good. Now lie back. I want to explore every inch of your body." He kissed her neck, nibbling down her jawline to her shoulder.

As he moved lower, she wanted to protest because his body wasn't pressed along hers and she couldn't feel his shaft pressed along her inner thigh any longer. Since he'd finally made it to her breast, she complied, lying back and letting her fingers trail along his sides. He lowered his mouth to her nipple, his gaze locked on her. She moaned in ecstasy when his tongue flicked over one hardened tip. Pleasure exploded through her as his tongue teased along her sensitive nipples. After working both nipples into hardened peaks, he moved down, kissing along her stomach until he reached the top of her panties.

"Naked." The one word camc out like a growl as he teased with deft fingers along the seam of the material.

"You know how to fix that." She arched up to allow him to pull her panties down.

In a blink of an eye, they were gone, leaving her as naked as he was, and the heat level within her rose with every caress. Her body craved his touch and it had been too long since she'd felt the gentle caress of a man, let alone another shifter. He pulled his mouth from hers and kissed a path down her neck. Sensations collided and threatened to overwhelm her when he teased her nipples. Pushing her gently back onto the bed, his bulky frame hovered above her and he stared down at her, desire burning in his eyes.

He caressed every inch of her body, sending moans of ecstasy from her lips. His touch was incredibly tender, as though trying to memorize every curve of her body with his hands and mouth. Heat soared through her blood, like a fire burning just below the skin, impatient and demanding.

He blazed a hot, wet trail of kisses across her belly and stroked her thighs with his fingertips. With every touch, she arched her hips, demanding more. She couldn't get enough of him. Nudging her legs farther apart, he delved his fingers inside her and she met the thrusts. A demanding moan she barely recognized vibrated in her throat. The trail of wicked kisses tingled over her thighs. He moved his hand and replaced it with his mouth. Tiny nips and gentle licks flicked over her sweet spot, nearly driving her over the edge. She grabbed his hair, torn between pressing him closer and dragging him up. She wanted all of him.

"Liam!" She nearly screamed his name before gaining a little control over herself. "Please, I need you." Even in the sexual haze, she realized what she'd said and those few words changed everything. Sex would complete their mating, forever uniting them as one. There was peace in knowing she would forever have someone by her side, and that he was hers. Mates.

"You don't know how good it is to hear that." He spread her legs farther, giving him the access he needed before filling her slowly, inch by inch. Halfway in, he slid out before thrusting back in, this time filling her completely with his manhood. Their animals sprang forward, mingling their magic together until the air was thick with it, and the hairs on their arms stood on end. Their animals didn't snarl at each other, but caressed one another as their human sides brought them together.

His hips increased pace, driving the force of each pump. Every glide of his shaft inside her seemed to set off another cascade of heat. Their bodies rocked back and forth, tension stretching her tighter as she fought for the release she longed for. This was what she had been waiting for, what she needed.

"Liam!" She cried out his name as she found her release. She dug her nails into his back, pressing her body into his. He pumped into her a few more times before he shouted her name in ecstasy.

With his shaft still deep within her, he smiled down at her. "My mate."

As her breath slowly returned to normal, she realized how much she liked the sound of that. She was his, just as he was hers. They were locked together for all eternity. Hopefully, they could manage to live with each other without killing one another.

Epilogue

Mating had been easier than Ginger had expected, even considering that she was stuck with not only a lion but also the Chief's main guard. She was even adjusting to tribe life and joined in on their activities. Garret had ensured her that it was nothing like the wolf pack they grew up in but she hadn't believed it until she'd returned not as Garret's visiting sister, but as Liam's mate. There was a difference between the two. As the former, she'd been treated more as an outsider, but as the latter, she was part of the family. That's what had changed; she wasn't just passing through, she was one of them. *Family.*

It still felt weird to consider anyone besides Garret family, but now she had a sister-in-law, Sin, her mate, Liam, and the whole tribe. She and Liam even had an extra special person they considered one of them—Billy. Billy and Becky Lane had kept in touch and Liam had been good on his word. His cousin, the lawyer, had been at Becky's side as they pressed charges of kidnapping. Things were beginning to look up for the Lanes, yet they continued to keep in touch.

One thing that hadn't changed was Swift. She had opened up a little to Ginger but she wasn't ready to put the past behind her. Vengeance burned within her, but there was no justice to seek. Everyone who had been involved in the murder of her family and leash was dead. Ginger wasn't sure how to help her. Even Jase and Sin seemed to be running out of options. If her fear and paranoia continued to progress, they'd have no option but to force her to leave. They couldn't continue to allow her to expose the rest of the tribe to her delusions.

"There you are." Liam came up behind her on the deck to their cabin and slipped his arm around her waist. "What are you doing out here?"

"Thinking." She leaned back into his embrace, resting her head on his shoulder.

"About Swift again." He didn't even bother to phrase it as a question.

"I don't know what to do for her."

"I told you before, she has to want to help herself. Right now she doesn't, but I think she's realizing that if she doesn't do something she's going to lose the only home she's ever known."

She glanced up to look at him. "Why? Has something happened?"

"She stormed into Jase's while Noah, Ari, Kaden, and I were having a security meeting. Jase was furious. The tribe members know better than to just walk into his house without knocking. He ended up laying into her pretty good. She cried that he didn't care about her, which only enticed him more. He's done everything he could think of for her, and now she's going after the one man that is on her side. If she doesn't give some, he's going to have no choice."

"That's what I'm afraid of. What will happen to her then?"

"I don't know, baby, but we're doing all we can for her." He hugged her tight against his body. "None of us are giving up on her."

"I know."

"Then stop worrying and let's go inside. We have twenty minutes before the barbeque at Jase's and I'd like to use every moment of that to explore my mate's beautiful body."

She spun around to face him and let her hands roam up his chest. "Is that all you ever think about?"

"No, but it's the highlight of my thoughts. And with Billy and Becky arriving next week, I want to make sure I don't miss a moment. I want you naked as often as I can before they get here." He tangled his fingers in her hair and stared down at her. "You're the woman I've been waiting my whole life for. I love you, Ginger."

No matter how many times he said those words, they still made her heart skip a beat. “I love you too, Liam.”

Swift Move

Unable to put the past behind her, Swift is overcome by terror and a thirst for revenge. Believing she has nothing to offer the tribe, she leaves behind the only home she's ever known, but in a world filled with humans, this only makes matters worse.

Brett Oaks has just joined the Crimson Hollow Tribe, taking a position in the guard. Things turn out much as he anticipated until he is sent to bring back one of the tribe members and comes face to face with his mate. She reeks of fear, but he also senses something else.

She's tired of living like she is but will she trust him enough to let him help her? There is more to life than what she has experienced. He's ready to show her, if she'll only open up her heart to him.

Chapter One

If Swift heard someone say she needed to let go of the past one more time, she would scream. How was she supposed to move past the memories when every time she closed her eyes, she could see the ground covered in blood? Screams from her family and friends echoed in her ears. Everyone she knew had been slaughtered. Why? Because a human fell in love with a fox shifter who couldn't return that love. They weren't mates and because of that, he'd sought his revenge on the group of animals that reminded him of her.

Sinking down on the chair, she squeezed the bridge of her nose. What was she going to do? She'd thought leaving Crimson Hollow would be the right choice but as she sat in her hotel room, fear rose within her, worse than ever. She couldn't handle it any longer, but she refused to go back to the tribe with her tail between her legs.

The cell phone she laid on the table vibrated and Sin's name displayed again. This was the fifth call and it wasn't noon yet but Swift wasn't ready to answer. What was she going to tell her cousin? That wasn't the only reason why she didn't answer. If she did, Sin would try to talk her into returning and her will was broken enough that she'd let it happen. The tribe was her family; maybe not biologically, but they'd accepted Sin and Swift when their leash—their group of foxes—was slaughtered.

"Now I'm on the verge of losing them too. I'll be alone again!" Tears pricked her eyes as she fought to keep her emotions at bay.

Leaning back in the hard high back chair, she focused on the pale yellow walls of the hotel room and tried to breathe despite the lump in her chest. She needed to find a way to move past what happened. Not just for a few hours at a time, like she had been able to do since she left. She needed to be able to put the past behind her for good. Otherwise, she'd lose her family, her tribe, and she didn't want that to happen. They had become everything to her—until her past was tossed back in her face with the slaughter of more foxes and the arrival of Zoe. Now, nothing was the same.

A pounding on the door had her jumping off the chair. *They've found me.* Only, she wasn't worried it would be someone from her tribe. No, she wasn't afraid of them, but of a dead man. How was that even logical? Rationality didn't matter when it came to her terror. It was all in her head and that made it worse. How did one convince themselves that everything was fine?

"Swift?" Another knock echoed through the room. "Open up. It's Noah. Jase sent me."

"Noah…" His name came out whisper soft, so she wasn't sure he could hear her.

"Yes. Now open up."

Swallowing the lump in her throat, she forced herself to walk to the door. Each step seemed to take more effort like she was moving in quicksand. No doubt it was Noah; she knew his voice and his scent.

Scent. That was what her fox kept trying to tell her, but the fog that had settled over her brain stopped her from comprehending. Noah wasn't alone, she realized. "Who's with you?"

"Brett."

She stood on the other side of the door, trying to make sense of the scent, but her fox was barking within her, distracting her. What was going on?

"He's from the tribe. We're drawing attention and that's the last thing we want right now. Now open up, Swift. You're safe, I promise." Noah lowered his voice as he said the last part, as if he didn't want to be heard by someone.

Trust. She had to remember, Noah was a friend. He wouldn't hurt her or bring anyone else to her doorstep that would. Her fox circled within her, excitement spilling off her animal and urging her forward. Quickly, she pulled back the latch and unlocked the door, before opening it enough to look out and ensure it was Noah.

As the two men came into view, it wasn't Noah that she noticed, but the other man—Brett. His lean body was pale, while his vibrant, emerald-green eyes had so much life in them, they seemed to sparkle at her. His dark brown hair was spiked back on top and the sides cut shorter, tempting her to reach out and draw her fingers through it to see the different shades of brown. The caramel highlights seemed to catch the glistening rays of sunlight the most, but the tawny brown ones drew her attention. Women would spend hours in the salon highlighting their hair and still not get those hues he naturally possessed.

"Can we come in?" Noah asked as she continued to block the doorway, staring at Brett.

"Um…" She took a step back but her gaze remained on him. "Yeah."

As they entered, the scent of his beast drifted toward her, exciting her fox further. A bear. There were plenty of bears among their tribe that she wasn't surprised by his animal. She was, however, surprised by the fact that this was her mate standing before her. Mating hadn't crossed her mind much since she'd come of age. She'd never sought one out or even hoped for one. How was she supposed to be a good mate if she couldn't even keep her life under control?

Noah inhaled deeply and his eyes grew wide before taking a step back from between them. "Swift—"

She cut him off before he could say whatever he had come to say. "Why did you bring him?"

"Jase's orders." Noah watched her carefully.

"We've come to bring you home." Brett's deep voice caressed over her skin like teasing fingers, stroking her and bringing the fire to raging levels.

"I don't have a home any longer." She stepped back until the back of her legs brushed along the bed and she sank down onto it. "I wasn't welcomed in Crimson

Hollow any longer and now I have nowhere else to go. This is my life now."

"Jase never asked you to leave," Noah reminded her.

"No, but he would have. I lost my home and the only family I have, but I don't even blame him. He would have done what was best for the tribe." She slammed her hand down on the bed, anger pouring through her. "If only I could have got my head together…"

"Your family wants you home." Noah stepped farther into the room. "Sin wanted to come after you herself, but Garret and Jase wouldn't allow that. The threats to our kind have increased recently. Humans are no longer only hunting us for sport but a group is putting bounties on our heads. Each week a new species is chosen as the target."

"I don't understand. Why does that change anything?"

"You're in danger out here." Brett leaned against the dresser, his arms crossed over his chest as he was careful not to knock over the television that sat on the surface. "The longer you stay out here, away from the tribe, the more danger you're in. None of the other members are close enough to be able to aid you in an emergency."

"You can't stay locked in your room all the time. Your beast wants to be let out so it can roam. It won't be long before someone figures out you're a shifter. You'll be in danger. You need to come home," Noah added.

The men shared a look before Brett stepped away from the dresser and came to squat before her. "Jase sent me with Noah for a reason."

"You mean because you're my mate?" Saying it aloud made her chest tighten. Again, she reminded herself she couldn't deal with a mate and everything that union meant when she found herself in this predicament. "Jase knows who will mate with whom as long as he's met both of them and he loves to throw them together in an unexpected situation. Like he did with Sin and Garret."

"I didn't understand why Sin and Garret stopped by my place right before we left. It seemed out of place for them to show up to tell me how they'd met but when you opened the door, the pieces fell into place. Jase knew we're to be mates and their story was to show me that if we allowed this to happen naturally, things would work out."

"You don't want me. Trust me, I've been through some awful shit and I'm messed up. That's why I can't go back to Crimson Hollow." She dragged her hand through her hair, tugging the ruby red strands away from her face. "I think both of you should leave now."

"Not a chance." Noah shook his head. "You two have some things to discuss. I'm going to make a run for some food. Anything special you want, Swift?"

"You're leaving?" She stared up at him, her eyes wide, and her heart beating a little too fast with fear.

"Yeah, but Brett will be here. He's not going to hurt you." Noah strolled toward the door. Grabbing hold of the door handle, he turned to face her. "Trust us and we can get you home again."

He opened the door but before he could step out, she hollered to him. "There's a delicious Mexican restaurant on the corner. Tell them it's for Swift. They know my order. I've been there every day since I arrived."

"A creature of habit." He shook his head and closed the door behind him.

Left alone with Brett, she sensed tension rising within the room, knotting the muscles in her shoulders. Her stomach rolled. What could the two of them have to talk about? He had to be able to tell she wasn't interested in mating or anything else, for that matter. Her mental stability was hanging on by a thread. She didn't need this.

Chapter Two

Every moment, Swift made it clear she didn't want Brett around and the tension from Noah's departure only made her edgier. His bear snarled at him, demanding that he do something to put her at ease. She was his mate, even if she didn't like that fact, and he didn't want to see her so full of anxiety that her body ached. He'd rather she ached for other reasons…

He had been at this juncture and his bear was eager to take over. He'd made it through and was determined to help her do the same. The first step was to get her to trust him. He rose from where he squatted before her, grabbed one of the two chairs from the small table on the other side of the room and brought it closer.

"What did Noah mean that we have a lot to discuss?"

"Jase planned to send me even before he learned I was your mate." He placed the chair close to her but far enough away that they were not touching, and sat down. "Actually, it was Sin who I spoke with about joining Noah for this trip. She wanted me to see if I could help you because I've been where you are."

"I've already been through that. Garrett's sister Ginger tried but I can't…"

"I don't know Ginger's story. I only know that according to Sin, it's different. You witnessed your leash get—"

"Don't say it!" She closed her eyes and shook her head. "Don't say it, please don't…"

"Shh, Swift." He reached out and took her hand in his. "It's okay."

"It's not okay. It will never be okay."

"I know." Without letting go of her hand, he moved his chair closer so that their knees touched. "What happened will stay with you forever. Nothing will erase the memories or the blood spilled. But you can move past it."

"How am I supposed to do that?"

"I'm not going to say it's easy, but it's possible." He rubbed his thumb over the top of her knuckles. "Mating will help, too."

She tried to pull back from him but when his grip on her hand tightened, she stopped. "I'm not mating with you just because you think it will help me. I don't even know you. It might be impossible for us to put up with each other and that would only make a bad situation worse. It's not happening, buddy, so if you think you can just stroll in here and claim me, you're out of your mind!" She tried to pull back again, but he gently yet firmly had her stay put.

"It's a pleasure to see that your temper is still intact." He gave her a smile and squeezed her hand. "Listen, feisty, that's not what I meant and you know it. Your fear reeked through this motel room when we arrived, but since I took your hand, it has subsided."

"Maybe I don't see you as a threat anymore."

"Noah and I weren't the ones you feared."

To prove a point, he let go of her hand and made sure their knees weren't touching. As soon as the contact between them ceased, the fear started to rear its head once more.

"What…what are you doing?" She reached out to him again but he pulled back.

"Focus on the fear."

"What?"

"Trust me." He wanted to comfort her but, with the slightest touch, the fear would pop around her. "Focus on the fear. What are you terrified of? What does the darkness hold? Whatever it is, I know it's not Noah or me."

"I can't…"

"You can. Now focus and tell me what you see. What do you fear?"

"They're coming for me. They know I lived and they want me dead." Her voice broke and tears welled in her eyes. "Guns and knives. They want to see the fear in my eyes as they kill me. I'm scared but there will be peace afterwards. No more running in terror."

Unable to take it any longer, he rose from the chair and went to sit on the bed next to her. He wrapped his arm around her, pressing her against his body. "It's okay, Swift; no one is here. You're safe." The details he gathered from Sin about what happened to her leash gave him further insight into his mate.

"They'll come back. Just as they did with Zoe's family."

"They're dead. They're not coming back." He smoothed his hand down her arm. "Jase and the others made sure they were dead. I know you don't believe it, but you're safe from them."

Even though he wanted to, he couldn't stop himself from adding 'from them'. The men responsible for the attacks on the foxes were dead but that didn't mean some other lunatic wouldn't pick up where they started. There was a terrorist group out to eliminate them and their kind. Each week, they picked a new target, but how long would it be before they chose foxes? Swift wouldn't see this as a random thing; she'd see it as a personal attack on her. He needed to get her back to Crimson Hollow where she would be safe and shelter her from news of these murderers.

They sat there in silence, mostly because he didn't want to push her further and make her kick him out. She was his mate and he needed to help her move past this if they were going to have any kind of future together. Jase and Sin were also counting on him to bring her back to the tribe. Being a new member, he was just getting them to trust him. Bringing her back would be a good stepping stone to making a home for himself in Crimson Hollow.

"Ginger tried to help me, but the murder she witnessed was to protect her. My family was slaughtered in front of me and I was paralyzed with fear. I couldn't save them."

"You're feisty but you'd have been no match for them." He laid his other hand on her leg, linking their fingers. "You were what? Five? Six?"

"I had turned seven the day before." She rested her head against his shoulder. "My parents arranged for everyone to come together in the courtyard. They had a bonfire, lots of delicious food, games, and a birthday cake that would rival a wedding cake. It was taller than me, with multiple layers. A beautiful thing; I almost didn't want to eat it but Sin's mother had baked it and I knew it would be the best damn cake I'd ever tasted. She was a hell of a baker."

"See?" He unhooked his hand from hers to gently lift her chin and bring her eye to eye. "Those memories are what you need to focus on when the fear returns. Remember your family at the party, having a good time. Surrounded by everyone you love."

"But they're dead now," she reminded him.

"Dead but never forgotten. They wouldn't want you to remember them the way you do now. They'd want you to focus on the good times."

"How do you know? You never met them. I don't know why you're even here. Why does any of this matter to you?"

"Let me tell you a story." Needing space, he stepped away from her. He could sense the fear beginning to creep back into her but she was doing her best to suppress it. "At eighteen, I was wild, running with the wrong crowd, and basically needed a good ass kicking from my old man. I wanted freedom. I was tired of being stifled by their rules and customs. I thought I was tough and, to impress a girl, I borrowed a friend's motorcycle. This didn't go smoothly and, needing time to lick my wounds, I went on a drive. There was an abandoned farm a few miles out of town where we used to hang out, drinking and partying. That's where I was heading."

When he fell silent, she probed him. "What happened?"

"I parked a few miles away, planning on going for a run in the woods, but something stronger was calling my name. In the master bedroom there was a loose floorboard which I'd turned into my hidey hole for the bottle of whiskey I kept there. My anger controlled my beast enough that I wasn't paying enough attention to my surroundings and I stumbled into something I should never have witnessed. Turns out I wasn't the only one who wanted to use the house that night. Two guys were there with an older businessman. Over the howling of the wind, I couldn't hear what they were saying but they must have heard me because they shot him and started to come after me."

He stood near the window but didn't pull the curtains back so he could see outside. It wouldn't have mattered because all he could see before him were the results of what he'd set into motion that night. "I was young and naive. They warned me if I said anything to anyone or went to the cops, I'd be the next one left for dead. But, did I listen?"

"Being Mr. Tough Bear, I highly doubt it."

When he glanced over his shoulder at her, she had a small grin on her face. "You're right, I couldn't. The man's family deserved to know what had happened to him. But I didn't know what I was getting into. I didn't know these guys were cops. They were on the take—"

"Huh? On the take of what?"

"They were being paid off not to do their jobs. Drug dealers were paying these guys to look the other way. The guy they killed was an accountant who skimmed money from his clients. He was late on a payment and they didn't like that." The scent of fear, sweat, and gunpowder filled his nose as if he had gone back in time. "I didn't know who they were but I couldn't sit and do nothing so I went to the one person I knew I could trust. Sergeant Black, a black bear I'd met a couple years before. They were gathering evidence on the guys and they needed my testimony to help bring them down. I had done some things I wasn't proud of and to me this was my chance to make amends. Doing the right thing meant I could save someone else from that same fate. Bad cops like that taint the whole force."

"Good, assholes like that don't deserve to be on the force. But I don't understand what this has to do with anything."

"My actions had consequences." He dragged his hand through his hair and down his face. "I expected them to come after me. Sergeant Black put me up in a safe house outside of town, leaving a careful trail for them to follow. We were ready for them when they made their move. What I wasn't ready for was them going after my family."

"Oh, Brett, I'm sorry."

"They called my cell phone and I could hear my mother screaming in the background. Without taking the time to tell Sergeant Black, I jumped into my car and took off toward home. They wanted me, not my family. If only I could get to them in time. Desperate to save my family, I raced across town. We had our differences, but they didn't deserve this. It was my fault they were in this situation." He slammed his hand against the wall and, once again, he could sense her fear spiking. "Time wasn't on my side. I was too far away and these assholes wanted to eliminate anyone that could be trouble. Mom, Dad, and Annie—they couldn't live because they had seen the officers' faces and could identify them. I wasn't thinking, just reacting. I arrived too late."

"Brett, you don't have to do this."

He ignored her and continued, "They saw my father as a threat and eliminated him before I arrived. The medical examiner said he'd been dead before I even received the call. I arrived just as another shot echoed through the air. When I opened the door, I found my mother slumped over and my sister screaming. She was bound to the chair; terror filled her eyes as tears streamed down her face. I offered myself up in her place." He could see himself back in the living room of the house he'd grown up in. His parents' bodies on the floor as the blood seeped out of their wounds…

"It's me you want, not her." Willing to exchange his life for his sister's, he moved farther into the house. "Let her go. I'll do whatever you say."

"We warned you. Did you really think it wouldn't come to this? You were off in a safe house protected, leaving your family vulnerable. We were within our rights to make them pay for your betrayal."

"Betrayal? That's what you consider this? You killed a man."

"Since you couldn't keep your mouth shut, your family will die and then so will you."

Officers descended on the house and chaos erupted. Shots rang out as he rushed toward Annie and his shoulder exploded with pain. This didn't stop him—he had to get to Annie; he had to save his sister. She was all he had left. Fifteen years old, she hadn't even started living yet. Reaching her, he sliced through the ropes that bound her to the chair, but it was too late. She was shot, her white t-shirt covered in blood. "Annie!" he screamed as he lifted her into his arms and ducked behind the kitchen counter. There was no way he'd make it out of the house. Not with all of the gunfire. "Annie, don't you die on me!"

"Brett…" Her words were soft as she reached out to touch his chest.

He couldn't do anything for her as the darkness still surrounded him. He needed to finish the story, to get it off his chest once and for all. This was the first time he'd told someone everything and there was a bit of relief to it. "Sergeant Black must have heard me leave because the next thing I knew, he and his officers descended on the house. I rushed toward Annie, but before I could get there, another shot was fired, striking her in the chest. She died at the hospital later that day. All because of me. If I'd have kept my mouth shut, she'd still be alive. If I had been home, they'd still be alive."

"Or you might be dead."

He blinked away the past and looked down at her. "We're both alive for a reason. While the memories of what we witnessed and the guilt will always be with us, we need to remember that we are alive and we owe it to those we love who died to take advantage of every moment. We have to live life to the fullest because of those who didn't have the chance to do so."

Some days, that was harder to do than others, but now that he'd found her, maybe that would change.

Chapter Three

Standing before Brett, Swift couldn't help but be amazed that he seemed so well put together. There was darkness in his eyes as he spoke, one that warned her he was dangerous, but she admired his ability to keep what had happened out of the present. She wanted to be able to do that. She wanted a normal life again.

"How do you do it? How do you get up every morning and go on living after that? Don't you want revenge?"

"Revenge…" His jaw tightened and she could feel his bear edge toward the surface. "Every moment of every day, but you can't get revenge on someone who is already dead. They didn't make it out of my house. More than just them—some good officers went down in the battle. Sergeant Black was gravely wounded but managed to survive. He forced me to carry on even when I didn't want to. There were days when I didn't want to get out of bed. Do you think he'd have allowed me to mope around? Hell, no. He worked my ass every day and because of that, I joined the police force three years ago."

"Why did you leave?"

"Ari and Kaden put the security system in my house in Texas. I wanted the best and they are the best. Over the years, we've stayed in touch and become good friends. They mentioned Jase was interested in recruiting guards for the tribe."

"You left Texas to come to Crimson Hollow? What about your job with the police department? Surely that would have been more rewarding than working for Jase?"

He reached out and put his hands on her shoulders, drawing her a little closer. "Sergeant Black died six months ago. Since then, things haven't been the same. I was alone in this world and seemed to have lost my reason for being. I stepped down, hoping I could find that again with others of my own kind. I spoke with Jase a number of times before making the decision but once I did that same night, I was on the road headed this way. My house is on the market, and I'm starting over. So far, the tribe has been what I needed."

She couldn't picture giving up everything to start over in another state. She might have left Crimson Hollow because she would have been forced out anyways, but she was only two hours away. While it seemed far, it was the nearest town she could find work in without everyone questioning her. No one knew her here and that was what she needed. But, it also meant she was alone. Or at least she'd been until Noah and Brett showed up.

"You asked me how I go on every day after everything that happened. The answer is simple." He slid his hands down her arms, teasing along her skin. "I do it because the only other option is failure. I won't fail my family. They died because of my actions and I've spent years trying to make amends for what I've done, by protecting others."

"You didn't know what would happen to them; if you had, you'd have done something." She ran her hand along his chest, giving him comfort where she could.

"It doesn't change the fact that their blood is still on my hands. That guilt is always with me but I've forced myself to move forward. You can, too. Let me help you."

"It's different with me." She stepped back, breaking their physical contact. "You couldn't get to your family in time to save them, whereas I stood there and did nothing. My brother shoved me down behind this huge tree and ordered me to stay. Before I could argue, he ran toward the fighting. I watched everyone I knew and loved die. I was paralyzed with fear and did nothing. How am I supposed to live with that?"

"You saved yourself. That's what is important." He took a step toward her but when she shook her head, he stopped. "Sin said your leash was outnumbered."

"We were a small leash, mostly family. We kept to ourselves."

"In the end, that was your demise. Foxes are small creatures. If it had been another shifter group trying to take over, you'd never stand a chance. With the humans, you would have had a chance if they hadn't eliminated your best men immediately. The guards on duty were shot before they could even fight back. There was no perimeter fence to keep them out. Your guards were unarmed because there was peace in our world then. Humans hadn't known about us as they do now. It's a miracle that you and Sin survived. In the other leash that was attacked before yours, no one survived, which is why nobody learned about it before the second attack. It was weeks later before anyone knew about it because they kept to themselves."

She knew everything he was saying was the truth but it didn't ease the tightness in her chest or the fear that ran through her veins. His words also sent a chill through her very core. *Foxes are small creatures…they'd never stand a chance against another shifter group.* He was a bear and even before he'd said these words, she knew she wouldn't win if she had to fight him. But now she wondered if he was a threat to her…

"Hey now…" He stepped closer to her. As she backed up, he continued to close the distance until her back was pressed against the wall and his body held her there. "Don't, Swift."

"Don't what?"

"You're looking at me as if I'm about to kill you and your fear stains the air. I'm not here to hurt you, so quit looking at me like that." He cupped the side of her face and gently traced his thumb over the curve of her jawbone. "I'll protect and cherish you, if you'll only allow me."

"Pro…protect me from what? You said it yourself: the men I fear are dead. Who do I need protection from? You?"

"Never me. I've put my old ways behind me. I've changed. I mean you no harm and you know that. You're scared and you're letting your fears carrying you away from reality. The men who hurt your family are dead, and so are the ones who went after

Zoe's. I can't kill someone who's already dead. If I could, there'd be a list, starting with the assholes who killed Annie." He took a deep breath and let it out again. "Trust me and I'll help you through this. Come back to Crimson Hollow where you're safe."

"You keep saying that. Why am I not safe here?"

"I hadn't planned on bringing this up but I feel it's the best way to prove to you that you need to come home." He looked down at her and their gazes locked before she closed her eyes to get away from the intensity of his scrutiny. "The attacks on shifters are getting worse. They choose a different animal each week and put a bounty on their head. If you can prove you've killed the animal of the week, you're rewarded handsomely."

Startled, she'd have stepped back if she wasn't pressed against the wall. Each night she watched the news but they never said anything. Since she had purposely avoided other shifters because she didn't want anyone to know she was alone, she hadn't heard about it from them, either. The news made her heart skip a beat. The world was dangerous and becoming more so each day. *Maybe it would have been better if I had died with my family.*

"Are you listening to me?"

"Are foxes…" She couldn't bring herself to finish the question.

"No." He slid his hand upwards to tangle his fingers in her hair. "Foxes haven't been picked yet but it's only a matter of time. We want to get you home before they decide to choose another animal."

"The threats to us…they never end, do they?"

"Not as long as there's scum walking this Earth." He dropped his hand away from her and stepped back. "Now, with so many other horrors in the world, how about you trust me and let me help you?"

"Why? Why would you want to help me? Because I'm your mate?"

"Why should I help you?" Without breaking eye contact, he took a few steps back. "Even if you weren't my mate, I'd help you. No one deserves what these bastards are doing. No one should have to live in fear. What happened to you is awful. You're alive and you need to cherish each moment. I ask you again: Come back to

Crimson Hollow where you're safe. Jase, Sin, and everyone wants you back."

"If I can't keep my emotions under control, Jase will have to ask me to leave." She dragged her hands through her hair, tugging the strands just enough to feel. "I left once but if I go back, I'll never have the courage to do it again. I've practically had to tie myself to the bed so I wouldn't go running back with my tail between my legs. I'm no good for the tribe like this."

"We'll work together; we'll keep your anxiety at bay. You have to keep telling yourself that the shadows in the dark—the ones you fear—are dead. No one is coming for you. This terrorist organization hunting shifters will be eliminated, but it's going to take time. I've reached out to my contacts and they're working on stopping them. Until then, we've got to do our best to keep each other safe."

"Safe. What a joke. Is anywhere even safe anymore?" Her voice rising until she was almost yelling—but she couldn't stop herself.

"Jase, Ari, Kaden, and everyone else have put a lot of work into making Crimson Hollow safe. We're stronger in a group. There are more of us to watch each other's backs. Come home."

The door opened and Noah strolled in with the food. Even as the delicious aroma of Mexican fare drifted toward her, she couldn't shut off her thoughts. *Home.* That one word sounded so heavenly. She wanted to be back there, surrounded by the people she had come to consider family. She wanted to see Sin again, and Jase, too. To be safely hidden behind the perimeter fence, with guards protecting the whole tribe. More than that, she wanted to be back in her own bed, in her own cabin.

Chapter Four

Brett respected Swift's need to think it over but he'd be damned if he was going to leave her alone in that place without protection. Since there were no other rooms available in the hotel and both he and Noah agreed that she shouldn't be alone, he was staying in her room. Thanks to some extra encouragement from Noah, she agreed to the arrangements, while Noah took a room at another hotel down the road. There were two beds and he was giving her time to think things through, but he wouldn't allow her to be at risk just because she was stubborn.

As she slept, he leaned against the headboard, scrolling through the channels, looking for something to watch. He hated the silence and downtime had never been something that suited him. He needed the action, to be on the go. Bears could be patient when they needed to be, but tonight wasn't the night. Something hovered in the air, keeping his beast on edge.

Tossing the remote on the bed, he rose and quietly crossed the room to the window. The light from the bathroom's cracked open door was more than enough for him to see his way around the dark room. He hadn't bothered to ask her why she'd left the light on, but the way she'd slightly opened the door so only a sliver of light streamed into the room let him know she wanted it on. It might have been because of the strange man in her room, or the unusual place—either way, if it made her feel more comfortable, he didn't mind the light even if it shined directly on his bed.

A glance outside to find the world peaceful would help to ease the tension rising within him. Not wanting the outside light to wake her, he separated the curtains just enough to look out. At the late hour, only a few cars passed by on the road, while off in the distance he could hear police sirens. They were rushing to a call, making him long for the action. To leave the police force had been the right decision, though. If anyone had found out he was a shifter, he would have put anyone who'd worked with him in danger. He was tired of living in the shadows and at Crimson Hollow he didn't have to do that any longer. For the first time in his life, he could embrace his bear.

"No! Please don't…" Swift tossed and turned, her arms pinned to the mattress as if some invisible force was holding her there. "Don't! Leave them alone!"

He crossed the room in a flash and sat down on the bed. "Swift, wake up. Come on baby, it's just a dream." He pulled her into his embrace, holding her hands in one of his to stop her from fighting him. "You're safe, Swift. Breathe, remember where you are. I'm here with you."

In between deep, heaving breaths and the tears, he rubbed small circles along her back. He wanted to take away the terror that coursed through her, and the memories that brought the nightmares to life.

"I'm okay…" She stopped fighting him and collapsed against him. "It was just a dream."

"How often do you have them?" Without releasing her, he adjusted so he could put his back against the headboard and cradle her against him, making the most of their body contact. "No wonder there are dark circles under your eyes if you're going through this every night. I'm surprised the people in neighboring rooms haven't called the police. Or at the very least, complained to the front desk."

"It's not every night, but they've gotten more frequent and have grown stronger since I've left the tribe."

"Because you've disconnected yourself from your Chief. Jase might be a bear but he's your Alpha; he can keep some of this at bay through your connection with him. You've shut him out. They will continue to grow in power for as long as you let them control you. We need to get you back home."

"In the morning." She rolled over to her side and laid her head on his chest, her hair brushing against his chin. "I'm so tired."

"Okay, baby, just rest."

"Stay." She draped her hand over his waist and let her fingers dig into his hip as she pulled herself closer to him. "Just hold me. Keep my demons away…just for a few hours."

"Just sleep. I'm not going anywhere." He pulled the discarded blanket over them and scooted down in bed, doing his best to make himself as comfortable as he could get. It didn't matter; he wasn't tired. As long as she slept, that's what mattered. It might be the first restful night's sleep she'd have had in weeks.

My sweet mate, I can't take away the memories of what happened, but I can help you embrace your feisty side and move forward with your life. You have more fight in you than you think. Trust me and we'll get you through this.

Vibrations jarred Swift from her restful sleep, forcing her to open her eyes. The urge to bitch at whoever was calling disappeared as she woke to find herself in Brett's arms. It wasn't her cell phone going off, it was his, and he already had it pressed to his ear. She glanced over him to the nightstand alarm clock and the bright red letters told her it was just before two in the morning. Whoever was calling wasn't bringing them good news. Calls in the middle of the night brought nothing but trouble.

Was Jase calling to bitch at him for not returning to Crimson Hollow? No, Jase would have chewed him out once they returned. Unless something had happened to the tribe. Terrible ideas multiplied within her thoughts as she waited for him to stay something.

He glanced down at her and pressed a soft kiss to her forehead. "Okay, we'll be ready. Meet you outside in ten." He ended the call and placed the phone back on the nightstand.

"What's wrong? Is Jase pissed?" Even though she doubted it, she wished this could be true. A pissed off Chief would be better than the alternatives.

"We've got to go. Get packed."

"I thought…" As he started to sit up, she was left with no choice but to slide out of his embrace. "What happened to me making the decision? You promised you wouldn't force me to return."

"I'm not." He stood and pulled her up onto her knees on the bed. "We don't have to go to Crimson Hollow but we can't stay here. Damn it, Swift. Don't fight me on this. Let me protect you."

"What do I need to be protected from? What's happened? Noah wouldn't call at this time of night if something hadn't happened. Was it the tribe?" Questions flowed from her, one after another, without giving him a chance to answer.

"Just get ready and let us get out of here."

"Don't shut me out. If you want me to trust you then you need to tell me what the hell is going on." Even as she fought for him to tell her, she got off the bed and began to throw her belongings in her suitcase. She didn't have much, just one duffle bag. Not having a car, she had been forced to walk from the tribe's land until she reached the bus station, so she hadn't wanted to carry much.

"There was a meeting for shifters in the area without their own groups or tribes." He grabbed his wallet and slid it into his pocket before grabbing his gun from the nightstand and attaching it to his belt. "They were killed."

Dropping the last of her clothes into the bag, she turned to face him. "Killed? All of them? I thought they were only going after certain animals."

"They were, but I guess they got tired of only getting one or two at a time."

Not being fazed by his presence, she slipped out of the cotton shorts she had worn to bed and into the jeans she'd tossed aside while she was packing. "Who are these people? They have to have a name."

"Humankind Saviors—they also go by The Saviors. They believe they're saving the human population from the filth."

"We're humans, too." She slammed the shorts she'd taken off into the bag and turned to go to the sink area and gather the rest of her stuff. "We have families and friends that would grieve for us. What makes them so much better than us?"

"Nothing, baby." He came up behind her and laid his hands on her shoulders. Rather than turn her around to face him, he stared straight at the mirror, watching her. "They're willing to die for their cause, which makes them much more dangerous. They're on a war path tonight so we need to get out of here. If you don't want to go back to Crimson Hollow, fine. We'll have Noah drop us off at another town, wherever you want, but we can't stay here."

"Drop us off?"

He wrapped his arms around her, holding her close as if to stop the panic blooming within her. "Their strategy has changed and with Noah being Jase's guard, he needs to get back to protect the Chief. I'll have someone bring my truck, so we can return to the tribe whenever you're ready—unless you're willing to come back for me to get my truck. I can have someone bring it to town and you won't even have to go to the compound or see anyone."

"I…" She leaned back into his embrace. As she'd fallen asleep earlier, she had made a promise to herself to trust him and allow him to help her. His touch helped keep the worst of her fears from overwhelming her, while she couldn't go around attached to his hip for the rest of her life, their mating would help. It would be selfish to mate with someone just to overcome the darkest parts of oneself, but they could help each other. They'd make each other stronger. Or maybe *he'd* make her stronger, but there had to be something she could do to make him a better person. They were meant to be together—that must mean something. She just needed to trust that. "I'll go…home."

Chapter Five

Crimson Hollow was just as Swift had left it weeks earlier. The only difference was, *she* had changed. It might have only been a week since she'd left but she'd survived. Years before, when Sin had begged her to leave with her, she couldn't do it. She had been terrified that they would be eaten alive out there alone without an Alpha to protect them. While she might have only left because she felt Jase would have forced her to do so eventually, she still survived and was stronger for it.

"Come on, Noah will speak with Jase and I'll walk you home." Brett opened the truck door before climbing out and offering her a hand.

"Surely, Jase would allow you a few hours off." She wasn't sure what she was doing but she didn't want to be on her own. The desire to be alone with him, as they'd been at the hotel, overwhelmed her. She wanted to be back there, curled up with him in bed. There was nothing sexual about it, but she needed the comfort and understanding she found in his arms.

"Jase knows how to reach me if he needs to but I'm not planning on going to him now."

"What are you planning?" She accepted his hand, even though she didn't need it to get out of the truck.

"What would you like me to do?"

Stay with me. Not wanting to admit she wanted him to come home with her, she brushed off the opportunity. "Do you always answer a question with another question?"

Outside of the cab, he pressed her against the extended cabin, letting his body brush along the front of hers. "Say it. Say you want me to stay with you."

"I…I…don't—"

"Don't deny it, beautiful." He leaned down until his face was just above hers and she thought he was going to kiss her. "You want me back in your bed, don't you?"

"Yes." The word came out breathier than she expected and she leaned forward, hoping to close the distance between their lips.

"Let's go." He took a step back, popping the intimacy that had developed between them in their closeness. Reaching into the back of the pickup, he grabbed their bags before turning back to her. "Your place or mine?"

"Do I even…umm…have a place anymore?" She had left; maybe someone had moved into her cabin. It was one of the nicer ones with two stories and close to the Chief's own home.

"Sin has it ready for you. Fresh sheets, stocked with your favorite foods, and everything you might need. Ari and Kaden have installed a security system. Everything is ready for you." He slipped his free arm around her waist and started toward her cabin.

"A security system?"

"Part of the changes happening here. Everyone is getting a system with panic alarms. They will all be connected to Jase and Sin's cell phones, alerting them if anything happens. Another precaution that Kaden suggested. Guards will be at the doorsteps of whoever is in trouble within seconds. Does that give you peace of mind?" He didn't look at her as they made their way to her place and she considered what he'd said.

It did make her feel safer, but it also made her wonder if there had been any attacks on the tribe while she was gone. There was a perimeter fence, guard houses with round-the-clock guards on duty, and others circling the perimeter. Wasn't having each house alarmed overkill?

"Why does the idea of an alarm make you tense?"

They climbed the two steps onto the deck of her cabin. She pulled her key from her pocket and turned to him. "Has there been an attack since I've left? Alarm systems on every house seems like a waste of time, money, and manpower."

"Nothing has happened since the drunk asshole plowed his truck through the back fence." He pulled the key from her hand, opened the door, and ushered her inside. "Security systems are just a precaution. It's Ari and Kaden's business. There's no reason not to utilize every option we can to keep everyone safe. The systems are not happening overnight and other things are taking priority as needed. Your cousin ordered this to be completed before you arrived because she thought it would make you feel safe."

"How is it that every time I close my eyes I see the horrors of what happened, while Sin is able to let go of the past and get on with her life?"

"That is something you'll have to ask her, but she did tell me not a day goes by when she doesn't remember what happened." He pushed the door shut behind them and dropped the bags next to the door. "She forced herself to continue living because that's what her family would have wanted. She had Jase to help guide her through it when you first arrived here."

"Jase." She shook her head. "I remember, just after we came here, I was curled up in a ball in the corner while they were playing. How could she do that? She'd just lost her family. We'd just lost everything but she was playing like there was nothing wrong."

"She was five." He took her hands into his and brought them to his lips where he laid a gentle kiss on her knuckles. "Everyone takes something like that differently. You can't blame her for needing the escape and wanting to be a kid again."

"I don't. I'm envious of it." She glanced around the living room of her cabin until her gaze landed on the photos on the mantel above the fireplace. "It took time but I was able to put my fears aside, at least for the most part. I had a relatively normal life for a while, except I was terrified to leave here, but when the attacks started again…"

"Zoe arrived and you wanted to help her but everything came rushing back to you," he finished for her. "That's when the memories and anxiety returned."

She nodded. "If I could do it once, I should be able to do it again."

"You're doing it." When she turned back to face him, he continued, "Back at the hotel, your fears were rising again but you batted them away. You're trying and while it might not be easy right now, each day will be easier. You won't be alone; I'll be by your side as you go through this. Sin, Jase, Garret, Noah, and the whole tribe are here to see you through it."

"I've screwed up so much and now I don't know how to make it right. Zoe blames herself and thinks I hate her. Camellia and I had a huge fight before I left and I accused her of sleeping with the enemy. Her mates, Ari and Kaden, did nothing to me but I couldn't stop thoughts of them being outsiders sent to kill us from entering my mind."

He placed his hands on her hips and brought her to stand in front of him. "Do you know the best thing about our kind? We're forgiving. Camellia, Ari, and Kaden won't hold what you said against you. They'll forget it because we're all family. We can go see her in the morning if you'd like? But first I suggest you get some sleep."

"What about you?" Her lips curled up into a smile and she shook her head. "Screw it. I'll just say it. Stay…stay with me."

"Well now, that changes things." In one quick motion, he scooped her into his arms. "Which way to the bedroom?"

"Upstairs." Her voice squealed a little with surprise. "First door at the top of the stairs. But this is only to sleep, nothing more. Not yet."

"I didn't try to have my way with you at the hotel, did I? Being in your home doesn't mean I'm going to become a ravishing bear." He climbed the steps two at a time, making quick progress to her bedroom.

For the first time in years, she felt alive when he was around. The heat in his eyes told her he desired her. All of it was giving her something new to focus on—to replace the bad with good for the first time since the tragedy. The excitement took over the terror that normally coursed through her.

Mating—maybe that's what she needed. Or maybe it was just Brett that she needed. Maybe they needed each other.

Chapter Six

They'd returned to Crimson Hollow a week earlier and Brett had practically taken up residence with Swift, yet they had not made their mating official. He had given her time to adjust and they were working on keeping her terror from overwhelming her. They'd made tremendous progress with that even as The Saviors were continuing their terrorist actions across the country. Swift was able to keep her fears from overwhelming her. All of these developments made him want his mate that much more. He wanted her for her, not to save her from the anxiety. He wanted to claim her as his and to make her scream his name until her throat was raw.

His cell phone vibrated with a text message from Sin. *Two new guards arriving tonight. They've worked for Ari's company and passed background checks. Break the news to Swift. Would be better coming from you. Don't forget dinner—my place at seven.*

After reading the message he tossed his phone on the cushion next to him and leaned back with his laptop on his lap, working on the guard schedule Noah had asked him to manage. But, his mind wouldn't stay focused on the rotation of the guards on duty; rather, his thoughts drifted toward his mate. How was she going to take the news? So far she had adjusted okay to the new members who'd joined while she was away, but having two new guards coming to them might unnerve her. He hated the idea of all their work being spoiled because of an adjustment within the tribe's dynamics.

"Brett, you here?" Swift called as she walked through the front door.

"In here, baby." He closed the laptop and set it aside. "How did lunch go with Camellia?"

"Good." She sank down onto the sofa next to him. "She says she forgives me and at first it felt like there was still tension between us but as lunch went on…I don't know, it was just different. We were at ease again. It's hard to believe she had any time to have me over for lunch when she's got two demanding bears as mates."

"Hey now, I'm not demanding." He wrapped his arm around her shoulders and pulled her near him until she snuggled against his body. She fit against him as if she was meant to be there. Her head rested against his chest and the scent of her vanilla shampoo drifted toward him.

"No, it's me who feels like I'm pushing." She tipped her head up toward him. "Do you want me…I mean this?"

"Is that what's been bothering you?" He pressed his lips to the top of her head. "You're feisty and beautiful. How couldn't I want you? You're my mate. I want to explore every inch of your body, teasing light kisses over it until you're begging for more. I want your legs wrapped around me as I'm fucking you and I want to hear you scream my name as your body gives into me."

"Then why haven't you made any advances?"

"We've been focused on getting you to come to terms with your past. I didn't want to pressure you into something you weren't ready for." He leaned into her, forcing her back on the sofa. "Are you ready, baby?"

"More than ready." She pressed herself to him, her voice low and seductive. "Kiss me."

He didn't need to be told twice. Closing the distance between them, he claimed her mouth. As their lips met, she wrapped her arms around his neck, drawing him closer to her. Their tongues mingled together to match the desire coursing within him. He wanted her with every ounce of his being.

When he finally pulled back, he stared down at her to see the need burning in her eyes. "Do you want to go upstairs?"

"Later. Right now I just want you right here." She looped her fingers through his belt loops and pulled him against her. "Please, Brett."

He hooked the bottom of her shirt and pulled, forcing it up her body, while she worked on undoing his jeans. As she slipped a hand under the fabric of his boxers, he paused, arching back to give her access to the full length of him. She trailed a hand down, applying just enough pressure to keep him on edge. Even through this, he managed to get her shirt and bra off, leaving her topless. Unwilling to be the only one on edge, he leaned down and let his tongue tease along the tips of her nipples. As he breathed cool air onto them, they hardened into tiny pebbles, calling to him.

"Naked…I want you naked."

"But I'm having fun," he teased letting his teeth graze over her hardened nub.

"I'll take away your fun if you don't get out of those clothes."

Her threat worked both ways but since he wanted her naked too, he rose up off her. "Take the rest of your clothes off before I tear them from your body." Not wasting any time, they stripped to bare skin. Sitting down on the sofa, he pulled her down on him so straddled him. "I want to kiss every inch of this body, but the need to bury myself deep within you is overwhelming."

"This is the first time of many. Take your time and explore later; now I just want you. I want this to be about both of us and I want to feel you inside me." She caressed along his chest.

Needing to explore her body further before he'd allow himself the pleasure of her wet core, he kissed her neck, nibbling down her jawline to her shoulder, working his way back down to her nipples. He trailed his lips over her nipple, flicking his tongue over the bud, drawing it to full hardness, before he teased over the other one, tweaking it until it stood at attention. He loved the way her body reacted to him, and the soft moans of ecstasy that escaped her throat as his tongue met her sensitive nipples made him harder.

"Brett." Her voice was full of desire and need.

Keeping her nipple firmly between his lips, he glanced up at her. "Yes?" He tried to keep his muffled voice innocent but there was a hint of cockiness to it. He caressed over her body, teasing every curve, until the heat soared through his blood like a fire burning within him. He needed her and his bear was growing impatient, demanding he speed this up. Stifling his animal, he let her nipple slip from his mouth and kissed a path up her neck.

"I want you…" She let go of his shaft and wiggled her hips over his manhood, making sure it slid between her wet folds. "Now."

Obviously not content to let him set the pace any longer, she arched her hips into him, demanding more. He couldn't blame her; the teasing had taken a toll on him and he wanted her more than ever before. Nudging her legs farther apart, he delved inside her and she met the teasing thrusts. A demanding moan vibrated in her throat.

"Brett…" she cried out, pressing her body again his.

"I know, baby." He spread her legs farther, giving him the access he needed before filling her slowly, inch by inch. Halfway in, he slid most of the way out before thrusting back in, filling her completely with his manhood. His strokes fed the fire until the heat between them blazed.

His beast's demands ate at him, forcing him to go faster. They had waited too long to complete the mating and his bear kept his foot on the accelerator, increased pace, driving the force of each pump. Their bodies rocked back and forth, tension stretching her tighter around him, until he wasn't sure he could hold back his orgasm long enough for her to find her own.

"Oh Brett, faster." She clenched her muscles tightly around him, so he did as she begged.

She rocked her body against his thrusts, making their hips slam off each other. He could feel her climax building within her. Tangling his fingers in her hair, he claimed her mouth. Swallowing her cries of ecstasy with a kiss, he shuddered when her nails raked down into his shoulders, as she found her release. With one final drive deep into her, his own climax followed.

"Fuck, that was amazing." He held her against his body, his shaft still nestled deep within her.

"You stole the words from me." She collapsed against him, resting her head in the crook of his shoulder, and pressed a kiss to his neck. "My bear, my mate."

"My feisty fox." He wrapped his arms around her, holding her tight against him.

The rest of the world didn't matter at the moment. This was where they belonged, lost in each other's embrace.

Epilogue

Weeks passed and Swift slowly found her place within the tribe. She had begun to work with her cousin, Sin, in an administrative capacity, helping to keep the tribe running smoothly. For the first time in her life, she wasn't terrified of what might happen, or of the dark. No longer did she have to leave a light on at night or wake up terrified, thinking they were in her room ready to kill her. The only one in her room was Brett, but now it was *their* room.

Even as outsiders came to their tribe, she embraced them as part of the shifter family instead of believing they were there to hurt them as she once had. Her life had done a three-sixty and it was all because of Brett. Her mate had helped her come a long way in a short amount of time and she owed him more than she could every repay.

She and Camellia had picked up their friendship as if nothing had happened. The five of them—Camellia, Ari, Kaden, Brett, and she—had developed a tight bond. They had dinner together at least twice a week, once at each of their houses. Camellia had also helped her restore things with Zoe. Since Zoe had been taken in by Sin and Garret, she'd become more than just a tribe member—she was family. It had meant a lot to Swift that Zoe understand that she wasn't upset with her.

Now, for the first time, she stood at the gravesite where her parents and brother had been buried, next to Sin's parents and the rest of their leash, and she was able to put the past to rest. "I'll never forget you." She placed the roses at the foot of the tombstone and stepped back into her mate's waiting embrace.

"Your parents would be proud of you," Sin said softly from where she stood near her parents' tombstone. "They'd be happy for you and glad you found Brett."

"I know." Her cousin's words touched her heart and brought tears to her eyes. She knew they were the truth; she only wished her parents could have been there to meet him and to see the woman she had turned into. But maybe if they had, she wouldn't have met Brett. As much as she wanted her parents and brother alive, she wouldn't want to give up Brett. "Thank you for coming with us."

Sin nodded. "It took me a while before I wanted to come here. I felt like I'd betrayed my parents because Jase's folks had accepted me into their home with open arms and I'd started to call them Mom and Dad. It took me a long time to figure out that, even with two sets of parents, I hadn't betrayed anyone. Mom and Dad always held a special place in my heart; they wouldn't have wanted me to grieve so deeply for them that I could never move on. Just as your parents wouldn't have wanted that for you."

"It took me a long time to see that, but you're right." She glanced up at Brett. "Thank you for showing me the way. Thank you for showing me there's a reason to live and love again. I love you."

"I love you, too." He slipped his hand into hers. "Now come on, we have a wedding to get to."

"Our wedding." For some shifters, weddings were a human tradition but others, like Sin's parents Swift's parents, had also adopted the custom. Although she hadn't expected Brett to go for it, he had, and today was the day.

"One thing first." Brett reached into his pocket and pulled out a small box. "Jase gave me this."

He opened the box and there, in the soft cotton, lay her mother's wedding band. "How?"

"Granddad had found it when they'd gone to collect our families for burial. It wasn't until Jase took over the tribe that we learned about them. Jase gave me everything they'd found to go through. Some of it I'm not sure who it belonged to but you can go through it sometime. Both of my parents' rings were there." Sin pulled a gold chain from under her shirt to reveal the two rings on it. "Mom's hands were so much smaller than mine, so I wear them around my neck. Also, I love the ring that Garret picked out for our wedding day."

"I thought you'd like to have this instead of something I picked out. This would mean so much more to you."

"Thank you. Save it until the ceremony." She pushed the lid shut and looked up at him. "I'm the luckiest woman to find someone like you."

"Damn straight."

Laughing, she wrapped her arms around his neck. "My cocky bear." She'd rather be stuck with a cocky bear for the rest of her life than spend one day without Brett by her side.

Purrable Lion

Noah Jones is adjusting to his new role as Captain of the Crimson Hollow's Deputy's guards. It's his duty to protect Sin, and with the new threats from The Saviors, that task becomes harder with each passing day, especially when his charge doesn't listen to his commands. When a call comes in about an attack near their tribe, he's sent to investigate. He expects to find carnage—just like with previous attacks. What he never expects is to find *her*.

Karri Mallory finds herself in the wrong place at the wrong time. A small party in the woods turns disastrous when gunfire erupts around her. Terrified as she watches her friends get shot, she cowers behind a group of trees, hoping no one will spot her. Even after the gunfire stops, she can't bring herself to move, until he comes along.

When The Saviors find out someone witnessed their attack, they won't stop until she's dead. Even if she doesn't trust him, it's Noah's job to keep her safe—but first he must prove he isn't her enemy.

Chapter One

The night was unusually silent as Noah Jones made his way deeper into the dense woods. The stench of gunpowder lingered in the air and the bangs from the gunshots scared off the animals, leaving only eeriness in the attack's wake. As he inched closer to where the incident happened, he scanned the area, searching for anyone who might still be lingering. He didn't expect anybody from The Humankind Saviors—also known as The Saviors—but he couldn't be too careful. They were determined to kill anyone they suspected might be shifters, but tonight's attack took it further. The party in the woods wasn't a shifter only event and innocent humans had been killed because of The Saviors' hatred for shifters.

He crept through the woods, sensing the only scent that hung in the air. He wasn't sure if the sheriff and his men had missed an injured or killed partier but as soon as he made it around these trees, he'd find out. As he moved on, he could hear the frantic heartbeat of someone. A faint hint of perfume made him think the person he was going to find was a woman—a terrified woman. He wanted to holster his weapon so he didn't scare her but to keep them both safe, he couldn't do that. If anyone from The Saviors happened to be in these woods still, letting his guard down would put both of their lives in jeopardy.

He eased around the tree, far enough away that he wouldn't terrify her any more than she already was. "Miss...are you injured?"

"Please…" She held her hands out in front of her, as if surrendering. "Don't hurt me. I didn't see anything. I won't tell anybody."

"They've been gone for hours. The sheriff and his men have already been here. Crime scene techs and medical examiners—they've already processed the area. How is it that no one found you?"

"I…I don't know." As he crept closer, she cowered against the tree. "Okay. I'll tell you, just please don't hurt me. I was up in the tree."

"Why?" Her blonde hair fell just past her shoulders, but it was her eyes that captured him. The fear shining through those deep brown eyes made him want to reach out and touch her. He could tell her that everything was going to be fine but he didn't know that to be true. Lying to her wouldn't put them on the right footing.

"I don't know. When I heard people coming, I thought it was them coming back, maybe to clean up the mess. I didn't want them to see me and the tree was the first thing I thought of. Once I realized who they were, I…I just couldn't bring myself to face them. They'd question me and if I told them what had happened, me being the only witness, the shooters would want me dead. I didn't go through everything tonight just to have them kill me." She put her hands down and looked at him. "Are you one of them?"

"No, and I'm not with the police either." He went towards her, wanting both to comfort her and interrogate her. "I need to know what you saw here tonight."

"If I tell you, I'm as good as dead. So why don't you just kill me? I'd rather die here and now where my friend did, than run and be chased like a mouse. I saw them tonight; the sheer number of manpower they had behind them. I don't know who they are but I know they're not people you fuck with."

"I can protect you." He couldn't smell any blood from her and if she'd been fit enough to climb the high tree so no one would see her, then she could stand. He held his hand out to her. "Let's get you out of here before anyone comes back."

"Who are you?"

"The name's Noah Jones. What's yours?" She took his hand and his lion surged forward. *Shit.*

"Karri...Karri Mallory." She rose to her feet. "If I didn't tell the police because I didn't think they could protect me from these killers, why do you think you can?"

His lion snarled. *You're mine, that's why*—but he stifled it. "I have resources the police department doesn't have."

"What are those?" Keeping her back against the tree, she glanced around into the darkness.

"There's no one else here," he reassured her. "I've already scouted the area before I came to you. But we should be moving on. There's no guarantee they won't circle back here to make sure they didn't leave any evidence behind that the police missed." It was doubtful but he didn't want to have this conversation with her while they were standing in the middle of the woods, with the scent of blood still lingering in the air.

"I...I'm not sure." She glanced around the area again but the vibes coming from her changed. She was nervous but he couldn't put his finger on any of it.

"Karri?" Needing to get to the root of her unease, he placed his hand on her forearm, intensifying the dull connection between them. "What is it?"

"I came with a friend. We're not even from here. We just drove down to see her boyfriend."

"Good." He slipped off his jacket and wrapped it around her shoulders. Not so much because he suspected that she was cold but to help mask her scent. If other shifters came into the area, he didn't want them to question the lone female scent that led away from the incident. The only scent that wouldn't have the stench of gunpowder or blood came from the emergency personnel that had shown up earlier. If he could keep her existence a secret from anyone outside of Crimson Hollow, it would ensure her safety. "No one knows you were supposed to be here, so no one will come looking for you."

"What?" She stepped back from him, her eyes wide with fear.

"That's not what I mean," he reassured her when he realized what she was thinking. "Karri, I'm not going to hurt you. I meant the people that attacked tonight. They don't know you were supposed to be here and that will make it easier for me to ensure your safety. But we need to go."

"Go where?"

"Back to my place where you'll be safe." He kept his hand on her back, partially to keep the jacket in place but also to help mask her scent. "You need to lay low for a bit until we're sure it's safe."

"I'm not going home with you. I don't even know you." She tried to pull away from him but he adjusted his position so his arm was around her, keeping her right there next to him.

"Listen to me, Karri. You're a witness to what happened here tonight; you're the one person that could possibly throw them in prison. Do you think they'd let you continue breathing if they found out about you? Unless you want to end up dead, you need to come with me."

"The police…" Her voice broke, forcing her to swallow before she could continue. "They can protect me."

"Not from these people." Crimson Hollow Police Department might not have any of The Saviors in their ranks, at least none the tribe knew about, but Noah wasn't willing to take the chance. Even if they were directly connected to the department, there was no way the local outfit could handle this murder investigation. Crimson Hollow was a quiet town; it had been more than ten years since someone had been murdered. There was no way they could handle a crime scene this big, or with this many dead. They'd have to seek help from outside agencies and that was where Noah's trust ended. He wasn't about to risk his mate.

"Who are they?" A howl in the distance sent a shiver through her and he wrapped his arm tighter around her in reassurance. "If you want me to trust you, then answer me."

"Not here." Keeping his arm around her, he took a step, forcing her to move with him. Garret's howl was letting Noah and the others know he had found nothing and would head back to the tribe's land.

"Why now?"

"Trust me for a little bit longer and I'll tell you what you want to know." His lion could sense no one around, but he didn't want to have this conversation here, not where it was possible for someone to overhear them. He couldn't tell her everything but he'd tell her what he could.

"I'm just supposed to trust you." She shook her head but continued to allow him to lead the way back to his car.

"Would you prefer I leave you here and when they come back they can find you waiting for them?" He voiced the question knowing there wasn't a chance in hell he'd allow that. He'd throw her over his shoulder and carry her back to the tribe if he had to.

"How do I know I'm not putting myself in a worse situation?" She stopped and turned slightly toward him. "Maybe you're part of this or maybe you're some type of serial killer who likes to torture his victims. If that's the case, I'm better off with them since they just gun down people."

"Bullshit, sugar." He stepped toward her, forcing her to take a step back. Exactly what he wanted, so he could trap her between the tree and his body. "Now you listen to me and you listen well. I'm not like those assholes. I protect those I care about. I'm not a serial killer and I sure as hell would never torture a woman for my own amusement."

"But you would torture them to gain something."

"Don't twist my words." It came out more as a growl than he planned. He'd never hurt a woman if he could help it. But if it came down to it and they were threatening his charge, mate, or lifestyle, he would end them as quickly as possible. There was no doubt in his mind that women could be just as deadly as men.

"What could you gain from me?"

Happiness. A mate. Rather than voice his thoughts aloud, he tipped his head. "We need to go. Let's get out of the woods and we'll talk. If you don't like what I can offer you, I'll drop you off at the police station and you can figure shit out on your own." Even though he knew he wouldn't do it, he made the suggestion to put her at ease.

A loud moan of a bear echoed through the air, causing him to pause a moment to listen for the second and third bear to join in. When they did, he was able to let out a deep sigh of relief and breathe easier. The Chief of the Crimson Hollow Tribe, Jase, was out searching the area because he refused to stay home and wait. Noah didn't like it; the Chief wasn't supposed to risk himself, but at least he had agreed to take Ari and Kaden along with him.

While the Chief was out searching for The Saviors, at least his charge, Sin, was safe back with the tribe. Sin had wanted to come and as the Deputy of the tribe she had tried to force Noah to take her. He was after all her guard and her orders were law, at least until Jase overruled her. Jase and Sin's mate, Garret, had vetoed her leaving their land. It would prove too dangerous and all of them were tired of her risking herself for little reward.

"Did you hear me?"

"What?" He stopped his in tracks and turned toward her.

"I asked what was that? Instead of answering me, you continued to move along toward the car as if you hadn't heard the sound when I know you did. Your body tensed for a moment before relaxing. So either you're going to tell me what's going on or I'm out of here."

"Where are you going to go? You came down with a friend and she's dead. You were too scared to even get out of the tree when law enforcement was hovering around, makes me wonder if you're not hiding something."

"Fuck you!" She pulled away from him. "I didn't even want to be here tonight. I told you I was here with a friend. She dragged me here." She squeezed the bridge of her nose and she could feel the throbbing pain behind her eyes, a warning of a nasty headache.

He took a deep breath and the chemical scent hit him full force. How he'd missed it before he wasn't sure but now that he smelled it, everything clicked into place. His lion snarled within, ready to attack whoever had done this to his mate. "You were drugged."

Chapter Two

The urge to deny his statement rose within Karri until she fought it back, pushing it aside. How did he know? The moonlight peeking through the trees was too dim for him to make out if her eyes were glazed. She wasn't stumbling, at least not that she noticed. What had given her away? Refusing to meet his gaze, she tried to regulate her breathing. *Don't give anything away.*

"At least you're not going to deny it." He wrapped his hand around her arm and tugged her forward. "Let's go."

As they came to edge of the woods and found the dirt road, she glanced around before turning to him. "How?"

"Get in." He nodded to the passenger door of the car park in the middle of the road.

"Answer me. I'm sick and tired of you constantly ordering me around. I'm not a dog you can expect to have at your beck and call."

"If you want to stay alive then you'll get in the car." He didn't wait for her to get in; instead, he climbed into the driver's seat and started the engine.

Standing in the eerie woods alone, she was suddenly terrified. What if the killers returned? Were they still lurking in the woods? Noah had told her he'd checked the area but how could he know without a doubt there wasn't still someone hidden within the thick trees. Maybe someone had climbed up into the safety of the trees and waited for everyone to leave like she had. A branch cracked not more than twenty-five feet away from her, but she couldn't see anything but darkness. Staying out there, she might end up dead, whereas in the car, she might have a chance. Something about Noah had put her at ease and she was willing to deal with his bossy attitude a little bit longer if it meant getting out of the woods alive.

She stepped around to the passenger side and opened the door before climbing into the empty seat. Movement a few feet in front of the car caught her attention as she pulled the door shut. "Something is out there."

"Someone," he corrected as a lion leaped through the trees to land on the dirt road a few feet in front of the car.

"What the hell?" she screamed, locking her car door as she did so. "A lion…here? This must be from the drugs…" She brought her legs up onto the seat to cradle them against her chest, her gaze fixed on the beast standing there. *Is he watching us? No, this isn't possible.* She blinked, wishing the animal away. Maybe everyone was right; maybe she was going crazy. Coming down to Crimson Hollow had been her friend's way of forcing her to relax and remember that, despite everything, she was alive.

Noah addressed the lion. "Roger, help Liam and watch over Sin for me. I'll be there when I can." Roger was one of the new guards, but he was proving himself worthy. If given the chance, Noah would have Roger as one of the guards for Sin. Not his First Lieutenant—he already had Brett in mind for that once Jase approved further additions to the team—but definitely the third in rank, Second Lieutenant.

The lion roared in answer to Noah's order and took off through the trees on the other side of the road.

"This can't be happening." She shook her head, sending her blonde hair flying into her face. "You see it too? He understood you. No, it's a hallucination."

"Roger's a lot of things but a hallucination isn't one of them." He put the car in gear and quickly did a three-point turn so they were facing the opposite direction. "Don't blame what you saw on the drugs; they're mostly out of your system. The headache you have is just a lingering aftereffect from mixing it with alcohol. You could have ended up dead for mixing them."

"I'm pretty sure I survived worse things tonight, so I'm not too concerned about the drugs and alcohol combination at the moment." She watched the side-view mirror, somewhat expecting the lion to emerge from the darkness again.

"He's gone."

Noah's statement had her looking over at him.

"How did you know what I was thinking?"

"There's a lot I know about you, Karri." He didn't take his gaze from the road, which made her uncomfortable. The implication in his words had her body tense. She'd never met him before so anything he thought he knew about her was just a guess. Yet she went crazy at the idea he might figure out her thoughts. Maybe she was back in her dorm, asleep in her own bed, and all of this was just a nightmare. None of this could be happening.

The drive passed in the blink of an eye as she tried to convince herself that this was all a dream. As much as she tried, she couldn't wake herself up. She pinched herself until she was sure she'd be left with bruises. Yet, despite all this, the more the dream seemed to solidify around her.

She blinked as the car came to a stop, and took in her surroundings. They were still in the middle of the woods but now they had found a paved road, and they were high enough that she could see the lights of a small town off in the distance, lighting up the night sky. "Where are we?"

"Down there the sheriff waits; he'd be eager to know a witness survived. Walking into the station, you'll have questions to answer and it will make your survival known. It won't be long before The Saviors find you and put you in the ground just like they did your friends. So, it's time to make a choice. Either you're willing to trust me or you're going to trust the sheriff to keep you safe from something he had no chance winning against."

"Why doesn't he have a chance?" If she wasn't dreaming, she had to believe that the sheriff would be the best choice. The man sitting next to her seemed to be connected deeply to this issue and knew more than he was saying. Sticking with him when he wouldn't tell her anything was out of the question.

"The Saviors are responsible for what happened tonight."

"The Saviors, but they're only after…" Her jaw slacked open and the air was sucked from her lungs. "You're a shifter…the lion…"

"Yes, Roger and I are both shifters. There were shifters within your group of friends tonight. Most of them were in hiding, not wanting anyone to know what they were, but somehow, The Saviors found out."

"But Kat was human."

"Associating with us—therefore, in their mind, as contaminated as a shifter," Noah explained. "The Saviors' goal is to wipe the world of the shifter disease."

"Scientists have discovered it's not a disease. The ability to shift is not something you can catch from being around shifters, or from receiving their blood through a transfusion. Body fluids can't transfer this ability. But you already know this." She shook her head. *What am I thinking, giving a science lesson on shifters to a shifter?*

"Some people don't understand or don't want to. They let their fears control them and allow them to act on it instead of researching it to determine the truth. Shifters have lived among humans since the beginning of time and have never been a danger to you. If anyone is in danger, it's the shifters themselves."

"How so?" She turned in her seat so she could get a better glimpse of him.

"Humans hunt us down not for meat as they would for another animal but as a trophy. Each week The Saviors choose a different animal as their target. In the United States, we're considered legal citizens but we have a long way to go before we gain equal rights. Even now, if we're shot in our animal form, the law sides with the shooter, not us. As the law stands, they're within their rights to shoot if they feel threatened. We don't have to be charging, preparing to attack, or anything, all we have to do is be within the same space at the same time. They might be fined but they'll never face murder charges."

"That hardly seems fair. How can shifters be considered legal citizens, yet be killed like that?" She stretched her legs back out so her feet rested on the floor. "Wait, wouldn't it be poaching then? There are certain times throughout the year when you can hunt certain animals. If you shot a bear when it's not bear hunting season, that's poaching and illegal."

"Except when that bear is a shifter." There was anger and sadness in his voice as he spoke.

"That's bullshit!" The same anger rushed through her. "How can they do this to you?"

"The legal battle is ongoing but that's how the law stands now." He took in a deep breath and let it out again. "The Saviors are taking things too far. Tonight, they didn't just kill shifters; they killed humans. Some of them I'm sure had no idea there were shifters mixed into tonight's crowd. No matter what company a human keeps, taking their life is against the law. If the killers are found, they'll be brought up on murder charges."

She stared at him for a moment, trying to take in what she was hearing. "Listening to you just now it seems that in your mind there's a divide between humans and shifters. You don't consider yourself human? Not even partially human?"

"I'm a shifter and I'm proud of that. While I look and act human most of the time, my beast is always just below the surface waiting and watching." The last bit of his statement came out as a snarl. She wasn't sure if that was to prove his point or to scare her.

"If you're doing that to scare me, don't bother. I've been through worse shit. Your animal growling at me while you're in human form does nothing to scare me." Even though her words made her sound strong, she had to stifle the bubble of fear that started to overwhelm her.

"Sugar, if I wanted to hurt you I can ensure you it would be more terrifying than what you witnessed tonight." He paused for a moment as if wanting that threat to sink in. "You should be terrified of an unknown shifter."

"I uh…" Watching his eyes change from dark brown to an amber that seemed to sparkle in the low light of the car, she pressed her back to the door, and the fear she'd felt before started to spread within her again. The air in the vehicle changed, as if now charged with electricity. Hesitantly, she reached out her hand between them as if expecting to be zapped, but nothing happened.

"Lesson learned." Whatever he was doing, he eased back to normal and slowly, his eyes returned to their normal color. "I'm not going to hurt you but you don't know about the next shifter you might encounter."

"What did you do?" Her tone was weak as she fought the emotions that threatened to overwhelm her. "It was…I can't explain it."

"My beast edged toward the surface, charging the air, but I never lost control."

"Your eyes…"

He nodded. "They changed."

"What are you?" She took a deep breath and tried to calm herself but the air remained different. The scent within the close confines wasn't the same as it had been before his beast peaked through. Now it felt like she was standing in the middle of the woods again, where a fire burned off in the distance and fresh leaves coated thc ground, reminding her of fall.

"Lion. Feel it." He reached over and took her hand in his.

She closed her eyelids and it was like she had been transported to the place she smelled in the woods. Only now she could see houses and people milling around. She couldn't make out any of the faces; they seemed quite blurred. The one thing that stood out more than anything was the lion trotting toward her. The big, golden lion had to be close to five-hundred pounds but he didn't seem intimidating. His mane was darker than the rest of his coat, allowing the dark browns to mix in with the lighter, golden color of his fur. His amber eyes watched her, not like she was prey, but as if he was waiting for a reaction from her. She allowed her gaze to continue downwards until she could take in his massive paws. There was no doubt in her mind that he could take her down in a flash and she'd be dead before she could even lift a finger to defend herself.

"It's not going to hurt you." Noah's soft words drifted toward her as the lion edged closer. "Touch it."

"I can't, I'm scared." She stood there, waiting for something to happen. Inch by inch, the lion crept closer until he was standing in front of her.

"Touch it," he urged her again.

She wanted to open her eyes and look at him to see if his eyes matched the lion's, but she didn't want this moment to end. The lion stretched out on the ground, as if to prove he wasn't a threat. Not realizing she had decided to listen to him, she was startled to feel the lion's fur under her fingertips. There was a certain softness to the mane that she hadn't expected. So full and beautiful, like that of the stuffed lion she'd had as a child. The toy lion had not possessed the dark mane and had been nowhere near as beautiful as the one that stood before her—but that was the first thing that came to mind. *This is so much better...*

With that thought, her body relaxed. She dropped to her knees in front of him and tangled both of her hands in his fur. Gazing into the lion's eyes, she could feel Noah there—and remembered when he'd looked at her with the lion's eyes. *They're one.*

But there was something more to it. She glanced around, as if she'd heard or saw something but nothing was there. *They can kill us without facing murder charges.* Noah's words played through her thoughts again and she realized she wasn't looking around for an active threat but the threat that lingered over shifters in general. Protective instincts rushed through her and she had the desire to keep him safe.

"Pretty stupid considering..." Her words trailed off when she realized she had spoken aloud.

"Not stupid; it's the connection." He caressed the side of her face with his free hand, teasing along the curve of her cheek. "Look at me, Karri."

Not wanting the moment with his beast to end, she fought against his demand and kept her eyelids firmly shut.

"Trust me, my lion will never be far away." He squeezed her hand. "Come back to me."

She forced herself to open her eyes and when she did, it took her a moment to realize she was still in the car with him. For a moment, she had expected to be in the middle of the woods with the houses and people nearby. The illusion was as clear as reality. "What happened?"

"You witnessed a glimpse of me and my life. You saw and felt my lion as if I shifted for you. Karri, you're my mate."

"I'm what?" She leaned back enough so he no longer touched her face.

"I understand it's a shock. Such news is better not delivered like this but I need you to trust me. What you witnessed tonight puts you in great danger; even if they don't realize that you survived, if you encounter anyone from The Saviors, you will have my scent on you."

"What does that mean?"

"We don't know if they're using a shifter to locate others, or how they're able to determine who is a shifter in order to kill them. If they're using one of our kind, they'll smell my scent on you and if they don't kill you for it, you'll be used as a pawn."

"Why would a shifter turn against his species?" She shook her head, amazed she'd asked that question and not what really plagued her mind right now. *Mate? What the hell does he mean by his mate?*

"If The Saviors are holding their mate hostage, or threatening them…a shifter would do whatever they could to protect their mate. We're not like humans; there's no divorce in our world. Once mated, it's for life. The connection between mates is so strong it could kill the other when one dies. The connection you just felt between us is nothing compared to what will someday be."

"You make it seem like I have no choice in this." Even as she spoke she felt no anger, just acceptance. *Is this connection already affecting me?*

"A human wouldn't feel the urgency of the beast within them, or understand the honor of finally finding their mate. You felt my beast now because I wanted you to understand. I felt your fear with Liam back there and I didn't want you to have that same fear when it came to me. You have a choice and it's my job to prove to you I'm the best choice."

"You wanted me to see your lion there in the woods as if you were no threat to me—"

"I'm not a threat to you and neither are the people where I live. I want to take you there but I need you to trust us, I need you to be accepting of those you meet there, and most of all, I need you to trust me."

"Why can't I feel your beast now? What are you hiding from me?"

"Nothing." He squeezed her hand as if to reassure her. "Until we are officially mated you won't feel my beast like you did unless I open the connection. Trust me—it would be too overwhelming to leave that link open continuously."

"And after the mating? I mean if it's too overwhelming now why wouldn't it be then?" *Am I really considering what he's saying?* Was she willing to at least consider what he said was the truth? It seemed too bizarre to make up but then again, people lied about all sorts of things.

She could definitely feel something between them—something strong and nothing like she'd ever felt—but how could she explain this? She had no point of reference; human relationships took a while to build, and while it was possible to experience attraction to someone straight away, this went far beyond that. Far beyond her understanding. Was she going crazy? It was almost as if a current was drawing her toward this man, and she had no chance of resisting it. Was it this mating connection he was talking about or did she feel this way because he had come and found her when she was terrified of what waited for her on the ground? He had been her knight, rescuing her when she was too scared to move from her perch in the trees. Maybe that was all this feeling was about—not some magical mating connection he believed they shared.

Even as she thought this, though, something told her she needed to face some other truth. Something she couldn't explain yet, no matter how hard she tried.

"Mating would give you the ability to control what you're feeling. Think of it as the volume on the television. You can turn it up or down, depending on the situation. If it's too overwhelming, you can turn it down so my lion wouldn't be as aggressive. Then, say, if we're in a situation where we can't communicate aloud, the link can be opened so we can connect and plan our move. In that same situation, you would be able to embrace the bond with my tribe and connect with Chief Jase, Deputy Sin, or her mate, Garret. They're the leaders of our tribe."

"I don't understand—why would I need to use the link to speak with them?"

He laced his fingers through hers, pressing his palm against the back of her hand and nestling both their fingers under her palm. "If I were unconscious or dead, this would be a lifeline for you."

The thought of him dead sent a wave of panic through her, which didn't make sense. She'd just met him; why did she care? She tried to tell herself that she would care, no matter who it was. The thought of someone so young dying should invoke sadness in anyone.

Rather than let her emotions rule her, she tried to take in everything he said. She knew shifters existed but she hadn't expected to actually meet one in person. Maybe she had met them before and they just kept their nature to themselves out of fear of what was happening to their kind. She'd definitely never expected to have one tell her she was his mate. *It's just too bizarre…*

Chapter Three

Noah had laid everything out for Karri, not holding anything back. He'd risked himself so he could find out where she stood on shifters. To take her back to the tribe's land before he knew without a doubt that she wasn't a threat to them was out of the question. It was his job to keep the members of the tribe safe, especially Sin, and he couldn't do that by bringing danger to their doorstep. Karri was his mate but that didn't mean she couldn't pose a risk to them now. After their connection was cemented in stone through their mating, she wouldn't turn on him or the tribe but until then, she was an unknown.

"I don't know what to say to any of this. It's all so much to take in. What are you expecting from me?"

"Nothing." He ran his fingers along her forearm. "Normally I would ease this information on you, but we didn't have time. I needed to tell you everything to determine if you were a threat."

"Am I?" She let out a light chuckle before he could answer. "Funny thing is, shouldn't I be the one to know that answer?"

"Sugar, you know the answer." He slipped his hand from hers so their connection couldn't influence her answer. "The answer to this question will allow you to know the truth that I already know. Think long and hard. Do you want to see me or my kind dead?"

Looking at him, she shook her head. "I don't need to think about it. The answer is no. What is happening to your kind is appalling and horrifying, and needs to be stopped. I don't know what I can do to make that happen but I'm willing to try."

"That's all I needed to know." With a smile, he reached back over and took her hand. It seemed impossible to be that close to her and not touch her, especially since their mating connection would only spark to life when their bodies were touching until he claimed her as his mate.

"I don't understand." She leaned her head back against the headrest and stared down at her lap. "I feel like I'm saying that a lot tonight. But while I'm at it, another thing I don't understand is why you took your hand away and then brought it back a moment later."

"There's nothing wrong with admitting you're unsure of something. My world is new and different. There will be many things you're unsure of until I've claimed you as my mate."

"I never said I would allow that to happen. I don't even know you." With wide eyes, she stared at him.

"Sugar, I'm not going to force anything on you but, one day very soon, you're going to want it as much as I do. Until then, I'll take things slow. Now, as for your questions: even though I could feel your anger over what was happening to shifters, I needed to hear you say it. I needed to know you weren't going to run off and try to find someone from The Saviors and turn any information over to them. If the slightest possibility even existed that you'd do such a thing, I couldn't take you home with me."

"You're a bit sure of yourself, aren't you? First, you think you're going to claim me as your mate. Now you want to take me home with you. Maybe I just want to go home—my home. I'm sure there's a bus station or something that can get me there."

"Do you want to live? If so, you will come with me. The Saviors don't know about you yet, but that doesn't mean they won't figure it out. We have no way of knowing if you were a target or just happened to be at the wrong place at the wrong time. Your friend—was she a shifter?"

"No…I mean I don't think…I don't know." She dragged her hand through her hair and tried to think of anything that might give her a better answer to his question. "What would that have to do with it?"

"If The Saviors knew she was a shifter, they might have been watching her. It's possible they could know about you."

"Guilty by association." The words clung to her tongue, making her mouth dry. "When they learn I'm not among the dead, they could come after me."

"Or they could already know and be waiting at your apartment." With his words, he felt the uncertainty and surprise within her. He had expected her to be terrified but there didn't seem to be even a hint of that within her emotions.

"I should be afraid but I guess after everything I witnessed tonight, I'm just numb. I overheard some of the police officers discussing survivors at the hospital. Those should be The Saviors' priority, not me. Surely, witnesses who might be able to give information to the police right now would be their first concern instead of them wasting time stalking my apartment, waiting to see if I return."

"Except you're a witness, too."

"I didn't see anything," she said before letting out a deep breath.

"You saw more than you're willing to say." When he let the connection between them flare to life, he used it to help him see into her mind. While she explored his lion, he searched her memories of what happened. She had them all walled off, as if trying to keep them from herself, but he caught a glimpse of people dressed in full black. The bulkiness of their outfits let him know they were in bulletproof gear. Their assault rifles mowed down the partiers quicker than anyone could react. The only thing that saved her was that she had been on her way back from the car. The vehicles had hidden her, giving her an opportunity to climb into the tree, out of harm's way. *If there had been a shifter with them, why hadn't he pointed her out to them?*

"So what now?" she asked, interrupting his thoughts.

"Now, if you're ready, I'll take you to the tribe's land. You'll be safe there." Taking his hand back from her, he turned the key to start the engine. "Everything is going to be okay. I'll get to the bottom of what happened tonight and we'll go from there."

"Can you find out, without causing too much attention, if Kat is dead? Maybe she's one of the ones in the hospital. Or maybe she was able to get to safety."

He nodded but he knew as well as she did, Kat was most likely dead. The cell phone in her pocket hadn't gone off. If her friend was alive, she'd have tried to find out if Karri was safe. He understood though that she needed closure so he'd reach out to his contacts for additional information once he got her to safety. Shifting into drive, he glanced over at her one last time as he kept his foot on the brake. "Are you sure you don't want to go to the sheriff?"

"I have a feeling he couldn't keep me as safe as you can." She ran her hand down her denim clad thigh. "Funny thing is The Saviors are after your kind but with you is the one place I'd be the safest. Seems like it should be an oxymoron."

"The tribe has taken precautions to ensure our safety. There is a perimeter fence to keep anyone from wandering onto our land and guards that patrol the grounds to make sure everyone is safe." He pulled away from where he was parked and headed home. Without knowing if there was a threat hanging over her head, he needed to get her to safety. Then he could learn what the others had found.

"This tribe of yours—are they all lions? I'm not sure if that's rude to ask or not. I was just wondering."

"Lions and bears mostly. There are a few foxes as well but Garret and his sister Ginger are the only wolves within our tribe. We're open to any shifter, but wolves are a pack animal; they prefer to stay within their own group. Garret and Ginger left their pack when they came of age and for years stayed out on their own."

"How did they end up with your tribe then?"

Pressing down on the gas pedal, he headed back toward the tribe's land. "Garret mated with Sin and settled here. Ginger came for a visit and ended up staying when she mated with Liam."

"So you can…never mind."

"Say it," he urged as they turned onto the dirt road and he could see the guards at the gate as he neared.

"You can date outside of your species."

"Shifters don't date, sugar; we mate. Yes, our mate can be anyone or even multiple people. Ari and Kaden have a high-profile security company and they were brought in to help us secure our land. While they were here, they found their mate, Camellia. They've made their home with the Crimson Hollow Tribe because Camellia is one of the tribe's teachers. Some shifters have human mates, as you might have already figured out." He rolled down his window as they came to the gate and eyed the older of the two guards. "Hey, guys. Has everyone made it back? Any issues?"

"Everyone's back and no issues, sir," the guard answered as the younger one opened the gate to allow Noah to drive through. "Jase wants to meet with you and the woman when you arrive. He's waiting at cabin two."

"Very well. Close down the gate; no one in or out until morning unless otherwise cleared through the leaders." Not waiting for the guard to reply, Noah rolled up the window and headed into the compound. "Time to meet the Chief."

"Are you in trouble because you brought me back? Maybe I should leave."

"Stop." He reached over and placed his hand on her leg. "I explained the connection between mates earlier. The one between me and my Alpha is very much the same. He knows who you are and that I am bringing you home. It's not unusual for him to want to meet with anyone coming to our tribe, so there's nothing to be concerned about. You have my word, Karri; you're safe here."

He parked the car near the guard's cabin, which he was the only one living at now that Liam had mated. There was another cabin on the other side being constructed for Liam and Ginger. The two main guards for the Chief and Deputy needed to be close by.

Two guards for two charges. He shook his head, not wanting to think about all the things that could go wrong with that. It was impossible for him and Liam to keep both Jase and Sin safe twenty-four hours a day. While his primary goal was Sin's safety and Liam's was Jase's, their duties overlapped. Each of them needed at least one additional guard, preferably four to six guards, working shifts, to keep them safe.

Both he and Liam had approached the subject with Jase, but he was unwilling to add guards until he knew for certain that they would protect Sin with absolute thoroughness. Until then, it was up to Liam and Noah. They had a group of potentials going through training and hopefully, before things got too out of control and unsafe, they'd have a strong team to keep the leaders of the tribe safe.

"What is your role in the tribe?"

He came around the car to where Karri was standing, her hand still on the door frame as if she wasn't sure she wanted to get out of the safety of the car. "My primary responsibility is to protect Sin, the Deputy of the tribe. If someone challenges her for her place within the tribe I can do nothing to stop that, but I keep her safe from all other threats, including The Saviors."

"You make it sound like there are other things to worry about besides them."

"There are many threats in your world, too; you just don't constantly consider them. You could walk out of your apartment and get hit by a truck. While you're shopping, there could be an armed robbery. There are always threats around; you just have to understand how to handle them." He wanted it to sound like everyday issues so that he didn't worry her further, but the truth was, the shifter world brimmed with danger. While The Saviors were making it more so, they were also bringing shifters together to stand as one and fight the greater evil.

A cabin door opened behind him and he started to turn toward it. Thanks to his shifter hearing, he knew where it was coming from and who to expect before he even saw who'd arrived. Sin stood in the doorway of her cabin, glaring at him, her anger drifting toward him. "Still angry, I see."

"You have no idea," she snapped. "Jase is waiting for you. A little male bonding, I suspect."

"Now Sin, you know we didn't keep you out of the fun to be assholes. We did it—"

"To keep you safe." Garret came up next to Sin and wrapped his arm around her waist as he finished Noah's sentence.

"The two of you gang up on me, but I'm supposed to be the Deputy here. Then you bring Jase into it, making matters worse, and you let him go out there."

"You know as well as I do that we couldn't have stopped Jase unless we were going to knock him unconscious or tie him up. He's the Chief and he believes strongly in not asking someone to do something he wouldn't do himself. He also had Ari and Kaden with him." Knowing he needed to calm Sin down before she could allow this to simmer longer and let her anger turn into rage, he stepped away from Karri and moved toward the cabin. "You're just as headstrong as he is, but the one person who can help me is Garret. Your mate knows the right words to say to you in order to keep you from doing something stupid. You're not just the Deputy; you're mated and have Zoe to look after. In the next few days, we need to all sit down and discuss this situation. You and Jase both need to let me and Liam do our job of protecting you guys."

"I already had that talk with her tonight, but you're right—we need to make some changes in that area," Garret agreed. "Both of them need additional guards."

"You're preaching to the choir." Noah shook his head. "That's something both Liam and I have brought to Jase's attention numerous times. Maybe you addressing the topic will make him see the urgency of the situation. The need for more guards for them is not something we can continue to ignore. Liam stayed here to protect Sin and the tribe while the rest of us were off looking for survivors and anyone from The Saviors who might have been still in the area. Because of that, we had to recruit Ari and Kaden for his protection. They're not even guards."

There was no doubt they could handle themselves and protect Jase but the point was, they had to rely on someone else to protect the Chief because they were failing him. It was beside the point that he wouldn't allow them to bring on additional guards. They couldn't continue like this. He was too important to the tribe to allow him to continue to risk himself.

"It's late, we're all tired, so go talk to Jase and we'll meet tomorrow to continue this discussion," Garret told him before looking down at his mate. "Come on, Sin. Everyone is back; now let's get some sleep."

As the door closed, he knew he wasn't done hearing from Sin about denying her the right to go with them. He could only hope that in the next few hours, Garret would be able to keep her from getting angrier; otherwise she'd be raging by the time of the meeting. Sin didn't like being kept on the sidelines but, with her position within the tribe, she needed to accept she couldn't be at the frontlines all the time. Jase needed to accept that as well, but that was more Liam's problem than his. He had to worry about Sin.

"She's not what I expected." Karri came up next to him, her voice low.

"Why not?" He didn't give her a moment to answer before he added, "Sin's red hair matches her feisty attitude. You never know what to expect with her. She's always a cannon ready to go off but not always on what you might expect. She's loyal and would do anything for this tribe, even after the hell she was put through."

Knowing she'd want to know what he meant, he put his arm around her waist and started toward cabin two as he explained. "You could say Sin is Jase's adoptive sister. She was born in a leash—a group of foxes—and when they were all killed, Granddad—Jase's Grandfather and the tribe's former Chief—took Sin and her cousin, Swift, in. They were the first foxes here and not everyone made things easy for them. Many considered them outsiders and the children were vicious. Jase stood up for Sin, but when she turned eighteen, she was tired of it all and took off. She just rejoined us a few months ago when Jase took over."

"Did her cousin leave, too?"

He paused at the bottom of the three steps that led to the cabin's porch. "No, Swift stayed. She was doing well until another leash was attacked. Things were rocky for a while but she's mated now and is working through her issues. I'm sure you'll meet her soon enough. Now come on, let me introduce you to Jase." Without waiting, he led the way up the steps into the cabin as excitement teased through him. Noah was anxious to see Jase's reaction to his new mate. *I wonder if he knew I'd be mated to a human.*

Chapter Four

The cabin had an open, airy feeling to it but did nothing to help Karri's claustrophobia. She found herself in a compound full of shifters with dangerous people after them—possibly after her. It all seemed like a nightmare she couldn't wake up from. Standing before the Chief, she seemed to dwarf before him. His muscular, wide frame and height made it seem like there was more of a difference between them then there actually was.

"Welcome to Crimson Hollow, Karri. I'm Jase." He held his hand out to her.

After a moment of hesitation, she reached out to take his hand, wondering if she'd feel the same connection she had with Noah's touch. As her fingers brushed the back of his hand, nothing sparked to life, allowing her to accept the handshake. "It's nice to finally meet you. Noah spoke highly about you."

"Now I know you're lying." Jase let out a deep laugh.

"I ensure you, he did," she pressed not wanting Noah to be in trouble because of her.

"It's fine, sugar." He laid his hand on her arm and the unease that had been running through her subsided. "He's messing with you. Jase is a good Chief."

"Better if I accepted your suggestions." Jase raised an eyebrow at Noah, as if waiting for a response.

"Well, we all know that's the truth." The other man spoke from where he was leaning against the wall in the background. "I'm Liam."

The third and final man had thus far stood silent, watching the exchange. "Though we kind of already met. I'm Roger, by the way."

"The lion from the…I'm sorry." She wasn't sure what to say around these people and it seemed that the filter between her brain and her mouth had been suddenly turned off.

"You're fine. Yes, the lion from the woods. I hadn't meant to scare you. I assumed you were aware of shifters, considering how many had attended that party."

"I was aware of shifters existing; I mean, how could I not? It's all over the news. I just never expected to meet one in person. Let alone be standing in the middle of their town." Noah's touch helped to keep the anxiety at bay. Though she wasn't sure why, she trusted him, and if he trusted everyone here, then she knew she'd be safe.

Kat had always told her to be more open to people and less judgmental. She could hear her friend's words playing through her thoughts. *Just because you came from a small hick town where everyone knew everyone else doesn't mean the world is as bad as your parents have made it seem.* Except maybe it was; she had just watched a group of people get murdered in front of her eyes, including Kat and her boyfriend.

Sitting there on the sofa, she ran her hand through her hair and tried to fight through the emotions running through her. For the last twenty minutes, Jase had grilled her on what happened, making her relive the horrible scene. She had cooperated because she wanted to help but she couldn't handle much more of it. No longer was she seeing the open space of the cabin; instead, she was back in the woods, dead bodies littering the ground around her and blood everywhere. She didn't want to be there, didn't want to look at the bodies at her feet, and she most certainly didn't want to find Kat's body in the carnage.

"When the shooting started, could you tell how many shooters there were?"

As if his question sparked the memory, she was back at the beginning. She was just returning to the party after fetching her phone from the car. Music blared, people danced, and liquor flowed freely. That party somewhat reminded her of home—there'd been a barn she and some friends used to party at in her teenage years. The barn backed to the woods, which left plenty of places for privacy. The difference was that back then they'd had country music playing and drank beer, rarely any hard liquor—unlike this last event. Gunshots rang through the air then, stopping her memory of teenage parties and bringing her back to recent past.

"Stop!" Pain laced that single word and her chest tightened.

"Enough." There was a touch of anger in Noah's voice, but she didn't have enough strength to look back at him.

"I can't do this! Not again…" She held her hands to her ears as if it would stop the gunshots but it didn't. They weren't real, but lived on in her mind.

"Sugar, it's okay." Noah, who had hung back through the whole questioning, came up to her and squatted in front of her.

"I'm sorry, I just can't…" Tears stung her eyes as she stared at him. He brought her hands away from her ears and held them together in his larger one.

"You did great." He glanced over to where Jase was sitting on the armchair. "She's been through enough tonight and you've got your information."

"If she remembers anything—"

"I'll let you know." Noah cut Jase off before he could finish. "I'm taking her back to my place tonight. She's too distraught to be alone."

"Take care of your mate. We'll see about what we can do with her information." Jase rose from the chair and tipped his head to Liam and Roger before going to the door.

"Karri." Liam paused by the sofa before joining Jase at the door. "I know that was rough, but I assure you it was worth it. The information you were able to give us, while you might not think it was much, will be a great help to us."

She didn't know what to say so she stayed silent. Instead, she tried to remember where she was and what she was doing there. She focused on Noah and allowed his deep brown eyes to ground her in the moment.

"Come on, we'll go back to my place and you can get some rest. I don't want to leave you here alone." He stood, taking her with him.

"Why can't we stay here?" She wasn't sure she wanted to go back out there.

Inside, she felt safe, but outside, even knowing about the guards' presence and the fence separating her from the rest of the world, she felt as if The Saviors might be watching, waiting for her to venture out so they could kill her.

"I need to be close to Sin and Jase in case something happens. My cabin is right next door. Liam used to share it with me as well, but once he mated, they wanted more privacy. Until their new cabin is built alongside mine, I'm the closest guard to Sin and Jase." He tucked a strand of her hair behind her ear and stared down at her. "It's going to be okay."

The moment might have seemed innocent to someone looking in from the outside but there was something very intimate about his touch and the way he slid her hair behind her ear. She wanted to lean into him and enjoy the moment but exhaustion ate at her. "Let's go."

"Liam's right. The information you gave us will be helpful."

"I'm glad I didn't go through Hell for nothing." She tried to make light of it, but her words were truthful. Reliving the memories over and over to answer Jase's questions had been worse than Hell. The whole time she kept thinking about what she could have done differently. What could she have done to save people? Could she have saved Kat? Somewhere in reliving the memories, she realized Kat was likely dead. She had no proof of this but in her heart, she sensed her friend was no longer alive. The horror of it clung to her. If she hadn't gone to the car minutes earlier, she'd have been standing next to Kat when the shooting started.

I'd be dead, too.

Early morning sunlight streamed through the bay window as Noah sat in his living room trying to pull together what he could from the police and news reports. According to the reports, the police suspected six shooters. What they weren't aware of was the presence of a seventh one, who, if he had a gun, didn't get to use it. They had only been able to gather that information because of the interrogation Jase had put Karri through. Noah had wanted to stop it, to protect his mate from having to live through it again, but the information she had might be what they needed to stop The Saviors. So, he'd hung back, giving Jase the chance to question her, forcing himself not to reach out and touch her. His touch might have influenced the memories she was recalling.

The night had been rough, but now with it over she was finally resting and he was able to do something to help his tribe. He'd missed the meeting with Sin and the others, but Liam dropped by to fill him in. The attack on the party close to home was enough to bring Jase to his senses. He agreed to adding additional guards to both his and Sin's protection details. Now, both Liam and Noah had to pick a First Lieutenant to be second-in-command of the charges' protection. After that, they could each chose two additional guards, to be used as needed.

Noah was hoping to convince Brett Oaks to take the position. As a former police officer, he was suited for the role and his size as a bear shifter added extra weight to the decision. He had also proven himself time and time again to both Noah and the tribe. He glanced at his phone and debated calling Brett to have him come over to discuss the promotion. The original plan had been for him to go over to Brett and Swift's place once Karri woke up so he wouldn't have to leave her alone, but having him come there might be easier since he wasn't sure she'd be up to socializing after everything she had been through. Getting Brett on board immediately would help to relieve some of the pressure on Noah, especially now that he had to worry about his mate as well.

Before he could make the call, a scream echoed through the cabin and he shot off the sofa, rushing up the stairs in a blink of an eye. "Karri!" As he opened the door to his bedroom, the stench of fear hit him full force, bringing his lion to the forefront. He glanced around the room but no one was there—not that be expected there to be with the guards patrolling the grounds, but one could never be sure.

"Karri," he called to her again as he sat down onto the bed. "You're safe."

"No! No!" Sitting on the bed, she shook her head back and forth.

"Karri." He wanted to wrap his arms around her but he didn't want to scare her further. Even though her eyes were open he wasn't sure she was awake or not. "Karri, look at me."

"No…not Kat."

Tears rolled down her face and he couldn't stop himself from going to her. He scooted farther onto the bed to lean against the headboard and wrap his arms around her. "Oh sugar, I'm sorry." The moment he held her, he could see the images in her mind that had her so upset. The pale woman with long black hair, thick black eyeliner, and bright red lipstick seemed to stand out more from the memory, as the rest of the bodies were hazier. In an instant, he recognized Kat from the picture he'd seen in the police report earlier when he'd learned she'd been among those listed as deceased. He hadn't been able to give the news to Karri since she had been sleeping, but it was a piece of information he'd had no desire to deliver.

It appeared Kat, her boyfriend, and the group that had been hanging around them were the first to die. He wasn't sure if they had been targeted yet, or if they just happened to be in the wrong area when the shooting started. He remembered enough from Karri's memories to know she had been standing with them only moments before. If she hadn't gone to the car for her cell phone, she'd be dead, too.

My mate would have died before I ever found her. He wasn't sure what that meant—if he would have found someone else. Or if he would have been stuck without a mate until his dying day. Either way, it didn't sit well with him. She was his. Now he had to figure out if she was in danger or not.

As much as he'd dug for information, he hadn't been able to determine if Kat or her boyfriend had been shifters or not. Surprisingly, the news had been keeping it quiet as if they didn't want to incite more riots. The police reports wouldn't state the nature of the person until a family member confirmed it or the autopsy report came back. If they had been in hiding, it was unlikely that a family member would admit the truth. He wouldn't be surprised if some of the family members went into hiding over the next several days. Those who didn't risked being hunted down and killed by The Saviors.

"She's really dead." She pressed her face against his chest, tears seeping through his shirt.

"I know." He squeezed her tight against him. "I've read the report. She didn't suffer. She probably didn't even know what happened."

"How can you say that?" She tipped her head to look up at him. "It was terrifying."

"For you, sugar, but you saw the whole thing. She was one of the first to die. It's possible she didn't know what was happening." He wasn't just saying it to calm her down, but because he believed it. From what he read in the police reports and the crime scene photos, it didn't appear as if any of those from her group had tried to run. Kat and her boyfriend landed together, her shirt half unbuttoned as if they had started to get intimate there in the middle of the party.

"Were they…were we targeted?"

"I don't know yet but I'm looking into it." He smoothed his hand down the length of her back. "You're safe here."

"You keep telling me that and you'd think I'd believe it but I'm just so scared." She leaned back against his chest. "I'm from a small town; where the worst crime we have is when someone gets rowdy at the bar. The most the cops have to worry about is speeders. There's never been a murder there as long as I've been alive. Maybe I'm sheltered or even naive but I almost expected it to be like that everywhere. I never watched the news and our paper rarely covered the horrible things that were happening outside of our little bubble. When I left to start college, I had a rude wakeup call. Kat helped me adjust and she protected me when I needed it, but she also pushed me outside of my comfort zone."

"She drugged you," he reminded her.

"That was her boyfriend's idea. He wanted her to come down for the party and she wouldn't come without me." She was silent for a moment before glancing back up at him. "He wasn't a bad guy, just used to getting his own way no matter the cost. Unfortunately, the cost this time was their lives."

"And it could have been yours." The idea was unsettling, making him want to hold her tighter to him, as well as get back to his research to make sure The Saviors were not after her.

She's safe here. The Saviors won't have a chance to attack here.

Chapter Five

A week had passed since the incident in the woods, and with each passing day, Karri felt even more unnerved. Noah and the others were following every lead, researching every aspect, and reading through every police and news report. Still, they hadn't determined if she was one of the chosen targets. *How hard is it to figure out if they were gunning for me?* Kat's autopsy hadn't come back yet either to let them know if Kat herself had been a target. Maybe it was the boyfriend? For all they knew, it might not have been any of them.

Only three shifters had been confirmed to be at the party that night. Two were dead and the third was in the hospital in critical condition. One of the shifters that had been killed belonged to Oswalt's Tribe—a neighboring tribe. The other two had been in hiding. The family of the shifters who had been killed had picked up and moved in the middle of the night for fear of their safety. While the family of the hospitalized victim had no choice but to stay or leave their son behind. Karri couldn't put herself in their shoes or even begin to understand what they were going through.

The shifter world was a whole new experience for her, unlike anything she would have thought it to be like. The Crimson Hollow Tribe seemed to be a family. They hung out together, played together, ate together, and most of all, they fought for each other. Everyone was protected. Only a few of the tribe members left for work, most of them either worked remotely or had another job within the tribe, because of that there were less risks being taken by the members.

As closely bonded as they seemed to be, they'd welcomed her as if she were one of them. Never once had she felt like an outsider. They had stopped by the cabin to meet her, usually bringing food by for her and Noah as the excuse. Turns out Noah was terrible in the kitchen and most of the time one of the other families sent food over for him, or he joined Sin or Jase for dinner. It didn't matter their animal; they were family. Too bad her own family wasn't half as welcoming and open.

"Sugar." Noah jogged down the stairs, tugging a shirt over his head. "We've got to go."

"Go? What's wrong?" She moved away from the window where she had been watching the tribe members move about with their daily chores.

"Garret's received new information and we're meeting at his place to go over it."

"We're…?" Even as she questioned him, she sat down to pull on her boots. "I've never been invited to one of your meetings before. Why now? Jase isn't going to question me again, is he? I don't remember anything else."

"Whatever he's found concerns you, so you need to be there." He came to stand in front of her and held out his hand to her. "Don't worry about it. We'll get through it together. Now come on, they're waiting for us."

Together. Enjoying the sound of that, she slipped her hand into his. She wanted to look on the bright side of this whole disaster and be glad that she'd found him but too much blood had been spilled for her to see anything positive out of this mess. In her heart, she believed that if they were meant to be, like he claimed, then they'd have found each other without so much death surrounding them. How was she supposed to be happy about their developing relationship with what she had to go through to get there?

She wasn't even sure she could call it a developing relationship. Most of the last week he had spent working. He had tried to make time for her but that time had been limited and she always felt like she was holding him back from what he needed to do. They'd spent an hour or so cuddled together on the sofa every evening, chatting about anything and everything, before she went to bed. Yet, a lot of what she learned about him had come from a second party. Too many times one of the tribe women dropped by and shared some gossip about him.

With every touch, the connection between them seemed to grow stronger. It wasn't that she could feel his lion more, but the air became charged around them. It was hard to explain even to herself. Most of the time she wasn't even sure it was happening until after their embrace ended and she missed that connection.

Stepping outside, she took a moment to enjoy the rays of sunshine on her face and the sweet caress of the wind. Days ago, she had been so close to death she could feel the cold fingers of the grim reaper but until that moment, she hadn't realized how thankful she was to be alive. She had a chance to go on with her life—one she couldn't waste. There had to be something she could do to help the shifters and their cause.

Still standing on the porch, she turned toward Noah. "I want to help."

"What sugar?" He pulled the door closed behind him.

"I don't know what use I'll be but I've got to do something. I understand now what's happening to shifters. Changes need to be made both with the laws and with the attitudes of people."

"Both of which are hard to change. They take time and those who are spearheading the movement are in more danger because their presence is known. There's no hiding that they're either a shifter or connected with them. The Saviors will make them a target. While we've been lucky so far with their safety, there are still great risks. It's why many lawyers will not take on this cause except Liam's cousin—he's an attorney and is leading the legal battle."

"Standing by and doing nothing will get you killed, too." A little girl with long brown hair ran by, catching her attention for a moment. The children were the reason why they had to do something. This was a time in their lives when they were supposed to be young and innocent. To preserve that innocence, they had to act soon. It was their job to protect the future generations. "Right there is the reason why we can't sit by and do nothing. Look at her carefree attitude; she doesn't realize the dangers that are lurking outside the fence, and I don't want her to ever go through what I went through."

"While my primary responsibility is to protect Sin, we protect everyone here. The children are safe."

"For now—but Ginger told me about the man that crashed his truck through the fence. There wasn't even a road there. What if that had been someone from The Saviors?"

"He was a drunk. Nothing more."

"That time." Her gaze continued to follow the little girl as she joined a group of other girls. "What about next time? You can't deny that The Saviors are a threat to their safety."

He leaned against the doorframe, watching her for a moment before finally nodding. "You're right, they're a threat. There are people working on changing the laws and we're not the only ones working on taking down The Saviors. None of this is going to happen overnight. In the meantime, we've got to do whatever we can to keep ourselves and our tribe safe. If you want to help with the cause, trust me, we won't turn away the assistance—but you're going to do it our way. You're not going to run out on your own and bring attention to yourself."

"I hadn't planned on rushing into town and drawing attention to myself by screaming that shifters saved my life. With my luck The Saviors would pick me up, and instead of killing me straight away they'd want information on your location." She stepped in front of him and placed her hand on his chest. "I'd never betray you."

"If you said that to another shifter they'd tell you you'd never have a chance to betray us." Goosebumps spread along her arm, which he quickly chased away by running his hand along her skin. "As your mate I can taste your words are the truth, so there's no need to frighten you into keeping quiet."

"Never have a chance…you mean…forget it." Needing space, she stepped back from him.

"If they had critical information and turned against us, we couldn't stand idly by if we had the chance to put an end to it. Killing is something we do our best to avoid whenever possible but if it means keeping our people safe from a traitor, then we will do whatever is necessary." He stepped up behind her, careful not to touch her. "We're more civilized than we are in the wild, but we're still dangerous if threatened."

"Noah." Liam leaned out of the door at Sin's cabin and hollered down to him. "We're waiting on you."

"One second," he told Liam before finally touching her back. "Karri, we need to go."

"Yeah…" She nodded and forced herself to move. The short walk to Sin's cabin, two doors down, happened in a haze. While she never expected him or other shifters not to act if someone was turning information over to the enemy, she also hadn't expected him to be upfront in telling her he'd kill them if it came down to it. There was something terrifying about that knowledge but the more she thought about it she realized something else also bothered her. The idea that Noah or someone she had gotten to know over the last week could get hurt or killed because of some traitorous asshole made her livid.

She wasn't sure what kind of person this made her but she accepted what he said. Did that mean she was becoming less of a human being? Were the shifters who had come into her life recently affecting her in a way that she was willing to accept murder might be the only answer? As they stepped into Sin's cabin and she looked around at the leaders of the tribe, she realized it wasn't hardness that made her accept things; it was compassion. Compassion for what was happening to shifters. This was war and unfortunately, in war, there would always be fatalities.

"Now that everyone is here, let's get started." Jase sat down at the head of the dining table.

"Before you do, I'd like to say something." She paused next to the chair Noah had led her to.

"Karri." Noah's voice held a touch of warning, as if he wasn't sure what she was going to say.

She wished that she had the same ability as he did to be able to open the connection between them and let him know she wasn't about to say something careless. Unfortunately, that was a one-way street, which did her no good.

"Go ahead," Jase encouraged her.

She slipped her hand into Noah's and allowed herself to let their embrace wash away her nerves. "First, I appreciate the welcome everyone has shown me since Noah brought me here. I was clueless before he found me and I appreciate how everyone has taken the time to answer my questions. I don't know how I can be of any use to you but I want to help in any way I can. I want to change what is happening although, obviously, this issue is bigger than any one person can manage. A few moments ago, while we were standing outside, I was watching a young girl. She couldn't be older than seven. I don't want to see her witness the same thing I did a few days ago, or worse yet, be one of those who didn't make it. She deserves to be able to do whatever she wants, without looking over her shoulder, wondering if The Saviors or some other lunatics are gunning for her."

"Hopefully we'll get to that point. Unfortunately, it won't happen overnight." Jase clasped his hands together in front of him on the table.

"Noah said the same thing to me." She glanced at him before turning back to Jase. "And I do realize that. Hell, it might be something that affects her most of her life, but hopefully, her children and her children's children will know a different world. I'm just one person and I'm human so I know I have limitations. Still, I want to help."

"Then help us." Garret turned the paper over in front of him. Revealing a photograph, he slid it across the table to her. "Do you know this man?"

"That's…" Her knees turned soft and her breath caught in her throat. As if knowing what she needed, Noah pulled out the chair and eased her into it. As she sat down, she couldn't pull her gaze from the jailhouse mugshot.

"Who is it?" Noah asked.

"Kat's father," she breathed out. Unable to look at it any longer, she reached out to turn the picture over. "I heard him…that night. He was there. Heaven help me! He shot them…"

Noah dropped into the chair beside her and forced her to look at him. "You heard him say something. What did he say?"

"I warned you, daughter, but you wouldn't listen." She remembered the way the wind had carried his words toward her and the chill it had sent through her bones from the hatred in his words. "He opened fire and the others followed suit. Why…why would he kill his own daughter? Was she a shifter?"

"No," Garret answered. "The autopsy report came back yesterday. She wasn't a shifter, but her boyfriend was. Turns out more than half of the people there were from a wolf pack. The guy who put together the party is from the area. He's human, but met some of the wolves through college. It was break and he was stuck here so he figured he'd throw a party in the woods, and no one would know."

"Regrettably, the wrong people found out about it," Sin added.

"They knew because Kat told her parents we were going. Shit, they knew I was supposed to be there." Even Noah's touch did nothing to subside the fear that rose within her. He'd killed his own daughter and there was no doubt in her mind that he'd come after her as well if he could figure out where she was.

"The police arrested him this morning. Here's the press statement and summary of his charges." Garret leaned forward, offering her what appeared to be a computer printout.

She read the text before placing the sheet on the table in front of her. "What about Kat's mother—did she know about this?"

"The police believe she knew nothing but you can't reach out to her," Jase told her before eyeing Noah as if giving him a silent message. "Have you spoken with your parents or any family members yet?"

"No." She focused her attention on the paper in front of her, her finger tracing the edge of the corner repeatedly, embarrassed to look at anyone in the room. "I haven't spoken much to them or anyone from my hometown in months. Dad was livid I left to go to college instead of working in the family's grocery store. Mom goes by what he says, so when he cut off communication, it went for everyone, including my younger sister. They know I'm friends with Kat and I'm sure the news reached them by now, yet no one called to see if I was okay. That's my family." She shook her head, disgusted by the fact that her family didn't seem to care if she was alive or dead.

"No, sugar, we are." Noah scooted his chair closer to hers and took her hand in his. "You're my mate and we're family here. That makes you one of us."

"He's right." Jase nodded. "Not to add pressure but you're going to need to claim her."

"Excuse me? Claim me? I'm not a lost dog." She glared at Jase but her words lacked anger. She wanted to lash out at her family for their lack of caring but since she couldn't do that, she picked the next easy target. Unfortunately for Jase, his comment came at the wrong moment and she couldn't help letting it all out on him.

"It's not meant in a disrespectful way," Sin explained. "Once the mating between the two of you is cemented, it will link you with us permanently. It will also give Noah the connection that will allow him to know where you are at any time."

"A tracking collar, then."

Next to her, Noah's muscles tightened and his body went completely still. His reaction made her realize she was lashing out through embarrassment and fear of what was happening, not because of Noah, the mating, or any objections to the claim. "I apologize, that was out of line. Noah—"

"Don't." He pulled his hand out of hers and the loss of touch sent a pang of regret through her.

"Please, Noah." She started to reach out for him but stopped. "I let my anger speak for me and I'm sorry."

Jase cleared his throat, forcing her to stop. "This is something you two should work out privately. Right now, we need to wrap this meeting up so Liam can make his appointment. One last thing, Noah, have you picked a First Lieutenant?"

"I plan to meet with Brett Oaks this afternoon about the position." Noah rose from his chair and stepped away from the table.

Her chest tightened as she watched him put distance between them. Never before had her mouth got her into so much trouble as she was in now. She'd hurt the one person who had been by her side, supporting her, all this time. He claimed she was his mate and while she didn't completely understand it, she knew there was something between them. It had been Jase's comment about Noah claiming her that made her uneasy. This was too close to what her father had done with her mother. At twenty-five, her father met her mother, who'd been seventeen at the time. He'd come into her life and taken control; two days after her eighteenth birthday, they were married.

"Let's go." Noah ordered, pulling her from her thoughts of her parents.

"One last thing, Karri." Jase stopped her before she could go after Noah. "We need you to not answer your phone if anyone calls. Right now, we're still not sure if The Saviors planned you as a target or not. It's possible Kat's father had planned to execute you that night was well. You were a friend of Kat's and her boyfriend's and you were at the party with numerous other shifters. It's possible they have their sights on you. You're safe here and right now we don't believe the police knew you were there. None of the survivors mentioned you. If you were one of the planned victims, your name is not on the list of the dead so they could be watching for you, if he told the others about you."

"You said it yourself, Kat's parents knew you were going to the party," Sin added before she could argue. "Right now, this is just out of precaution."

"Whatever, my phone is almost dead anyways." She pushed back from the table and quickly hurried after Noah who had already started for the door. She didn't care about being cut off from anyone outside of the tribe. Her parents obviously didn't care and the only friend she'd been close to was now dead. What she cared about was Noah, and he'd just walked out on her. Somehow, she needed to make him understand where she was coming from. Speaking out of anger might have been one of the worse things she could have done but she'd be damned if she allowed her anger to cost her his love. *I've already lost so much; I'm not going to lose him, too.*

Chapter Six

Outside, Karri followed Noah, mentally preparing herself for what she expected would be a fight. The short distance between the cabins seemed to take longer than before, until finally they were far enough away from Sin's place that they wouldn't be overheard—or so she hoped. It didn't matter because she needed to make things right with Noah before he went inside and back to work. "Noah, stop for a minute, please."

"According to what you said in there, I'm the one who's supposed to be giving the commands," he snapped without turning to look at her. The anger in his voice didn't surprise her but the pain his words caused in her chest did.

"That's not what I meant. It came out wrong." She let out a deep sigh and stepped back from him. "No, maybe it didn't come out wrong; maybe I said what I thought I meant, but I was wrong."

"How could you compare yourself to a stray dog? Do you really think you mean that little to me?" Anger and sorrow mixed into his tone.

"During my senior year of high school I had to put this project together and to add a personal aspect I decided to include some family photos. I was looking through an old photo album when my mother came home from work. This album was hidden behind some things and you could tell it was old from the yellowing on the page and the warn material that Mom used to cover it. Inside I found pictures of her and her family. She was smiling and happy. Do you know I can't remember a single day when my mother looked as happy as she did in the photographs?"

"What does that have to do with now?"

She glanced around the grounds, taking in those who were around, especially the family gathered at the picnic table sharing lunch. Yet another thing she'd had never done with her folks. It wasn't until she'd left home that she realized how unusual her family really was. "That's how things were with my parents. He barked and she'd cower in fear or run off to do whatever would make him happy. For a long time, I thought it was normal and it took me nearly two years to realize it wasn't. I don't want that for myself."

"Have I ever ordered you around? Forced you to do something you didn't want to do? I didn't even force you to come back here with me even though I knew it would be the safest place for you."

"I know." She turned back to him. "But sitting there having Jase tell me that you need to claim me made it seem like a demand. It seemed like either complete the mating or leave. It was a shock and I reacted without thinking. I don't want to be stuck in a relationship like my mother was. She might love my father but no man is worth being a doormat for."

"And you think I'll treat you like one." He leaned his hip against the handrail leading up the stairs to the porch of his cabin and watched her. There was no question in his statement, leaving her for a moment unsure of what to say.

"No." She closed the distance between them to stand in front of him. "I'll be honest and admit I'm concerned about this relationship. What can I contribute to it? I don't want it to be something that developed because some lunatics are after me and I need your help to stay alive."

"That's not what's happening here and if you thought about this for a minute, you'd know that."

She already knew this of course but hadn't wanted to accept it. This wasn't what she'd thought it would be like. She always imagined they'd meet, date, and then have this connection. With Noah, the connection was instant and this attraction to him seems almost magical.

"What's the problem, Karri? Is it that I'm a shifter?"

Glancing back up at him, she was met with his amber lion eyes, reminding her of the lion she'd petted days ago. If being a shifter had any impact on her feelings for him, it certainly wasn't a negative one. She was intrigued by his second nature. Any holding back on her part was from her wanting a relationship where she was an equal and not something like her parents had. She wasn't willing to settle for anything less. As she'd only known him a short time, she couldn't yet accept that she wouldn't end up in a situation that replicated her mother's. He didn't seem like that type of guy but if she didn't take her time, she might find out she was wrong too late.

"No." She brought her gaze to meet his as she tried to put her uncertainties into words. "You have to understand this idea of being claimed because you believe I'm your mate is new to me. Where I come from, it doesn't happen like that. Upon meeting you, you told me I was your mate and I've been trying to adjust to that but it won't happen overnight. What you're talking about is a lifetime together because of this mating, but I barely know you. What if once we know each other better we find out that we don't like each other? Then what? For shifter mates, there are no divorces, so does that mean we're stuck together? Do you really want to live miserably for the rest of your life?"

"We're a perfect match."

"Who says?" Feeling overwhelmed, she took a step back from him. "Your lion?"

"Fate. What's happening here is similar to what two humans would experience with love at first sight. The connection seems instant, like they've known each other their whole lives, and neither of them wants to spend a day apart from the other. Are you denying you feel that way?"

Part of her wanted to be able to tell him she didn't, but it would be a lie. The connection was there and stronger than anything she'd felt before. Maybe that scared her the most. She wanted what he was offering but fear plagued her. Did she want him too badly? Since they'd met, she found herself constantly seeking him out. Whether it was a moment of his time as she brought him fresh coffee while he was working, or the cuddling on the sofa in the evenings, those meant everything to her.

Even asleep, her subconscious put him in her dreams, as well as her nightmares. It didn't matter if she was back in the woods surrounded by blood and gore, or there at Crimson Hollow—Noah was there, with her.

"I feel it," she admitted. "I'm just scared."

"Letting fear hold you back from what life has to offer is like going on a roller coaster and keeping your eyes closed the whole time. It's the adventure you don't want to miss—not how you got there. We have our whole lives to live and I want to do it with you."

When he put it like that, it sounded amazing. She was a risk taker; otherwise she'd have never left home to make her own path in life. Why was she letting fear hold her back from something she wanted now? She didn't know but her best guess would be all the unknowns. After her near death experience, she should be grabbing life with both hands.

"I know you're right but…" Exhaling, she dragged her hand through her hair. "It's hard to explain everything I'm thinking and feeling. Does that connection of yours do anything useful?"

"Such as?"

"I don't know. I mean if you can know where I am, can't you use it to feel my emotions? Maybe feeling them would allow you to better understand why I'm holding back."

He straightened himself from where he was leaning on the porch railing and tipped his head toward the house. "Let's go inside and finish this conversation."

"Noah…" Unsure if going inside was the best move, she called after him. If they made it inside, would he be tempted to go up and sulk in his office? They needed to get through this before it brewed strong, causing hatred.

"Inside." His tone held command, leaving no question that he expected her to follow. "There are too many people around to be having this conversation outdoors." Without waiting for her, he went to the front door and held it open.

She glanced around her; more of the tribe members seemed to be milling about now. They hadn't even registered to her; all she'd thought about was Noah and making things right between them. This tension between them was like a brick in her stomach. Was this because of the connection they shared or her own emotions? Not wanting to question this, she followed him. Whatever was happening between them would continue to happen. He had explained the mating connection would continue to grow until he claimed her and that would be the final piece needed to light the circuit between them completely. Once lit, it would never be extinguished, becoming a connection far beyond what humans shared.

Inside, she dropped down onto the chair and waited. She needed to see what he would do. Would he rush back to his office or would he stay and fight? There was something to be said about staying and fighting and while she expected he would, she knew he also had work waiting for him. The Saviors' attack in the woods had been the first large scale attack against them but everyone suspected it wouldn't be the last. Noah and the others were digging into every possible avenue and since Kat's father was a part of the big picture, that meant tearing apart Kat's family. How many others did she know who were part of this war on shifters?

Noah's lion snarled at him, demanding he do something to convince Karri that this mating needed to happen. He wanted this, not for Jase's reasons—the logical ones—but because his lion was growing restless. A week might not seem long to humans but for his lion, it had been an eternity. They had searched so long for a mate and now his beast was growing impatient with the need to make her his. The urge to carry her up to his bed to show her what a tease he could be ate at him. He wanted to make love to her until she cried out his name and then he'd officially claim her as his.

With a long night ahead of him, he snatched a beer out of the refrigerator and headed back to the living room where he had left her. "Want one?" He twisted the lid off the bottle.

"No, thanks."

"The connection isn't, let's say, fully operational mode yet, so your emotions are hazy to me." Hating that his mate's emotions were obscure to him, he took a long drink from the beer bottle. "The lion within me can smell certain emotions but with you, it's a knotted mess. The ball of emotions makes the cat in me want to tug at it and dissect it."

"What about what you did to show me your lion? Would our touch make things more clear for you?"

"The touch connection allows me to see things clearer between us but it's still like opening your eyes in murky water. Once you're mine it will be clear but that doesn't help this situation." Chuckling, he came around the sofa to sit close to her. "For the first time in my life, I got a tiny slice of understanding as to what it would be like to be human."

"We don't go around knowing everyone's emotions and, in a disaster, we can't know for certainty where our loved one is. I guess that's why there can be such a panic in those cases. Everyone trying to find their loved ones or at least get in touch with them to make sure they're alive." She reached down to unlace her boot when suddenly, she shot up straight. "Wait. Will this mating make me…"

"No, you won't become a shifter. We're born, not bitten. We cannot give our ability to someone else, not even our mate." Carefully, he watched her, trying to determine if she was relieved.

"But how can I be human and still have the connection with you?"

"A number of things will change but essentially you'll still be human." He set his beer on the coffee table and leaned forward, resting his elbows on his thighs. "You're not all of a sudden going to start changing into an animal. You will only have your abilities because of your connection with me."

"This is a lot to take in but it would have been even more mind-blowing if I found out I'd shifted once the mating happened."

"When both mates are shifters there's no issue explaining the mating because each of them know instantly they were meant for each other. In most cases, we've searched so long for our mates that once we find each other, our beast is eager to make it official so we can start our lives together."

"Is that what it's like for you? Is your lion eager to claim me?"

The question held the warning of being a trap and the longer he thought about it, the more it seemed that either answer could have a negative impact. In the end, he decided to be truthful instead of holding back something she would feel for herself later. "My beast is on edge wanting to claim you. He's growing impatient with the delay and wants his mate. Times are dangerous for my kind and the mating will make it easier for me to protect you. I can control my beast so you don't have to be concerned that I'll force this mating upon you."

"I hadn't considered that." She tugged off her boots and looked at him. "I'm not sure how we got off topic. This wasn't what we were discussing."

"It is. We were discussing our mating."

"Yes, but my hesitation to it, not anything else. I guess in a way it all ties together. I wish there was a way to explain my reluctance better. Until you came into my life, I hadn't realized how much my parents' relationship affected me."

"We'll get through it," he assured her as he picked up his beer again. "I need to finish a few things upstairs but how about you give me an hour and then I'll make dinner."

"You'll make dinner? I've been told that the last time you tried to cook you almost burned down the house."

"I see Ginger has been around." He chuckled at Liam's mate and her extravagant stories. "It was just a small fire…"

"You admit it then?"

"Well…" Reluctantly, he nodded. "I'm a disaster in the kitchen but I can reheat. Camellia brought us a chicken and rice casserole this morning, I can manage to pop it in the oven without setting the place ablaze, I promise."

"You go work. I'll put the casserole in the oven and let you know when it's done." She ran her hands down her thigh and stood.

"I swear I can manage that much, but thanks. We'll have a nice meal and tonight; instead of watching a movie, we'll talk. Forget about me being a shifter, The Saviors, and everything else. We'll get to know each other as if we were just two people out on a date."

Before his beast could decide that he was unwilling to wait, he had to get himself out of there. Without wasting another moment, he polished off his beer and rose from the sofa. His office was the only safe place at the moment. There, he could dive into the research the tribe needed him to do and hopefully get his mind off wanting to claim Karri. Inside, his lion snarled at him, demanding his mate. Soon…

Chapter Seven

A night like a normal couple should have taken the tension out of the air but it only made Karri want him more, which in turn only made her more uneasy. This mating idea felt like she'd walked into a booby trapped building blindfolded. Something was coming but she didn't know what it was. Her body told her to just do it, accept the mating because it was her destiny, but her thoughts wouldn't turn off long enough for her to allow it to happen.

Now, hours after she'd turned in for the night, she stood in the living room staring out the bay window. Noah was back in his office working and part of her yearned to go to him. Surely, with his lion demanding he claim her, he wouldn't mind the interruption so she'd give him just that. Yet, rather than going ahead with it, she paced back and forth in front of the window.

Her thoughts traveled from one thing to another quicker than she could put all the pieces together. Kat's boyfriend had been a shifter—did that mean she'd been his mate? Had she been resistant to it as well? So many questions but no answers and no way to even get the answers she sought.

"I thought you were in bed."

She turned to find Noah standing at the bottom of the stairs. The heat of his gaze lingered on her as he waited for some response but she couldn't speak as she took in the man before her. His shirt was gone, revealing a toned chest that appeared to be chiseled out of rock. The only stitch of clothing he wore was a pair of faded jeans, sitting low enough on his hips that she could see the curve of his pelvis. "And I thought you were working."

"I was…am. Shit, I need more coffee." He dragged his hand over his face as if that would wipe away his exhaustion.

"What you need is sleep." *No, what we both need is each other. Sleep, work, and worry could all wait.* Something sparked within her and she held out her hand to him. "Come here."

"You're not still having nightmares, are you?" He came to stand in front of her and took her offered hand in his.

A nightmare had indeed woken her but she didn't want to think about that; she wanted to focus on *him*. Leaning into Noah, she looked up at him, their lips inches from each other. "No more hesitating." Then, without giving him a chance to respond, she pressed her lips to his. Instantly, the connection between them sprang to life, allowing the warmth of what he'd explained to be the mating desire burn within her. He ended the kiss all too soon, leaving her craving more.

"Are you sure?"

"Positive." She looped her arms around his neck. "What about work?" As the words left her mouth, she wanted to take them back. She was giving him an opening to stop this before it started. While she might have wanted that before, she didn't want it now.

"It can wait. This can't. I want you now." Slipping his thumb under her chin, he forced her head up enough to give them a better angle as his lips found hers again. He traced his finger down the curve of her neck before coming back up to tangle his fingers in her hair, drawing them closer as his tongue slipped between her lips. "I knew it."

"Huh?" she asked breathlessly.

"I knew you'd taste like sugar. Sweet, sinful, and delicious."

With each kiss, her longing seemed to grow until she met his kisses with an eagerness of her own. She hooked a finger through his belt loop, pulling him against her until she wasn't sure where he ended and she began. This heat and desire was what she had been waiting for. Whatever had changed, she welcomed because she wanted him with every ounce of her being.

He took her hand in his and led her toward the sofa. "We could go upstairs but I need you now."

"I don't care where we are but this is prefect." Every night she had curled up in his bed, since the spare bedroom that had belonged to Liam was now Noah's office with an extra bed just pushed into the corner. It only seemed fitting to have him claim her there in the living room where they spent most of their time together.

Suddenly free of all the things that held her back before, she made quick work of getting his jeans undone enough that she could slip her hand between the rough material and his bare skin. She freed his shaft from the constraints of his boxers, running her hand down the length of his hard-on. Teasing along the length of him as his pants dropped to his ankles, she gave him a moment to step out of his jeans before pushing him down on the sofa.

"What are you doing?"

She slid her hand along his chest, feeling his smooth skin and tight muscles. Then she dropped to her knees before him, trailing her palms down his chest until she could take hold of his manhood. Gently, she caressed down the length of him.

"Sugar." Catching on to what she intended, he wrapped his hand around her wrist.

"Let me." She leaned forward to kiss the tip of him before taking him into her mouth while working his erection at the base with her hand. Groaning, he tangled his hand in the strands of her hair, holding her close. She worked up and down the length of him, milking the life out of him.

He moaned her name before placing a hand on her shoulder. "I can't claim you as my mate like this and I've waited too long for you to hold on much more. I need to be inside of you."

Eagerness filled her now. Letting him go, she straddled his lap. With one quick tug, she pulled the nightshirt she was wearing over her head, leaving herself naked, like him.

He kissed her neck, nibbling down her jawline to her shoulder. She let him have a few more minutes of exploration, since he finally made it to her breasts. Wrapping his mouth around her nipple, he flicked his tongue over the bud, drawing it to full hardness. He teased over the other one, tweaking it until it stood at attention. She moaned in ecstasy when he licked one hardened tip.

"Noah," she gasped, desire rushing through her.

He let her nipple slip from between his lips as he gazed up at her. "What do you want, sugar? Ask and it will be yours." His eyes gleamed and his lips curved up into the cocky grin. He grabbed her hips, adjusting her quickly so she was arched above his shaft. "Ride me, sugar, so I can give these beautiful breasts of yours the attention they deserve."

Purring softly, he caressed every inch of her body, sending moans of ecstasy from her lips. His touch was incredibly tender, as though trying to memorize every curve with his hands and mouth. Heat soared through her blood, like a fire burning just below the skin, impatient and demanding. He kissed a path down her neck, his thumb playing over her nipple. Sensations collided and threatened to overwhelm her. She wiggled her hips, his shaft rubbing against her folds.

"I want you." She arched her back, pressing her chest against his to feel the soft purrs coming from within him through every ounce of her body.

With every touch, he seemed to ignite the fire within her until she was ready to beg for more. She couldn't get enough of him. Dropping his hand between them, he slipped a finger between her folds, finding her clit. Teasing along that bundle of nerves with his thumb, he then delved a finger inside her. A demanding moan she barely recognized vibrated in her throat as she arched toward him, meeting his thrusts.

"Noah!" His name echoed off the walls as she rode his hand. The need for him to be buried deep within her core increased with every stroke.

"Are you ready for this, sugar?" He pulled his hand away before quickly adjusting himself so he could slide his shaft into her.

"Yes. Noah, I need you now!" She dug her nails into his shoulders as she tried to keep from screaming her desire for all to hear.

She wasn't sure if it was her own need or his that had him giving her what she needed. Halting the teasing caresses, he grabbed hold of her hips and eased her down onto him. He kept the pace slow, taking it slowly, filling her inch by inch.

"Faster…please Noah, faster." Halfway in, he slid out before thrusting back in, filling her completely with his manhood. His strokes fed her with heat until a wildfire spread within her. She rocked down on him, increasing the pace as he continued to pump into her.

The tension between them was gone, replaced with a unique understanding of what the other wanted. He'd warned her that the connection between mates was unlike anything she had ever experienced and now that it was beginning to fill her, she understood what he'd meant.

Lean forward. His voice drifted through her thoughts as if he'd said it aloud but he'd gone through their mental link. Even before she did as he asked she knew he wanted to claim her nipple with his mouth, to suck the hardened bud and allow his teeth to graze over the soft skin.

Their bodies rocked back and forth, up and down. Never once did he lose contact with her nipple, nor did he pull too hard to cause her pain. When they moved, they were as one. Her muscles clenched around him as her release neared.

"Noah." His name came out on the edges of a moan as he tangled his fingers in her hair, pulling slightly.

He let her nipple go and brought his mouth up to hers to swallow her cries with a kiss. Their breaths became ragged as he rocked in and out, finding the perfect rhythm, bringing ecstasy within reach. Upon that release, she dug her nails into his shoulders, arching her body into his, her head thrown back in pure ecstasy. He continued to drive his shaft into her, until with one final slam home, his own release followed.

"My gorgeous mate." He held her against his body, his shaft still nestled deep within her as their breathing began to return to normal.

Mate. I'm his mate now. She expected the same feeling of fear to rush through her, but it didn't. His soft purrs vibrated through her, making her want to make love to him all over again while also comforting her, as she adjusted to the new connection between them.

"You okay?"

"Yeah, I'm fine." Exhaustion peeking through, she snuggled against his body. "It's weird. Almost as if I'm looking at the world for the first time. I see things so differently now…clearer."

"You'll get used to it."

While it saddened her to think she'd get used to this—lose the newness of it—she knew she would. Until then, she'd enjoy the fresh insight and allow her outlook on the future to shift to what her life now become. Noah had come to mean something special to her, and while she wasn't ready to admit she was falling in love with him, she understood their lives would revolve around each other until they took their last breaths.

Mated and linked for eternity.

Epilogue

They were no closer to bringing down The Saviors than they had been a few months ago but Noah, Karri, and the others weren't giving up. They hunted down every lead and sought out every witness. They turned what they had over to the police and dealt with what they could handle themselves. This was a shifter problem so they preferred to deal with it on their own. If they wanted to appear as if they were accepting the human law as their own, they needed to delegate some of the work.

Some—not all of it. There was no way Jase, Noah, or any of the others were willing to have their livelihoods decided by someone who didn't understand what it meant to be a shifter. To protect themselves and their kind, they had to defend themselves from threats like The Saviors or others would continue to come after them until all shifters were dead.

Amid all this chaos, Noah and Karri had found some time to celebrate their mating. The doubts she initially had were gone, thanks to the mating bond between them, which allowed her to know she'd never be in the same position her mother had been in. That had taken away a tension that had knotted itself around them.

He slid his hand along his mate's naked body, caressing her sweet curves as she snuggled against him. The caresses had nothing to do with sex, but offered a touch of comfort. Only hours ago they'd received notification of something no one had expected. She had tried to cover up the rage that boiled within her blood by giving her body to her mate. Sex and cuddles afterwards could only do so much. The intimacy had taken her mind off things for a bit, but now it was back and he wanted to be able to take away her pain. "I'm sorry, sugar."

"Me too." She draped her arm around his chest and squeezed him tighter against her. "I never expected my parents, my whole town to…"

There were no words to express the treachery her family and friends had performed when they put a bounty on her head. Once the news that Kat's boyfriend was a shifter reached her hometown, they quickly realized Karri had been keeping company with shifters, and their hatred oozed out. Karri's younger sister, Arlene, had been the one to deliver the news.

"What are we going to do about Arlene?" She tipped her head up toward him. "I can't tell if she's lying. If they're after her because she left home to warn me, then we must do something. But if she's a plant to get to us, the tribe, or any other shifter, I'd rather turn my back on her than have anyone get hurt." After two years of no contact with her sister, for her suddenly to show up was a surprise, to say the least. The whole situation left Karri with mixed emotions as she tried to decide whether she could trust Arlene or not.

"I have Brett watching her now."

"What?" She leaned up onto her elbow.

"She's your sister and she might have risked everything to warn us you were in danger. I could not let her continue to risk her life. Kaden is looking into what Arlene said and if there's anything questionable about it, he'll find out. Kaden's very good at what he does and can find dirt on anyone, no matter how deep it is buried." He caressed up from the small of her back. "If she comes back clean, we'll bring her to the tribe's land. If she's a danger to you…" He let his words trail off, rather than finish off saying what he meant.

"The mating bond doesn't stop communication just because you stop talking." She dropped back onto the bed next to him and rested her head against the curve of his shoulder. "I know that if she's a threat, she'll be handled. I doubt you'd turn her over to the police. Correction—I know you won't. You'll want to deal with it yourself."

"If that's the case, then yes." Appearing surprised, she took in a deep breath if she wasn't expecting him to make the admission, then he added, "Did you expect me to lie? You can feel what I would do so you know I would kill her for bringing danger to my mate."

"Not just me, but the whole tribe."

"But you, sugar—you're the target." The very thought of that engaged his lion, making him want to go after every single person who was part of the bounty on his mate's head. Before his rage got the best of his beast, his cell phone rang. He reached over and grabbed it from the nightstand and read the display. *Kaden.* "And the answer is…" He tried to make light of the situation as he brought the phone to his ear. "What do you have?"

"We have evidence to take to the police that her parents and many in her hometown are funding The Saviors." Kaden's bear was close enough to the surface that his words held a twinge of growling in them.

"Arlene?" His mate went still in his arms at the brief pause, which seemed like minutes ticking by.

"She's clean. She's been in contact with some shifters in hiding and was doing her best to warn them of any activities The Saviors and her parents were up to. They were then getting the information out to others through the Internet. If anything, I'd say she's on our side."

"Call Brett and have him bring her back here. It's already been cleared with Jase that as long as she's clean, she needs protection. Have him put her in cabin two." Noah let out a deep breath that had gotten stuck in his chest. "Thanks, Kaden."

"Anytime, man. I'm glad she's clean."

"Me, too." He ended the call and turned back to his mate. "I told you everything would be okay."

"Not everything. We will have to deal with my parents. If they're funding The Saviors, it has to be stopped."

"We will, but for tonight, let's celebrate having your sister here with us." He pressed his lips to the top of her head. "Trust me, sugar. I'll deal with them."

"I love you, Noah." She tipped her head up so instead of him kissing her head, they could share an actual kiss. "Kiss me."

"I love you too, sugar, and every chance I can get I'll kiss you so you'll never forget you're mine, now and always." He pressed his lips to hers, claiming her mouth with more than just desire, but true love. This was where he was meant to me, where they were meant to be…together.

Bearly Alive

When Becky Lane was introduced to the world of shifters, she found it wasn't as dark as she'd expected. Actually, there seemed to be more good in their world than in her own. So, she accepted them into her life with open arms, but never thought this would bring danger to her and her son, Billy. Without warning, the quiet life she had made for them ended, suddenly blown up. Literally.

After almost a year as Chief of the Crimson Hollow Tribe, Jase is ready for more. He wants his mate. He has so far stood aside as Becky dealt with the demons of her past and opened her heart to shifters—but when his bear alerts him to the peril she's in, he knows it's time to intervene. All the fluctuations in their lives can't hold him back from his mate and the one thing he refuses to compromise on is her safety. He must claim her now or risk his bear going rogue to eliminate the threats to her and Billy.

As the world of shifters turns upside down, Crimson Hollow becomes a beacon of safety for its inhabitants and their allies. Will Jase and Becky's union bring more death and destruction, or is this fated mating of human and shifter just what the tribe needs to beat the enemy once and for all?

Chapter One

The kitchen had never seemed this lonely, Becky Lane thought as she sat sipping her mug of coffee. The newspaper spread out before her on the table reported nothing but negativity. She was tired of the hatred and ignorance contained in nearly every article, especially those concerning shifters. It seemed as if the whole world was against them but it was just one group—The Saviors.

After more than a dozen of their members had been arrested weeks ago, some thought they would begin to crumble but as she read the morning paper, she was beginning to doubt it. There was too much hatred in the words she read for there not to be Savior supporters in the media. Too many articles highlighted shifters in a negative light. She suspected in many of these reports and incidents, the shifters involved had only been protecting themselves or their loved ones.

With each day that passed, she wondered if she shouldn't have taken Jase's invitation to stay in Crimson Hollow with his tribe. The tribe had quickly become family for her and her son, Billy. Now that her mother had passed away, they were all she had left. She had declined the invitation not because she didn't want to be closer to them, but because she was unnerved by her developing feelings for Jase. Feelings she wasn't sure were returned from him.

After saving Billy from his father, Liam and Ginger had been the ones to bring her into their world. Liam's cousin was a lawyer and assisted her when it came to pressing kidnapping charges on her ex. Those kidnapping charges added years to the twenty-five-year sentence he had been serving before escaping and snatching Billy. After the escape, he'd been sent farther away to a maximum-security prison, which gave her more peace of mind thanks to the greater distance between them.

Even with everyone's help getting through the last few months, it was Jase that stood out in her mind. He had been in the background a big chunk of the time, but always seemed to be there when she needed him the most—appearing out of nowhere with a comforting embrace or an encouraging remark. The day her mother died, he'd come to her. He'd never explained what he had been doing there in her area, or even at the hospital. One moment she'd been sitting alone in the waiting room, tears streaming down her face as the doctors rushed her mother in for open heart surgery, and the next he'd been there, comforting her.

"Mommy!" Billy called down to her from his room, where he was in timeout. "I'm sorry. Can I come down yet?"

"Not yet. I'll be up in ten minutes to talk to you about what you said. In the meantime, clean up your room." She leaned forward, placing her forearms on the table and cradling the coffee between her hands. "What am I going to do with him?"

At eight she hadn't even considered swearing in front of her parents because she knew there would be hell to pay if she did. Did the fact that Billy just dropped the f-bomb in front of her mean she was too relaxed as a parent? Being both mother and father to him meant she couldn't afford to screw anything up. If she wanted a well-behaved, respectful child then she needed to keep him in line. She couldn't go soft on him because she was feeling sentimental over the loss of her own mother.

If she had taken Jase's offer and moved to Crimson Hollow, maybe this wouldn't be happening. With Jase, Liam, and the others, Billy would have had strong role models around him. But, she had to be independent and stay there. The trips to Crimson Hollow every other weekend were the highlight of her days, even if she wasn't sure where things were going between her and Jase.

Her cell phone vibrated on the table, pulling her attention back to the present. Jase's name appeared in bold letters across the screen. She should go upstairs and have the conversation she needed to have with Billy, but instead, she found herself sliding her finger across the screen and unlocking the phone. "Hello Jase, I was sitting at the table, thinking about you."

"Get out of the house! Grab Billy and run! I'm on my way."

His words chilled her to the bone, sending dread through her. She didn't think of herself as someone who overreacted but the fear in his voice was something she had never heard before. "Jase?"

"Listen to me, Becky, you have to get out of there."

The mug of coffee fell out of her grasp as she scooted the chair back from the table. "Billy!" With the phone still in her hand, she shot up from the chair and headed toward the stairs. Brushing past the china cabinet, she could see the foot of the stairs in front of her. The short distance seemed to take too long to cross as if she was moving in slow motion, which she knew she wasn't. "Billy, come down—"

The first explosion rocked the house, sending her stumbling backward, away from the old windows that shattered, sending glass through the air. Tripping over something that had fallen, she slammed back into the wall, her head slamming on the china cabinet as she went down. "Billy!" She fought to get up and go to her son but it wasn't over yet. Another explosion rocked the house, collapsing the wall behind her, and sending more debris down on her. Something crashed down on her head or maybe she fell into it, she wasn't sure, but as the darkness closed in around her, she could only think of her son. *Please let Billy be all right…*

It was too late by the time Jase arrived; the damage was already done. In the distance, sirens blared but he wasn't waiting for them. He wasn't even waiting for his guards, Liam or Brett. Brett was the First Lieutenant to the tribe's Deputy's guards, but he was filling in as one of Jase's guards for this rescue. The only thing filling his thoughts was getting to Becky and Billy.

He hopped out of the truck and took off for the house. The front porch had collapsed, blocking the entrance and forcing him to go around the side. His bear raged within him, demanding they find who attacked his mate. *Later*, he promised his beast. The person responsible would suffer immensely for what had happened. *I'm coming, Becky…hold on.*

"Damn it, Jase, wait." Liam jogged after him with Brett directly behind him.

The side of the house didn't look as bad as the front, but there was no telling if more bombs had been set to go off. He could have taken the time to smell the air in search for ammonium nitrate and other materials used in bomb-making, but that would take time he didn't want to waste.

He turned the handle of the back door, expecting it to open, but it was locked. He cursed inwardly at that. But he knew Becky was smart; she wouldn't leave her doors unlocked. He should have realized that and wouldn't have wasted precious seconds trying the handle.

"Get out of the way. Let me get that," Liam hollered as he came to the backdoor.

"Let me check the—"

Jase didn't let Brett finish before he slammed his shoulder into the door. The wood splintered away from the lock, making it easy for him to push it out of the way. The broken door separated from the frame with ease and no explosions followed.

Liam pulled his gun from his holster and pushed Jase to the side. "Don't even."

Jase snarled but didn't stop his guard from doing his job. As long as Liam moved quickly, so Jase could get to Becky, he wouldn't fight him on this. Liam and Brett weren't being led by their animals as he was, so they'd be able to sense any traps before he stumbled into one. The last thing they needed to do was set off any other bombs if they could help it.

Dust and smoke filled the inside of the house, making the air thick and hard to breathe. But that wasn't all they had to worry about. Walls were beginning to collapse around them, and from the looks of things, it wouldn't be long until the whole place was nothing but a pile of rubble. They had to get Becky and Billy out of there before the structure came down around them.

"Are you sure they're here?" Brett took a deep breath, no doubt searching for her scent, but it was hidden by the thick smoke.

"She was screaming for Billy to come down when the first explosion happened. He must be upstairs." Jase scanned his surroundings, searching for any sign of Becky or Billy. His senses weren't able to focus on one thing, which would allow him to quickly single them out, so he took in the whole picture.

"I'll check upstairs." Brett climbed over the debris that littered the area, quickly making his way toward the stairs.

"She's got to be around here somewhere. She'd have gone for him."

"I'll check this way." Liam nodded toward the hall that would lead to the kitchen. "The fire is spreading rapidly. We need to hurry. Another explosion and this place is gone."

"The call…" If Liam heard Jase, he didn't take any notice as he headed the opposite way in search of Becky. If she still had her cell phone on her, they might be able to locate her quicker. Or it could have him searching in the opposite direction. Not seeing any option other than either calling the phone or digging through the already unstable debris, he grabbed his cell out of his pocket and dialed her number. *Please let this work.*

It took a moment for the call to connect and her soft ringtone to echo through the space. Narrowing in on where the noise was coming from, he ended the call and shoved his device into his pocket. Debris surrounded a collapsed wall, but what had him concerned was the support post, which was barely hanging on.

"What was that?" Liam hollered from the other room.

"Keep looking." He wasn't sure if she was under there and until he was certain, he didn't want to pull Liam away from his own search. "Come on, baby." He hopped over the end table that had been knocked over and made his way toward where he thought she might be. Part of him wanted to find her there, while the other part was concerned what shape she would be in if that wall had come down on top of her.

As he lifted a chunk of drywall from the top of the pile, his bear lunged forward, slamming off the internal walls of Jase's body. *Faster.* Her scent drifted toward him, along with the stench of blood. "Fuck!"

"Did you find something?" The sound of Liam's hard sole boots stopped, as he waited for Jase to answer.

"I need your help. Get in here, Liam." Jase didn't wait for Liam. He continued to shift the debris from around her until the beam started to shift, threatening to bring down the rest of the already unstable ceiling. "Hurry."

"Of fuck, tell me she's not under that." Liam came toward him, the gun he held earlier now holstered. "If we don't find something to support this beam, you're going to bring the ceiling down on us."

"No shit. Find something." He shoved more drywall out of the way to reveal Becky's arm. There in her hand she held the cell phone, his name displayed on the screen, alerting her to the missed call. Ignoring the phone, he pressed his fingers to her wrist, feeling for a pulse. Under his touch, her pulse was strong but the sight of the blood that stained her shirt and her limp body urged him to move quicker. He needed to get her uncovered and to safety before anything else could happen.

"I've got Billy!" Brett shouted down from upstairs. "He's alive."

"Get him out of here!" Jase hollered in reply. They might need Brett, but right now getting Billy out of there had to be his priority. "Liam, find something to brace that beam with." Carefully, he continued to move rubble from on top of Becky. Piece by piece—until he found her slumped against the wall. Only a few things stood in the way of lifting her out but before he could move them, they had to brace the beam.

"Becky?" He touched the side of her face, careful to avoid the cut just above her eye. "Baby, can you hear me?"

"Mommy!" In the background, Jase could hear Billy screaming but his attention was on his mate.

"Get him out of here. Take him to the truck and stay with him. If there's any sign of The Saviors, get in and drive. We'll find another way," Liam ordered.

"No, I want to stay with my mom!" Billy fought against Brett's embrace but was no match for the bear.

Jase spun around to face the young boy, careful to keep his body in the way of his view so he couldn't see how bad Becky was hurt. "Billy, the house is unstable and if I'm going to get your mom out of here quickly, I can't worry about you being in danger. Now I need you to go with Brett and I'll bring her out to you in a few minutes."

"Is she going to be okay?" Tears swam in the boy's eyes, making Jase want to go to him.

"Yes." Hoping he wasn't wrong, he tipped his head to Brett, letting him know to get moving.

"Promise?" Billy's gaze stayed on Jase.

"I promise." He waited until Brett and the boy disappeared around the corner before turning back to Becky. "Once I'm sure you're going to be okay, I'm going to hunt down these fuckers and kill them myself."

"Let's get her out of here and keep your promise to that little boy before we worry about that." While Jase was busy, Liam had braced the beam the best he could with the objects on hand. "We're only going to have a few seconds to get this done."

"Are you sure that's going to hold?" Jase took in the brace and he wasn't sure the couple of two-by-fours Liam had used would do more than give them an additional second or two. There was no way they'd hold back the second floor that threatened to come down on them.

"I'm going to hold onto the beam, while you grab her and get the hell out of here." Liam held up his hand, stopping Jase before he could interrupt. "It's the only chance we have. The fire is spreading and the smoke is thick. Wait too much longer and she's not going to have a chance."

"The fire department—" Before Jase could finish his thought, Liam cut him off.

"If we wait for them, the news of her surviving will be all over the place within the hour. This was a direct attack on her and Billy because of her association with us."

"Mr. Mallory. Son of a bitch!" Jase exclaimed, everything seeming to fit now.

Karri Mallory had recently mated with Noah, the guard in charge of protecting Sin—the Deputy of Crimson Hollow Tribe. Only weeks earlier, with the arrival of her sister, they'd found out that not only her parents but most of the town she'd grown up in were tied in with The Saviors. They were working with the police, at least as much as they could, to bring down the terrorist group, but it wasn't an easy task.

Many of the members had been arrested and were currently in jail awaiting their trial. Until they could take down the leaders of The Saviors, they would be a threat to all shifters.

"If you were thinking clearly, you'd realize we need to keep their survival under wraps until we can deal with the issue." Liam tipped his head toward Becky. "Waiting to claim her has been good for her, but your bear has been growing impatient. Now he's angry because of the threat to her. She'd have been safe if she stayed in Crimson Hollow…"

"I'd have known where she was if I had mated with her," Jase snapped, angrier with himself than with Liam. "I know all this."

"Let's do this before you lose your opportunity with her altogether."

"Not going to happen." He crouched down beside Becky, ready to pull her out of the last of the rubble and lift her into his arms. The moment his hand slid along her skin, he knew the injuries were minor compared to what they could have been. She had a concussion, broken arm, bruised ribs, but between the cut above her eye and the gash on her thigh, the worst of her injuries was the blood loss. There was nothing the tribe's doctor couldn't handle. He just had to get her out of there.

"I'm glad Sin sent the others along." The doctor, Ari, and Kaden were waiting at a hotel a few towns over. After Jase and the guards had taken off, Sin called to tell him that she had sent others after him. She knew it was too long of a drive for them to make it back if Becky or Billy had been hurt. Having the doctor close by would give them additional options besides going to a hospital. At a human hospital, there'd be no way to keep The Saviors from finding out the Lanes had survived.

"You ready?" Liam stepped to the side of the beam, preparing himself to hold it up while Jase grabbed Becky. It was dangerous but with the shifter strength, it took some of the risks away.

"Let's do this." As Liam braced the weight, Jase kicked the last chuck of drywall out of the way and tugged her away from the rubble before quickly lifting her into his arms.

"Go!" Liam roared as a piece of the ceiling came tumbling down upon them.

Holding her closer to his body and doing the best he could to shield her from the falling debris, Jase dashed back toward the door they'd come through. The door was in sight when the ceiling gave way, bringing the front of the house down with it. The noise of the walls collapsing was almost deafening and when he glanced over his shoulder he was unable to see his guard through the smoke and dust. "Liam?"

"I'm here. Go!"

Liam's footsteps sounded behind Jase as he jogged toward the truck. The fire department could be seen off in the distance and in moments, the fire engine turned onto her road, several blocks up, leaving their escape window to mere seconds. "We've got to go."

Brett started the engine and unlike before, when Liam was driving, he stayed behind the wheel.

"Get in the back with Billy," Jase ordered Liam as they climbed into the truck. He silently wished for the boy to remain calm.

"Mommy!" Billy hoisted himself up on the back of the seat, trying to swing his leg over so he could get up front.

"She's fine, just sleeping." Liam climbed into the truck, hooked his arm around Billy, and pulled him back into the seat. "Buckle up."

Jase shifted in the seat, using his body as a shield so Billy couldn't see the full extent of Becky's injuries. He hadn't had time to check her thoroughly before he'd moved her but thanks to the connection between them, he already knew there were no spinal cord or neck injuries he had to worry about. With a broken arm, dislocated knee, a couple of bruised ribs, and numerous other cuts, though, she was in bad shape. The loss of blood from her head wound and the deep gash on her thigh had him the most concerned.

The strong pulse that had beat against his fingers when he'd found her was lighter now. They didn't have much time.

"Brett—" Jase hadn't meant to snarl at him but his bear was too close to the surface.

"I'm hurrying." Without braking, he turned the wheel sharply to the left, allowing them to make their turn onto the highway without missing a beat. "Put pressure on it."

Applying pressure, he stared down at her pale face, cursing himself. If he had only claimed her as his mate when his bear wanted him to, none of this would be happening. "Stay with me, baby."

Chapter Two

Two hours had passed and Jase was about to lose his control over his beast. Waiting for Becky to wake up was torture. At first, he was there by her bedside, refusing to leave even when the doctor told him she was okay. There were things he needed to take care of if he was going to take down The Saviors, but he couldn't leave his mate's side.

Liam leaned in the doorframe between the two adjoining hotel rooms, his thumbs hooked in the corners of his jeans pockets. "Billy's asleep."

He glanced behind the guard toward the bed in the other room, but in the dim light he couldn't make out more than a lump on the mattress. The young boy was terrified his mom was going to go away and he'd be all alone. No matter how much Jase, Liam, or even the doctor tried to explain to him she would be okay, he wouldn't believe it. The only thing that would convince him was Becky waking up.

"We need to get back to the tribe. If this was meant as a direct attack on me, they're in danger."

"Soon." Liam glanced at Becky before turning back to Jase. "Once she's awake, the doctor said she can be moved. Until then, it's best if we just wait. Home can wait a little bit longer. Sin and Garret have it under control and there are extra guards on duty. Oswalt's tribe called to offer their help and support. If we need anything, we're supposed to contact them. After Sin and Garret had gone over to help them find the missing child, they feel they owe us."

"They owe us nothing." Even as he said this, he knew if he were in Oswalt's position, he'd feel the same way. Maybe banding together, assisting each other, was what they needed. It would make them stronger and hopefully, he'd be able to take down The Saviors before more people could end up dead at their hands. There had already been too much death, pain, and suffering because of them.

"I told them that, but they insist that they're there to help."

"We might need it." Brett leaned back from the desk where he had been working on Jase's laptop that he just happened to have in his hands when they took off to save Becky.

"What did you find?" Jase was eager to learn anything that could bring The Saviors down and end this war on shifters.

"I hacked into The Saviors' online discussion group and it would seem that they've picked a handful of tribe leaders to go after. From what I can tell, they've selected the easiest ones to target first."

"How the hell are the leaders easy targets? If anything, with the constant guards, we should be harder to get to. Otherwise, Liam is taking his job too seriously. I can't take a piss without reporting it to him." More anger infused Jase's words than he intended. While at first he might have despised having personal guards, they had now become part of his life.

"Sir—"

"Don't give me that sir shit, Brett. You've been with us long enough to know I hate that crap." Jase dragged his hand through his hair and leaned back against the wall. "I don't need it sugar coated; just spit it out."

"They knew about Becky." When Jase snarled again, Brett seemed to stumble over his thoughts for a moment before getting back on track. "I don't just mean that she was connected to the tribe. They know she's your mate. Even though you haven't claimed her, you've marked her, letting any shifters who came near her know that she was under your protection. That is all another shifter should have known. They shouldn't have known she was your mate."

"I'll ask what none of us wants to." Liam stepped out of the entryway and shut the door behind him. "Could it have been a leak?"

"I considered that and would have said it was likely, except it's not just Jase and Becky. Not even just our tribe, though they have Sin and Garret on the list as well. They even have Zoe on there as a target and she's just a child. There are other tribes on there and the information they have on each of them means they either have a lot of spies working for them or…"

"Spies are unlikely. The only ones who know about Becky are people I trust—Sin, Garret, the guards, and Ginger. None of them would have turned on me. I'd know it."

"Are you sure about that?" Liam turned to Jase, watching him for a long moment.

"Am I sure that they wouldn't betray me? You're damn right I am. Otherwise they wouldn't be with the tribe." Jase's bear roared within him. He was already barely hanging onto his control by a sliver of a thread and now that his best friend and lead guard was questioning him, the thread began to fray.

"I meant are you sure you'd know? Delaying the mating has made you preoccupied, not to mention all the issues we've dealt with lately, including The Saviors. Before we consider the alternative to leaks within the tribes, we need to rule out every possibility. Maybe someone said something to someone—"

"Bullshit." Jase stepped away from the wall and went to stand in front of Liam. "Even if I did miss something, you know damn well Sin would have caught it. She'd have known if there was a traitor in our tribe. You standing there saying this bullshit is not only pissing me off, it's making me question if you're in the right position. Your job details do not include questioning your Chief." His fists clenched, he fought to keep his rage at bay.

"Wait a moment." Brett rose from the desk and came to stand by them. "Liam didn't see the rest of the information yet. He's going with the spy possibility because he doesn't want to think of the only other option."

"What option?" Jase didn't take his gaze from Liam as he waited for Brett to answer.

"That they are forcing shifters to work for them."

"Shifters working with The Saviors." Jase voiced the statement to make the words sink in. They had discussed this as a possibility before but to actually believe this was happening was a different matter. The anger disappeared and he stepped back to drop down onto the empty second bed. "Fuck."

"Are you sure we've ruled out the possibility of a traitor?" Liam asked.

Brett gave him a quick nod. "Eight different tribes have their leaders on the hitlist. The likelihood of a spy in each of those tribes is doubtful. You might question if Jase is preoccupied by the delayed mating but I know Sin; she wouldn't have missed it. If we had a turncoat on our land, she'd know it."

"Even if Sin and I weren't as connected with the members as we are, there's no way seven other tribes missed a traitor within their tribe. That's fourteen other leaders. No matter how much we might hate the other option, this one is impossible." Jase glanced back at Brett. "What I don't understand is how we're going to be easy targets."

"Not easy targets compared to shifters in general, but in the case of the leaders, the ones selected are easier to get to than some other tribe Chiefs." Brett tipped his head toward Becky. "She was alone, no protection and no guards."

"Because I didn't claim her." Jase turned to look back at Becky. "I wanted to give her time to accept everything, then her mother became ill and passed away. Everything continued to pile up against us and the timing never seemed to be right. After her mother died, I wanted her to move to Crimson Hollow but she wouldn't. Getting away from the tribe to make the trip up here to see her proved difficult and my bear was growing tired of it. He wanted her but I forced him to wait and now…look at her."

"She's going to be fine," Liam reminded him.

"She was barely alive when we found her." Jase blamed himself. Not only for leaving her where she was in danger, but for what The Saviors had done. They were after shifters and she had been dragged into the mess because of him. Billy had been through enough with his father going to prison and now, he'd lost everything in the explosion. They could never go back there and until The Saviors stopped being a threat, they couldn't go out into the human world without them being in danger. "If it wasn't for your insane driving, Liam, Becky would be dead."

"But she isn't. Sin would tell you to be thankful that your bear alerted you to the danger she was in. If you hadn't called her when you did, she'd be dead. One of the bombs had to be in the kitchen because it was nothing but rubble and fire when I went in."

"They're going after us because we've taken down some of the controlling forces behind them. Their organization is crumbling and this is their last-ditch effort to bring us down with them." Brett stepped over to the computer. "I don't like to admit it but every target on there is someone with opportunity to be eliminated. Becky was alone without guards. Dave Eckhart—"

"The Alpha of the wolf pack outside of Lincoln, Nebraska?" Jase shook his head. "Other packs have tried to take over his pack and failed. He's not an easy target."

"Except he is for The Saviors. They're not looking to take over the wolf pack so they don't have to challenge him legally." He tapped a few keys on the keyboard, bringing up a picture of Dave strolling up a flight of steps outside with a briefcase in his hand, appearing completely unaware that his photograph was being shot. "Businessman by day and Alpha by night. Every time he leaves the wolves' den for work, he leaves behind his guards. He can't appear to be the average businessman if he has pack members following his every move. He'll be eliminated quickly, a victim of opportunity. They know when and where to hit him, just as they did with Becky."

"The discussion group has all of that online?" Liam stepped closer to the desk. "Maybe we can get the police to use it to take down more of The Saviors, or at the very least to protect those that are on the list."

"A former coworker of mine took a position with the FBI. He's a shifter so he understands what's happening here better than some. Unfortunately, due to his position, he's unable to come out as a shifter. So, he'll do what he can. Until then, we're on our own." There was a touch of disgust in Brett's voice that he was unable to keep hidden.

"Do what he can…what does that mean? Is the FBI going to help or aren't they?" Jase was tired of the government trying to play both sides of that matter. Either they were going to give shifters equal rights or they weren't. They couldn't say shifters had the same rights as humans but still allow hunters to murder them and do nothing

"They're having a meeting to discuss the situation because if they send agents to protect those on the list they'll lose their opportunity to take down more of The Saviors. Some of the higher ups are concerned protecting shifters will be seen as the government agencies taking a stance on shifter rights. That could incite further issues because there are some in power that are determined to keep it legal to hunt shifters." Brett let out a deep sigh and shook his head. "They have a fine line to walk and while I've been in their position, I'm not sure which way they'll lean. Damn, I'm glad I'm out of that shit now because it's only going to get worse."

"Then it's our responsibility to alert them to this threat." A soft moan came from behind Jase and he shot off the bed to face Becky. "Brett, I want you to get in touch with everyone on that list; alert them to what is happening so they can take precautions. Tell them they need to continue their day to day lives but to make sure they're safe. If they can take down The Saviors that are sent after them, they should do it. The more threats we eliminate, the more people we can keep safe. Liam, help him get the job done quickly. Then I want the two of you to dig through that discussion board and find out who did this to my mate. I want them dead."

A second moan slipped from her lips and he crossed the room quickly, coming to stand next to her. "Becky…"

"We'll take this into the other room." Liam tipped his head toward Brett who was grabbing the laptop. "We'll leave the door ajar, let us know if you need anything."

Jase nodded at them as he took her hand into his. "Come on baby, open your eyes."

Gently gliding his thumb over the curves of her knuckles, he sat down on the bed next to her. This was the moment they had been waiting for. Doctor Graham assured him that she'd wake up; she only needed time. To wait patiently had taken everything he had in him and nearly drove his bear to the edge. If he had claimed her as his mate back when he needed to, she'd be healed. Instead, he'd let everything get in the way.

Her eyelids fluttered, not quite opening yet, but she was coming to. "Becky?"

"Ah…"

"Stay still baby, I'll get the doctor." He turned to holler toward the door but remembered Billy was still asleep. "Just a minute, Becky. I'll get him."

"Billy…you have to…" Opening her eyes, she stared at him, her eyes full of unshed tears.

"He's fine." As she started to lean up as if to get out of bed, he placed his hand on her chest, gently holding her in place. "Listen to me, Becky. I promise Billy is fine. He's in the other room with Liam. Both of you are safe. You were hurt so you need to stay still."

"Jase." Her fingers tightened around his, holding his hand tight. "Oh, Jase!"

"It's okay, baby, you're safe." He wanted to wrap his arms around her and hold her tight.

"You knew…but how?"

"Later." Now that she wasn't fighting to get up, he removed his hand from her chest and brushed her long blonde hair away from her face. "What matters now is that you and Billy are safe. I want you to rest for a bit longer and then I'm going to take you back to Crimson Hollow."

"My house…"

"I'm sorry." He brushed his thumb along the curve of her cheekbone.

"Excuse me." Doctor Graham stood in the doorway. "I heard Ms. Lane was awake. If you'd like I could examine her now and we could be on our way home soon."

Jase wanted to tell him to come back later, that he wanted to be alone with her for a bit longer, but he had to put her safety above his needs. The longer they stayed at the hotel, the higher the chance of someone finding out she and Billy were alive. He needed to get them back to Crimson Hollow where they'd be safe. "Becky, this is Doctor Graham; he's the tribe's doctor. He's going to check out your injuries and if he okays you for travel, we'll get you and Billy somewhere safe."

"It won't take long." The doctor came forward carrying his black medical bag. His short black hair held strands of silver poking through, and he told anyone that commented on them that they were from the stress of medical school. The silver made him appear older than he really was, while giving him an air of confidence that set his patients at ease.

"I'm just going to step into the other room and check on Billy. I'll be right back." With a gentle squeeze of her hand, he rose from the bed and allowed the doctor to step in and take his place next to her. Walking into the other room and leaving his mate behind in the bed only enraged his bear further.

What did his beast think? That she'd wake up and he'd claim her as his within minutes? That might have been something his bear would have done in the wild but his humanity kept him from even considering it. Good thing, since he was mating with a human and no doubt she wouldn't have appreciated being jumped on after everything she'd been through already. He had to keep it together a little longer and then he'd have his mate.

Chapter Three

Leaning back against the pillows, Becky was thankful she and Billy had survived. According to Doctor Graham, Billy had only received a few scrapes and bruises; for the most part he was uninjured. Becky's injuries were extensive but none of them life-threatening. The pain medication he had given her made her brain foggy and exhaustion was sneaking up on her again.

"The medication I've given you should be enough to get you back to Crimson Hollow. You'll most likely sleep through the ride, but if you wake up and the pain becomes too much, let Jase know." He patted her hand before rising from the bed. "You're very lucky."

"Do you know what happened? I mean, why did someone try to kill us?"

Without meeting her gaze, Doctor Graham dropped the container of pills into the bag. "You'll need to talk to your mate about that."

"Mate?" She'd heard that term before. Liam had used it, but the drugs coursing through her bloodstream made it hard to think straight.

"Ask Jase." He took hold of his bag and marched toward the door.

There was something very military about the way he held himself and walked. She almost asked if he had served in the military, but he was gone before she could get her mouth to work. He disappeared quickly enough that it made her wonder if he was hiding something. Why wouldn't he answer her questions?

She let her eyes close and gave in to the drugs, rather than her fears. Something was off but she couldn't figure it out. She trusted Jase and Liam enough that she believed she and Billy would be safe, but what if the people who'd blown up her house found them?

"Becky." She opened her eyes to find Jase. She'd hadn't heard him come into the room, but there he stood, looking down at her from the side of the bed. "I know you're tired, baby, but let's get you into the SUV before you go to sleep."

"Fir…st…" Her tongue seemed heavy, making the words cling to it. "Why co…come after…me?"

"Becky, the medication Doctor Graham gave you is making you tired. Let's get you into the SUV and you can sleep. When you wake up, I'll answer all of your questions."

"Now." Her eyelids threatened to slam shut and not open again. "Pleas…"

"Because of me." He slammed his hand against the wall, causing the drywall to crumble around his hand. "It's my fault, baby, but I'm not going to let them get anywhere near you again. I'll keep you safe, I promise. You and Billy."

"Bil…"

"He's fine. He's going to ride back to Crimson Hollow in my truck with Liam. They'll be right behind us." He leaned down to adjust the covers around her. "Brett has already made you a bed in the back of the SUV, but I'll tuck you in so you don't get cold. Hopefully, when I lift you, the pills will keep you from feeling anything."

"So tired."

"Close your eyes and rest. It's going to be fine." He lifted her into his arms before she had time to protest.

She tipped her head to the side so that it rested against his chest. Though her ribs ached from the position, she stayed where she was. The spiciness of his cologne drifted toward her, making her want to snuggle in against him.

"Everything is going to be okay." His voice drifted through the fog.

The drugs were pulling her under and she couldn't keep her eyes open, let alone get her mouth to work. *I know. I trust you, Jase.*

Crimson Hollow was the safest place for them right now but even when they were safely tucked behind the perimeter fence and armed guards, Jase couldn't get his bear to settle. He wanted to get them out of the area, away from The Saviors, but there was nowhere safe. The Saviors had groups spread out across the United States, if not the whole world. Even if there existed somewhere secure to send them to, he wasn't sure his bear would allow him to do that without claiming her first.

Now. Mine.

He understood what his bear wanted, but he'd have to wait. Becky was in no shape to allow him to claim her and with the drugs coursing through her bloodstream, it was likely she wouldn't even understand what she was agreeing to. He couldn't force his life on her. If they weren't able to eliminate The Saviors, she and Billy would always be in danger. What kind of life was that for them?

Unable to sit still, he rose from the chair where he had been perched most of the evening and put his laptop aside. Becky was asleep in his bed and every time he looked at her, the urge to go after the bastards who'd hurt her overwhelmed him. He wanted them to suffer for the pain they'd caused her. With Brett, Liam, and Garret working on a lead for who was responsible, Jase was stuck waiting.

The idea behind having Sin's ward, Zoe, watch after Billy for the evening, was for Jase and the others to be able to get some work done. However, for Jase, that was proving impossible. When Jase and the others had arrived home, they found fourteen-year-old Zoe outside waiting for them. He wasn't sure if that was Sin's doing or not, but Zoe had occupied Billy while Jase dealt with Becky. While there were a few years between Zoe and Billy, she seemed to be able to connect with the boy. If she was using her past trauma to connect with him, it was working because he spent the evening safe and content watching movies with her until he passed out.

Even at the late hour, he grabbed the insulated coffee pot that Ginger had brought up to him hours earlier and poured himself another cup. The caffeine had his bear edgy but it was the only thing keeping him going. Exhaustion tugged at him, making him want to curl up in bed next to Becky and sleep. But, the surprise of her waking up next to him might be enough to make her forget about her injuries and try to get out of bed. He couldn't take that risk. She was in enough pain; he didn't need her hurting herself further.

Leaning against the long waist level oak dresser, he closed his eyes and took a sip of the coffee. He hoped the warm caffeinated liquid would be enough to start his circuits firing again. Rather than feel the motivation he needed, though, he only found liquid refreshment. There was no energy to initiate. Nothing left for his body to give. The stress of seeing his mate lying injured and near death had stolen more from him than he'd realized. Closing his eyes, he let his thoughts drift back to Becky's last visit.

"You cooked dinner for me?"

The voice stole his attention away from the candle he was lighting, for long enough that the match burned his finger as it went out. Dropping the match onto the table, he let his gaze slide over her, taking her all in with only the candlelight to light the room. The short black dress she was wearing made him want to strip it off and claim her right then and there. He had to remind himself that this was the start of their relationship. He needed to take it slow with her, not force her into a mating she wasn't ready for.

"It's not much. Spaghetti is about all I know how to cook but my homemade tomato sauce is amazing if I do say so myself. My grandmother taught me how to make it years ago and told me that one day it would be the way into the heart of my girl." He grabbed the bottle of wine off the table and began to pour. "Can I interest you in a glass of wine?"

"Convincing Ginger to watch my son, cooking dinner for me, and now wine. Are you trying to seduce me?" A soft laugh teased into the words as she took the glass from him.

"You deserve everything you want out of life. If you wish to be seduced, I'm eager but I doubt my cooking is going to win me the grand prize. No, tonight is about showing you that shifters are better than what the news portrays us as being."

"I already know that." She brought the wine glass to her lips and took a drink. "I know the people here are nothing like the media makes out. If The Saviors could see this, maybe they wouldn't start this war."

"The war has already begun. The Saviors don't care about us or our loved ones; they only see

us as animals they wish to destroy. It doesn't matter who gets in their way. I believe the government is starting to realize that and hopefully they'll take action before my people have to do something that will no doubt make things worse." He closed the distance between them and took her hand in his. "Tonight we're not going to worry about all the crap that's happening in the world."

"Jase?" Becky's soft voice drifted toward him, forcing his back ramrod straight as he came off the dresser, the memory popping like a bubble.

"I'm here." He sat the mug aside and went to her. "Are you in pain?"

She turned her head so her cheek was resting against the pillow and she was looking at him. "I remember."

"Remember what?" He sat on the edge of the bed, careful not to disturb her.

"I remember what a mate means to you." Her eyelids fluttered shut before she was able to force them back open so she could look at him. "Doctor Graham said I needed to ask my mate. He was talking about you, wasn't he?"

"Ask what?"

"It doesn't matter." She paused before answering his question. "I asked him why they wanted to kill us? What did Billy and I do to have our house blown up with us still inside?"

"Becky…baby, I'm sorry." He reached out to hold her hand. "I should have known…I should have protected you." All the years while Sin was away from the tribe, out in the world all alone, she had been safe. A few months had passed since he'd marked Becky, and she was in danger because of his connection to her.

"So he was right, you know why they attacked us? Did this happen because…I could be way off base here…"

"Because what?" he pressed, wanting to know what she had figured out.

"I'm your…mate."

With a nod, he leaned forward and brushed a few wayward strands of her hair away from her face. "I never meant for you to find out like this."

"So you meant to tell me? How long have you known?"

"I knew the moment I met you." His thoughts drifted back to the first time she'd arrived to visit Liam and Ginger. The moment she'd stepped out of her car, her long hair blowing in the wind, her scent drifted toward him. Realizing who she was, his bear had him strolling across the land toward her. "Your scent drew me to you immediately. I wanted to pull you aside and tell you everything then but I knew what was happening in your life. Billy's father had broken out of prison and kidnapped him from school."

"That's how I met Liam and Ginger. They invited me here, welcoming me into something I never knew before—a family. I mean I had Mom, but that's all. Even growing up, it was just Mom and me. I had always hoped to give my kids—or well, I guess in my case, Billy—more. I wished my husband would have a big family."

"Now you have that." He dropped his hand away from her face. "I screwed up, leaving you unprotected. When you turned down my offer for you to come here to Crimson Hollow, I should have assigned round-the-clock guards to you. Then this wouldn't have happened." With guards, no one would have been able to get close enough to hurt her. Guards would have also smelled the bombs before they went off.

"Do you really think I'd have accepted that? I have a life. I can't have people following my every move. What would the other kids think if Billy had people shadowing him?"

"You're my mate. It's my duty to protect you."

"You say *my mate* like I'm your property."

He took a moment to think about his words before he opened his mouth. If he said the wrong thing, it would only make things worse. She wasn't property, but she was his. To a shifter it was so simple, but when a mate was human it made things more complicated. After witnessing the tension between Noah and Karri as she adjusted to shifter life and accepted him as her mate, he would do whatever he could to make things easier.

"Should I take your silence as admission?"

He dropped her hand and stepped away from the bed. "It's not the same thing. You're not a possession but you're mine. I don't know enough about your culture to explain it better. You're mine to cherish, to love. It's my duty to see that no harm comes to you. We'll be a team. I have a beast within me—my bear—but that doesn't make me different from you. I lead my tribe like I would lead a family…or maybe a better word is an army. Not everyone is trained for duty; some have other responsibilities, but we work together like a well-oiled machine."

"Where do I fit into that?"

"At my side." He wasn't sure if he was getting through to her or making her doubt him more but this was the best way he could explain shifter life and mating to her. "We would lead together."

"What about Billy?"

"He's worried about you." He turned back to her, grinning as he remembered his earlier interaction with the boy. "You've raised a strong little man. He's angry that you're injured and wants to go after the people that hurt you."

"You told him what happened and why? Where is he?" Her eyebrows knitted together and heat filled her eyes.

"Children shouldn't have to face the evils within the world until they're older. No details were shared with him. He begged to see you. After he promised he'd stay with Zoe for the evening and watch movies, I brought him here for a short visit. Don't worry, I had you covered enough that he didn't see your injuries. He only knows you were hit on the head and saw you sleeping."

"He'll find out about them soon enough." She lifted her arm slightly off the bed and looked down at the cast. "I don't understand. Why an air cast?"

"Doctor Graham was unsure about the stage of our relationship." Uneasily, he shifted his weight from foot to foot. "If I could mark my claim on you as my mate then it was pointless to cast the arm. Our bond would heal you quick enough that an air cast would be ideal."

"He said my arm was broken. I can't remember the name of the bone running to my wrist but it's broken. That doesn't just heal in a few days."

"A few minutes for shifters."

"That's great for you but it doesn't help me." She used her good arm to put another pillow behind her, raising her up higher.

"You would be connected to your shifter mate. That connection would heal you—my bear would heal you."

"You think we're ready for that?"

I'm ready. I've been ready since you strolled into my life. Rather than tell her these words, he went around the side of the bed so he was closer to her. "Life is short. Without question, I would love to claim you as my mate right now. I've been working my way to that point with you, trying to move at your pace, because I didn't want to force you into anything. Mating is a big commitment. The connection between mates is unlike anything you've felt before. The bond is deep, allowing you to know what the other is feeling or doing. With you being human, it will come as a shock at first but within minutes of the connection, it will feel like it was always there."

"Is that how you knew I was in danger?"

"Somewhat. There's a fuzzy connection between us now. Do you remember the rabbit ears for televisions? No matter how much you try, the channel won't come in properly; it's mostly a black and white snowy picture but occasionally you get a glimpse of the show. That's what it's like for me now. My bear had been uneasy for the last few days. I assumed he was getting restless about you being unclaimed still. It wasn't until this morning when I woke up that I knew you were in danger. I grabbed Liam and Brett and we raced toward you. I thought you'd be safe at home until I got to you. It wasn't until we were getting off the highway that I knew I wouldn't make it to you in time. I was terrified I was going to lose you."

He was on the edge of scaring her away and instead of calming the situation, he kept on rambling. This woman did something to him no one else had ever done; she knocked him off kilter. When they were together, he wasn't sure what to stay. Going with his natural instinct would only send her away screaming because his bear would lead the way and frighten her away from the shifter world. Not that he was going to let her go. She was his mate and somehow, he'd convince her they belonged together.

Chapter Four

Alone in the bedroom, Becky couldn't untangle her jumbled thoughts. She wasn't sure how to react to what she learned. Part of her thought she should be scared but Jase didn't provoke that reaction from her. He was caring and the way he put his tribe's needs above his own was admirable. When Liam had invited her there, Jase was the one who made her feel welcomed. He'd made sure she knew she was part of their family, even going as far as inviting her and Billy to a family dinner he'd had with his sister Sin, her mate, Garret, and their ward, Zoe. Before then, she'd thought the reason for the invite was just so she could see them interacting together, to put her mind at ease about shifters. Now she was realizing he'd done it because he believed she was his mate.

Her thoughts flashed back to a conversation she'd had with Ginger on her last visit.

There was a slight breeze in the air, warning them that winter would be there before she knew it. As much as she looked forward to their trips to Crimson Hollow every other weekend, she expected this to be their last visit before the snow came and she hated it. Once winter set in, she wasn't sure about making the drive. It took too many hours on the road with just her and her son. Too many things could go wrong.

"You look like you could use this." Ginger sat down next to her on the bench and handed her a glass of wine.

"Thanks." Watching Billy play with some of the other children, she took a drink of the wine. "There's something peaceful about life here."

"There is. It's so unlike where I grew up, but I guess that's why I love it here." Ginger sipped on her wine before glancing over at her. "I know Jase asked you to stay. Why don't you?"

"I can't..." She wasn't sure why she couldn't. Maybe she was too independent or maybe she wanted more from him. Even knowing she might not see these people for months, she couldn't bring herself to agree to stay there.

"I've never been happier than I am here. Some of that is Liam's doing but there's more to it than that."

"You have a special relationship with Liam." Becky tried to keep the jealousy from her voice. She wanted what the two of them shared, but all she found were men not worth her time.

"Mating is something you can't deny. It's in your bones and every ounce of you wants to be with that person. When I found Liam, I wanted to run, but when I saw him with Billy, I knew he wasn't like the other lions I'd known in the past. It forced me to open myself up to him. I'll never regret that."

Ginger was right; there was something between her and Jase that she couldn't deny. An electrical pull that tugged her toward him. With each visit to Crimson Hollow, she found herself looking more and more forward to spending her time with Jase. The one time when he had been called to a neighboring tribe and hadn't returned until she was in the car ready to leave had seemed like the loneliest visit. She'd spent time with other tribe members but the one she really wanted to be with—Jase—was nowhere to be found.

Days later, he showed up at her doorstep, just minutes after she'd put Billy to bed. Those hours they spent together then brought them closer than all of her visits to that point. There was something different about him coming to see her and just being alone with her. No interruptions from other members or tribe business coming up. It was as if they were alone for the first time.

That night, as she was lying in bed, her thoughts full of Jase, she realized she was falling in love with him. Excitement bubbled within her at the thought of him staying at a nearby hotel so they could spend the following day together before he had to get back to his tribe.

That had been his first visit to her but it wasn't his last. He was there whenever she needed him. The moment that stood out in her memories was when he showed up at the hospital after her mother passed away. He'd never explained why he'd driven there, hours from his home, and at the time she let it go because she was grateful for his presence. That night he'd gone home with her and held her until she fell asleep. He had been there through every moment of the days that followed, helping her get through the grief, and doing what he could with funeral arrangements for her. To some it was just an extra hand; to her it was something she'd always be grateful for.

Jase hadn't been just there for her; he had been there for Billy, too. Since Billy's father was in prison, he had been lacking a male role model until Jase came into their lives. It wasn't just Jase that stepped into the role, but also Liam, Noah, and the other tribe members. Everyone had become a rock for both of them. Knowing that they'd accepted her son helped to ease her mind when it came to having a relationship with Jase.

"Relationship, is that even what this mating is?" She let out a deep sigh, wondering how she was going to handle things when Jase came back from getting her a drink.

"It's a closer relationship than anything you've ever experienced." She turned to find Jase standing in the doorway, a glass of water in his hands and a small prescription bottle in the other. "Doctor Graham has left pain medication for you."

"I'm fine for now." As he came into the room, she sat up enough to be able to take a drink. There was too much for her to think about to take any medication. Less than twenty-four hours earlier, her life had seemed normal. Her biggest problem was Billy swearing and her wondering where things were going with Jase. Now she still hadn't had the conversation with her son about swearing; not that it seemed like that big of an issue any longer. Things with Jase seemed to be clearer yet more confusing all at once. There was something between them—this mating; she just wasn't sure how to move forward.

He waited for her to take a drink before setting the glass on the nightstand. "I understand that mating is new to you. Besides the connection that's shared between us, it's no different than what human couples have. You'll still have a relationship; it will just be on another level, a deeper one. Mating would bring us together as husband and wife. I would be a father to Billy and hopefully, in the future, we can have another child or more. I understand if you're concerned about Billy but he already knows I'm a shifter and doesn't seem to have a problem with it. The time you've spent here has gone smoothly."

"Billy likes you. When we're home, you're all he ever talks about. He marks down the days on his calendar until we can come back here." Her fingers played along the seam of the blanket as she realized Billy would be happy in Crimson Hollow. "Last week he had an issue at school; another kid was making fun of him for not having a dad. When I picked him up that day, he wanted to know why he couldn't go to school here. This is where all of his friends are and he was angry at me for keeping him where he wasn't happy."

"Doug is the same way. On Friday when you're coming for a visit he sits at the picnic table where he can watch the gate and waits. During the week, he seems lost without Billy here."

She could picture the little redheaded boy sitting there waiting until her car came through the gate and then he'd come charging toward them. During each visit, Doug and Billy were inseparable, spending the whole weekend together, so much so that one would sleep over at the other's house. From the first day, the two boys had formed a quick friendship that only seemed to grow with time.

"So, that's why he's always the first to greet us." She let out a lighthearted laugh, sending pain sparks through her chest, until she reached up to grab her bruised ribs.

"You okay?" He reached toward her, laying his hand over hers where she held her side.

"Damn ribs, they're more painful than my broken arm."

"I'm just glad the ribs aren't broken. I thought they were but Doctor Graham ruled that out back at the hotel." His thumb teased over her knuckles. "Why don't you take the pain pill and get some rest?"

"Not yet." She moved her hand away from her ribs and took his hand in hers. If he was surprised by this move it didn't show on his face; instead, he slipped his fingers between hers. "Do you know why I refused to stay when you asked me?"

"No. If I did, I would have done whatever was necessary to change your mind."

"I couldn't stay without knowing what was happening between us." Nervous, she kept her gaze on their interlocked fingers and away from his face. "We were spending more time together but I wasn't sure where things were going. There was this connection between us, drawing me to you, but I needed more. You were busy with the tribe and trying to take down The Saviors…I wasn't sure where I fit into it all."

"I already told you. You belong by my side. We're supposed to lead this tribe together and together we'll be stronger."

"I don't see how. If anything, as a human, I'm a weakness to you and your rule. You need someone strong by your side." It pained her to say the words but she needed him to consider what he was saying.

"You're not a weakness." He took his hand out of hers and reached up to cup the side of her face. "You're the woman I want by my side. You'll keep me grounded and sane. Your humanity will make sure my bear instincts don't rule me, making me rash. While the world is screwed up, our lives together will be filled with happiness. I let The Saviors get to you once because I was stupid, but I'll spend the rest of my life keeping you safe. I'll make this up to you."

"You have nothing to make up for. The Saviors made their own choices. They are the ones who attacked me and they will have to pay for that. Not you." She took a deep breath and let it out again. "At first the idea of mating with you scared me. I wasn't sure what to make of your bear. Ginger said you had a tendency to be grumpy but I don't see that. Your bear is always there and when you're angry I can hear the snarl in your voice. Even with all of that, I've never once worried you'd lose control and hurt me. What I'm trying to say is that I've known for weeks that I'm in love with you. It's just the next step that seems overwhelming."

"Nothing has to be decided tonight. Sleep on it." He slid his fingers down the curve of her neck before teasing along her collarbone. "We can wait as long as you like. Mating only came up now because of the air cast. It could have waited. You've been through enough today. I'm not demanding that you submit to me claiming you."

"You'd like that though, wouldn't you?"

"Shit, baby…" He dragged his hand through his hair. "Damn right I'd like that. I've wanted to make you mine since you stepped foot in Crimson Hollow. My gorgeous mate, you fill my dreams every night and hopefully soon, you'll fill the empty spot in my bed."

"Umm…" A cocky grin stretched across her lips. "I believe I've already accomplished that." She was in his bed but she was alone. She knew he meant them sleeping together but she couldn't stop herself from making a smart ass comment and easing some of the tension that lingered around them. "How about we start with that and go from there? I know that your guest bedroom is empty and you're not sleeping on the sofa. Come to bed and get a good night's sleep. Tomorrow all our problems will still be there."

"I need to—"

She reached out and pressed her finger to his lips. "The stress of the situation and worrying about me has left you exhausted. More than that, I want to feel your touch as I go to sleep. Maybe it's the mating bond or whatever but when you touch me, I know everything is going to work out. I need that right now." She needed him without all the strings, mating, and stress surrounding them.

Chapter Five

Waking up with his arm slung over Becky's waist should have been a joyful moment for Jase, but his first thought wasn't about his beautiful mate; rather, it was about the bastards who'd hurt her. He wanted revenge and his bear was eager to dig his claws into whoever was responsible. When he'd found her under the rubble, her pulse was weak from the loss of blood due to the deep gash on her thigh. Now, her color was returning and her injuries—concussion, bruised ribs, broken arm, and dislocated knee—were minimal compared to what they could have been. Even if she let him claim her, it would take time for her to get better, but the important thing was, she *would* heal.

Lying there when there was work to be done wouldn't stop The Saviors from going after one of the others on their list. He needed to go and get some work done. If luck was on their side, they might be able to save someone else from suffering the same fate as Becky or worse yet, get killed. "Sleep well, baby. I'll be close by." He pressed his lips to the top of her head and slipped out of bed.

Thankful she didn't stir, he quickly dressed and grabbed his laptop that was still sitting on the dresser where he'd set it before. Picking up his cell phone nearby, he shot Liam a text message. *Need an update now. I'll put the coffee on.*

The hour was early enough that he questioned if Liam was awake but he needed to conduct a meeting with his team before Becky woke up. He'd be briefed by Liam before meeting with the rest of the team to see what everyone had gathered throughout the night while he was busy attending to his mate.

Downstairs, he placed his laptop down on the table. Even though it was in his dining room off the kitchen, he couldn't consider it a dining table. This was where he met with the rest of the leaders of the tribe—Sin, Garret, and their trusted guards, Liam, Noah, Brett, and Roger. Sometimes, Ari and Kaden joined them to iron out the security aspects of things, since they handled that business for the tribe. This space was more for handling tribe matters than for eating. He pressed the brew button on the coffee pot that was ready for him and wondered if that would change now that Becky and Billy were in his life.

Numerous times during the week, everyone would gather together. There were enough picnic tables for everyone, as well as a large outdoor kitchen that some of the wives used to prepare the food for everybody. Barbeques could be fired up and since Garret had joined them, he'd taken over as barbeque king. He managed the grill like no one ever had and everything came off tasting delicious. On other nights though, he suspected that with Becky and Billy in his life, he'd be expected to have family meals just like Sin, Garret, and Zoe managed, as much as her schedule would allow. No longer could he just grab a quick bite in the middle of handling things. He'd have a family and he wasn't about to neglect them. He had waited his whole life for them and now that he had them, he'd find a way to balance tribe business with his instant family.

Standing in the kitchen at the back of the house, he could hear the key turn in the lock as Liam let himself in. He turned back to the coffee pot and paused it so he could pour two mugs for them. "Back here."

"How's Becky?" Liam strolled into the kitchen looking as if he hadn't slept.

"Resting. Worried about Billy. Stressed about the attack on her and her son." He could go on but that seemed to cover it. Instead, he focused on stirring the honey that he'd added to his mug, into his coffee.

"Billy's good; we had a chat last night before Zoe put him to bed. As a shifter, that boy would have been an Alpha. He's strong willed and determined to make the bad man pay for his sins. His words." Liam leaned against the counter and shook his head. "Sin offered him the guest room but when he didn't seem happy about that, Zoe said he could stay in her room. They used a blowup mattress and fell asleep while watching movies. But before he'd go in there he made me check the room for the bad man."

"Did you explain…" He wanted to say that the bad man couldn't get to them, but as safe as the tribe's land was, there was always a chance they could be attacked. No matter how much he wanted to, he wouldn't make promises to Billy that he couldn't keep.

"I told him we were safe here. That with all the shifters around we'd smell any bad men before they got to him."

"Creamer is in the fridge." Jase handed Liam a mug of coffee. "Then join me at the table."

"Black…strong and black is what I need this morning. It's been a long night." Liam followed Jase, bringing his laptop with him. As he sat it down, he pulled it open, bringing it out of sleep mode. "The night brought good and bad news."

"Right about now I'd take the good news but something tells me that after I hear the bad I'll need something positive, so give me the bad first." Needing the caffeine, Jase brought the mug of steaming hot coffee to his lips and took a long sip. The heat burned his tongue but it barely fazed him.

"I know you want to go after The Saviors for those who blew up Becky's house, but the two responsible have already been apprehended by the police."

"What?" Jase roared. "Who gave the cops the information?"

"It wasn't…"

"Jase?" Becky called out to him from the upstairs bedroom. "What's going on?"

He sat his coffee aside and went to the bottom of the steps. "It's okay, baby. I didn't mean to wake you. Are you okay? Do you need a pain pill?"

"No." Her voice held a touch of pain. "I'm fine. I just…are you sure everything's okay?"

"I swear, baby. Liam's here, I need a few more minutes with him but I'll be up shortly and I'll fill you in. Holler if you need anything." Cursing himself for being so loud that he'd disturbed her rest, he gripped the banister until he was concerned the wood would splinter.

"Jase." Liam calling his name brought him back to the moment. "It wasn't us. The neighbors called two weeks ago. While Becky was visiting us, someone was lurking around her house. I guess they were scouting out the place because they're the ones that returned yesterday. Minutes before the house exploded, the neighbor saw the guys leaving. She didn't think much of it, figured they were visiting Becky, but when the police questioned her, she mentioned it. Turns out the market at the corner caught them on camera as they walked back to their getaway car. She identified them."

"Fuck!" Jase walked back to the table and took a long drink from his coffee as he tried to figure out their next move.

"The police served a warrant before we could have done anything. The house they lived at was a front. They rented it a month ago but neither of them had much there, at least not personal possessions. Bombs, tracking devices, an arsenal of guns, grenades, and pretty much anything else you could think of. They were ready for war and the targets were us." Liam clicked a button on the computer, bringing up images of the supplies that were found. "Immediately after the police arrived at their place, they announced they were doing the work of The Saviors. They were saving humanity from shifters and even if they were arrested, there would be more death. It didn't take the police officers long to get a full confession from these assholes."

"Have the other targets been alerted?"

"All except Dave Eckhart. He had left for work before we could get in touch with him but he never arrived. There's no sign of him. His brother Derek, the pack's Beta, has people out searching for him."

Jase glanced at the microwave clock. It was too early to call Derek, but he'd make sure he did it soon. His men had been in touch with the man but it wasn't enough; Jase needed to make contact himself. If there was anything they could do, he'd get someone on it. "Can't Kaden track Dave's cell phone?"

"We've already tried that. The phone's off but Kaden will be alerted if it's turned back on. We're doing all we can." Liam polished off his coffee before rising and pouring himself another mug. "I know it doesn't seem like it but we are. Besides Dave, everyone's safe. They're taking precautions."

"You're damn right, it doesn't seem like enough. How many more will die before we can stop The Saviors?" Movement out the kitchen window caught his attention. Members of his own tribe were at risk but he hadn't considered alerting them until that moment. *Shit!* "The members that leave for work, have they been alerted?"

"None of them are on the list but Sin wasn't willing to take the chance one of them would get hurt because we didn't tell them. Late last night she took matters into her own hands and, with Garrett's help, they've been alerted." Leaning against the kitchen counter, Liam took another sip. "A couple of them are going to work from home or use personal days. There are a few who have to leave. We've given them a tracking bracelet so if anything happens, we'll know where they are. The guards on gate duty have a list of names of those who can exit the territory. If their name isn't on the list, they're not allowed to go. No one is leaving here unless it's cleared through us."

"Let's hope it won't come to that but if it does, are you sure the trackers will be good enough?" Jase didn't want a repeat of Dave's cell phone. If one of his members went missing, he wouldn't stop until every rock was overturned and they found the missing member. These were his people; it was his duty to protect them—no matter the cost.

"The trackers are better than anything on the market—Ari and Kaden designed them." Jase felt Liam's lion edge forward, aggravated with the situation, before he regained control. "I know you're frustrated; I am, too. I wanted the fuckers that went after Becky and Billy. The need to tear them limb from limb is as close to blood lust as I've ever had. This is personal; they fucked with our family."

"We have to remember that it was done on the orders of The Saviors. They're the ones we need to go after. They'll feel our rage soon enough." It was either that or Jase was worried his bear would break through his control and go on a rampage. The rage that burned within him had his bear ready to kill anyone who looked at him the wrong way. Anyone who hurt his family was in danger. Where Liam wanted to rip them limb from limb, Jase wanted to tear them into little pieces. To identify the body, someone would have to put the world's smallest piece jigsaw puzzle together. When he was done, it would be nearly impossible to tell that the pile of blood and gore had at one time been a human being.

Run, fuckers. I'm coming for you.

Chapter Six

Three days after the attack, Becky had reached the end of her tether. Enough of the pain, and also fed up with not being able to do everything she needed to do. A little thing like going to the bathroom had suddenly become a challenge. With the dislocated knee, Doctor Graham had ordered a leg split and she wasn't allowed to put her weight on it. Crutches were impossible to hold with her broken arm, leaving her stuck in bed unless someone was around to help her.

The loneliness was getting to her more than anything. Jase tried to spend as much time with her as he could and when he couldn't, Ginger or some of the other members would stop by, but it wasn't enough. When she was in Crimson Hollow, she was used to being surrounded by everyone. Being stuck in bed with her leg up was making her stir crazy.

Now that Billy knew about her injuries, though they'd sugarcoated how bad they were, he'd stop by a couple of times through the day to check on her. He'd stay for a bit before he grew tired of being cramped up in the room and want to go play with Doug. Ginger and Zoe had agreed to watch over him, so she knew he'd be fine. At least she tried to tell herself that. They were safe there, but after everything she had been through, she'd rather be watching over him herself.

Most of the time she was alone with her thoughts, which gave her lots of time to think about what was happening with her and Jase. During one of the times Ginger had stopped by for a visit, Becky had questioned her about mating. She needed to know everything about it before she could commit herself to Jase. Asking Jase would have given her the answers too but she needed time to sort through it all on her terms, without his influence. Ginger allowed her to do that.

"I'm back." Ginger strolled into the bedroom, a brown paper bag in her hand.

"It's about time."

"Liam wasn't thrilled with my run into town, so this better be worth it. You've got to tell me what's going on before I give you this." She pulled a tub of cookie dough ice cream and two spoons out of the bag. "Otherwise I'm going to stand here and eat this whole carton by myself, teasing you with every bite."

"Too bad I don't have crutches or I'd beat you with them to get that ice cream." She tossed the book she had been reading aside and held out her hand. "Get over here and give me a spoon."

"I'd love to see you wobbling after me on crutches." Ginger let out a lighthearted laugh as she tossed the bag on the dresser. "Forget that, Jase would kill me if you got hurt over ice cream."

"Jase…" The very mention of him sent her heart fluttering. "Things are complicated there."

"You mean because he's your mate?" Ginger sat on the edge of the bed and pried the ice cream container lid off.

Becky's jaw dropped open in surprise and she could feel her eyes widen. "How…I mean…"

"Don't act all flabbergasted. Any shifter could have smelled his mark on you from a hundred yards away." Ginger held out one of the spoons to her before digging her own into the ice cream.

"Mark? I don't even know what you mean."

"He didn't tell you that he marked you?"

"No." Becky looked down at the spoon in her hand and suddenly wasn't in the mood for ice cream any longer. "Does that mean he claimed me as his? If so, why's he saying he needs to claim me? How could he do this without my permission…without even mentioning it to me?"

"Marking isn't the same as completing the mating." Ginger stuck her spoon in the ice cream and set the carton aside. "When he marked you, he did it with his scent. Once you're mated, his scent will mix with your natural one and it will be something you always carry with you. Any shifter that comes in contact with you would know you're his mate and that messing with you would bring Jase down on them, not to mention the whole tribe. I know it sounds confusing since marking and mating can overlap, but what he did by marking you was for protection. It would let anyone who could smell you know that you were under his protection. Sometimes, shifters mark friends of the tribe to keep them safe."

Silence stretched out between them as Becky tried to take everything in. How long had she carried Jase's mark? Was that why she had been attacked? Had Billy been marked? Or didn't Jase think that Billy needed the protection? She had more questions than she had answers but she would figure it out. "If friends of the tribe can be marked, then how did you know I was his mate?"

"Being tribe members, we're connected to Jase; it was just something we knew through the connection. It was never announced to everyone and, to be honest, Jase tried to hide it at first. I think he wanted to see how everyone would react to you without him interfering. Not that he had to worry; everyone here loves you. You fit in like you always belonged. Look at Billy and Doug—they're best friends."

"Is this mark the reason we were attacked? I know The Saviors will attack humans if they associate with shifters, guilty by association in their minds, but did they find out because of Jase's scent on me?" Even though the answer wouldn't change anything, she had to know. Could she have somehow stopped this all from happening? If he had told her about the mark, maybe she could have done something. She doubted that because it wasn't like she could tell who was a shifter and who wasn't just by looking at them. That train of thought led her to wonder how The Saviors knew who to attack. Surely, they couldn't stalk each prey before they went after them. If anyone knew, it would be Jase. She made a mental note to ask him about that later.

"We don't know how The Saviors found out about your relationship to us or to

Jase, but Jase and the others are working on it. You carrying his scent was just one of the ways someone could find out." Ginger paused for a moment, as if debating what she wanted to say next. "Every time you left here, another shifter would have been able to tell you had been around us. There would have been a lingering odor of our beasts on you. It would have worn off in a few hours, since it would have just been from brief close contact, but it would have been there long enough for anyone you encountered on the way home to realize where you had been."

"So, I set this in motion from the start." It came out more as a statement then a question but before Ginger could reply, Jase strolled into the bedroom.

"Bullshit, Becky. You know better than that. Those assholes look for any excuse to go after us and to them you were just as bad as a shifter because you were friendly to us." He dropped the bag on the bed and ran his hand through his hair. "Shit, there have been attacks on humans from The Saviors for less than what you did. Do you remember the mechanic that was attacked in his shop after hours a couple of weeks ago? The Saviors did it to send a message. Any association with a shifter will get you killed. All he'd done was change their flat tire. Yet, he nearly ended up dead for that."

"I should go." Ginger rose from the bed and grabbed the ice cream carton. "I'll put this in the freezer for you."

"Thanks." A twinge of guilt hit Becky as Ginger got up to leave. The idea that Ginger had gone into town to get the ice cream and they were supposed to talk, and now Jase was here and she was running off, made Becky feel terrible. But they had a few things to discuss.

Ginger paused next to Jase. "Sorry. I didn't realize you hadn't told her that you marked her."

"Go." His commanding tone left no room for questioning and Ginger scurried past him.

Becky wanted to say something but she didn't know what would make the situation better. Jase was in charge of the tribe and the last thing she wanted to do was make things harder on Ginger, so she kept her mouth shut. At least until the front door banged shut and she turned her attention to him. "What was all that about? If anyone here should be angry it's me. Why didn't you tell me? Better question yet, why didn't you ask me?"

"I was giving you time to handle—"

"Don't give me that shit." She dropped the clean spoon that she still had in her hand onto the comforter and looked at him. "Everything I've learned about this mating process showed me it's not easy to hold back the urges of your animal. You were taking things slow, spending time with me while I was here, coming to see me at my home, and all the while your bear was demanding that you claim me. Why would you suffer with that without even telling me?"

"When would have been a good time? Should I have blurted it out the first time we met? Or perhaps during the court case as you fought to make sure Billy's father could never hurt him again? Would your mom's funeral have been a good place? Tell me, Becky, when would you have been open to this news?"

"How dare you?" Angry and not thinking, she grabbed the pillow on the other side of her and threw it at him. Those might have been the worst days to tell her but there had been other days that presented a better opportunity. When her ex had escaped from prison and kidnapped their son, she had been shaken to the core. She'd thought he wouldn't be a threat to them any longer, then all of a sudden, that danger had resurfaced out of the blue. She hadn't been sure how to deal with that, so she'd confided in Jase.

Now here he was, making excuses. Without hesitation, he grabbed the pillow midair and tossed it back on the bed, but far enough out of her reach that she couldn't get to it without causing herself pain. "How dare I what?"

"How can you turn this around on me? There were plenty of occasions when you could have told me. What about the countless dinners we shared together? The long chats we'd have once Billy went to bed? The day you were visiting and we took Billy to the zoo?"

"There was no perfect way to tell you about the mating. I've considered it a hundred times since you came into my life but I always put it off. Maybe I'm selfish but I wanted to spend the time with you. I wanted those visits to be special. I didn't want to fight about marking you because I needed to do that for your protection." He came around the bed to sit next to her. "Becky, it's not just my bear that wants you. *I* want you. I love you. Every moment I spent with you, I wanted to be special."

I love you. With those three little words, the air from her lungs escaped at once, leaving her breathless. If she had taken one of the pain pills from Doctor Graham, she'd have thought they were playing tricks on her ears but she hadn't had one since the night before. She needed a clear head to figure out what was happening between them and now that he'd just said he loved her, she was glad none of the medication was still circling within her bloodstream. She wanted this moment to be something she would always remember.

"I love you, too." The words came out in a low whisper but from the glistening in his eyes, there was no doubt he'd heard her. "I wish you'd have told me about all this sooner. If I'd have known I was your mate, it would have changed things. For weeks now I've been trying to determine where things were going with us. I knew what my feelings for you were but I wasn't sure if things were the same for you. There were times when we were alone that I thought there was something happening but other times I wondered if I'd imagined the whole thing."

He took her hand in his and let his thumb glide over the knuckles. "I never wanted you to question things. You were going through so much that I didn't want to add to it. Billy's safety had to be our priority. The last thing you needed during the trial was additional stress."

"What's a little stress?" She tried to make a joke of it, but it fell flat. "I was a mess then. After what happened I was terrified to allow Billy to go back to school. I was terrified of a rehash of what had happened. I couldn't trust them to keep him safe—not until the principal showed up on my doorstep a few days after the incident."

"I know." He squeezed her hand. "Kaden and I went to speak with him."

"You what?"

"Hear me out. We went to speak with Mr. Howell because Billy needed to be in school. Kaden's presence and the fact his security company is well known helped Mr. Howell accept our suggestions. We had a couple of guys who were able to install the fence around the playground that day. Even though Billy was taken from the playground, Kaden repaired the card readers at the doors so they could be secured. This made sure visitors to the school had to go through the office before gaining access to the building. After the children were dismissed, the teachers were briefed on security measures. There are always going to be threats out there, but we did what we could to make it a safer environment to ensure Billy's safety."

Silently, she sat there and took in his words. He had gone out of his way to make sure her son was safe and that meant the world to her. More than that, he'd never told her, never sought out the credit for it. "He never said…you never said."

"I told him we were there representing you, so I'm sure he figured you already knew."

"Why didn't you say something?"

"I didn't go see Mr. Howell to win points with you. I went because I wanted Billy safe. No parent should have to worry that their child could be kidnapped from the playground during a school day. Billy's father was back in prison and there wasn't a chance they were going to let him escape again, but the peace of mind you received from the new security measures made it worth it." He paused, letting his gaze meet hers for a moment. "I wanted you to come here. Billy could go to school with the other kids and both of you would be safe."

"Does that offer still stand?" Nervous, she bit her lip. One thing she'd realized since she woke up to find him by her bedside was that she wanted to be there with him and the tribe. Not simply because she was safe there—because maybe it was no safer than anywhere else, except they took extra precautions. She wanted to be there because they were her friends and family. With them, she felt as though she belonged.

"Always, baby. Always."

He leaned forward to press his lips to her cheek as he had done before. This time, she wanted more. At the last second, so he wouldn't stop, she turned her head, allowing his lips to find hers.

There's no going back…

Chapter Seven

As their lips met, Becky grabbed the front of his shirt. She had planned to only stop him from pulling back but instead, she drew him closer to her. Just that fast, the kiss tore away all her hesitation and opened a door between them. She'd wanted him before but now, there was no holding back. "Don't stop."

"Becky…" Her name escaped his lips on a growl. "You have to be sure about this."

"I'm sure." She tugged his shirt out of the waistband of his jeans, dragging it up to reveal his chest. "I want you, Jase. All of you."

"Is this because I went to speak with Mr. Howell?" He pulled back enough that he could look at her.

"No." She continued to tug his shirt upward but with one hand it was impossible to get it over his head. "I've been thinking a lot about this mating and while I was upset that you marked me without talking to me about it first, I want this. I want *us*. Ours might be a relationship that's out of the box, nothing like the kind I was raised to expect or believe they should be like, but that doesn't change anything. I know you'll treat Billy as if he were your own son; otherwise I wouldn't even consider this. He's been through enough and doesn't need me getting involved with someone who will treat him as less than he deserves. Especially if we have more children."

"You don't have to worry about him. He'll be my son. As for more children, there's no if, it's only when. One day I'll have to pass the tribe on to our child and as much as I love Billy, it can't be him. A Chief can be challenged for his position and Billy would never stand a chance against an Alpha shifter. He will always have a place here with the tribe but I will not put him in a position where he'd have to fight for his life against a shifter wanting to take over the tribe."

"Challenged? You mean fight to the death? Someone could challenge you for the role of tribe leader? What if you're killed?"

"Shh, baby." He scooted closer to her and ran his hand down her arm. "Nothing is going to happen to me. For someone to come here and challenge me, they would have to have a death wish. I'm a strong Alpha and my tribe follows me. They're not revolting and they'd never follow an outsider."

"Did I ever tell you parts of the shifter world are downright barbaric?" Her hand stilled, no longer trying to pull the shirt over his head. "It's scary."

"There are differences in every society and every group has their own brutal ways. Your world is dangerous as well but you accept it because you've never known anything else." His fingers brushed along the top of her air cast before moving back up her arm. "I should have kept quiet about that but I wanted you to understand that I couldn't hand the tribe over to Billy. It would be too dangerous for him…and for everyone."

"I never thought of him taking your position here. Heck, I didn't even consider it for a child that we created together. I guess if you'd have asked I would have said you worked for that position, not given it because of family ties." It was clear and not for the first time that she didn't know everything about his world. To be with him, she was ready to learn and accept it.

"Trust me, it's something you have to work for. Granddad, made me work hard for it. I chose Sin as my Deputy, so she got off easy, but I worked hard to get to where I am. My mother is Granddad's daughter but she never wanted the position and when she mated with my father, he was content in his role. Granddad had never considered who to leave the leadership to, but he wasn't ready to step down then, either. Tonight, I'm meeting with Sin and our guards. Come with me. You can see firsthand what it's like. After all, as my mate, you'll be part of the leadership here."

"Mate." That brought her back to her senses and reminded her just what she had been planning to do. "I know there will be obstacles in the future that we'll have to overcome. I don't mean just The Saviors, even though they might be the biggest issue right now. I might not understand everything about your world, but with your help, everything will be fine. I want Billy safe and one day, we'll have to sit him down and tell him about his limitations within the tribe. It's only one door that's closed for him. Many others are and will be open, so he can do anything he wants. One day at a time. Right now is about us."

She wasn't sure if she wanted any of her children to step into Jase's role for the tribe but that was an issue for another day. No use worrying about children that weren't even born yet. Maybe they wouldn't even be interested in leading the tribe. Even if they were, she didn't see Jase giving up control anytime in the near future. This worry could be put on hold for another time.

"What do you want, Becky?"

"You." She tugged on his shirt that she was still holding, halfway up his chest. "Claim me as your mate."

"There's no going back from this."

"So you've said but that doesn't change anything. I want you today, tomorrow, and for the rest of my life. Now take this off." She pushed the shirt up a little further before he grabbed hold of the thin material and pulled it over his head.

"Happy?"

He tossed the shirt toward the foot of the bed and she took in his toned, sun kissed chest.

"Not yet; you've still got your jeans on." He rose from the bed and slipped his jeans off, letting them fall to the floor. "Now your boxers."

"Hardly seems fair. You're still dressed."

"You can help me out of my shirt once you're naked." She wiggled her eyebrows. "Come on, don't make the battered and bruised woman wait."

"You won't be that way for long." He dropped his boxers to reveal his already hard shaft. "Once I claim you, the injuries will begin to heal. By the time we go to the meeting, your knee will support your weight. Your bruised ribs will feel better and by tomorrow they'll be healed, as will the gash on your thigh. The broken bone in your arm and the concussion will take a little more time but, in a few days, you won't even know you were injured."

"I'll never forget, just like I'll always remember the fact you rescued me." She reached out to clasp his hand and pull him closer. "Thank you."

"I wish I could have been there sooner."

"Come here." Her voice was raw with need as she lifted the blanket to reveal the shirt she was wearing was pulled at her waist and she was naked below it. "What do you say about helping me out of this shirt?"

"Are you sure you're up to this?"

"I'm fine." She grabbed the hem of the shirt and pulled it up. Inch by inch, she slowly revealed her lower stomach, working the material up tortuously slow.

He slipped onto the bed next to her. "Do you want a pill…a mild one to keep the pain at bay?"

"The pain hasn't been bad but even if it was, those pills make me loopy and I don't want to miss a moment of this."

"You'll tell me if it's too much?" He pulled the shirt over her head before carefully sliding it over her air cast. "Just keep this arm off to the side. I don't want to bump it."

"Don't worry so much."

He leaned up on his elbow so that he was looking down at her naked body. "Damn, baby, you're beautiful." He brushed a hair out of her face and tucked it behind her ear. His touch was gentle but caused an inferno within her; with every caress, the flames burned hotter. When he teased his fingers down her neck and along her collarbone, she moaned.

"Jase…"

"I know, baby. The connection between us is starting to come to life. The fire within you is the mating desire." He slid his hands softly down her mostly uninjured side. "Lie back."

Doing what he asked, she scooted down on the bed so she was lying flat. "This has been burning within you all this time. Oh Jase, you should have told me." The idea of him suffering with this fiery need inside and nothing he could do to quench it bothered her. If she were honest with herself, she felt guilty about it.

"Don't, baby. No guilt." He caressed every curve of her body, watching her closely. "It's allowing me to feel your emotions stronger."

She felt her cheeks heat with embarrassment. "Then you know how badly I want you."

"Are you sure you're up for this? I don't want to cause you any pain." Even as he asked, he slipped his hand between her legs, easing them apart.

"It will be fine as long as we're careful. We've waited too long already. I don't want to wait anymore." She arched forward to bring her face inches from his. "We both want this."

As if he was giving in to her, he pressed his lips to hers. Instantly, everything seemed to brighten around her and she was aware of things that never seemed to register before. A strong scent of maple and oak trees hit her in full force, quickly followed by the aroma of wet leaves and soil. If she hadn't felt the bed under her, she would have wondered how they got outside so quick.

With his tongue, he gently pried her lips open, turning passion to deep hunger with a kiss. The scent grew along with the heat. Something brushed along her skin, soft and light enough that it tickled. *Hair…it's hair.*

Her eyelids sprang open but there was nothing to see. Where she felt the touch along her arm, Jase wasn't near. "Jase?"

"It's okay, baby. I swear to you I have control." Adjusting her injured leg so he could slip between her legs, he looked down at her.

"What?"

"My bear…that's what you're feeling. He's eager." Kneeling between her legs, he crouched to kiss along her stomach. "I'm not going to shift. He's just close to the surface; that's why you can feel it. The gentle caresses, the strong forest scent that lingers in the air, and the craving for honey."

"Honey…" Saying the word had the craving rise within her. "Oh, I can almost taste it. Sweet, sticky, and oh so heavenly."

"Trust me, Becky."

"Always."

With her acceptance, he continued to kiss his way back up her body, taking his time. "I'll never get enough of you."

As his tongue teased along the hardened bud of her nipple, she moaned and arched into him. "Jase, please!"

"What, baby? Do you need me to stop?" His gaze found hers and she shook her head.

"It like the fire within me is consuming me. I can't stop the urges and as much as I enjoy foreplay, it seems like too much right now. I need you inside of me."

"Okay, baby." He crouched over her and leaned in to kiss her neck and gently rub his cheek against her neck, like a cat nuzzling her.

"What are you doing?"

"Marking you. I want my scent all over you so everyone knows that you're mine."

"I thought you'd already done that." She dragged her fingers along the curve of his hip, wishing there were just a little more room between them so she could slip her hand in and wrap it around his shaft.

"I did but until the mating it needed to be redone or it would wear off. Now it's just part of mating and my bear needed it. Now, baby, it's all about you."

"Then please…" Her words died off when he adjusted his weight to balance on one side and slid his hand between them to find her core. He let his fingers slip between her lips and enter her. "Oh, Jase!"

"I know what you need, baby," he said, tantalizing her until she was arching into him and moaning his name. After laying a line of tender kisses down her neck, he gently bit the flesh just below her collarbone. With deft fingers, he delved in and out of her, stoking the fire that burned within her.

"Then don't make me beg."

"Soon, baby." He took her nipple in his mouth, sucking gently, before letting it slide out again. His cool breath made her nipple harden. "My beautiful mate."

"Not if I don't get what I want soon." She raked her hands through his hair, fisting a handful of the silky strands to pull them back until she forced him to look right at her. "This isn't our only night. Please, Jase, don't make me wait any longer. Give into your bear and claim me."

She ran her hands down his chest, feeling his tight abs, then slid her hand between them and wrapped her fingers around his hard shaft. Without breaking his rhythm, he arched up and claimed her mouth. Their kisses grew deeper as she worked her hand up and down his warm, hard length.

He pulled back enough that he could look down at her. "Okay baby, you've made your point." Caressing her clit one last time, he adjusted until she could feel his shaft against her folds.

The light touch of it had her arching forward, pressing herself along his body, her fingernails digging into his back. "Now, Jase…please now!"

Without forcing her to beg anymore, he arched forward, gliding himself into her tight channel. As the muscles stretched to accommodate him, she cried out in pleasure. While she might have just beg him to go faster moments before, he seemed to understand right then that she needed a moment to adjust to him inside of her. Easing out of her, he thrust back inside. Gentle at first as he worked his way in and out her, allowing her body time to adjust to his size and for her own juices to slick the passage.

"Oh, Jase!" She cried out his name as each thrust came deeper and faster. Desire bloomed, sending every nerve within her on full alert. She arched her body forward, meeting his thrusts. They rode back and forth until they exploded together in unison. His bear growl mingled with her own moans of ecstasy and the connection between them intensified until it nearly overwhelmed her.

Breathless, she collapsed back on the pillows and ran her hand down his side, teasing her fingers along every contour of his body. "Your bear…he's like a fur coat."

A growl shook his chest, sending vibrations through his shaft and making her muscles tighten around him. "Don't think about it."

She let out a light laugh and dragged her nails along his back. "I wasn't thinking of stripping him of his fur. So maybe that wasn't the best way to describe it. He tickled my skin but also warmed me. Even now I can feel him there. As if he's encompassing my body."

"He'll always be there, connecting us." He slid out of her to lie next to her. "I'm not sure I like you thinking of him as a fur coat, but I guess it's the best metaphor. After all, he'll keep you warm and safe when you're not in my arms. He'll be like your sixth sense. You'll understand what I mean soon enough. Anytime you're around a tribe member, you'll automatically know anything you need to know. Welcome to the leadership team. I can't promise it will be the easiest job, but it will be worth it. And I didn't mention the best part of the job." Pulling the blanket over both of them, he cuddled along the side of her body.

"And what's that?"

"Sleeping with the boss." Her giggles quickly ended as he dragged his teeth along the curve of her shoulder. "Every chance we get I'm going to show you that you're mine and how much I cherish you. Not just your beautiful body, but every aspect of you. I love you, Becky."

"I love you too, Jase, even though you add honey to your coffee." She gasped. "How did I know that?"

"My bear." He pressed his lips to her shoulder. "You'll have to watch what you say in the future. The leadership team has information that other members don't. Trust me, you'll get used to it. He'll warn you if there's something you can't tell someone."

"It's all so overwhelming. It's like my senses of smell and hearing have increased tenfold. This connection between us is something amazing." She hooked her fingers between his. "I was afraid at first but with you by my side everything is going to be fine. My mate…"

Chapter Eight

What was supposed to be a check-in visit had turned into an unexpected afternoon. The work Jase was planning on doing before the meeting was forgotten as he spent the time in bed with Becky. They cuddled and discussed their future. More than that, he let her adjust to the new bond between them. She had questions about the shifter culture, the tribe, and the plan to take down The Saviors. He was able to answer most of them, but in regards to what they were going to do to take down The Saviors once and for all was still something he didn't know.

"Maybe the others have discovered something that will help." She rubbed her hand along the contours of his abs.

"Maybe." He wanted to give her some hope but he knew, if they'd found something, they'd have called. "We should get dressed. They'll be here soon and I want Doctor Graham to examine you."

"Why?" Pushing the blanket aside, she sat up and looked down at the gash on her thigh that she'd taken the bandage off of an hour earlier. "Look at this, it's almost healed. My knee feels fine, and even my arm isn't throbbing like it was. My ribs are tender but the pain is nearly gone. I'm good. This mating has done wonders for healing my body."

"I don't want you to overdo it. Your knee might not be ready to handle your weight yet." He ran his hand down her back.

"There's only one way to find out." She hopped out of bed before he could stop her. "It feels fine."

He rolled over to look at her standing naked next to the bed. "Baby, you need to take it easy."

"It's a little stiff but there's no pain." She paced back and forth.

"You're stubborn." He sat up and swung his legs over the edge of the bed. Silently, he watched her for a moment, taking in her beauty. "Trust me on one thing: your arm might feel better but it's not healed. Don't take your air cast off."

"The throbbing pain might be gone, but I know it's not healed." She came to stand in front of him and touched his shoulder. "Now stop worrying. I'm not going to do anything stupid."

"I'll never stop worrying about you." He placed his hand over hers. "Tonight, after the meeting, if you're up to it, we'll go to Sin's for dinner. Billy's there with Zoe."

"I owe Zoe for watching him."

"Nonsense. She loves watching over the kids around here. She sees it as her part of the leadership team, though she keeps begging to do more." He shook his head.

At fourteen, Zoe already wanted a bigger role within the tribe. By the time, she reached eighteen, there was little doubt she'd earn one, not because she happened to be Sin's ward but because of her ambition. Those thoughts led him back to Billy, who also had ambition, but at only eight he had a longer road to travel before his time came.

"Tomorrow we'll bring Billy home." He grabbed his shirt off the foot of the mattress and slipped it over his head. "I've already sent Liam and a couple of guys to pick up some things for his room. Ginger went with them and picked out some other stuff he needs, such as clothes and toys. Ginger, Camellia, and Swift set up his room while the rest of us were busy with other things. We can welcome him home to his own room."

"Thank you."

"There's no need to thank me. He's our son and I want him to feel at home here."

The front door opened and Liam's scent drifted toward Jase, followed by some of the other trusted members of the team. "Jase?"

"I'll be there in a minute." He grabbed his jeans and boxers from the floor and slid them on. "In the closet, you'll find some clothes for you. Ginger forced the guys to stop so she could get some things for you as well. Once you're feeling better, we'll go get anything else you and Billy need. If there's anything missing that you need now let me know and I'll have someone get it for you."

"You think of everything." With a nod, she disappeared into the walk-in closet.

"I can't take credit for that—it was all Ginger. I'd have kept you naked if I had a choice." He tugged on his boots and laced them up, smiling to himself.

"There's too much to be done. We can't be spending all of our time naked in bed together." She came back into the bedroom wearing a pair of jeans that hugged her curves and a sweater in hand. "But I'm pretty sure we can make time for it."

"Trust me, baby, we'll make time for it. I can be a grumpy bear if my needs aren't met." He went to her and wrapped his arms around her waist, drawing her tight against his body.

"What about my needs?"

"Those are first on my priority list. You're going to be a very happy and satisfied mate." He pressed his lips to hers in a quick kiss before stepping back. "This meeting shouldn't take long but if you're not up for it, I understand."

"I'm fine." She slipped the deep forest green sweater over her head and ran her hand through her hair, fluffing it the best she could. "I'm your mate and it's time I help where I can. Plus, I want to know if they've found anything new. The Saviors need to be stopped."

"Let's do this." He slipped his hand into hers and headed down the steps to where everyone was waiting for them. They had barely reached the bottom of the stairs when they were met with commotion from the dining room, which also acted as their meeting space.

"Have you lost your mind?" Noah snapped.

"Hear me out…" Karri begged.

"Lovers' quarrels need to be handled before you come here." Jase and Becky entered the room to find Noah and Karri squared off, while Liam, Sin, Garret, and Roger were already seated at the table. "We're about to have a meeting here so Noah if you need to deal with this now, take it outside. We've got bigger problems to worry about than your mating struggles."

"Jase," Becky hissed, squeezing his hand.

With a glance in her direction, he realized she thought he was being insensitive. Maybe he was but his team knew this wasn't the place for things like couples' disagreements. If there was an issue he could help with, then his door was always open but most times, newly mated couples had quarrels over minor issues that could be worked out between themselves. Right now, they had a bigger problem to deal with—The Saviors.

"Sir…" Karri stumbled over her words as Jase eyed her. Everyone knew he didn't like to be called sir. It might have been out of respect but it only served as a reminder that every single member of the tribe was relying on him.

"Karri," Noah growled in warning.

She didn't even look at him; instead, she kept her attention on Jase. "I'm sorry and while Noah disagrees, I need to speak up. I need to make this right. Please—"

"Why doesn't everyone sit down and we can bring Jase and Becky up to speed?" Sin suggested before glancing at Karri. "Once he knows what we've found, you can tell him your suggestion."

"*Our* suggestion." Arlene stepped into the room from the living area. "I apologize for intruding but I knew Karri would go against Noah's wishes and speak with Jase. My sister is hardheaded but this won't work without me."

Jase's gaze narrowed in on Noah as he wondered just how much the Captain of Sin's guards had told her. Arlene was human with no connection to the tribe except through her sister Karri. Jase had opened the tribe to her after she'd brought them information concerning The Saviors but he wasn't about to trust her with the same information the team had. She was barely eighteen and without being mated to one of his members, there was no way to ensure her loyalty.

"Nothing, Jase, I swear," Noah told him as if reading his thoughts.

"It's my fault." Karri took a step to the side, so that she was in front of her mate. "You approved me to assist him in whatever way I could. He had me following up on leads. That's when I found out that Pat Guttenburg was responsible. I was arguing with Noah when Arlene came down and overheard us. In my anger, confidential information was leaked and for that, I apologize. I accept responsibility and whatever punishment you feel is necessary, but leave Noah out of this. He worked too hard to gain his position here; don't take it away because of my negligence."

"Karri." Noah stepped up behind her and placed his hand on her shoulder.

"This topic isn't closed but we'll deal with this later. Now tell me who Pat Gutternburg is and what you've found." Jase led Becky over to the head of the table and pulled out the chair for her. After she sat down, he grabbed another one, pulled it alongside hers, and sat.

"What about her?" Sin nodded toward Arlene who was standing in the entryway leading from the living room.

"Seems that she already knows about this part so I guess let her stay." He turned to face the young girl. "Anything you learned in Noah's house or here needs to be kept in the strictest confidence. You cannot discuss any of it with anyone outside of this room and even if brought up in conversation with one of us, it needs to be done in private, where no one can overhear you. If you don't take this seriously, it will put all our lives in jeopardy. Do you understand?"

"I'm not stupid. I know what's at risk." Arlene crossed her arms over her chest.

"Arlene," Karri snapped at her sister's rude tone.

Jase let go of his mate's hand and rose from the table to stand in front of the young girl. "Listen to me, Arlene. I might not be your Chief, but I still demand your respect. My tribe put themselves on the line by bringing you into our home. We protect you—"

"Because I brought information to you," she snapped. "Evidence that kept Karri alive when people put a bounty on her head."

"Those people…you mean your parents." He paused briefly to let that sink in.

"Yes, you brought us information that your parents and other members of your hometown were aiding The Saviors. Those same people demand for Karri to be killed because she was friends with Kat and her shifter boyfriend. The people you considered family and friends would have done the same to you as soon as they learned you were passing information to shifters about their activities. That's why some of The Saviors' planned attacks were unsuccessful. Do you not think that after the attack in the woods, that you claim you didn't know about beforehand, they would have become suspicious? Other attacks you did know about turned out to be a failure but this one was successful. Seems to me it wouldn't have taken long for them to figure out you were leaking information. So how long before you had a bounty on your head?"

"I…" She shook her head, unsure what to say.

"Fine, I'll tell you then. The Saviors had a bounty on your head the minute the attack in the woods was over. Kaden found your name on the discussion board. They wanted you dead because they suspected you were betraying them. How long could you have survived out there on your own?"

"Enough." Karri stepped away from Noah and came to Arlene's side. "I thought you weren't going to tell her."

"You knew about this and didn't tell me!" With tears in her eyes, Arlene pulled away from her sister. "How could you?"

"I was trying to protect you." Karri took a step toward her sister but stopped before going any further. "I know what it's like to realize your family turned their backs on you. That hatred toward shifters overtook the love that was supposed to be there. I didn't want you to have to deal with that."

"You still never said anything when I said I would go back there. I would have gone there and told them I made a mistake by going to you and trusting shifters, that they were right. You knew they would kill me and you never said a word. Talk about betrayal." Arlene moved toward the door but Karri caught her arm.

"I'd have never let you go."

"Screw you, Karri!" Arlene stormed out of the house, leaving an eerie silence in her wake.

Noah went to his mate and wrapped his arms around her. "She'll come around."

"I'll go talk to her." Roger rose from the table, only to have Jase raise a hand and stop him.

"Stay. Liam asked you here for a reason and I'd like to get down to business. You can talk to her after the meeting." Jase came back over to the table.

The silence stretched on for a moment before Becky slipped her hand into his and looked over at Noah. "I guess Jase and I are the only ones who don't know who Pat Gutternburg is, so maybe we could start there."

"He owns a tactical supply store in the town I grew up in." Karri took a seat at the table but wouldn't look at Jase. "The store always seemed out of place to me. What did our small town need with something like that? Some of the men would hunt in the winter but that wasn't enough to keep the shop afloat. It wasn't until a few days before I left for college that I learned what he did in that backroom."

"Pat Gutternburg created the bombs that blew up Becky's house." Noah nodded to Roger who placed an e-table in front of Jase from his seat across the table. "He started supplying The Saviors with their weapons months ago and is now providing them with bombs."

"You've got to be kidding me." Jase stared down at the information displayed on the screen. "How did we miss this?"

"Garret and I went through every aspect of that town and found nothing about it." Sin leaned forward, placing her forearms on the table, and watched Jase. "We only found it now thanks to our team. Kaden showed Roger how to access The Saviors' discussion board online without them knowing we were watching them and he's been monitoring it."

"There was an increase in the information on the online board so Noah asked me to help Roger," Karri explained. "While we were digging through all of it, we found the post that mentioned the bombs for Becky's house were ready. It didn't say her name, just BL and the location, but it was obvious."

The knowledge of who'd supplied the bombs comprised a big part of bringing down the bastards who had hurt his mate. Jase wanted to jump in his truck and go after Pat Gutternburg but he couldn't. They needed a plan. It would be easy to turn this information over to the police and allow them to handle things, but it wouldn't be nearly as satisfying. *My mate, my responsibility.*

Chapter Nine

All the information hit Becky like a freight train, overwhelming her, but the one thing she could make out through all of it was Jase's rage. He wanted to go after Pat and anyone else they could link to the attack on her. She knew he wanted to do it for her, to protect her and Billy, but she was terrified of losing him. She'd rather direct the focus to the ones who'd carried out the crime. "Do we know who received the bombs?"

"Polo Gutternburg, Pat's brother." Roger nodded toward the e-tablet that was still in Jase's hands. "Second tab is an image of both brothers. The one on the left is Pat and the other is Polo."

"Is he one of the two the police arrested? Has he rolled on his brother, Pat?" Becky stared down at the pictures, taking in the two siblings in it.

"That was what I didn't understand at first." Roger shook his head. "The two in custody haven't mentioned either of the Gutternburg brothers. I figured these two were fall guys and The Saviors must still need the brothers for other plans. The nagging question was, how did your neighbor miss Polo?"

"Are you sure he was even there?" Jase asked.

"The discussion board has a post from him, describing things. If he wasn't there when the bombs were planted, he was there sometime. He knew too many details about the house, which he wouldn't have known unless he was inside. Still, I couldn't let it go, so I dug deeper. Turn to the next image; you'll see proof he was there." Roger nodded to the tablet. "He coordinated planting the bombs with the two guys already in police custody. Your neighbor and the police both missed him because he came in a different way, parking several blocks away, and using the alley as cover."

"Jase, I know you're going to make your move on them. To drain their financial accounts so they cannot support The Saviors is not sufficient any longer." Karri let out a deep breath. "I request to be part of it. These are people I've known my whole life. They betrayed me and Arlene, and they've come after the people I care about above all. I can't stand by and do nothing."

"We've already talked about this, Karri; it's out of the question," Noah growled. "I will not have you putting your life on the line."

"But it's okay for you?" she snapped.

"Stop it, both of you." Becky pushed back her chair and stood. "These people are dangerous and I don't want anyone to get hurt. There's got to be another way. Can the authorities do anything to stop The Saviors?"

"With pressure from Brett, they've been working on it but there's only so much they can do until the laws are changed," Garret told her.

"You're right, Karri. We're going after them." Jase took his mate's hand in his. "I'm going to ensure you and Billy are safe and that what happened to you doesn't happen to someone else."

What if something happens to you? Fear coursed through her but she couldn't voice her uncertainties before he turned back to the team.

"I want you to gather everything you can on every resident of that town, especially Pat and Polo. See if you can pinpoint where the key supporters of The Saviors will be tomorrow evening. We'll meet back here at eight tomorrow morning to put together a plan of attack. Tomorrow night this town will be all but a memory." He glanced at Karri before shaking his head. "I'm sorry, I truly am, but they've left us no other course of action."

"Let me go with you," she begged.

"No." There was no wavering in Jase's tone. "Sin, Becky, before either of you get any ideas, you're staying, too."

"Then so are you." Sin shot up and slammed her hands down onto the table. "I'm tired of you rushing out there to deal with whatever comes up. You're the Chief here and you have a duty to this tribe, which means you can't keep risking yourself."

"I agree." Becky turned in her seat to face Jase. "I don't want you doing this for me. If you really want to do something for me, stay here. We're about to begin our lives together; don't rip that time away from us before we even get started."

"I can't." He cupped the side of her face. "Baby, please understand, I have to do this."

"That's what you always say," Sin argued.

"I'll make you a promise." He lifted his gaze to eye his sister—the tribe's Deputy—before finishing. "After this, I'll stay here and allow the others to do their job. This time it's personal."

Becky didn't know what to say, but she couldn't sit there any longer. She needed to get out of the room and allow herself time to process all of the madness. Shifter life was dangerous enough without Jase risking himself to extract revenge. She didn't want or need it. What she desired was a quiet life for her and Billy.

"I need some air." She stepped behind his chair and headed toward the front door. As she wrapped her hand around the handle, the door came open, someone pushed it toward her and she was forced to step back. "Ahh!"

"Jase." A man stepped into the house before his gaze landed on her. "Becky…I'm sorry, I didn't mean to startle you. I'm Brett—Brett Oaks. Is Jase here?"

"Kitchen."

"What's going on?" Jase stepped up behind them. "Brett, what are you doing here?"

"Arlene took off. She said she had things to take care of and you knew about it. The guards at the gate didn't stop her. I only found out because I caught her scent at the gate while I was out doing rounds and asked them about it."

"We've got to go after her!" Karri turned to Noah. "She'll go home and get herself killed if we don't find her first."

"Roger." Jase spun back around to look at him. "Go with Brett; follow the scent. Find her before she can do anything stupid. If you haven't found her in thirty minutes, stay on the trail but give me a call." Roger nodded and then headed for the door with Brett.

"I'm going, too." Noah pressed his lips to Karri's forehead. "Don't worry, I'll find her."

Jase shook his head. "No, you're going to suit up. They've got thirty minutes to find her. If they don't, we won't be able to wait until tomorrow night. We'll have to take care of this tonight."

"I need—" Noah's tone and ridged body warned Jase that he was going to argue.

"I already told you what you need to do. Now go." He turned away to find Sin behind him. "Sin, I need you to find Kaden. I want financial proof the bombs were purchased from Gutternburg. Then I want Karri and Arlene's parents' account drained. Make it look like they sent it all to The Saviors. Put the funds in the account that Kaden started last time for the sisters. They can do what they want with the money. Obviously, our last warning wasn't enough so hopefully this will make things clear for them. I want to know if there's been any further financial payments to The Saviors from anyone else in that town. When this is over we'll give the financial information to the police, including all evidence gathered of the multi-business fraud that they're part of, and let them deal with it. Give a little, take a little. But first we're going to deal with Pat and Polo Gutternburg. We're going to bring them down, every single one of them."

As Becky stood there listening to Jase, she wanted to applaud what he said because she knew what he meant by bringing them down. He wanted them dead. These were human beings and yet she couldn't feel anything more for them than she would feel if she'd stepped on an ant. Had she lost her humanity? No, it wasn't she that had lost her empathy; it was them. They chose to attack shifters because they were different. How long had they thought shifters would just sit back and take it all without doing something? Now, shifters were fighting back and the humans responsible for the threat to them were becoming the hunted. How could she feel sorry when they were getting exactly what they had done to shifters?

In that moment, she accepted that she might be losing part of her humanity and she was okay with it because something better was growing within her. She wasn't just human, at least mentally, because through Jase, she could connect with the shifter mentality. For the first time, she was seeing things clearly. Attacking shifters because they were different was like attacking someone with an accent. Things couldn't continue like they were and if shifters had to stand up and fight back in order to make the needed changes happen, then that was what would happen.

This also meant that she had to stand back and let Jase do what needed to be done. He wasn't a leader that would stand on the sidelines while his people were out there risking themselves. No, her man would be on the frontlines. While that scared her more than the moments in her house when the bombs were going off, she would allow him to do what he needed to.

"I worked technical support; maybe I can help Kaden." Becky hadn't realized Garret was speaking when she made her statement until everyone looked at her. "I'm sorry…I was…"

"I'll take you over there before I head out and we'll see what you can do to help him." Jase rubbed his hand along the curve of her back. "You okay?"

"Yeah." She forced herself to give him a smile even though she was scared about what might happen in the coming hours. "I got lost in my thoughts and didn't realize you were talking. I'm sorry, Garret."

"No apologizes necessary." He rose from the table and took Sin's hand. "I'll get my gear and meet you back here in ten minutes."

As Garret and Sin headed for the door, the others took it as their cue to leave as well, leaving her alone with Jase. Part of her pleaded for her to argue with him about going. Even beg for him to stay if that's what it took. Yet, she knew it wouldn't help. Even though Arlene wasn't a member of the tribe, Jase believed it was his duty to go after her. Becky remembered what she'd been like at Arlene's age and the trouble she'd gotten herself into. She'd been wild at that age, but it all changed when she got pregnant with Billy. She'd turned her life around for her son. Now they had to give

Arlene a chance to change things and they could only do that if they saved her before something happened to her.

Jase leaned back against the bar separating the kitchen from the dining room. Looping his arms around her waist, he brought her to snuggle against the front of his body. "I know you're worried but nothing is going to happen to me. I'm taking a team of excellent men with me. We go deal with what we need to, get Arlene, and come home. We'll be back before you have a chance to miss me."

"I doubt that. I already miss you." She placed her hand on his chest, just above his heart so she could feel the rhythmic thump. "I was thinking, since you'll be gone, I'd like to go ahead and bring Billy home. There's no reason for him to stay with Zoe again tonight. Maybe she could stay with him while I talk to Kaden about helping him and then, if there's an extra laptop around, I can do whatever he needs done here."

"Then let's go. We'll do it together and after that, I'll suit up." He pressed his lips to her forehead.

Twenty minutes after the team left, Jase was finally suited up for the mission. Billy was settled into his new room and Becky had a project from Kaden to work on. His family would be occupied while he was gone, which would hopefully make the time pass quicker for them. As he headed downstairs to meet with his men, he caught a glimpse of Billy playing in his room.

"Hey, little man." He sat his weapon bag next to the door and strolled into the room. "Your mom tells me you like the room."

"I sure do. I can't wait to show Doug. Thanks." Billy dropped the action figure he was playing with and looked up at Jase. "Mommy said you were leaving. Are you going to fight the bad man that hurt her?"

"Yeah." Jase squatted down in front of Billy. "I'm going to take care of it so you and Mommy are never hurt again. But while I'm gone I need you to look after her for me. Think you can do that?"

"I didn't do so good last time." He dropped his gaze to his lap. "I'd been bad and she'd sent me to my room. That's why she got hurt."

"Billy, look at me." He waited until the boy did what he asked. "A bad guy is responsible for what happened, not you. You being in your room saved you from getting hurt. Though since you brought it up, I have to say I'm not impressed with your choice of language. The F word shouldn't be something you say, especially not to your mom. Okay?"

"I know," he mumbled. "Is Mommy still mad at me about it? Is that why I had to stay with Zoe?"

"She's not mad at you and between us I think she forgot about it, so don't bring it up. You had a sleepover with Zoe because your mom was healing. I told you about the bump on her head. Well, she needed to stay in bed for a couple of days and rest. Both of us wanted you here with us but with her resting and me looking for the bad guy, I needed someone to watch out for you. Don't you like Zoe?"

"Even though she's a girl, she's okay. She let Doug come over and we had popcorn and chocolate."

Jase let out a light chuckle and ruffled Billy's blond hair. "I remember that age when girls are yucky. Trust me, son, you'll grow out of it. Now I've got to go, but you watch out for your mom, okay?"

"Okay." Billy grabbed his action figure but before he went back to playing, he looked at Jase again. "Unlike other kids, I don't have a daddy. Are you going to be my new dad?"

"Would you like that?" Jase's chest tightened. If the boy said no it would make things difficult, since Becky was his mate and he wasn't going anywhere. He was also beginning to see Billy as his son, so the rejection would hurt on another level.

Billy nodded. "Mommy likes you. She's happier when you're around. I like you, too. You taught me how to pitch and hit a ball. Can we play ball again soon?"

"Once I get back." With a weight lifted from his shoulders, Jase rose and retrieved his bag. "You be good while I'm gone."

"Jase," Becky hollered from the bottom of the stairs.

"I'm coming." He jogged down the stairs and when he reached the bottom, he was surprised to find the living room empty. His team wasn't waiting for him, which was unusual.

"They thought we'd like a few minutes alone so they're waiting outside." She slid her hand over the curve of the banister.

"Good." He stepped closer so they were nearly touching. "You smell so tempting, it's hard to leave."

"I want to say 'then don't', but I know you have to do this." She glanced up at him. "Promise me you'll be careful."

"You have my word." He traced the curve of her jawbone, slowly making his way up to her ear. "I'll make this quick and be back soon. I wouldn't miss a day with my beautiful mate if I can help it. I love you, Becky."

"I love you, too."

Their lips met in a quick but thorough kiss before she stepped back. He hadn't been ready for it to end; maybe he never would be. The urge to reach out and draw her back tingled within him. Their time earlier in the day had been too short. He hadn't realized he'd have to leave so soon after claiming her, but he was thankful they'd had the time together earlier. She was his and through that connection, he'd know she was safe.

"See you soon." He strolled toward the door but paused before taking hold of the handle. "When your fear becomes too much, focus on the connection between us, focus on me, and you'll know I'm safe."

"Really?" She sat down on the step and watched him.

"Yes, but you'll also have part of my bear here with you, which will leave no doubt." He didn't add that if he were to die, his bear would no longer be with her. The connection between them would be gone, leaving her alone once again. Though she would never truly be by herself, she had become part of the tribe when they mated and Sin would make sure Becky was welcome there. "If you need anything, Sin is right next door. The two of you are in charge of things until I return. Don't do anything crazy."

He chuckled and headed for the door. To leave proved difficult enough but a moment longer and wouldn't be able to force himself to walk out of the house.

Epilogue

Becky had been without a man by her side for more years than she cared to count, but Jase's absence felt like half of her heart was missing. Every moment he was gone seemed like an eternity and now he was on his way home. It had only been hours since they'd left but something had happened—something he wouldn't tell her about over the phone. Even the connection between them wouldn't give her any insight as to what was going on.

The work Kaden had given her was done and until he came back from the security job he went to check on with Ari there was nothing for her to do. So, Becky was left sitting there, waiting for Jase to return to answer her nagging questions.

"Mommy!" Billy came running down the stairs. "Doug's outside. Can I go?"

She got up to look out the window to see Doug had just stepped off his porch "Were you watching out your window for him?"

"Uh…" Billy refused to meet her gaze. "So can I? Can I go outside?"

"Little man, Doug's mom said she'd send him over after lunch and you've been up there watching for him while you were supposed to be cleaning up the toys you left all over the floor at bedtime last night."

"It's clean, I swear." He bounced around, inpatient for her to let him out.

"Okay, but if I go up there and find one toy not put away, I won't let you stay over at Doug's tonight." It was a good threat but as much as Billy was looking forward to his sleepover, Becky was looking forward to it more. It would give her time alone with Jase and even though he had only been gone a few short hours, she needed that.

"Everything is put away." Billy didn't even flinch at the possibility of not going to Doug's for the night, so either the toys were back in the toybox or he didn't have faith in his mother's threat. She hoped it was the first one.

"Go on." The words barely left her lips when Billy pulled open the front door and took off.

When she wrapped her fingers around the door handle, the air shifted. She didn't need to look at the gate to know that it would be sliding open. Jase was home and she couldn't withhold her excitement. She stepped out onto the deck and waited. It took everything she had in her not to run to the gate to meet him there, but she wanted their homecoming to be private. Seconds ticked by before the SUV came to a stop in front of the house and Jase hopped out from passenger seat and strolled toward her.

"Hey baby, did you miss me?"

"Every moment since you left." As he stepped onto the deck, she wrapped her arms around his neck, careful of her arm that was still in the air cast. "It's good to see you again."

"Kiss me." He didn't give her a chance to argue as he closed the distance between them, pressing his lips to hers. His tongue slipped between her lips and the hunger of the kiss burned through her, leaving her breathless.

"Ahh." She moaned as he lifted her off the ground; she wrapped her legs around his waist, and held on as they moved inside. His mouth never left hers until they were in the house and he kicked the door shut. "Jase…"

"I've missed you." Pressing her back against the wall, he slid his hands under her shirt. "Now I understand what others mean when they've said it's hard to be away from their mates. Every minute away from you was torture."

"Is that why you're back?"

His hands stilled, no longer inching up under her shirt. "I'm back because there's nothing we could do."

"What?" She unwrapped her legs from his waist and he lowered her back down to the floor.

"Pat and Polo Gutternburg were no longer any use so The Saviors killed them. They were the reason we were going and with them dead, our job is done." He stepped back from her. "The financial evidence that was gathered has been sent to the authorities. Karri and Arlene's parents have been arrested, along with other members of the community."

"Arlene...did you find her?"

He shook his head. "Roger and Brett are still searching for her. But with the community torn apart, they are no longer a danger to her. Karri's beside herself with worry but we have no idea where she is. I left two of my men near her hometown in case she makes it that far. They have to lie low because if anyone finds out they're a shifter there will be trouble. It's the best we can do for now."

"I should go talk to Karri." She had just started to get to know the young woman but she felt like she had to do something.

"Later. Noah's with her and her mate will be able to help her more than we can right now." He moved farther into the house and shook his head. "I told Billy I was going to take care of the bad man that hurt you two but I didn't. The Saviors are still a threat. You're still in danger."

"All of us are." She stepped up behind him and placed a hand on his back. "I never expected this to be over with one move. This is a war and I'm afraid there are many more battles to come."

"Jase..." Ari banged on the door. "It's important, open up!"

"It's open!" Becky hollered, not stepping away from Jase.

The door swung open and Ari rushed in. Kaden followed closely behind with his laptop opened. "It's happening."

"What?" Jase turned to them and as he did so he slipped his arm around her waist, pressing her along his side. "What's happening? What are you talking about?"

"The Saviors." Kaden put the laptop down on the coffee table. "Before Pat and Polo were killed, Pat dropped a package off at his sister's. By the time, she opened it, he was already dead. With no reason to protect her brothers any longer, she took everything that was in the envelope to the police. All the evidence they needed to take down The Saviors was in that envelope. Pat knew he was a dead man walking and he wasn't going to go down alone. Polo had got him into this mess and if he was going to die, he wanted to make sure everything went down with him."

"It's all over the news. Hundreds of people all over the country have been arrested." Ari dropped down on the sofa. "It's over."

"We don't know that for certain," Jase reasoned.

"Between Brett, Kaden, and me reaching out to our contacts, we do. Believe it or not, the law enforcement agencies across the country worked together, sending out teams to make the arrests before word could spread through The Saviors' ranks. Most of the key players are already behind bars; a few minor ones are still out there but the authorities are sure they'll catch them before long." Ari let out a deep breath. "This is huge."

"You said most of the key players. What about the others?" Becky asked.

"There's a standoff in California with four members. They have hostages. Law enforcement are not sure if the hostages are part of The Saviors or not, but they're working on a peaceful surrender."

"There's also another one that is believed to be in New York," Kaden added. "When they went to his hotel room, he was gone."

"Maybe it really is over." Jase slid his hand up her back. "But until we know for certain, we don't let our guard down. The few that are left out there might regroup."

"Let's hope not." Ari shook his head. "This should be something we celebrate. Even if they're not out of the game completely, they're knocked down. We're winning the battles and in the end, we'll win the war. We'll take them down, each and every one of them."

"I hope for all of our sakes it's over." Becky sighed.

She leaned into Jase's embrace, yearning to feel a little relief but none would come. It might have been different if Arlene had been found but with her still out there alone, Becky was uneasy. The Saviors might be on the verge of going down but there were still nut jobs out there that could pick up where they left off. Only time would tell how things would go. For the moment, she would embrace the news and hope for a better future for all of them.

Saved by a Lion

Angry Arlene Mallory left the safety of the Crimson Hollow Tribe in search of revenge. Her family and friends put a bounty on her head because of her so-called betrayal. Screw them—she couldn't stand by while they supported The Saviors and their determination to wipe out shifters. Her quest for revenge, however, isn't going as planned.

For more than a year, Roger has been working his way up in the Crimson Hollow Tribe to become a trusted member of the team. His first big assignment is to find Arlene before she gets hurt. As a human with known ties to shifters she is in danger, so he needs to act fast. Failure has never been an option for him; not after all his hard work and dedication to his job.

Arlene wants the same love that her sister has with her mate, but when the opportunity presents itself, can she accept it? Can she put the images of him murdering someone with his bare hands out of her mind and accept him as the man who saved her from Hell?

Chapter One

Pain exploded through Arlene Mallory as her captor's steel-toe boot slammed into her ribs for the third time. Unable to hold back the moan, she let it out. Every inch of her body hurt and blood caked her skin, but she wasn't going to give in to his demands.

"Just make the call and tell them you're in danger. They'll come for you and after we kill them, I'll let you go." His anger was marked with another kick, this time to her lower abdomen, and the throbbing pain sent waves of nausea through her. "If you continue to deny me, you'll experience true agony until you're begging to make that call. I'll give you time to think about it and when I get back, be ready or else."

The tiny overhead light bulb on the other side of the room was switched off, sending her into total darkness again. The light held mixed emotions for her. There wasn't much to see in the dim light, just concrete walls and shelves on the far wall where he kept his tools that he promised to use on her, but it was better than complete blackness. She might not be able to see the tools but she knew they were there, waiting to cause her pain. If only she could get one of the knives, but the chain around her neck wouldn't allow her to reach that far. The chain too offered another reminder—she was his prisoner, at his mercy until he ended her life.

She held herself together until the door clicked shut behind him, metal rubbing on metal as he slid the lock into the hole. The basement had been her prison for how long? Days? Weeks? With no windows to see through, she couldn't be sure how much time had passed. At least a day or two from her guess, but it could have been longer. The frequent beatings had left her in so much pain, the only way to escape was sleep and she took advantage of every chance she had to do so. Staying awake staring into the pitch darkness would make her go crazy.

Shivering, she curled into a ball on the cold cement floor and cursed herself for her actions. In a fit of rage, she'd embraced the need for revenge and left safety and security behind. As she'd convinced the guards on duty to let her through the gate, she hadn't thought about the danger she might be putting herself in; she'd only focused on confronting her parents. They put a bounty on her head and she was going to let them know face-to-face what she thought of that. What kind of parents did such a thing to their child? Hers, obviously, but why should she be surprised? These were the same people who'd supported The Saviors attacking the party in the woods. The very party they knew her sister, Karri, had been at. They'd specifically wanted her to die that night. Luckily for her, she'd survived and found Noah—her mate.

Finding Noah hadn't only been a good thing for Karri, but for Arlene, as well. Because of Noah's position in the Crimson Hollow Tribe and him mating with her sister, he had gotten Jase to allow her to go and stay there, too. Before then, though Arlene had known her parents and most of the residents in her hometown had taken a stance against shifters and supported The Saviors, she'd felt that her place remained there, at home, where she could spy on everyone and learn what she could. Any information she'd gathered, she'd passed on to a couple of shifters in hiding. In turn, they would get it to those who could help. She hadn't been on the frontlines of the war, but she did her part.

It wasn't until the attack on Karri she'd realized she couldn't continue this way anymore. While it had been a few years since she'd seen her sister, they had been close before she took off for college and life outside of their hick town. She wasn't about to lose her just because her parents wanted her dead. So, she'd risked everything to go to Crimson Hollow and it paid off. The weeks she'd spent there had turned out to be the happiest and most carefree of her life. At least now she could die with happy memories.

And she *was* going to die. Death didn't bother her as much as the pain she knew would come with it. Accepting her demise was one thing, but it was quite another to know that the last minutes or hours of her life would be spent in agony. She didn't want to suffer another minute under that man's hands, but the only way out was to turn her back on the people who had welcomed her into their home, and she wasn't about to do that, either. She would take their secrets to the grave.

"I'm sorry, Karri." Shivering, she hugged her legs to her chest. Darkness etched in at the corners of her vision and she gave into it. *It will all be over soon.*

Before sleep could take a hold and let her drift off to paradise where there was no agony, a loud bang sounded from upstairs. Every muscle tightened in her body, making her moan out in discomfort. Something wasn't right; she'd never heard anything more than footsteps. His anger would only mean pain for her. What had happened to send him into a rage that had him slamming things around upstairs?

She forced herself to move, to feel the ground in search of something she could use to defend herself. It wasn't the first time she'd searched the space, but she never found anything there. She hoped he'd drop something, but he never did. Even on the rare occasions when he'd show kindness and bring her a drink of water, he always took the cup away. A plastic cup wouldn't be much of a weapon against him but it would have been something. Maybe she could have broken it apart and filed an edge to a point. Then what? She'd still be chained to a wall with no way out. The man didn't care about her screaming so there was obviously no one to overhear her. No one else inhabited the house, except her captor.

"This is stupid." She scooted back against the corner and kept her legs bent in front of her. With the chain around her neck, she couldn't even stand up straight. She couldn't go more than four feet and that was only because she had been tied to the table when she woke up, the chain already around her neck. The blood from the slices he'd carved into her during her first hours there had seeped into the unfinished wood, leaving behind a reminder of what was no doubt in her future. "Maybe, in his rage, it will be quick?"

The door handle rattled and metal clanked against metal, confusing her more. Her kidnapper had a key to the door but what she could make out over the sound of her own frantic heartbeat didn't sound like he was using it. What if it was someone else? She wanted to holler for help on the chance that it was someone else but if it wasn't, it would only make her predicament worse. Biting on her lip to stop herself from crying out, she waited.

Whoever it was didn't have the key and was hell bent on getting in. With a few swift kicks, the door splintered and fell down the stairs. She couldn't see but pictured the door lying destroyed at the bottom of the staircase. *Please let it be the police.*

"Arlene? You down here?" A flashlight sliced into the darkness and someone descended the stairs.

Terrified, she pressed herself tighter to the wall, wishing it would just open up and swallow her. The voice was different, but she wasn't sure if the person was friendly. She wanted someone to come for her, but now that it was happening, she couldn't bring herself to move, let alone answer him. Her captor was unknown to her but she suspected he was somehow attached to The Saviors. Was this mysterious man coming down the stairs part of the same group? He knew her name, and while there should have been comfort in that, she couldn't help the rising anxiety.

The pounding of her heart and the tightening in her chest made her wonder if she was about to pass out. Unconsciousness would allow the stranger heading for her to do anything he wanted to her. While that could mean a quick death, she couldn't allow herself to give in to the darkness and be helpless. She might have been going crazy but she could have sworn she heard her sister's voice. *Don't give up. Fight. We're coming for you.*

The footsteps paused halfway down the steps, directly where she knew the staircase opened up into the room. He scanned the room with the flashlight, searching for anyone who might be down there, until the glow of the light landed on her. "Arlene." There was a hint of relief in his voice.

She couldn't see who was there but she cowered from the brightness of the light. The dull glow proved too much for her eyes, making them ache.

"Why didn't you answer me?" He shifted his hand so the light was no longer in her eyes and continued down the stairs. "Come on, I'm getting you out of here."

"I…I can't." The idea of getting out of there was enough to push back the panic. She reached up and grabbed hold of the chain attached to the collar around her neck, holding it out for the man to see. If he hadn't had a key for the door, he certainly didn't have one for the padlock on the collar. But, he'd found a way into the basement; surely, he could find a way to get her out of the restraints.

She might not trust the mysterious man but if she got out of the basement, maybe she could get away from him. Getting free would be the first step; the second step she was unsure about. Calling Karri would mean she'd send Noah or convince Jase to send someone from the tribe after her. But if anyone from The Saviors was following her, it would mean the death of anyone who'd help her. That's what she'd fought against since she'd been kidnapped, and she couldn't allow that to happen now.

"It's okay." He crouched down next to her and sat the flashlight on the ground, so it was pointing up.

As her eyes adjusted, she finally caught a glimpse of her rescuer. The short black hair with a few stray pieces down on his forehead while the rest was spiked in kind of a natural, carefree way was familiar—but it was the dark, penetrating eyes that made her recognize him. She couldn't forget that gaze, the way he looked at her as if she meant something to him. It wasn't possible; they had barely met, but it was the only thing she could think of to describe the look.

"Roger…" Her throat tightened as she reached out and wrapped her arms around his neck. Even the pain that had nearly paralyzed her earlier proved no match for the happiness she was feeling now. His body was still under her embrace but he didn't force her to let go. "Oh, Roger…"

"Shh, it's going to be okay." He caressed the side of her face, his thumb tracing over the curve of her cheekbone. "I'm getting you out of here."

"The key…he has a key…the collar…we've got to hurry." She wasn't sure she was making any sense but her thoughts were going a mile a minute and she couldn't keep up with them.

"I'll get it off you." He grabbed the flashlight and turned it back on her. "How bad are you hurt?"

"I'm fine."

"Bullshit," he snapped before gaining control again. "The stench of blood is in the air. Answer me this, are you able to walk?"

"If you get this chain off me, I'll beat you out of here. Please, Roger, I just want out of this basement. He might come back."

"You don't have to worry about him. He's dead." He slipped his fingers under each side of the collar. "Good, this is loose. Now I need you to stay still."

Knowing that he could see her better than she could see him, she nodded and closed her eyes. Her thoughts shifted from Roger to her captor. The news of his death didn't seem to have any effect on her. There was no happiness, relief, or even sadness in knowing that Roger had killed someone in order to save her. He'd had to do this because of a decision she'd made. The choice to leave had been hers and if that wasn't bad enough, she was ignorant of her surroundings, which had allowed her to get kidnapped.

Roger had managed to free her now but would others from The Saviors come after her? Would they come after Roger, too? Yes, and she didn't know how to stop it or them.

With his hands wrapped around the metal collar on either side, he pulled, tearing the metal apart where it hinged with the padlock. "There you go." He tossed the collar, at least as far as the chain would let him, and slipped his arm around her back, helping her to her feet.

The muscles in her legs protested and she realized how weak they had become. He must have felt her swaying because his arm tightened around her waist, keeping her on her feet. She wasn't sure if she had been there longer than she thought, but the weakness in her limbs was something she had to overcome so they could get out of there. She couldn't risk him carrying her in case they encountered someone else on their escape. She forced herself to keep it together but as she became steady on her feet, the lightheadedness kicked in and she realized she wasn't sure when she 'd last eaten anything.

"How long have I been here? Never mind, let's just go." She wasn't sure she wanted to know the answer to that question, at least not yet. At that moment, she needed to stay focused on getting out of there. "What if there's someone else upstairs?"

"I've only caught one scent in the house. His." Keeping his arm around her, he handed her the flashlight.

"Don't you need…" The words died in her throat as she caught sight of him pulling his gun out. "Are we…do you…"

"Sweets, it's a precaution. Keep the flashlight. I'll be able to see fine once we're upstairs. There's plenty of moonlight shining through the windows up there."

"Weapon…I need a weapon." Using the flashlight, she scanned over to the workbench where he had kept his tools. There had to be something there that she could use.

"I got you. Nothing is going to happen." He escorted her toward the stairs and she didn't resist. "Let's get you back home. Karri's going crazy with worry."

"My sister always was a worrier." When she'd left, she had been angry with Karri but now, all of that, seemed so childish. She wanted to put the whole thing behind her and find some way to patch things up with her sister. Newly mated, Karri was supposed to be having the time of her life, not worrying about her sister. Arlene would find a way to make this whole fiasco up to her.

If she weren't still fearful for her life, she'd have laughed at her train of thought. She'd been tortured but she was now more worried about Karri being stressed out over the situation. *That's just like me. Not even a near death experience can stop me from worrying about everyone around me.*

Chapter Two

For three torturous days, Roger had followed Arlene's trail. For a short time, he'd lost her scent, which only enraged his lion further. Going back to Crimson Hollow without Arlene wasn't an option. It wasn't that he'd worked for years to get Jase and the others to trust him or that this was his first big mission. Leaving her behind wasn't an option because she was his mate.

At least his beast told him that she was his. Roger hadn't allowed himself to touch her to know for certain. Not wanting to screw things up when the tribe needed him, he'd forced himself to keep his distance. Even though their flirty comments were slowly getting the best of him, making it harder to keep his distance. When she took off it hadn't mattered to Roger whether he'd been assigned to find her or not. He'd have gone after her anyway, even if it meant he'd lose the position within the tribe that he'd worked so hard for. If she was truly his mate like his lion claimed, he wasn't about to lose her.

Every hour he'd searched for her but didn't find her only served to enrage his lion further. By the time, he found the house where she was being kept, he was ready for a fight. Too bad it ended too quickly to ease some of the rage within him but the human kidnapper was no match for a shifter. Especially not an angry mate. The blood and fear that marked the man's clothes had only made him livid, so the man's death came much too quick to please his lion. He needed to get to his mate and that spared the kidnapper from suffering for too long before he ended his life.

Finding Arlene in the basement meant he wasn't simply dreaming of rescuing her—he was doing it. He hadn't failed her. He'd reached her in time and she was alive. Injured and bleeding, but alive. He wanted to scoop her into his arms and rush out of the house that instant, so they could begin to put this whole ordeal behind them. It wasn't until she wrapped her arms around his neck that he got the final confirmation that his human side needed to have. The tingle that rushed through his body, bringing his lion to the surface, let him know she was his.

Inside, his lion roared, demanding he claim her as his. This disaster had been enough for him to realize it was now or never and he wasn't about to wait another day. Things might not be as dangerous as they had been weeks before but he wasn't about to risk losing her again.

"Roger?"

Arlene's whisper pulled him back from his thoughts. He took a deep breath, filling his lungs with air, as he searched for the scent of anyone in the area. "It's okay, we're alone." Keeping his arm around her waist, both to help support her and to satisfy his own lion, he led her through the house.

"Ahh…"

Confused, he glanced down at her only to find her eyes wide and her jaw hanging open. He didn't need to look to know that her attention had drifted to the dead body on the kitchen floor. "Shit! Sweets, look at me." Still holding his weapon, he used the back of his hand to force her to look at him and away from the bloody body. "Arlene?"

"You killed…"

"I told you downstairs that he was dead." There was no other way out of the house besides walking through the kitchen and out the backdoor. The front door had been boarded up and even with his strength, it would take too long for them to get out. If they stayed in the area any longer than absolutely necessary, they'd risk someone coming to check on the kidnapper's progress and finding them. Since he refused to wait for backup, he had to get her out of there before anyone could find them. "Don't look, just keep your eyes closed or focus on me. We've got to keep moving."

"We have to go in there?" She pulled back from him but he kept his arm around her. "What if he's not…"

"Does that not look like he's dead?" When she tried to turn back to the body, he spun her around to face him. "Listen, sweets. That asshole is dead; he's not going to hurt you again. Now we've got to go. My truck is a half mile down the hunting trail. If we get moving now, we'll be out of this area before anyone is the wiser."

He would have loved to take his time, comfort her as he should, but they just didn't have the time to spare. "I know you're scared and you've been through Hell but Karri trusts me to bring you home so you've got to let me do my job."

"Job…yeah…your job."

He watched her closely. Her light blue eyes held a sadness that hadn't been there moments before and she seemed to sink in disappointment. The sudden change was surprising enough to leave him confused. Why did mentioning Karri and his duty to the tribe force such a change? Did she not want to go back to Crimson Hollow? Was she still angry with her sister? He wasn't sure but lingering to ask her now would put them in jeopardy, so he'd have to put it off for a bit longer.

"Come on." Keeping his arm around her waist, he forced them forward through the dingy kitchen that only had room for a table, small prep space, and refrigerator, leaving the owner able to make little more than sandwiches. He stepped wide, avoiding the dead body and the blood seeping over the dirty linoleum floor. Two steps from the door, he caught the scent of something and froze.

Even through the closed door, the stench of sweat, alcohol, and gunpowder drifted toward him. Someone was coming and there was nowhere for them to go. He couldn't get her out of the house and into the woods without being spotted or, at the very least, overheard. Their best chance was for them to wait in the cabin for the man.

"Roger?" She kept her voice low but the stiffness in her body let him know she'd been alerted to the change within him.

"Sweets, it's going to be okay." As much as he hated it, he had to take her past the dead body again; there was nowhere she could hide in the kitchen. At least, in the living room, she'd be out of the way and he could handle the situation before she could get hurt. "I just need you—"

"What? What's going on?" Her words were laced with panic but she kept it together.

"I need you to stay hidden." There was no good place in the living room to keep her hidden but at least the intruder wouldn't have a direct aim on her the moment he made it through the door. He escorted her toward the corner of the room and forced her to squat down, making her harder to spot. "Stay here."

"Don't leave me." She grabbed a hold of his arm before he could rise.

"I need to take care of whoever is outside, then we can leave. I'll be right back." Without thinking it through, he pressed his lips to her forehead. "I promise."

The cabin door opened and, without a choice, he moved back from her. His gazed stayed on her until the last second; he let his lion essence drift out toward her, to caress along her skin, reassuring her. She might not understand what was happening but the reassurance would keep her from making her presence known. Soon, she'd know that she was his.

Being saved should have meant the ordeal was over but instead of riding off into the sunset, Arlene found herself in another deadly situation. The whole time she had been kept there, she'd never seen anyone besides the man who'd tortured her. Why was there someone else showing up now? Had he been there before and she hadn't realized it? The basement made it hard to hear what was happening upstairs. She'd only heard the scuffle between Roger and her kidnapper because of the intensity of it.

The vision of her captor's dead body popped in her thoughts—the last thing she wanted to picture because it made her also imagine Roger like that. He could die and she'd be alone again. The idea of being at someone's mercy again terrified her but it also sparked her will to live. She'd fight. If Roger had found her, someone else could find them. They just had to stay alive long enough.

She had already taken in her surroundings and decided there was nothing she could use for a weapon besides the old heavy box television and a five-foot lamp. She wished he had let her grab something from the tool bench in the basement. One of the knives would have come in handy right then but she wasn't about to go down there unless she was left with no choice. Right now, she'd rely on Roger and hope he could get them out of this situation.

She let her gaze find him again. His back was toward her as he focused on the intruder coming through the cabin door. *Don't you die on me, Roger. Not now. Remember your promise to Karri…to Noah…to me.*

She wasn't sure how long she repeated those words in her mind before reality snapped back into place with a deafening bang. The intruder came inside and Roger attacked, slamming the man against the wall hard enough that it left an impression.

"Who the hell are you?" The man grabbed the butt of his gun and pulled it from the holster.

Roger! She wasn't sure if his name came out verbally or not, as all she heard were his snarls.

"What are you doing here?" Roger had his hand wrapped around the man's neck.

"Where's Wayne? The girl?" Roger's grip must have tightened because the other man's eyes bulged as he brought his gun up.

Wayne? She hadn't known the name of the kidnapper but somehow, that seemed to fit.

"Dead." He swatted the gun away, sending it out of the man's hand but not before a shot was fired. The bullet went wide, not hitting either of them. Instead, it found its home in the old television, sending sparks flying through the dimly lit space. The gun clattered to the floor a few feet away from them.

Moonlight glistened off the weapon and even with her human vision, she could see it. She considered going after it, but it would make her presence known. After Roger answered the man's question with one word—dead—she wasn't sure he wanted the man to know she was alive. She forced herself to stay there. Roger had the situation under control at the moment and she could go for the gun if she needed to.

"You're a fucking disgusting shifter, just like that bitch downstairs."

"Watch it." Roger slammed the man back against the wall again.

"We're going to kill all of you. So many have died but more will come. That whore gave us the location of your people. There's a bomb—"

Roger's snarls echoed through the space and the air around her grew warm, as if charged with his anger. "I didn't…" she started, trying to deny the man's claims, but the words couldn't be heard over the scuffle. She couldn't see what was happening as much as hear it, but the man's words proved sufficient for Roger to not question him any longer.

Even knowing the man was about to die, she wouldn't do anything. He was part of the problem, part of the group that had kidnapped her and killed too many shifters and human supporters. He was getting what he deserved but deserving to die and seeing it done in front of her were two different things. Still, she forced herself to not look away.

Somehow, during the struggle, the sofa was pushed to the side and with the moonlight cascading over the floor to where they fought, she could see what was unfolding better. The man struggled to get free, bringing his fist up to connect with the side of Roger's face. Roger shook it off but that was enough to give the man another inch and he reached for the abandoned gun.

In a split second, Roger shifted, transforming seamlessly into a lion. Members of the tribe shifted often and there wasn't a day she had spent there that she hadn't seen at least one of them in their animal form. Including her sister's mate, Noah, who enjoyed lounging in his lion form. But, she'd never witnessed Roger transform. His mane was lighter than Noah's, more golden blond with sun kissed strands through it.

A massive paw pressed against the man's chest, pinning him to the floor, and in the glow of the moonlight, she could see the fear in the man's eyes. His claws dug in, leaving groves in the skin and blood seeping through the white shirt. As if the man realized he wasn't going to reach his gun in time, he froze, his hands up in surrender, but Roger wasn't having any of that. The lion snarled as he lowered his head, his jaws opening.

"Pleas—" Teeth sank into the man's neck, cutting off the words, and in one quick move, Roger ripped the man's throat out.

A squeal escaped from between her lips and the lion turned toward her. Blood dripped from his mane and reality set in. She brought her hand up to her face and pressed it to her lips—not so much to stop her from making another sound but to keep herself from speaking her thoughts aloud. *The blood on his hands…or fur…is because of me. He's killed two people to save me…*

Chapter Three

Being away from the cabin where she'd been kept should have dispelled the weight from Arlene's shoulders, but there wasn't enough distance between her and that hellhole yet. She wanted to get as many miles between her and that place as she could but Roger had other ideas. He called Kaden and asked him to locate a place nearby they could use to get cleaned up without anyone asking questions. His recommendation turned out to be an abandoned hunting cabin a couple of miles away.

Roger's idea to get cleaned up was logical. No one wanted to stay covered in blood, especially blood that wasn't theirs. The idea of cleaning some of the grime and gore off her was appealing but the urge to get farther away strengthened within her. The second man had found them before they could even leave the cabin; what would stop more from catching up to them?

"How far are we from Crimson Hollow?" She dropped down onto a folded metal chair.

"A few hours' drive." He sat the duffle bag he'd carried in from his truck on the coffee table and shook his head. "After days of being stuck on cement and now with the choice of any seat in this cabin, you sit on the hardest surface."

"I…I didn't…" She ran her hands down her thighs over her jeans and winced in pain. "Look at me. I'm a mess. I'm not going to dirty up someone's home just for some comfort. Someday, someone might come back here. I hated getting into your truck, too, but what choice did I have? You weren't going to let me ride in the back."

"Then let's get you cleaned up."

"Excuse me?" She stared up at him with wide eyes.

"Yes, both of us. You'll need my help." He took hold of the duffle bag again and held his other hand out to her. "You're injured. Let me help you clean your wounds and from the way you're holding your side, I'd say you have a broken rib, if not more than one. You're going to need help binding them."

"Fine." She slipped her hand into his and rose from the chair. Every muscle in her body was so stiff she could barely move, so why not accept the help? Shifters were destined for their mate; no substitute would do, so she didn't have to worry about him wanting anything from her. "It's not going to mean anything to you anyways."

"Really, sweets?" He led her toward the back wall where they found a small kitchen.

"I know how it works with you guys…I mean with shifters."

"I figured that's what you meant." He tossed the bag on the counter and turned toward her. "I'm going to lift you up onto the counter, so why don't you take off your jeans first?"

"Let's not worry about—"

"Take them off or I'll do the honors." He watched her for a long moment, neither of them giving in. "I know you have a deep wound on your thigh and if we don't take care of it, the infection is going to sink in. Then you're going to be feeling the pain. So how about we do this the easy way?"

"Fine." She unzipped them but when she went to lean over and pull the material off, pain shot through her. A hiss escaped from between her teeth and he reached out, taking hold of her arm.

"Let me." Slowly, he eased the jeans over her butt before stopping. "Place your arms around my neck. I'm going to lift you up onto the counter and then finish taking your jeans off. It will be less painful for you."

She did as he asked and he cupped her ass before gently lifting her off the ground and sitting her on the cool countertop. "It's stupid to take my jeans and shoes off when I'm going to have to put them back on. You might have a change of clothes but I didn't think things through when I left. I threw some money and my ID in my pocket and left."

"I've got you covered." He peeled away her jeans and unlaced her shoes. "I knew when I found you that we might need supplies, so I picked some things up." He tugged down the zipper of the bag and began to pull the contents out.

"You think of everything."

"Not everything but hopefully I have the essential items. I'm sure glad I had the foresight on these." He pulled out a package of baby wipes, followed by a couple of bottles of water and towels. "No running water means we're limited to these." He unscrewed one of the bottles of water.

"It's more than I've had in days." She still wasn't sure how long she had been in that basement but she was beginning to believe it might have been longer than she had thought before. "How long...?"

"You left Crimson Hollow eight days ago."

"Eight..." Her throat tightened, stopping her from speaking.

"Drink." He held the bottle of water he had opened out to her, which she accepted. "We found out you were gone less than an hour after you left. That's when I set out to find you. I've been following your scent and leads for days. Early yesterday afternoon I found out about the cabin but it was the first solid lead I've had in days."

As he spoke, she polished off the bottle of water. It might not have been cold but it was the first time she'd had more than a few sips of water in days. "You've been looking for me all this time?"

"I wasn't the only one. Brett Oaks was sent out with me the night you left. Jase and some others were going to deal with your parents and the other people in your hometown but..."

"But what?" she pressed when he let the words trail off.

"It was already taken care of." He pulled out a first aid kit from the bag. "Noah was out here searching for you, too. None of us were going to give up."

"'Cause Karri wouldn't let you? I bet she threatened to do it herself if you didn't stay out here searching for me." She knew her sister Karri would have felt like she owed it to Arlene not to give up. She'd have searched every inch of the world, turned over every rock, and threatened anyone who got in her way. Karri was strong; she'd have never let herself be taken. *Just another way that shows I'm a failure.*

Roger's clenched jaw and the way his gaze seemed to narrow down on her made her go still under his watch. His eyes shifted from their normal dark brown to light amber. "Don't."

That single word came out more like a growl, accelerating her heart rate. He could smell the panic rising within her and hear her heartbeat speed up, but the more she thought about gaining control over them, they seemed to elude her. She forced herself to close her eyes and picture herself anywhere but there. Karri trusted him and that was enough for her to allow herself to do the same. With a couple of deep breaths, she could almost see herself standing in the meadow, the window blowing her hair back from her face. Everything was perfect.

"You've done nothing wrong. There's no reason to think like that."

"Huh?" Startled by his words, she opened her eyes. "Think? You can hear my thoughts?"

"No, sweets. But wouldn't that be nice?" He chuckled.

"No."

"Come on, I know you've got some dirty little thoughts floating around in that brain of yours. Wouldn't you like me to know about them so I can make your deepest desires come true?" Saturating a towel with water, he eyed the wound on her thigh. "Do you have any more cuts like that one?"

With a shake of her head, she glanced down at her thigh. The jagged wound was red and to say it was painful wasn't a strong enough description. The pain had been bearable in the basement but now that she was moving, it felt worse than her broken ribs.

"He did that. Obviously…I just mean…" Images of her being kidnapped flashed before her eyes. Now she could see how useless her struggles had been. He had outweighed and dwarfed her, making her look like a tiny woman compared to him. Her fight ended when he'd driven the knife into her thigh, making it too easy for him to hold the rag to her mouth, forcing her to breathe in the chemicals in it.

"You're upset and you've been through a lot. There's no need to explain." He wrung out the rag into the sink and came to stand in front of her. "I'm just going to wipe off the blood so I can see what I'm working with."

"You can do it if you tell me how you knew what I was thinking about."

"I'm doing it either way, but I'll tell you." He brought the cloth to her leg, starting farther away from it and slowly working his way closer. "Sometimes when your thoughts are stronger I can catch a whiff of them. It's like a quick breeze but gives me an insight into what you're thinking."

Air hissed out from between her teeth as he wiped along the open wound. "Why tell me?"

"Why not?" He set the rag aside and dug through the first aid kit.

"If humans knew, they'd have less reason to trust you. It would be another thing The Saviors could use to get more people on their side. With this skill, they'd find you more dangerous." Didn't he realize that what he'd just admitted could bring more trouble down onto his kind if he said it to the wrong person? Her sister was part of their tribe and he was risking her with being so free with the information.

"Sweets, haven't you figured it out yet?" He placed everything he needed on the counter and turned back to her. "The tip of the blade is lodged in your leg."

"What?" She wasn't sure if she was questioning the first or second part, but as he picked up the forceps she realized she was more concerned about her leg than whatever she was missing.

"I've got to get it out before I can stitch up the wound." He reached out and tucked a stray hair behind her ear. "Sweets, I'm sorry. This is going to hurt."

"Why do you call me that?"

"Sweets?" He brushed along the curve of her cheek with a gentle hand. "Because that's what you are. My sweets. Still confused, aren't you?"

"About more things than I care to admit." She put her hands on the counter behind her and leaned back.

"Then let me clear something up for you. Knowing what's on your mind, I will say my perception wasn't a general shifter thing. At least not in the way you think. Others don't have that ability, so there's no need to concern yourself with it being used against us. I knew because you're my mate."

The air stuck in her throat and her jaw dropped. *Mate?*

Chapter Four

Rational thinking proved impossible for Arlene until after Roger had pulled the last stitch closed and wiped away the blood that seeped from the wound. Every second of the process had been agonizing and her stomach heaved the whole time. If she'd had anything but the few sips of water in her stomach, she had no doubt it would have come up by now. Her skin felt hot and her mouth was dry but she was too afraid to move in case she sent another wave of agony through her.

"I'm sorry." He pressed a cool rag to her forehead, cooling her down before sliding the rag down to her cheeks to wipe her tears away. "I hate to see you this way."

"I'm fine." She didn't feel fine but she didn't want him to worry about her. His concern through the ordeal had been something she hadn't expected. He'd offered to stop but she wanted the bleeding to stop. The last thing they needed was for her to pass out from loss of blood. If something happened and she was kidnapped again, she needed whatever strength she might still possess, not to be reeling from low blood levels.

"Are you ready to take your shirt off now and let me attend to your other injuries? Or do you need a few minutes first?" He tossed the last of the bloody towels and gauze into a plastic bag he'd pulled out of the duffle bag earlier before cracking open a new bottle of water.

"I..." Her voice cracked, forcing her to swallow and try again. "I don't think that's such a good idea now."

"Why?" He cocked an eyebrow at her and waited.

"We're…umm…you said…we're…" she stammered, unable to get the words to come out.

"Mates," he supplied. "Why does that change things? If anything, it should make you more comfortable taking your clothes off in front of me."

"It complicates things." It made a tangled mess out of all the emotions she thought she was feeling and after everything else she wasn't in the right frame of mind to try to make sense of what was happening between them. The tingles of excitement when she'd seen him around the tribe's land, or how her gaze had found his moments before her sister announced their parents wanted her dead. Even as she'd argued with Karri, she'd kept Roger in sight. From the way she'd caught him glancing at her, she would have thought there was something there between them—but he was a shifter. There wasn't an 'if' when it came to shifters; they were either mates or they weren't. If they were, then why hadn't he said anything about it during the weeks she'd lived there?

She needed to get back to Crimson Hollow and talk to Karri. Maybe she could explain things better. Otherwise, she was feeling her way in the dark and after everything else, she was tired of the darkness. If anything was supposed to be clear cut, it should be a relationship. He'd saved her and that had to mean something but then again, it could mean Jase had ordered him to do so. It was possible she was overthinking this mating situation. It wasn't like he would lie about it. Yet, she wasn't ready to just accept it at face value.

"Listen here." He put his hands on either side of her and leaned toward her. "We've got a long drive ahead of us and you're going to want those ribs wrapped. Now let's do this so you can put on a clean pair of clothes and rest for a bit while I clean the blood off me and change."

The mention of blood on him made her look at him again. Dried blood coated his neck and splattered over his arms. She suspected there'd be more hidden underneath his shirt but she wasn't about to venture down that road. "Roger—"

"Don't apologize again." He lifted his hand off the counter and slid it down her uninjured thigh. "What happened to that flirty vixen that floated around the tribe for the last few weeks?"

"She got a rude wake up call." Memories of the teasing comments they'd shared clenched her chest.

"You're stronger than that, sweets." Sliding his hand up to where hers rested in her lap, he let out a soft breath of air, almost purring. "Nothing's changed since you left home to come to us. The world was shit then and it's still the same. Evil exists everywhere you look but what's happening right here, right now—that's what it's all about. That's why we wake up each day and fight. Shifters have no doubts when it comes to finding their mate. I found you and I'm not letting you go. I'll protect you. I promise."

"That's the second promise you've made to me." She met his gaze and forced herself to give him a smile, even if it was halfhearted. "I trust you, Roger; it might be crazy but I do. It's not because I know Noah would kick your ass if you let something happen to me."

"Just Noah?" His lips curled into a cocky grin. "Here I thought Karri would have my hide before anyone else got a chance. Jase would have to wait his turn, though I'm not sure how the Chief would like that."

"Jase…he must be pissed at me. I snuck into his house while he was having a meeting with the leaders and then Karri and I got into it. I bet he doesn't even want me back there. He only wants me safe so Karri doesn't do anything crazy." The easiness between them disappeared as her tension returned. "I really screwed things up."

"Your thoughts go a mile a minute and without the mating connection, they're hard to keep up with." The grin disappeared as he took in what she said. "We're going back to Crimson Hollow. Jase might not be happy about what happened or how the situation was handled, and I know he's livid you went off by yourself, but none of that means he doesn't want you there. You're part of the tribe now. Even if you weren't Karri's sister, you'd still be welcome. You're a friend of the tribe, which means you have our protection. You risked your life for us. It's the least we can do."

"I could have betrayed you while I was captive." She sucked in a deep breath and shook his head. "The tribe…oh fuck, how did I forget? The bomb…"

"Shh…" He spread her legs so he could get closer to her, scooted her to the edge of the counter, and wrapped his arms around her waist. "Everyone's fine. There's no bomb."

"But he said—"

"Stop, Arlene." He pressed his finger to her lips. "He was bluffing, hoping to turn my attention on you so he'd have his opening. We both know you didn't give them any information. Even if they somehow found out where the tribe is, I already alerted Jase. I shot him a text as we were on our way through the woods. They've done a thorough search and there's no bomb, but, as a precaution, they've added more guards to ensure the safety of everyone."

"You never said, never asked. I was their prisoner for days…I could have told them everything."

"I know you wouldn't have given them information about us." He slid his hand into her hair, cupping the back of her head. "You're smart enough to know that it wouldn't have changed anything. They weren't going to let you go no matter what you told him. When you were no longer any use to them, they'd have killed you."

"Death would have been the easy way out." Unable to deal with her own weakness, she closed her eyes. "It wasn't just Karri I would have betrayed by answering their questions. I'd have betrayed you…everyone. Betrayal is worse than any pain he could have caused me. No matter what he did to me, I couldn't do that. I've been on the other side of the treachery and I'd rather be dead than do the same thing to someone."

In her heart, she knew Roger was the reason she would have taken their secrets to her grave. She would rather be dead than have him attacked or killed because of her. She might not have realized what was happening between them but there had been something there even before he'd found her. Their teasing comments and chemistry had been progressing, and if she had stayed, it wouldn't have been long before she'd learned he was her mate.

Realizing there was more, she opened to eyes to look at him again. "I never gave up on you. I knew you'd come for me. Not because of Karri but because…" She wasn't sure how to finish her thought. "I just knew."

"Because subconsciously you recognized the connection between us. You might not have realized it meant mate, but you understood enough to know there was something linking us together." He leaned into her, his lips hovering just above hers, and his breath brushed along her face. "Trust me, sweets, I was coming for you no matter what. I'm not here because of Jase's orders; I'm here for you, and I wasn't leaving without you. You're mine."

The possessiveness in his tone should have sent fear rushing through her but she found herself relaxed. "Kiss me." She needed to feel his lips, to know for herself if there was truly this mating connection between them.

With his hand still pressed against the back of her head, he pressed his lips to hers. It was gentle at first, barely a peck as if he was holding back, but when she reached out and placed her hand on his chest, it seemed to light something within him. His tongue slid between her lips, opening her mouth so he could invade and explore. Their tongues danced together and she clenched her fingers around his shirt, drawing him closer. The heat and desire seemed to spread within her and she forgot about everything else. A soft moan escaped her throat and with one final kiss, he pulled back.

Not wanting him to pull away from her, she held tight to his shirt. That kiss was everything she thought it would be and more. The surge of energy and desire exploded from every cell in her body. Her body vibrated from the purr of his lion along her skin, teasing along until she could swear she felt fur brush along her skin as his fingers traced down her arm. His other hand, still in her hair, kept her close but she wanted to be closer. She wanted his body pressed along hers until there was nothing between them.

"Wow."

"Sweets, that was nothing. Wait until I get you back home." He leaned back enough to grab the hem of her shirt and carefully slid the material up her chest until it was off. His eyes widened as he stared down at her sitting in only her bra and panties. "Fuck!"

"Disappointed or dying to get your hands on me?" She tried to determine what the answer would be but his features were rock hard and he wasn't giving anything away.

"I'm fucking pissed." He snarled, shaking his head. "Damn it, sweets. Why didn't you tell me you were hurt this bad?"

"I'm fine." She didn't need a mirror to know how bad it looked; she could feel every cut, bruise, and broken bone. The knife had sliced through the skin on her stomach, over and over again, without cutting deep enough to do more than bleed her. Her shoulder was sore from her kidnapping, when he shoved her into a tree, nearly dislocating it. The bruises were more of an eyesore than anything else. They were the least of her worries.

"Bullshit." Gently, he pressed his hand to her ribcage, feeling along the curve, until she hissed out in pain. "Broken rib but at least it didn't puncture your lung. The bruising…what the hell?"

"What?" She tried to see what he was seeing but he placed his hand on her shoulder and gently pressed her back.

"What the fuck did that asshole do to you?" His fingers caressed right above her hipbone.

"What's there? What do you see?" She tried to wiggle to see what he was talking about but the pain in her ribs stopped her. "Damn it, Roger, tell me."

"Shh, sweets. I'll show you." He grabbed his phone from his jacket pocket, snapped a picture, and held the screen out to her.

The image displayed took her breath away. She wouldn't have believed it was her skin if she hadn't seen the flash go off when he took the picture. Her normal pale skin was an angry shade of purple, with hints of reds and blues. It looked like a child's art project that got out of hand but there, within the horrid bruise, was a tread mark. He'd kicked her so hard that the bruise held the mark of his shoes.

"We're going to have Doctor Graham look you over when we get back to Crimson Hollow. We need to make sure you don't have any internal injuries."

"No."

"Excuse me?" His back straightened, until he was standing ramrod straight in front of her.

"Don't look at me like that and don't pull away from me. I know more about your kind than you obviously think. If there were internal injuries, you'd know."

"We're not mated yet. I can't feel your pain like that," he reasoned, but she wasn't accepting it.

"Mated couples can feel the other's pain and injuries, unless they're shielding, and being human I wouldn't know how to. But that's not what I meant." She watched him for a moment, waiting for him to understand what she meant, but he remained silent. "Shifters can smell that type of injury. If I had internal trauma, you'd smell it. Just like you could smell the copper scent of blood. I don't need Doctor Graham or anyone else and you know it."

"I don't." He took a step back from her. "I need to know. We need to know. I won't risk you."

"You're not risking me. Trust your lion, you'd know." She sat up and held out a hand to him. In a flash, he took her offered hand. "Come here."

"You're my mate. I need to know you're okay."

"Trust your lion," she repeated. "Has your beast ever been wrong?"

"How do you know we can smell things like that?" he asked, avoiding her question.

"Noah…" In an instant, she was back in Crimson Hollow, hours before she'd taken off, standing there in her sister's living room as she learned the news. *I'm pregnant.* Karri's words echoed through her thoughts. It was too early to tell and pregnancy tests would come back negative, but Karri and Noah knew without a doubt that she was pregnant. Noah could smell it in his mate's scent. Other shifters would know soon enough, but Karri had wanted Arlene to be the first to know.

That news gave her an extra dose of strength as she thought about her sister and the coming birth. In less than three months, she'd be an aunt. She still couldn't wrap her mind around how quick the pregnancy would be but since Karri wasn't having a human child, but a shifter, that meant the gestation period would match their animal's—in this case a lion, so it would be a short three and a half months.

"Arlene?" His voice brought her out of her thoughts and back to reality.

"Karri's pregnant. They wanted to tell me before everyone else knew." She met his gaze and smiled. "Thanks to you, I'm going to be alive to see my niece or nephew."

"Nieces or nephews. Plural, sweets."

"They know?" The idea of more than one baby had her jaw dropping open. Shifter pregnancies were completely different and with them lasting a shorter amount of time she wasn't sure what else was different. Maybe Doctor Graham could do a sonogram and know for certain how many she'd have, or even the sexes. For all she knew, maybe that was something Noah and the others could smell.

"In the wild, lions have three to six cubs. As shifters, we favor that aspect of our animal. It's extremely rare, especially for a lion, to have a single baby. Multiples are the norm for us." He grabbed another bottle of water and began to wet a rag to wipe down her skin. "It's a lot to take in."

She wasn't sure what she thought of multiple babies at once but she was going to take things one day at a time. Today that was her sister's predicament, though she had a feeling that in the future she'd be in the same position.

"Especially when you're mated to a lion."

Chapter Five

The drive back to Crimson Hollow had allowed them some alone time without any pressure. Roger was glad to be almost home. He wanted his mate to be safely tucked away behind the fence and additional guards. More than that, he wanted her home where she belonged. His home. There was just one thing he had been putting off since he'd found her and he was running out of time. He had to tell her now, before they pulled through the front gate, and Karri or one of the others had a chance to tell her first.

"You got quiet on me." Arlene fiddled with the string that went through the hoodie. "If you're worried about what Jase is going to do to me, don't. I can handle myself. If he wants me to leave—"

He pulled his truck to the side of the road, shoved it into park, and turned toward her. "I told you that's not going to happen. Even if it did, you're not alone. We're in this together."

"I can't do that to you. You've worked hard to prove yourself to Jase and the others. I won't have you risk your position for me. You've already done too much."

"Sweets." He stretched his arm across the middle divide and took her hand into his. "You're my mate. I'd risk my life to keep you safe. This—"

"You've already done that."

"We've got this, you and me, we're a team. But there's something we need to talk about before we get home." His thumb teased over her knuckles and his gaze stayed locked on her. "I told you Jase and the others went to take care of your parents and the other members of your hometown."

"Yeah, you said they had to turn around because things had been taken care of. Honestly, I didn't care about it at that moment, but I thought about it a little since then. Very little, but still. They're dead, aren't they? The Saviors…"

"No."

"Jase?" she asked before he could explain.

"No. Your parents and most of the town was arrested. Evidence of their support and plotting with The Saviors was turned over to the police department. Law enforcement agencies were able to swoop in before Jase and the others had a chance to deal with the situation."

"Deal with the situation? What does that even mean?"

He took his gaze away from her and stared out the window of the truck for a moment. There was nothing to see but darkness and trees. They were in the middle of nowhere with another thirty-minute drive ahead of them before they'd reach Crimson Hollow. The driver side window was cracked and he couldn't smell anyone out there, yet unease settled onto his shoulders. Was it because of the conversation? Or was something coming? He wasn't sure but his lion was edgy.

"Your silence is enough of an answer." Her tone sounded cold, holding no emotion, but her eyes held a hint of sorrow.

"They weren't going there to kill your parents." He squeezed her hand, offering her a little comfort. "Kaden stripped their bank account so they could no longer financially support The Saviors. The money was placed in an account for you and Karri. Jase and the team were going to deliver justice to someone else."

"The Gutternburg brothers."

He nodded. "Pat and Polo Gutternburg were the target that night. Pat made the bombs and Polo planned them at Becky's house. Jase couldn't stand by when they'd attempted to kill his mate. None of us could."

"I wanted to go. When I learned what they did, I thought I could go back to uncover more evidence, I guess you could say. Evidence that we could take to the authorities and bring them down. There were financial records detailing the activities of my parents and other members of the community but that would only do so much. They wouldn't see as much jail time as they would for bomb-making, blowing up Becky's house, and whatever else I could have found."

"I know but you didn't have all of the information." He hated bringing up a topic that hurt her deeply. She'd mentioned her parent's betrayal earlier and what it did to her; it was part of the reason why she could never turn against the tribe. "The bounty on your head wouldn't have allowed you to return home. Even if there wasn't that, I don't think they'd have believed your story that you realized how dangerous shifters were and wanted to be on the right side. Your loyalty would be in question. They knew you'd saved your sister and while your parents might have accepted that as a sisterly bond, the rest wouldn't and The Saviors sure as hell wouldn't have. You'd have been walking into a trap. A death trap."

"Doing nothing would mean Pat and Polo might walk free."

"They're not walking anywhere." He lifted the middle divider and pulled her hand. "Come here."

She scooted closer to him and he wrapped his arm around her shoulders, pressing her against his body. "The Gutternburg brothers are dead. Once they were no longer any use to The Saviors, they were killed. But something good came out of all of this."

"Really? What? Because I don't even see a ray of sunshine in this dark nightmare." She rested her head on his chest and relaxed into his embrace.

"Pat knew something was going to happen. He suspected he was going to die. The night before it happened, he dropped an envelope off at his sister's house. She wasn't home but there was enough evidence in the package to make sure The Saviors would no longer be a threat. Law enforcement agencies across the country swept into action and arrested people."

"What about Wayne? Why wasn't he arrested?"

He rubbed his hand lightly down her arm, careful not to hurt her. "Kaden is looking into that. I'm not sure if he was one of the main characters in the organization and therefore, he wasn't one of the first picked up. Or if he was one of the few that escaped arrest so far. It doesn't really matter right now, as he's dead. The second guy, I wasn't able to ID but, based on my description, Kaden discovered that the police have been unable to locate him. They checked his home and office and he wasn't at either. Now we know he wasn't even in the same state."

Silence filled the cab of the truck for several minutes before she tipped her head to look up at him. "So, what does all this mean? If The Saviors are being arrested, does that mean there's no longer a threat to shifters?"

"Sweets, I'm sure there will always be a threat to shifters. We're different and until something else comes along, someone will always take offense to that." He pressed his lips to the top of her head. "The threat from The Saviors is diminishing. There are still small groups that have survived; some of them have gone into hiding, but they've lost their power. That certainly diminishes the danger to us now."

"That is some good news. Though we have to make sure they don't regain their power. We can't let our guard down now."

"Even after everything you've been through, you're still ready to fight for us." Part of him loved the strength and courage to stand on the side of shifters, while the other part of him wanted to protect her. Keep her safe and hidden away from the dangers that might always be coming for his kind. She was his mate and it was his duty to protect her. They had been given a second chance when he found her and their lives together were just starting. He wasn't going to lose her now. This was their chance and no matter the dangers they'd face in the coming days, weeks, or even years, they'd overcome them together.

"Do you expect me to just sit on the sidelines?" Holding her side and careful not to jar her ribs she twisted on the seat so they were facing each other. "These assholes kidnapped and tortured me to get information about you. I want to see their organization destroyed, so they can never do this again."

"I don't expect you to do anything, but I'm not going to stand by while you take off again like you did this time." The idea of her taking off again was enough to enrage his lion but what gave him the most pause was the fear that next time he might not be as lucky to find her before she ended up dead. After he claimed her as his mate they'd have the connection and it would be easier to track her—but that didn't mean they couldn't kill her before he could arrive. A mate would be perfect bait to lure a shifter out. No matter what the Alpha ordered, a shifter wouldn't be able to stop him or herself from going after their mate.

"It took me a while to find you, but it would have taken longer if Brett hadn't seen you leaving. We got lucky and your scent trail was easy to follow, at least until you started hitchhiking." He shook his head. "What the hell were you thinking? Hitchhiking? Do you realize how much danger you put yourself in?" He hadn't wanted to fight with her about it and had tried to let the whole situation go because there was no doubt that Jase would give her a lecture of his own. Karri would add in her voice and most likely Noah, too. She didn't need it from him as well but now that the subject was out in the open, he couldn't drop it.

"I was angry and the only thing I could think about was confronting my parents." She looked down at her lap and let out a soft chuckle. "Look at me! Don't you think I realize that now? It was stupid and I've been berating myself for it for days. I really don't need you bitching at me, too."

"You can't just rush off in anger. Not now, not when you're connected to shifters. It's too dangerous for you. If we sprang to action every time something happened, more of us would be dead. You need a plan first." He cupped the side of her face, tangling his fingers in her hair as he did. "Just like we were going to deal with the Gutternburg brothers, we weren't going to let your parents get away with their part in things. You're family and we fight for our family."

"Jase would have never let me go." The anger in her voice disappeared.

"You're right, and if you're going to be pissed at him you might as well be mad with me as well. I wouldn't have let you go, either." He rubbed along her temple, working upwards toward her hairline. "I've known for weeks that you were mine, but I wouldn't face it."

"Why?"

"I thought about that a lot over the last few days." He took his hand away but kept his arm resting on the back of the seat, leaving the offer open for her to cuddle against him again. "At first I assumed it was because you're young, just left home for the first time, and you were catching up with your sister after two years apart. I didn't want to intrude on that. I wanted you to get your feet under you before you realized what you were to me. But when I thought I might have lost you, I realized I was denying what was happening because I wanted to keep you safe, as if you not being my mate would have kept you safe. It wouldn't have; you were connected to the tribe, and The Saviors knew you were a shifter supporter. You were in danger, even if you weren't my mate."

He took his gaze from her and stared out the windshield, watching nothing and everything. His lion crept forward, torn between wanting Arlene and yearning to go after any of The Saviors left alive. The urge to end it all and make her safe overwhelmed him. They were supposedly safe from The Saviors now but it had been so long since he didn't have the constant worry of something happening, he wasn't sure how to handle the change. To him, it still felt like there was something coming, a threat lurking, waiting to attack.

"Our playful flirting was not enough…" She scooted toward him.

"I know. My lion was growing irate because that was as far as things went."

"I found myself making excuses to go outside when I knew you were out there. Early in the morning, I'd sit by the window in my bedroom, so I could watch you train with the other guards. It had become my morning ritual to watch the sun come up and glisten across your naked chest." She slid her hand up his chest, teasing along the contours. "The day I left, that was the same day I watched as you…"

For a moment, he wasn't sure if she stopped talking or if the sound of her frantic heartbeat drowned out what she had said. It wasn't until the rush of mixed emotions poured off her that he realized something was wrong and he reached out to put his hand on her shoulder. "Arlene? What's wrong?"

"Blood…" She took a deep breath and shook her head. "Forget it."

"No, tell me what's going on. What blood? What are you talking about?"

"That morning you were stabbed. I saw the blood. The training…that's all real. Real weapons. You could have been killed."

"Oh sweets." Instantly, he knew what she meant and he slid his arm around her shoulders and drew her closer to him. "Not all the time but yes, sometimes we use the knives or swords as we would in battle but we never do it at full strength. We're careful and guns are never used on each other."

"You were stabbed!"

"It was a scratch that healed shortly after." He wanted to press her tight against him but with her injuries, he couldn't risk hurting her. "We have to train for different situations so we're ready when a threat comes. Those training sessions made sure I was prepared to do what I had to in order to save you."

"They prepared you to kill." She shook her head, gently hitting his chest. "I should be appalled by that. You killed to protect me. No one should have to do that. Even though my brain tells me that others would be horrified, I'm not."

"You've witnessed enough to know life isn't a bowl of cherries." He rubbed a soothing hand down her arm. "If I hadn't killed them, they'd have killed us. I wasn't planning on dying today and Karri would be pissed at both of us if you weren't there to see her children grow. We've all got to do what we've got to do."

"How did I go from a protective little community where the worst crime we have is a drunk getting rowdy at the bar, to living with the threat of violence around every corner?"

"It's a change for you, I understand that. No one is pressuring you to accept this life." In that moment, he realized he'd go anywhere for her. As a lion, he wanted to be part of a group of shifters, a tribe or a lion pride, but if it meant losing his mate, he'd give it all up. Even though it would cost him deeply, he'd keep his beast hidden from the rest of the world, because it would cost him so much more to lose her.

"I'm terrified of what the future holds for us and all shifters, but I want this. I look at what Karri and Noah have and I want that same kind of love and relationship. The devotion they have for each other can be seen every time they look at one another. For them, it's like the world revolves around their family. I know Karri worries about Noah, but he does what he can to eliminate her fears. Every moment they have together, they cherish. I want that."

"We'll have that." He pressed his lips to the top of her head. "Our world is different but everything you want is still possible."

Her face was unreadable when she glanced up at him. "Not completely…I can't have a white picket fence."

"Huh?"

"Did you know, every little girl dreams of a house with a white picket fence, two and half kids, and a husband who will always be faithful?" She chuckled. "At least, that's what I've always been told. The girls I went to school with wanted that. Heck, I'm pretty sure they had their weddings planned out, the ages at which they'd have their children decided, and their damn dream home decorated. None of that ever mattered to me."

"What matters then?" In the back of his mind, he worried she'd want something he couldn't give her, like a safe world. He wanted it too but it wasn't possible, at least not yet. Hopefully one day.

"I wanted a husband who would not only love me, but would listen to me. I don't want to be controlled like my mother is. A marriage doesn't give a husband the right to control every aspect of his wife. I want children but I also want a life. I didn't realize some of this until Karri went off to college. That's when I woke up. I started sneaking out just to get out from under my parent's thumb, but a whole new world opened to me when I met a couple of shifters. Anytime I had information that might help, I passed it to them. I made a difference and now that I have nieces or nephews about to join the world, I can't sit back and do nothing."

"See, all your dreams can still come true. I'll make sure of it. Now why don't we get you home?" When she started to scoot back to the other side of the truck, he took a hold of her hand. "Stay."

He wanted her close and even that small space of the middle divide seemed like too much for him. They'd be back with the tribe and divided soon enough. Karri would want to see her and he'd have to report to Jase. In the meantime, he wanted to spend as much time as possible with her. He would have loved to put off returning to Crimson Hollow. Time for them to be together, to cement their mating, but things were still too uncertain and he wasn't going to put her at risk. Home was where they needed to be. *Home in my cabin and in my bed.*

Chapter Six

Even though it was only early evening, Arlene was tempted to go upstairs to her room. The only thing that stopped her was the hope that Roger would come by. They arrived home to Crimson Hollow hours before and it had been nonstop since. He'd warned her that he'd have to have a debriefing with Jase, but she hadn't expected it to take hours. He had been gone for days, looking for her, and now he had to fill the Chief in on everything that had happened, including the two men he'd killed. Every time she glanced out the window and didn't see him in sight, she couldn't help but wonder if he'd got into trouble for what he did. What were the consequences for his actions? Would Jase demand his life as payment for the two he killed? Fears continued to multiple as the minutes ticked by.

"So, with the babies…" Karri dropped down onto the sofa, stealing Arlene's attention back from the window where she was looking for any sign of Roger.

"What?"

"I'm going to need the bedroom for the nursery."

"Oh…" She should have seen that coming but after everything else that had happened, it had slipped her mind. "I'll…"

"I've already got your stuff packed." When Arlene's gaze narrowed on Karri, she stumbled over her words for a moment. "I mean since Noah and I already purchased the baby furniture, we need a place to set it up. I don't want to wait until the last minute."

"You have three months." She couldn't believe Karri would just pack up her stuff and basically kick her out right then. "Forget it. I'm sure Jase can let me stay in the cabin I was supposed to stay in before. Remember it was you who wanted me here in the first place, but now you're just chucking me out like the rest of the trash."

"Arlene…I…didn't know if you were…"

"What? You didn't know if I was coming back?" She rose off the sofa and stared down at her sister. "Neither did I and now that I'm here, I'm not sure it was the best thing. Maybe Roger should have never found me. Then you wouldn't have to worry about what to do with your little sister who's obviously in the way. Well, don't you worry. I'll find somewhere to stay."

"You'll stay with me." She'd recognize that voice anywhere and spun around to find Roger standing in the doorway next to Noah. "Come on, sweets. Let's go home."

Home?

"Your stuff has already been moved," Noah told her as he strolled toward his mate.

Before she could wrap her mind around what was happening, Roger came to stand in front of her. He didn't touch her but the nearness of him made every nerve tingle. She wanted to feel his hands caress along her body. More than anything, she wanted to feel his lips on hers again.

"You ready?"

Not trusting her voice, she nodded and slipped her hand into his.

"Have fun!" Karri hollered behind them as Roger escorted her to the door. There was a light, carefree tone to her voice that should have annoyed Arlene, but it didn't. Had this been her sister's plan? To get Roger to take her home with him? Surely Karri wasn't manipulating them, but if she was, Noah was in on it, too. And Roger?

Once they were outside and far enough away from Karri's cabin, the need to know if he was part of this became too great and she stopped, turning to face him. "Did you ask Karri to pack up my stuff and move me out?"

"Seriously, Arlene?"

The sound of her name made her pause. She had grown used to him calling her sweets and the change was enough to throw her off-balance for a moment.

"The whole way back I dreaded the moment you'd go back to Karri's and I'd go to my cabin. I wanted to ask you to stay with me but I wanted to give you a little time with your sister. I didn't know how long things would take with Jase and after everything, I thought you needed a good night's sleep, so I said nothing." He stepped closer and slipped his arm around her back. "Don't think you were getting rid of me. I was planning on convincing you tomorrow to stay with me. The idea of another night away from you drives me crazy. You don't have to let me claim you, yet. I just want you near me. I want to know you're safe."

She wanted that, too. That's why she hadn't gone up to her room that evening. She had hoped he'd come to her, ask her to come home with him, or at the very least give her a kiss goodnight. Karri's sudden change just made her feel as though something else was at work. "I don't understand Karri's sudden change. Did she really think I was dead so she packed up my stuff so the kids' room could be set up?"

"No." Needing further explanation, she looked up at him and he continued. "On Karri's request, Ginger and Swift packed up your stuff this afternoon."

"What?" This was worse than she expected because Karri knew she was alive and coming home, yet she wanted her out. "The lie about the baby furniture…"

"Before you get angry, listen to the whole thing. Jase has the ability to know who will be mated with each other. The only requirement is that he's met both people. So, he knew from the moment he met you that you were mine. To comfort your sister, he told her that we're to be mated." His fingers teased under the hem of her shirt, caressing along the small of her back, soothing her.

"I don't understand. How would that be of comfort? Why would she care who I might have been with if I lived? There's no way he could be sure I'd live or that I wouldn't betray you guys."

"Except he could. Knowing that we'd be mates was all the confirmation he needed to know you'd be alive when we found you. We weren't mated when you left and if they would have killed you, then we'd have never mated, and he wouldn't have known we were mates. Make sense? He dropped hints to me too but I didn't listen to them. I was too afraid I had lost my chance with you."

She tried to wrap her thoughts around everything he said but there were still pieces of the puzzle missing for her. "So why kick me out? Jase had me staying in one of the cabins but Karri wanted me closer, so she'd asked me to stay with them. Now she kicks me out…"

"Forcing us together. Come on." He moved toward his place, forcing her to come with him or let go of his hand. "She wanted you to embrace your mate without feeling like you were abandoning her. We're just a few doors down but you'd have felt like you owed it to her to stay, at least tonight. She wanted to give you this opportunity."

"I don't know if I should thank her or kick her ass for messing with my life." Stepping into Roger's place, she found her suitcase and other belongings sitting inside the entryway. "I can—"

"Don't you dare say leave." He shut the door and stepped toward her, gently pressing her up against the wall. "I've waited too long to have you here. Tonight, I want you in my bed. You know you'll sleep better with my arms wrapped around you, and I'll know you're safe. We both need a good night's rest."

"What if I want more than to just sleep?" With her body pressed against his, she wasn't given many options, so she slid her hands up his sides. "The whole time you were gone you were the only thing I could think about. Carrying on a conversation with Karri was nearly impossible, when I just wanted to walk out the front door and over to Jase's. You were gone for hours and I couldn't help but think the worst."

"I told you it was just a debriefing."

"Hours? That seems unnecessary. Are you in trouble for what happened? So many things went through my mind but I kept seeing Jase order your death because of what happened. He has to know that it was self-defense. They came after you. I heard the first one and saw the second guy. I'll testify…"

"You're getting worked up over nothing. Everything is fine. Do you need me to have Jase come over here and tell you himself? Nothing is going to happen to me."

"I was terrified..." She clung to him and pressed her face against his chest, breathing in his scent. The idea of losing him was more terrifying then being kidnapped and tortured again. Losing him would kill something inside of her that she hadn't known existed.

"Everything is going to be okay. Come on, let's go upstairs."

This time, she didn't stop him. Upstairs was where things would begin for them. They could put the dark, tormenting past week behind them and move on to brighter things.

It was still dark when Arlene's eyelids popped open. Terrified to move in case he was there, she listened to her surroundings. It took her a moment to realize she wasn't chained up in the basement but in a bed. The soft glow of the muted television should have been her first clue but it wasn't until she pressed the blanket to her chest that she realized she was at Roger's.

"Arlene..." Roger's hand slid up her back. "Sweets, are you okay?"

"Better than okay." She lay back down and cuddled against the side of his body, and he slid his arm around her until his hand rested on her hip, holding her close.

"Bad dream?"

"I don't know why I bolted up like that but it wasn't a dream." She ran her hand down his bare chest. "I can't remember the last time I slept this well."

"You needed it and there's still plenty of night left." He lifted his head off the pillow and glanced toward the alarm clock on the nightstand next to her side of the bed. "We've got hours before the sun comes up. It's only a little before two." He dropped down onto the pillow.

She took a deep breath, pushed her nerves aside, and let her hand slide down his chest. "I can think of a good way to spend it. That is unless you're too tired." Her fingers brushed against the waistband of his shorts and she debated for a moment whether to go under or over the material. *You almost died. Live dangerously.* She scooted her hand under the waistband and found him rock hard.

"Arle—"

She leaned up and pressed her lips to his, silencing him. She didn't want to hear that she should rest, or be careful with her injuries; she wanted him, and she was ready to claim him. It wasn't like he didn't want her. He did, but he didn't want to force her into anything she might regret later; and while she appreciated that, she also knew what she needed. What they both needed.

Karri had told her that she'd just known Noah was the one she was supposed to spend her life with but until Roger, she hadn't truly understood her words. Chained in that basement, she'd never lost hope she would be rescued. Logically, she couldn't explain it but part of her knew that Roger would find her. She just had to stay strong until he arrived.

Now, this was her reward. They wouldn't waste another minute denying what was happening between them. With the future unknown, she wanted him to know how she felt about him and she needed the connection linking them to be strong so that, no matter what happened, they'd be together. More than any of that, she craved him. The sweet caresses they'd shared since he found her weren't enough; she needed to feel him inside of her.

Wrapping her fingers around his shaft, she broke the kiss. "I want this and it seems like you do, too."

"There's no denying I want you, but you're hurt." He tucked a strand of her hair behind her ear. "Even though you're trying to hide it, I can feel your pain pulsing along my skin. Your muscles are tight, your body is sore, and your ribs are throbbing. I wish you'd take something for it."

"I'm fine. I don't like how medication makes me feel. But I know one way you can make me feel better." She slid her hand down the length of him before letting go and pulling down the top of the shorts to free his erection. "Your shorts are in the way."

Without a word, he lifted his hips off the bed and grabbed hold of the material, quickly pulling them down before kicking them off under the blanket somewhere.

"Anything else, sweets?"

"You gave in easier than I expected." Now free of the restraints, she continued to caress along the length of him. With every stroke, he seemed to grow harder in her hands, but she never sped the pace.

"I've been denying what I feel for you long enough. I want you as my mate and my wife."

"Some would say that's the most unromantic proposal ever but for us it fits. I know well enough that, for your kind, mating is what's important, not marriage."

"You mentioned wanting a husband—"

She pressed her lips to his, kissing him softly before drawing his bottom lip between her teeth and nipping lightly before letting go again. "Mate is the same thing, just a different word. I've never dreamed of a wedding with me in a white dress. Hell, I hate dresses. I just want a man who's mine, one who loves me."

"That you have." He tangled his fingers in her hair. "I can't get you out of my thoughts. Nearly every thought I have is about you. When you were gone, I thought I'd go crazy with rage. You're all I want. I love you, Arlene Mallory, my beautiful mate."

She could feel her cheeks heat with embarrassment, but before she could say anything more, he closed the distance between them. His lips held just the faintest traces of something salty, making her want more of him. She let her tongue slip into his mouth. They kissed as he slid his fingers under the hem of the shirt he'd given her to sleep in after her shower. When he tugged it as far as he could, he broke the kiss and pulled it over her head.

"You've got me naked. Now it's my turn to see your beautiful body."

As he tossed the shirt aside, goosebumps danced across her skin. The warmth of his body against hers and the notion of what was to come proved enough to set her on fire. Not even the pain held a candle to that feeling—all of it now relegated to the back burner. Anticipation had her still her hand as she caught her breath and focused on her next move. "I need this…I need you."

"Eager?" he teased.

"More than you know." Numerous times since she'd come to Crimson Hollow, she'd pictured herself in his arms. Now that she was there, eager didn't begin to describe the urgency flowing within her. "I bet you didn't know that the very first time I saw you, I thought about doing this."

"Really now?"

"Brett escorted me to cabin two and told me that Karri would be over in a few minutes. He left to deal with something else and when I heard a sound coming from the bedroom I figured it was Karri; instead, it was you."

"I was making the bed." He caressed his hand over her hip, ever so slowly sliding down her leg. "Does a man knowing how to make a bed turn you on?"

"A man who can do things around the house has his uses but no." She let go of his shaft and ran her hand up his chest. "It's you that turns me on. To some it might seem strange but I never thought twice about it. Rather, my dreams and fantasies were filled with you, though I blame that on the fact your scent was all over the bed."

"Sweets, I'm going to make all your fantasies come to life."

She stared at him, running her hand back down his chest until she found his shaft. Her attention had only been diverted for a few minutes but she already missed how his body reacted to her touch. She wrapped her fingers around it before rubbing down the length, painstakingly slow. She applied just enough pressure to make him arch toward her. She loved the soft moan escaping his lips, which held just enough of a growl to let her know how much he wanted her. "I have no doubt," she whispered.

"Good." He pulled gently away, lifting up on his elbow and turning toward her, which forced her to let go of him.

"I was enjoying myself. Now, get back here." She was unable to keep the smirk off her face.

"Later. First, I want to take in all of you. I've been picturing you naked in my mind and I want to see the beauty of your body." Careful to avoid her injuries, he placed a hand on her shoulder and lightly pushed her back down against the bed. He pressed his lips to hers with such desire that she moaned around his unrelenting embrace.

When the kiss ended, leaving her breathless, he whispered, "Beautiful and sinfully sweet, just like I imagined." He kissed down her neck and chest until he feverishly claimed her nipple. With that went any thoughts of taking it slow and enjoying the moment. Instead, she needed it all right then.

"Please…" She reached out, placing her hand firmly on his chest. His shaft pressed tight against her thigh. In his arms, she felt safe and desired for the first time. She raked her nails over his chest, her need escalating.

He slipped his fingers between her legs, sliding over her clit, pulling the pleasure from her inch by inch. Then, he thrust his fingers into her as his thumb continued to pull more pleasure from her core.

"I need you. Please, Roger."

He rolled over. As if she knew what he wanted, she gingerly moved with him, careful to avoid hurting her ribs. With her on top, he slid his hands over her hips. "Mmm." He caressed her clit one last time before returning to her hips and lifting her gently.

"I've never…I mean," she stammered, unsure how to say it. She wasn't a virgin but her sex life had been rather limited, and never involved her being on top. The only man she had been with had wanted to control every aspect of their relationship. Their short stints in the bedroom had been unadventurous and he had never allowed her to ride him like this. It was always him setting the pace and foreplay had been all but non-existent. Sex had been about him and his control over her. She'd been nothing more than a means to an end. That shouldn't have surprised her since her father had arranged for them to start seeing each other. It had almost been like an arranged marriage, without the marriage part—though she thought that would have been the next step if she hadn't turned her back on everything and traded sides.

Excitement shot through her like an electric current. She was nervous but there was something about being on top that made this extra special. This would be their first time and there was a freedom in knowing that he was open to more. The bedroom wasn't about control or about one person imposing over the other.

"I could tell you it would be easier on your ribs but honestly I want to see you above me," he said. "We'll take it slow, and I promise you'll enjoy it."

She tucked a lock of hair behind her ear and nodded, giving him permission to continue lifting her gently. Once he got her into position, he slid his shaft along her folds, teasing her until she arched her back and a moan escaped her lips.

"Oh, Roger!"

Without further delay, he slid his length into her until he buried himself to the hilt inside of her. He kept his hands on her hips, helping her work his shaft up and down. With each pump, she began to find her own way. As she became comfortable, she picked up the pace and drove herself up and down, the rhythm intensifying with each thrust.

He moved his hands away from her hips, leaving the pace up to her, to explore her body. Reaching up to fondle her breasts, he thrummed his fingers over the hard buds of her nipples. Pinching her nipples, he had her arching toward him, needing more.

"Oh…" She tipped her head back, growing closer to ecstasy.

Grabbing her hips, he drove his shaft into her harder and faster. The pain in her ribs seemed to disappear as her desire rose. The frenzy had her brain fog until she screamed out his name and groaned as her climax sent her over the edge. His hands on her hips, helping her movements, were the only thing that kept her going as her orgasm washed over her. His own climax followed moments later as he buried himself deep within her one final time, followed by a roar that had her eyes opening.

He let out a light chuckle as he caught her surprise and pulled her carefully down onto him so her face was just above his. "What can I say, sweets? You've got a lion in your bed."

"My lion." She wiggled her hips; his shaft twitched, and her core tightened around him. "I wouldn't have it any other way."

"Good because you're mine now and I might never let you out of this bed." Kissing her neck, he stayed buried deep within her, kissing a line along her neck and working his way to her ear.

A soft moan escaped her throat. "I like the sound of that."

Mated to a shifter…Dad would love this. I thought he wanted me dead before, but now there's no doubt as to what he'd think.

Chapter Seven

In the weeks since Roger and Arlene mated, things had been calm, at least as calm as they got in his world. The Saviors were no longer an active threat and their online discussion board that Brett had hacked into had gone silent. Even Kaden's automatic internet keyword search hadn't produced any alarming results. Any hits received came from news or police reports, nothing that posed any threat to the tribe. Without so much as a blip on the radar from The Saviors, and most of their members' arrested, Roger couldn't help thinking that something was still heading their way. Things were quiet—too quiet.

"Man, you need to quit worrying." Noah slapped him on the back. "Our women are safe, the tribe's safe. Everything is going better than we could have planned. So why do you look like you just received the worst news of your life? You should be celebrating."

"I just can't shake the feeling that something is wrong." Watching his mate, he took a swig from his beer bottle. "The Saviors have been wreaking havoc on our lives for a long time and now, with the government sweeping in, we're supposed to believe they're no longer a threat? It doesn't make sense. There's no way all of them are in jail. Some of them have got to be lying low, waiting for the heat to die, then they'll make their move."

"When they do, we'll be ready," Noah reassured him. "In the meantime, we need to cherish the peace we have now."

Jase strolled up to them, his arm around his mate, Becky. "It's not like we're sitting around doing nothing. We're still preparing in case there's more to this war, but Noah's right, we need to enjoy what happiness we have."

Becky nodded in agreement. Even after everything she had gone through, she seemed to be accepting of how things worked out. He suspected that at least some of it had to do with fact that The Saviors had killed the Gutternburg brothers after their usefulness ended. The brothers had both played a major role in blowing up her house with her and her son Billy in it. In the end, Pat Gutternburg had played a part in bringing down the organization, giving her a piece of justice.

"Tonight, we're supposed to be celebrating. So, let's forget about all this bullshit, even if it's just for a few hours." Becky tipped her head toward the party that was happening all around them.

All around them, people were chatting at the many tables, couples dancing, kids running around; everyone was having a good time. There were tables with more food on them than even a tribe of shifters could eat. This was the first time they'd had a chance to come together as a tribe, to relax and mingle. Tonight, they'd gathered to celebrate. In the next several months, their tribe would be growing.

Karri's triples were due in just over a month. Sin had announced just days ago that she was expecting but Doctor Graham was still trying to determine if she'd have a wolf or fox pregnancy and until he did, there was no way of knowing if she was due in two or three months. Lioness Camellia was expecting with her bear mates Ari and Kaden but unlike the others, her pregnancy would last longer—seven months—so they had a while to go before their cubs would be due.

"I hear there's more good news that we should be celebrating tonight." Becky's comment brought Roger back from his mental drift.

"Huh?" He turned his attention to the Chief's mate.

"Don't play coy." Becky slapped his arm. "Your mate already told me."

"You mean I'm going to be an uncle?" Noah let out a deep laugh before squeezing Roger's shoulder. "My man here is a little overwhelmed with the news. He hasn't exactly been shouting it from the rooftops like his mate."

"Maybe that's where your sense of doom is coming from," Jase joked before growing serious again. "It's going to be great. Fatherhood is unbelievable. Billy is giving me a run for my money and preparing me for when Becky here gives me another little one."

"I'm going to be a father." Even as the words came out of his mouth, Roger still couldn't believe them.

"Don't worry about him; he's still in shock." Arlene came toward him and he instantly pulled her into his arms, embracing her. "I thought he'd pass out when Doctor Graham explained why I've been so tired the last few days."

"I could smell something different about her scent. It was as if she was part lion, but I knew that wasn't right. I refused to consider the possibility…it's only been a few weeks." He hugged her tighter against him, as if he was afraid she'd float away.

"It only takes one time." Circling her arms around his waist, she looked up at him. "It's not so bad, is it?"

Hearing the concern in her voice, he smoothed his hand up along her back. "No, sweets, it's wonderful, just shocking."

If he could have planned it, he might have held off until they were certain that things were over with The Saviors, but he didn't have any say over that now. She was pregnant and ready or not, they'd be parents in a few months. Now, all he could hope for was an easy pregnancy and healthy cubs. At least their cubs would be surrounded by other children their own age, including Karri's children. They'd have a tribe full of people who loved and cared for them, as well as parents who adored them. Arlene was going to make a wonderful mother; he could only hope he'd make a decent father.

"What do I know about parenting?" He thought about his own parents and their hands-off way of life. He wouldn't have been surprised if he'd learned to change his own diaper because they were too busy with their own lives. Such a detached approach wasn't what he wanted for his children.

"Don't worry, we've got this." She rose onto her tiptoes and hooked an arm around his neck. "You're a great mate and you'll make an amazing father."

"As long as I've got you by my side, I know things will be okay." Pressing his lips to hers, the idea of lifting her into his arms and strolling back to the cabin danced in his mind. Before he could act on it, Karri and some others joined their group, interrupting the moment.

"If anyone should be worried about being a parent, it's me." Karri rubbed a hand along her stomach. "I've never spent much time around kids. I wanted nothing to do with Arlene when Mom brought her home from the hospital; I was angry she took their attention—whereas Arlene was babysitter of the year. All the neighborhood children loved her; parents would rearrange their schedules to get her to stay with their kids. She's going to be amazing."

"None of this talk." Sin leaned against one of the tables, her mate standing by her side. "We're all friends and we're in this together. Zoe expects to babysit for all the new babies, so anytime anyone needs a break or some help, you know she'll jump at the chance. We've got this. Our tribe needs new blood and we're doing it. This will be the generation that will one day lead our tribe, so we better raise them right."

"Nothing like a little pep talk from the Deputy." Jase shot his sister a grin. "She's right though. The Saviors have been living over our head for far too long. We need to start living again. Babies are just what we need."

"Besides Ginger who says she's not ready, I guess I'm the last one standing. The last one without the exciting baby news." Swift leaned back into Brett's embrace.

"Don't worry, Swift. It will happen for you, too," Sin told her cousin. "You've been going through a lot and finally rejoined the tribe. I'm just happy to see you smiling again and not letting fear overtake you. Brett's been good for you. As for babies, you're always welcome to come play with mine, though you might have to fight Zoe off."

"We'll get there." Brett slid his hand down his mate's side. "Maybe we should go work on that."

"We're supposed—" Swift's words were cut off by a squeal as Brett lifted her into his arms and strolled toward their cabin.

"Okay then." Sin chuckled at her cousin before turning back to the group.

"Doctor Graham is going to be busy in the next few months."

The conversation around him continued but Roger's thoughts drifted off. Watching his friends and mate interact, like one big family, he realized this was why they fought against The Saviors, to get the laws changed, and everything else they kept going through. Family was important. For some of them it wasn't the one they were born into, or even the tribe they were raised in. It didn't matter what brought them together, but right there, the bond they shared was one of family. Blood didn't make that connection; friendship, loyalty, and love did. He'd lay his life on the line to protect them and this tribe, just as he knew they would. If something were to happen to him, or any of them, their mates and cubs would always be looked after. That's just what they did.

No matter what the future held, they'd get through it because none of them were alone. They had each other. The Saviors didn't stand a chance as long as they fought as one. Divided, they'd succumb to their deaths, but together, they'd live to make this world safe for future generations.

The thought of his children living in a world where they didn't have to hide their animal filled him with excitement. He was beginning to accept the fact that he was about to be a father, but this also made him more determined to make sure the peace they'd recently found became permanent. As he thought about his children, he slid his hand over his mate's stomach. A new surge of protectiveness rushed through him. These were his cubs and it was his duty not only to protect them but also their mother.

No harm will come to my family. Not today, not ever. Mine…

Marissa Dobson

Marissa Dobson is a USA Today Bestselling Author of more than sixty books in different genres of romance, including Alaskan Tigers series.

Being the first daughter to an avid reader gave her the advantage of learning to read at a young age. Since then she has always had her nose in a book. It wasn't until she was a teenager that she started exploring writing.

Marissa lives an hour from Washington D.C. with her supportive husband, Thomas—who puts up with all her quirks and listens to her brainstorm in the middle of the night—and her writing buddy Pup Cameron, a cocker spaniel.

www.MarissaDobson.com

Marissa@MarissaDobson.com

Also by Marissa Dobson

Alaskan Tigers:

Tiger Time

The Tiger's Heart

Tigress for Two

Night with a Tiger

Trusting a Tiger

Alaskan Tigers Box Set Vol. 1

Jinx's Mate

Two for Protection

Bearing Secrets

Tiger Tracks

Healing the Clan

Alaskan Tigers Box Set Vol. 2

Her Black Tiger

Tiger Trouble

Alpha Claimed

Roaring to be Claimed

Forever Creek Shifters:

Forever's Fight

Protecting Forever

Crimson Hollow:

Romancing the Fox

Loving the Bears

A Lion's Chance

Swift Move

Purrable Lion

Bearly Alive

Saved by a Lion

Furever Mated Box Set

SEALed for You:

Ace in the Hole

Explosive Passion

Operation Family

Marine for You:

Lucky Chance

Back from Hell

A Marine's Second Chance

Phantom Security:

Different Sides

Undercover Agent

Takeover Agent

Cedar Grove Medical:

Hope's Toy Chest

Destiny's Wish

Leena's Dream

Cedar Grove Medical Box Set

Fate:

Snowy Fate

Sarah's Fate

Mason's Fate

As Fate Would Have It

Half Moon Harbor Resort:

Learning to Live

Learning What Love Is

Her Cowboy's Heart

Half Moon Harbor Resort Vol. 1

Tanner Cycles:

Until Sydney

Stormkin:

Storm Queen

Blessing Montana:

Smoke

Touch of Home

United Homefront Ranch:

Destination Heaven

Beyond Monogamy:

Theirs to Treasure

Reaper:

Touch of Death

Clearwater:

Winterbloom

Unexpected Forever

Losing to Win

Christmas Countdown

The Surrogate

Clearwater Romance Volume One

Small Town Doctor

Stand Alone:

Road to Kaytlyn

SEALed Rescue

Past Comes to Light

SEALed Outcome

Starting Over

Secret Valentine

Restoring Love

Made in the USA
Lexington, KY
30 November 2019